What had I done?

Mira was a vampire. She was my enemy, always would be. She and all of her kind were evil, and yet I had just wrapped my body around hers and wanted to bury myself so deeply within her that we could never be parted. I could blame the bori within me, but if I was honest with myself, it was more than that.

I was fighting a battle with myself to continue hating her, and tonight proved only one thing.

I was losing.

Praise for JOCELYNN DRAKE's DARK DAYS

"An intoxicating mix of jet-setting action and sparkling turns of phrase. . . . Filled both with action and satisfying characters. I wanted to slowly savor it, but I reached the end far too soon, left hungry and impatient for the next adventure."

Kim Harrison

"Darkly suspenseful and blessedly surprising . . . with prose as silky and enticing as her protagonist."

Vicki Pettersson

By Jocelynn Drake

The Dark Days Novels

NIGHTWALKER
DAYHUNTER
DAWNBREAKER
PRAY FOR DAWN

Coming Soon

WAIT FOR DUSK

pray for dawn

THE FOURTH DARK DAYS NOVEL

JOCELYNN DRAKE

An Imprint of HarperCollins*Publishers*

EOS
An Imprint of HarperCollins*Publishers*
10 East 53rd Street
New York, New York 10022-5299

Copyright © 2010 by Jocelynn Drake
Cover art by Don Sipley
ISBN 978-0-06-185180-3
www.eosbooks.com

First Eos paperback printing: July 2010

HarperCollins® and Eos® are registered trademarks of Harper-Collins Publishers.

Printed in the U.S.A.

10 9 8 7 6 5 4 3 2 1

To my family
You are a source of endless inspiration.

ACKNOWLEDGMENTS

I wish to give a special thanks to my amazing agent, Jennifer Schober, for helping to keep me sane through the years. I also wish to thank my brilliant editor, Diana Gill, for constantly pushing me to be a better writer than I thought possible.

pray for dawn

ONE

The bastard was fast.

The hard soles of his shoes echoed off the cobblestones that lined the alleyway, leaving the sound to bounce off the tall brick walls that rose up around us. He wasn't even trying to be quiet any longer. He was hoping to outrun me, but he didn't realize that just because he was faster didn't mean I wouldn't finally catch up to my prey. I could sense him now, smell him out like a hound to a hare. Even if he went to ground, I would find him.

Popping suddenly out of the alley, we darted across a barren street, cutting between parked cars before shooting through another trash-strewn alley that fed into a network of back ways and dark streets. I took a corner too fast and my feet slid, sending my shoulder crashing into a building on my right. The steel of the blade in my right hand scraped against the brick as I pushed off. My prey was gaining distance on me, darting down one dark alley after another until I had finally lost sight of him. But then I was there again, just over his shoulder, ready to plunge my knife into his chest.

A breath exploded from my lungs in a white puff as I leaped over an overturned trash can, and a bead of sweat trickled cold down from my temple along the side of my face. The cold bit at my fingertips and my legs despite the fact that my blood was pumping from the chase. Sliding my left hand down to my waist, I grabbed one of the small blades that I kept in a holder there and pinched it between my thumb and index finger.

I had caught sight of the vampire as he strolled out of a dark alley on the other side of town. The scent of blood and death hung heavy in the air as I slipped after him to find a young girl lying limp among the bloated bags of trash, her breathing labored and her skin an unhealthy shade of white. She had lost too much blood and the vampire had left her for dead among the rotting garbage. He hadn't even tried to hide her. I had spared a quick call on my cell to the local authorities, but I didn't have much hope that the ambulance would reach her in time. From there, the chase was on.

Taking only a moment to aim, I hurled the small blade at the vampire, embedding it right between his shoulder blades, deep into his back. He cried out. His right arm reached back for the blade, his fast gait slowing as he struggled to maintain his balance. Clenching my teeth, I fought back a smile as I moved in for the kill.

Nearly two millennia had passed at the blink of an eye, most of the time spent hunting down vampires, wiping their evil from the face of the earth. Each time, each kill, seemed to come just a little bit easier. They were getting younger, less experienced, careless, and I was just hitting my prime. Only one had eluded me so far, but I'd get Mira eventually. I had eternity on my side.

The vampire exited the alleyway and skid to a stop in the middle of the small town circle. Despite the cold of winter, water still bubbled and danced in the center fountain, though the lights had been put out. The area was empty, but then it was after two in the morning. We had yet to run across any pedestrians or even a stray car during our long chase.

Pulling the knife from out of his back with a grunt of pain, the vampire turned to face me, tossing the blade aside. It made a metallic ping as it bounced off the cold pavement. The cocky bastard didn't realize who he was up against, and thought he could easily dispatch me. He hissed, baring his bloodstained fangs at me. Tall and lean, he looked as if he were made of pure muscles and sinew, and yet the power that rolled off him spoke of a vampire that had seen only a few centuries of nights at best. He was young by most standards, a fledgling, but a killer nonetheless.

"What the hell do you want?" he snarled at me in roughly accented Spanish. He wasn't a native of the area. "Are you a hunter or something?"

"Something like that," I said in a low voice.

The vampire took a step backward, clenching his fists at his sides. "You're out of your league here, hunter. This is Sadira's domain. She won't take hunting in her domain lightly. If you wish to survive, I would leave here while you still can."

A soft snort escaped me as I took a step forward, keeping my legs spread wide and my stance ready for any kind of attack from the bloodsucking monster. That explained why there had been so much activity in this area recently. The mistress was gone, so all the children had decided to play. I had no problem exacting a little punishment for their carelessness. "Sadira was killed by the naturi in Peru months ago. Arrow through the heart."

The vampire's shoulders slumped slightly at this news and surprise actually flashed across his narrow face. He hadn't known that his mistress had been killed. He was simply enjoying her extended absence.

In a flash of movement, I launched my attack, taking him by surprise. Of course, that didn't mean that his reflexes weren't still faster than mine. I slashed the blade in my right hand down, moving from right to left, hoping to catch him across the chest, but he jerked just out of my grasp. I managed to only clip the side of his hand as he moved away from me. As he jumped backward, I grabbed another knife.

The vampire swung his hand at me, looking to take advantage of my apparent slowness. The palm was open, revealing a set of sharp fingernails that could easily shred me with the sheer force that was behind them. Twisting awkwardly, I dodged the nails. At the same time, I swung the blade in my left hand, slicing his right arm before he could move away from me. The vampire howled and jumped backward several feet, clamping his left hand over the wound. His blue eyes glowed in the darkness and I could feel his power filling the night air. Apparently, he was finally seeing me for the threat that I truly was.

Yet, at the same time, a second power filled the air. It swirled around us before seeming to settle just at my back like a heavy cloak hanging from my shoulders. It bore the same icy energy touch as any vampire I had ever encountered, but this was infinitely more powerful than I had ever felt before. I reached out with my own powers, but the energy couldn't be pinned down to any one place. It seemed to be everywhere and yet focused on me.

I kept my eyes locked on the vampire that stood before me, but he didn't flinch, didn't give anything away to indicate that there was something dark and evil standing just at my back. In fact, he launched himself at me, hands balled into fists. I dodged the first blow aimed at my jaw, but wasn't fast enough to evade the punch to my stomach that cracked at least two ribs. The impact was enough to send the air from my lungs, but it didn't stop me. Pushing the pain aside, I slammed the short blade in my left hand into his chest, just missing his heart.

The creature lurched away from me. Wrapping one hand around the handle of the blade, he attempted to pull it free as he dodged a series of swipes of my sword aimed at removing his head from his neck. A low growl rumbled through the circle, rising above the splash of water, as he pulled the blade free. Yet, instead of dropping it like he had the other, he kept this one tightly clenched in his bloody right hand. He finally had a weapon that he would wield faster and harder than I could, but not by much. My half-breed ancestry did give me a leg up when it came to fighting vampires. Not only could I sense them, but I was nearly as fast and as strong as they were, and could heal nearly as fast. Still, without actually becoming a nightwalker, I was just a poor cousin. I wasn't complaining, though. I still had an ace up my sleeve if it came down to it, but I wouldn't need it to take down this fledgling.

We circled each other, each looking for the perfect opportunity to insert a blade between the opponent's ribs. My heart hammered in my chest and adrenaline surged through my veins, giving me the only high that I could find after all these years. Hunting vampires was the only challenge I had left, the only thrill when the rest of the world seemed to have faded to a sickly shade of gray.

Yet, to my surprise, the vampire pulled the blade back, hiding it partially behind his body as he took a step away from me. "We're not alone," he muttered, but this time the words were in English. His brow was furrowed and a frown pulled his mouth into a downward slash across his pale face. Something about our guests had disturbed the vampire.

And a quick scan with my powers easily revealed the reason. My adversary would normally have been happy to continue this fight in full view of the public since he could easily cloak us. Our world was kept apart from the human world at all times, separate and secret. Yet, I knew that the vampire feared he could not cloak us from our new companions because he could not sense them. But I could. A trio of naturi had descended upon our scuffle and I suddenly found myself caught in the middle of two separate battles.

"Naturi," I murmured. I turned to my left, back toward the alley we had just come out of moments ago, so I could see both the vampire and the three naturi that were approaching our location, weapons drawn.

"Naturi?" the vampire demanded in surprise. He took a step backward and for a moment I was sure he was going to run. He had no problem chancing a quick scuffle with a creature he counted as simply human, but the idea of taking on three naturi at once was more than enough to send him scurrying for cover. And in truth, I couldn't blame him.

A second later, the energy that had been hovering just

at my back flowed toward my right and the vampire, who was slowly edging away from the naturi and me. The night-walker suddenly jerked to a stop as his face went completely blank, his eyelids falling shut as if consciousness has been ripped from his grasp. To my left, the naturi halted and even looked at each other for a second in confusion.

A smile grew across the vampire's face as he lifted his head. A red glow brightened his eyes, replacing the blue that had been there earlier. He tightened his grip on the dagger he had in his hand and slashed at the air a couple times.

Something was suddenly off here, and I couldn't begin to guess what had convinced the vampire to stay when running was the smarter option. If he wasn't killed by the naturi, he still had to face me, and that fight was bound to end poorly for him.

To confuse matters even more, the vampire said something to the trio of naturi in a language I had never heard before, but it was enough to cause the hair on the back of my neck to stand on end. It sounded as if I should recognize it, that it was something my deep subconscious understood but could no longer remember. It didn't matter, because the naturi understood it and replied with a pair of poison-tipped darts aimed at the vampire.

Jumping backward a step to put more room between my-self and the nightwalker, I watched as he easily deflected both bolts from a wrist crossbow with a couple swipes of the dagger, like swatting away flies.

Two of the naturi rushed the vampire then, while the third hung back, glaring at me. He raised one hand above his head and the black, midnight sky began to churn with dark clouds. It was cold enough to snow, but that wasn't what this wind naturi was summoning up. I had seen this too many times before. I had to kill him before lightning bolts began to plummet from the gathering storm clouds.

With sword in hand, I rushed the naturi, forcing him to stop his spell and pull his own short sword in hopes of defending himself. The blond-haired naturi was fast and skilled, blocking each one of my attacks while managing to sneak in a few blows of his own that I narrowly avoided. Blocking one blow and holding his sword trapped above his head, I slammed my fist into his face. The impact shattered his nose and forced him to stumble backward a couple of steps. I jerked my sword free of his and slashed downward, cutting through his neck, leaving his head hanging on by a thin flap of skin. The wind naturi fell dead at my feet, leaving the storm brewing overhead to slowly dissipate.

Turning on my heel, I found the nightwalker dueling with both of the remaining naturi at once. The air was thick with energy, almost crackling around them. By their broad shoulders and thick build, I was willing to bet that the vampire faced a pair from the animal clan. They seemed to be the foot soldiers of the naturi race. The first into any battle and generally the most brutal.

I was about to insert my sword into the fray when I hesitated. I didn't need to. The vampire had this fight completely within his control. In fact, by the devilish smile playing on his lips, I was willing to bet that he was only toying with them, drawing out the fight in order to crush their hopes. But it didn't make any sense. Moments earlier, the vampire had seemed lucky to know which end of the knife to be holding. Now, watching the vampire move was like watching an intimate dance of light and shadow intertwine. The blades flashed red in the lamplight, as he had scored more than one hit on his opponents. And then, to my complete consternation, the vampire turned to look at me as he sliced the throat of one naturi and then, in a flash, plunged the dagger through the heart of the second. The vampire's wide-eyed, red gaze never wavered from me as the naturi fell to the cold pavement, struggling to heal from their individual wounds before death finally stole them away.

My hand tightened on my own blade as I watched the two naturi writhing on the ground. "Finish it," I commanded.

"You've always been too compassionate," the vampire

said in a voice that barely rose above a growl. However, the vampire heeded my wishes. Kneeling down, he cut the heads off the two naturi, killing them. At the moment of their deaths, he sucked in a deep breath, his eyes rolling up into his head as if he was savoring the exact moment of their demise. He then looked down at the blood covering his hands and smiled to himself.

"We're not finished, vampire," I reminded him, lifting my sword slightly.

The vampire turned on the balls of his feet to face me and easily rose, leaving the dagger on the ground next to the dead bodies. He took a step toward me with his arms out and hands open, revealing that he was completely unarmed. But no vampire was ever unarmed. They were deadly fast and amazingly strong whenever the sun was down. I would not be drawn in by whatever ruse he was trying to pull on me.

"It doesn't have to be like this, Danaus," the vampire said in a low, soothing voice. "You've been fighting a good fight for many years, my son, but you've been fighting the wrong side."

"You may have helped with the naturi, but it doesn't matter. They would have killed us both regardless. You can't save your hide from me," I replied. Unwilling to let him stall any longer, I lunged at him, but he dodged as easily as if I were moving in slow motion.

The vampire chuckled at me and shook his head. "You think you can kill me now. Did you not witness how I so easily destroyed the naturi? What is one mere man against a creature such as me?"

"You're a vampire. A young one. You can be destroyed." Again, I came at him with a barrage of moves, faster than I had moved the last time, and still he dodged me. It was like he was inside of my head and knew exactly how I was going to move, and yet no nightwalker could read my thoughts without my knowledge. I would sense their presence.

Panic began to take hold as sweat trickled down my brow and ran along the edge of my jaw. My heart thundered in my chest and I tightened my grip on the sword. He was too fast for me to kill by conventional means. Hell, I couldn't even touch him. Something had changed in that moment when the naturi arrived and his eyes switched from a sky blue to a ruby red. I didn't understand it, but somehow the vampire has come into possession of the energy that had been swirling about me just before the naturi arrived.

I had to kill him before he finally decided to kill me. Taking a step backward, I lowered my sword slightly and raised my empty left hand toward the vampire. To my surprise, his grin grew even wider as I summoned up the power that bubbled within me. My body came alive with a fresh surge of energy and within me something roared with delight. The power left me in a rush and slammed into the vampire. His head fell back and he laughed maniacally for only a moment.

And then the red glow left his eyes. Whatever power that had possessed him for a brief period of time had left him. The nightwalker clawed at his arms and chest, stumbling backward away from me, but it was too late. His skin undulated and started to blacken. I had already begun to boil his blood within his lithe frame and there was no escaping it now. The vampire let out a high-pitched scream as he fell to his knees. His nails scratched at his face, tearing away chunks of flesh before he finally collapsed into a darkened husk that flaked away in the breeze.

Gritting my teeth, I pulled the power back inside of my body, struggling to cage the energy all over again. Once it was set free, I could relax for the first time in so many long centuries, but I couldn't let the power remain unleashed. The desire to kill grew as my body relaxed until it felt as if I would lash out at the first creature that crossed my path, nightwalker and innocent human alike.

I drew in a deep, cleansing breath while I tapped the power back down around my soul like a snake coiling around its prey, pushing away fear as well. The fear that I would lose control of the insidious power and kill everyone.

Shoving one trembling hand through my hair, I slipped the sword back into its scabbard on my back. My mind had just started to turn to disposing the body when a white glow began to grow out of the cold mist surrounding the fountain. I took a couple steps toward it, keeping my right hand lightly wrapped around the hilt of my sword. I couldn't imagine what I was seeing. A light clan naturi? But I couldn't sense any naturi in the area.

The energy pulsing through the air felt like every nightwalker I had ever encountered, and yet it wasn't a nightwalker. Slowly, a man became encased in the light, standing more than six feet tall with pale blond hair and shining clear blue eyes. Then in a brilliant flash that left me struggling to shield my eyes, a pair of white wings expanded from his back, spanning more than twelve feet across.

I jerked my sword from my back and stepped away as my heart skipped a beat. It felt like a vampire, but it had wings like a wind clan naturi. Neither was a friend of mine and neither wanted me alive.

"Hold, Danaus," the figure said in a deep, booming voice. "I am no threat to you." He held up one hand and I took a step backward, a frown tugging at the corners of my mouth.

"Who are you?" I demanded, still poised to attack.

A beatific smile spread across his face, a look of peace and joy. "I am your guardian angel," he claimed. "Gaizka."

A fine trembling started in my arms, causing the tip of my sword to waver. Was I truly faced with an angel? I had spent centuries studying and meditating with monks, priests, and other holy men, searching for some divine direction to save my soul from the demonic bori that darkened it, demanding violence. And now standing before me after more than eighteen hundred years was a creature claiming to be my guardian angel and I could not make myself put my sword away.

"Why have you come to me now?" I asked, tightening my grip on my sword. Something felt wrong.

"Because now is the time that you need me the most," he replied. His smile never wavered as he ignored my sword and took a step forward. He wasn't solid, but a figure comprised entirely of light and shadow. "We must join together to defeat that naturi that infest the earth once again. If left unchecked, they will destroy all of mankind. They must be stopped."

I stared at the creature before me, slowly lowering my sword. "You possessed that vampire. You fought the naturi."

"Yes, I can take possession of lesser creatures to accomplish certain tasks when necessary."

"And yet you let me kill the nightwalker," I pressed, more confused by the second.

The angel shrugged his shoulders. "He had his own sins to atone for."

"I've spent a lifetime hunting nightwalkers. They are an abomination feeding off the lifeblood of humans and tossing them aside like used livestock. Have I been wrong in my mission?" I asked. A shiver swept through me and my gut twisted. How could I be wrong? My soul depended upon it. But after centuries, could I finally find the salvation I prayed for now, here?

"The nightwalkers are not our enemies. They are our brothers-in-arms against the naturi. They will fight with us to destroy them. Let me join with you, body and soul, and we will become an unstoppable force in ridding the world of the naturi," the angel pressed.

"Join with me?" I demanded, taking a step backward.

"You are a powerful figure, Danaus. I need your consent. Together, let us cleanse the world and make it safe for mankind once again."

Frowning, I looked away from the angel as my mind turned over his questionable words. My gaze tumbled over the remains of the naturi on my left and I recalled the red glow to the vampire's eyes and devilish glee that he expressed as he slaughtered the naturi. Was that what I would be turning myself over to? Losing all control over myself as I became a puppet for a higher being? It didn't feel right. No angel would torment his intended prey or feel such enjoyment in their destruction.

The creature before me stood in the guise of an angel, but stank of the powers that flowed from a nightwalker. There was no heavenly light to be found here, no matter how I prayed.

"I've fought vampires for centuries to save my soul from the demon that possesses part of it. Have all those years of struggle been for nothing?" I demanded, drawing my gaze back to the creature that glowed before me. For a split second, the expression on the creature's face twisted and his eyes flashed red.

"No demon possesses your soul," he snapped. "That is a gift from me, from the heavens. Strength, longevity, and amazing power. You've used that power to destroy nightwalkers when you should have been hunting down the last of the naturi."

My jaw clenched and I tightened my grip on the sword I was still holding. This was all a lie. My mother hadn't made a deal with an angel. She admitted just before I killed her that she had made a deal with a demon for her powers. This was no angel hovering before me. It was the bori that owned part of my soul, and it had come looking for the other half.

"You're not an angel. No heavenly creature would accept what the vampires are doing to the human race. You're a bori," I growled.

The creature before me smiled an evil little smile as the white glow around it faded. The white wings immediately dissipated and a black shadow seemed to wrap around the creature like a black cloak. I raised my sword again as its flesh seemed to melt away to reveal a white skull with a wide fanged grin. It pointed a bony finger at me, trembling slightly. "Is this a little closer to what you were expecting?" the creature cackled.

I could still see through the creature as it shifted, a classical representation of the grim reaper. I was beginning to wonder if this monster had a specific form or if it was a formless creature that took whatever shape that fit its needs.

"No heavenly creature would condone nightwalkers," I snarled. "No heavenly creature would ask me to become a puppet in order to destroy naturi."

"But you have been a puppet of heaven, Danaus," Gaizka corrected. "Wrapped in your archaic ideas of truth and righteousness, you've been slaughtering nightwalkers in the name of God. You've been his puppet for centuries. I'm just asking you to eliminate a more immediate threat: the naturi."

"No."

The bori growled at me and glided slightly closer, but I held my ground. "I'm asking politely, Danaus. Do not make me force your hand. Those you care for could suffer a horrible fate because of your failure to cooperate."

"I will not be your puppet." I raised my sword and plunged it through the center of the creature, but it was like puncturing open air.

With a wave of its hand, a force slammed against my chest, throwing me backward several feet until I hit the side of a car. My body dented the door before I slid to the ground. "Sadly, I expected this from you," it said with a shake of its head. "Expect my first gift shortly for your lack of cooperation. More will follow. I'll destroy your world until you finally agree to bend to my will. I'm done waiting for you."

And then he disappeared, leaving me sitting on the cold pavement surrounded by the dead bodies of the nightwalker and the naturi. The bori that possessed half of my soul waited out in the darkness like a living nightmare, ready to take what little of my soul I still owned. Blood was going to wash over the world as I fought him for my freedom and I didn't know if it was even possible for me to win.

Two

I knelt before the fountain and ran my blood-covered hands through the icy water until my fingers grew stiff and numb. In the darkness, the water looked black, but by morning it would carry a slight pinkish tone. The four bodies had been crammed into a nearby car, but I hadn't yet set the explosive charge attached to the fuel tank. All evidence of nightwalker and naturi existence had to be wiped clean—the secret of their world had to be maintained if order was to be kept in the human world.

On my knees, I sent my powers out of my body before finally breathing in a sigh of relief. There was nothing supernatural close to me: not nightwalker, naturi, bori, or even lycanthrope. I closed my eyes and bowed my head, but the words would not come. It had been more than two centuries since I had last spoken to God. And even after tonight's encounter, when I was sure my soul was on the line, I could not bring myself to be the first to break the endless silence.

In the beginning, after finally leaving the Roman legion, I had fought vampires as a way of avenging the death of a friend's child. I fought them as a way of fighting the strange emotions that I felt whenever they were close. It wasn't until I had wandered the earth for nearly five centuries before I finally found a sense of peace and purpose while living with some monks. They said I would only regain my soul through fighting against the darkness that surrounded mankind. They spoke of salvation and giving order to the chaos that seemed to be constantly swirling about in my brain. They even seemed to forgive me for being born.

But I couldn't remain with the monks, no matter how I wished it. Vampires needed to be slain and I had more questions than they had answers. So I traveled the earth searching for answers that matched with the God I was fighting for and the soul I was desperate to reclaim. Yet, after more than a millennium of fighting, I discovered that there were no answers to be found. I painted most of Europe and parts of Africa and Asia in blood, and yet there was no answer from God signaling that I was at least on the right course; that I was one soulless nightwalker away from reclaiming my own soul. There was only silence.

It was only when I had grown too tired to continue on alone that I found a new purpose. Themis was barely thirty members strong huddled in a rundown house in Paris, but they were determined to understand the dark paranormal world that surrounded them. They watched nightwalkers from afar as they lured their prey into dark alleyways. They ventured into the woods during a full moon and listened to the werewolves baying at the moon as they prepared to hunt. Their lives were short but determined. They carefully cataloged all their findings in these great volumes for others to read and understand. Briefly, I thought that I might find my answers among them.

Sadly, Themis had offered only more questions with no answers. However, they needed a hunter, a dark hunter who could take on the vampires and the lycanthropes. I filled that role and was content to train others to follow in my footsteps, those who would carry on the knowledge I had accumulated over the long centuries.

Ryan, on the other hand, seemed to twist the early intentions of the research group. The white-haired warlock quickly assumed the lead of the group when his awesome powers and superior knowledge became apparent. Themis

had been confident that he could lead them further into the
world of the paranormal than ever before. Instead, nightwalkers seemed to die at a faster pace and old knowledge
was restudied. Fewer researchers were released into the field,
for their own safety, and the number of hunters that I trained
steadily grew. Through the centuries, I never questioned his
motives. I only saw that he was helping me to build an army
that would protect the world from nightwalkers. But kneeling beside the fountain now, I wondered not for the first time
in recent months if he was simply building an army.

The annoying jingle from my cell phone shattered the
night's silence, causing me to cringe as I quickly reached
inside my jacket. The little glowing LCD screen revealed
that it was my assistant, James. Perfect timing.

"I'm impressed," I said after flipping open the phone.

"Excuse me?" James stumbled, obviously surprised by
my rare compliment.

"Your timing. I'm ready to come in. I'm finished here,"
I replied, pushing back to my feet. I wiped my free hand on
the leg of my pants, drying it as best as I could before reaching into my pocket to find the remote detonator. I needed to
be at least a few yards away before setting off the miniature
bomb. The car would be destroyed along with the nearest
storefront, but no one would be harmed in the explosion, and
the remains of the nightwalker and three naturi would be
incinerated. It wasn't the prettiest way of disposing of bodies, but I didn't have Mira's flare or ability to simply set the
bodies on fire at will while cloaking the entire event from
the view of the public.

"Nightwalkers?" James inquired.

"A total of six throughout the area the past couple nights.
Apparently, this used to be part of Sadira's domain. With
her gone, they decided to play. Things should be quiet now."
Turning a corner and heading back down the alley. I hit the
switch, detonating the miniature bomb. The explosion rattled windows and set off car alarms.

"What was that?"

"Disposal," I replied.

"Oh."

"I also encountered three naturi while I was here," I admitted, but kept the appearance of the bori to myself. I had never told Ryan the origins of my abilities and I didn't want him to be able to use this newest development against me.

"Did you have any problems?" James asked, jolting my thoughts back.

"No, none. The area appears to be clear now. When can you have a flight ready for me to come in?"

James was silent for several seconds, causing me to stop in the middle of the dark alley. Off in the distance, the sound of a fire engine and police sirens could be heard echoing through the streets. I frowned and leaned my shoulder against the brick wall while rubbing my eyes with my free hand. This wasn't a good sign.

"You can't come in yet," James said softly.

"What are you talking about?" I snapped. "I've been going nonstop for nearly three months now. I want to come in. Clean clothes, a soft bed. Sleep for a couple days before the next round of slaughter."

"I know."

"What could Ryan possibly need from me?"

"He needs you to go to Savannah."

"That's Mira's domain. She can take care of her own problems. She doesn't need me in her area," I argued, pushing off the wall to continue to walk down the alley toward the hotel I was staying at. It was a small place with the lumpiest mattress I had ever had the displeasure of sleeping on. I had hoped that tonight I would be on a plane headed back toward my own bed, but it seemed it wasn't to be.

"I don't know too many details. The most immediate problem is the murder of a young girl the other night that has attracted the attention of the world media. It looks suspicious."

I bit my tongue against the first argument that came to mind and continued to walk down the street in silence. Mira should be able to cover up her own messes, but now that Themis had established a "relationship" with the night-walker, it seemed we felt it was in our best interest to be nosing around her domain at the first opportunity.

And in truth, despite my growing fatigue and aching body, I was beginning to see the benefit myself. Whether she liked it or not, Mira was a member of the nightwalker coven. The four Elders were the ruling elite among the vampires along with their liege lord. Maintaining my association with Mira kept me close to the coven and one step closer to their liege. If I had any hope of being able to take down the elite of the vampire race, it was going to be through my continued association with Mira.

"When will a plane be ready to take me to the New World?" I muttered after a lengthy silence.

"I should be able to have something waiting for you within the next few hours," James said with a sigh of relief. "I'll have more information waiting when you land. Ryan asked that you check out the city."

"I know," I grumbled. "See if I can get a sense of the chaos."

"Try to keep a low profile—Ryan wanted me to stress that this is a delicate situation."

I resisted the urge to snap. James was simply relaying Ryan's instructions, no matter how unnecessary they were. I knew how to keep a low profile and observe from a distance. This wasn't my first mission for Themis.

"Am I to contact Mira when the sun sets?"

"No!" James cleared his throat awkwardly. "No, that's not necessary. She'll be in contact with you."

Something was wrong with this whole situation, but I doubted that I was going to get any kind of valuable information out of James. Ryan had a habit of keeping those around him in the dark about his ultimate plans until it was far too late.

"Are the naturi involved?" I asked suddenly. I could only guess that the dark race of nature lovers was once again causing havoc within Mira's domain.

"We don't know yet. It's a possibility. It's why we need you on the ground in Savannah. You're the only one we have that can clearly read the situation."

"I'll grab my stuff from the hotel and head to the airport," I said. "Once I get a handle on the situation in Savannah, I'll call again."

"I have a feeling that you'll be hearing from us sooner than that." James sighed softly. However, before I could ask him about that comment, the phone line went dead. Snapping the phone shut, I shoved it back into my pocket. This did not bode well at all. Ryan was definitely up to something and I had a feeling that Mira was involved as well. I couldn't have Ryan interfering. I may be able to control Mira's powers, but I wanted more from her. I wanted her help in destroying the coven, and I couldn't allow the warlock to become involved in my plans.

Three

It was barely after nine in the morning when I hit the street in Savannah. Squinting against the bright sunlight, I rubbed my eyes and stifled a yawn as I stepped out onto River Walk. The wind sweeping up from the river was cold, cutting through my leather jacket, which sported a few new tears following last night's encounter. In fact, by the way the tourists were looking at me, I realized that I looked little better than a semi-crazed homeless person. My hair was wild and unkempt, and my clothes were dirty and wrinkled. I hadn't bothered to shave in more than three days and I hadn't slept in two nights. My flight from Spain to Savannah had been plagued with turbulence.

I walked down the street, taking in the handful of tourists popping in and out of the gift shops and hopping on the trolley that trundled around the historic district of the city. All seemed quiet enough. Of course, at this moment, all the nightwalkers were safely ensconced in their secret lairs, the lycanthropes were their day jobs, and any other creatures would be acting like normal human beings. I wouldn't be able to find out much until the sun actually set once again.

Pausing at one corner, I contemplated walking back and catching a few hours of sleep. However, a bit of yellow police tape flapping in the wind caught my attention. I turned

the corner and headed up the hill toward a wide alleyway
known as Factors Walk. James had not mentioned where
the girl had been murdered, but the one place it would
make the biggest stink would be near River Walk, where
most of the tourists flocked during the day.

"You don't want to go up there," called a young voice at
my back.

I twisted around to find a young girl of no more than
fourteen years sitting against the side of a building. Her
hands were tucked under her arms against the bitter wind
and her arms and chin rested on her bent knees. She was
staring straight ahead at the building across from her as if
some part of her was still trying to ignore my presence, but
for some reason she had spoken up.

"Why not?" I asked.

"The Dark Walk ain't safe anymore," she said, still refusing to look up at me. "Stay down by the river."

I turned and took a couple steps closer to the young girl
so that I was now standing directly in front of her. "What's
changed? I've been on Factors Walk before."

The girl shrugged one shoulder. A quick glance over the
young woman revealed that she honestly didn't look much
better than me. Her clothes were dirty and worn, just a motley collection that worked to keep her warm against the cold.
Her brown hair was pulled back in a ponytail and a smudge
of dirt covered some of her freckles.

"Is it just at night that the Walk is dangerous?" I pressed.

"Night. Day. It really doesn't matter. It hangs out there,
waiting."

"Is that where the girl was killed?"

The girl seemed to shrink in on herself, as if trying to
protect herself. "Yes," she whispered.

"And the killer is still around here somewhere?"

"He's always around somewhere," she replied.

"Then that's exactly what I want to hear."

Turning, I started up the hill again only to feel a sharp tug
on the right sleeve of my jacket. I looked down to find the

girl tightly holding onto my arm with both hands. Her head remained down, her eyes locked on the ground.

"You can't go up there," she commanded, raising her voice for the first time.

"I'll be fine," I said, trying to use my most reassuring voice. "I've faced all kinds of dark things and survived. I can handle this."

"There's been nothing like this in Savannah before," she replied, finally looking up at me. Her brown eyes went wide and she released me so fast that she nearly fell backward. I reached for her, but she quickly darted away from my reaching hand. She ran back down the hill, pausing only long enough to grab a worn backpack before disappearing out of sight.

Something about my appearance had scared her, but I couldn't begin to guess at what. I wasn't exactly looking my best, but she'd been talking to me before running in terror.

With a sigh, I resumed my trek up the hill to Factors Walk. As I reached the wide alley, I spotted a remnant of the police tape that had once cordoned off the area, tied to a lamppost. Even in the early-morning light, the alley was bathed in thick shadows thrown down by the buildings on one side and the high stone wall on the other side.

Factors Walk was a lonely strip of ground even in broad daylight. At night, River Walk was a hot spot for both tourists and locals with its trendy restaurants, bars, and nightclubs, and I had followed more than one vampire and its prey from the waterfront to the shadows of Factors Walk. Yet, I had never encountered anything there that would cause me a moment's fear.

Standing in the middle of the alley, I closed my eyes and allowed my powers to stretch out to the cover the immediate area. I could sense humans milling about the River Walk nearby, more humans up in the building beside me. There were no naturi near, but there was at least one lycanthrope standing still at the far end of the alley, most likely watching me. So much for an unnoticed appearance within the city. At this rate, the only thing keeping Mira unaware of my presence in her domain was the fact that the sun was up.

I opened my eyes and frowned. I wasn't surprised that I couldn't find anything because I wasn't even sure what I was looking for. Only when I saw the exact place where the girl was killed would I be able to possibly sense something, and even then it was a slim chance. But first I needed more information, and a local newspaper was good a place to start as any.

Unfortunately, it appeared that I first had some other business. As I reached River Walk again, I stopped in the middle of the sidewalk several feet from the three lycanthropes stalking me. I extended my arms from my body, hands open and my palms facing them. I could handle them, but I didn't want a fight with three werewolves in downtown Savannah in broad daylight. It would go against my vow to preserve mankind's ignorance of the supernatural species. It would also cripple the fragile peace within Mira's domain.

Ignoring the two other werewolves, I turned my gaze on Nicolai. A few inches taller than me, he had thick blond hair and his copper-colored eyes were narrowed against the sun that was rising between us. Nicolai had been another of Mira's unexpected acquisitions in Venice. She had claimed him after defeating him in a fair fight. She pressed her claim in an effort to keep him out of the hands of the naturi, and maybe even to tweak Jabari's ego.

"Gromenko," I said with a slight nod.

"Danaus. It's been a while," Nicolai matched my nod.

"Not since Venice."

Nicolai frowned, deepening the lines that cut through his face as a soft grunt escaped him. The man appeared to be in his early thirties, but lycanthropes generally aged more slowly than normal humans. He may have been quite a bit older. Judging by the power rolling off of him, Nicolai was considerably stronger than his two companions, making me wonder if Nicolai had been close to alpha status in his last pack. Some werewolves were natural born alphas, while some could grow into the role under the right circumstances.

Nicolai shoved his hands into the pockets of his navy jacket, his eyes darting away from my face. "We were hoping we could talk to you about an important matter."

"Of course."

His jaw muscles jumped for a second before he finally spoke again. "Privately." There was no missing the disgust in his voice.

"Naturally," I replied, as my mouth twisted in a smirk. Nicolai's eyes returned to my face and his frown eased. It was obvious that he didn't want to be here, but he had most likely been stuck with this task because we knew each other. They assumed I would be more willing to cooperate with someone I was acquainted with than the two thugs hovering behind him like anxious shadows.

With a stiff nod, Nicolai turned. I followed behind Nicolai, and the two silent strangers fell into step behind me. I had nothing to worry about as long as we were on a public street, but a knot of anxiety twisted in my stomach when Nicolai stopped beside a plain white Toyota Camry and pulled open one of the rear doors. I slid into the backseat of the car. Nicolai closed the door behind me and got in the car on the other side of me, while his two companions climbed into the front seat. Wordlessly, we pulled out into the steadily growing traffic and headed farther east toward the edge of the city and the river. I was surprised no one had bothered to take my weapons away from me before I got into the car. This obviously wasn't a social call. I kept my hands on my knees and stared straight ahead, memorizing where we were headed.

"Should I reschedule my other appointments for the day?" I asked, turning my head toward Nicolai. The driver jerked his head up so he could see us both in the rearview mirror.

"No, this won't take long," Nicolai said. His eyes remained out the window to his left.

"For who?" I mocked.

A half smile twisted on his face as his gaze jumped to my face. "Either of us."

"Jabari?"

Nicolai winced, his shoulders stiffening. He met the gaze in the rearview mirror then looked out the window again. "I've not heard from him in a couple months. Not since before Mira left for Peru." His voice was low, little more than a growl.

Prior to coming to Savannah, he had been a pet of sorts to a very old and powerful vampire named Jabari. Despite this, Jabari had attempted to give Nicolai over to the naturi, but Mira quickly claimed the werewolf and shipped him back to her domain. We all knew she was prolonging his life, not saving him. Jabari was even older than I was, and when he decided to strike back, his first act would be to kill Nicolai while he was under Mira's protection.

The white Camry slipped outside the inner city onto the gray ribbon of highway that cradled Savannah to her east. But after only a couple minutes we pulled off onto what appeared to be a service road and turned south. The lycan stopped the car in front of a pair of enormous steel doors attached to a giant tan stone entrance that seemed to go under the city to the right of the highway.

The werewolf in the passenger seat jumped out and jogged over to the door. He quickly unlocked the padlock and shoved the doors open enough to let the Camry pass through. The driver flicked on the headlights as we pulled inside, but they barely made a dent in the darkness that swamped the underground room. And it got even darker when the shifter closed the doors behind us.

Leaning forward, I could make out the dirt floor and the rock walls that had been carved under a part of the city. Here and there crumbling red brick arches and pillars struggled to keep the ceiling from caving in. The ground was littered with large stones and the occasional beer bottle from its random and temporary occupants. The tunnel looked to be as old as the city itself and probably was. I had heard tales of pirates and rumrunners using tunnels that ran from the river to secret coves under the city. In fact, one was supposed to still run from the Pirate House restaurant not far from where we were sitting.

I felt a mocking smile rising within me. The tunnels explained why on more than one occasion I had sensed the presence of a vampire or werewolf moving around underground. I had initially thought that maybe a couple of the buildings downtown had secret tunnels connecting their underground parking garages. However, some of the locations had seemed too far-flung from the main core of the city to hold to that logic. Now that I knew, the creatures of the city had one less place to hide.

Beside me, Nicolai slid out of the car. I climbed out as well and walked around the back of the car over toward Nicolai, staying away from the headlights. My eyes had finally adjusted to the darkness of the tunnel. My night vision wasn't as keen as a lycanthrope's or a vampire's, but it still was better than a human's. As I slowly stepped closer to Nicolai, I let my powers sweep over the immediate area. I didn't know how deep the tunnel ran or in which direction, but I could at least get a feel for who was close at hand. To my surprise, it was just the four of us and the rats.

"Why are you here?" demanded a rough voice from behind me. I turned to find the lycan that had driven the car circling me, edging into the shadows. Nicolai was leaning against the hood by the front left wheel. His arms were folded over his chest and he was staring down at the ground. He had done his part, and gotten me there.

I turned my back to Nicolai and stepped away from the car, searching for some open ground. The other shifter stood nearby, off to my left.

"You brought me here," I called into the darkness. The palm of my right hand itched, urging me to grab the knife that was nestled against my lower back, but I wouldn't be the one to start this fight.

"Why are you in Savannah? Why did you come back?" asked the second lycan. His voice was younger, with a slight Southern accent, as if he'd been born and raised in South Georgia.

"Vacation." I flexed my hands against the bite of cold in the damp, musty air. The enclosed tunnel was several degrees colder than the sun-kissed River Walk, causing my breath to fog as I exhaled.

"Is that why you were here during the summer?" asked the first. "Vacation? Kill a few vampires and catch a couple ship shots down at Tubby's," he suggested, mentioning one of the restaurants down along the River Walk.

"I don't do shots." Behind me, Nicolai snickered.

"Look, man, I personally don't care if you stake a few bloodsuckers while you're in town." The easy, placating tone from the younger werewolf instantly put me on edge. "Hell, wipe out their whole fucking kind if it's how you get off, but since you didn't kill them all, we gotta keep the peace."

The lycanthrope to my right circled closer, his feet scuffing the dirt-covered floor. The scent of earth and rain started to drift into the air as if a breeze had run across a field and gotten lost in the tunnels. He was dipping into his powers. "What did you do with Mira?"

Every muscle in my body stiffened. James had made no mention that the nightwalker wouldn't be here when I arrived. In fact, I'd almost anticipated an awkward reunion once the sun set. But she wasn't here?

"I haven't seen her." I widened my stance slightly.

"You attacked her in July, and now you're back to finish the job. Where is she?" the first lycanthrope demanded.

I knew they wouldn't believe me. "If Mira's missing, it happened before I arrived. I just stepped off the plane this morning. I've been in Europe the past three months. I haven't seen her."

"What about Themis?" Nicolai demanded. A soft whisper of cloth rubbing was my only indication that the blond werewolf had moved. "Don't they have other hunters like you?"

I kept my attention on the lycans I knew were a threat. "No one has been sent to Savannah. I should know. It's my job to issue the orders. I'm the only Themis member in town. If some other hunter got his hands on her, I would know it."

"Our—" Nicolai was cut off by a low growl from the right. "Something happened two nights ago and she has yet to answer our calls. With your sudden appearance in town, one has to wonder if Themis is playing in our neck of the woods now."

So I was, naturally, their prime suspect. I was probably the only suspect. "I don't know where she is," I snarled.

A subtle shifting in the air was my only warning, the scent of earth and rain intensifying as the shifter to my right rushed me. Bending my right knee, I lowered my right shoulder and put it into his stomach. I used his own momentum to flip him over my back. The crunch of the car's side panel giving under the weight of the man as he crashed into it filled the silence. My attention shifted to the second lycanthrope, who was inching closer, his eyes glowing reddish brown in the darkness. I felt confident that he wouldn't change. It would take too long and it left him vulnerable for several minutes. But that didn't mean that his strength and speed weren't already enhanced by being a werewolf in the first place.

As I tensed for the attack, I was hit from behind. The lycan I had thrown into the car recovered faster than I had expected. I hit the ground hard with him on top of me, my shoulder slamming into a large rock. His fist crashed into my jaw, hitting my head against the ground. Stars lit up the darkness, momentarily distracting me from the pain that exploded in my stomach as he landed a punch to my gut. I twisted beneath my attacker, grabbing his neck with my left hand. Pressing my thumb into his windpipe, I closed off his throat. The lycan grabbed at my wrist with both hands, desperate to loosen my grip. With him distracted, I finally pushed him back so that I could roll to my knees.

The second shifter took the opportunity to wrap his arm around my throat as he tried to pull me off his companion.

Releasing the first werewolf, I kicked him hard in the chest, sending him back into one of the columns as his companion pulled me away. In surprise, the younger shifter loosened his grip briefly. Grabbing his arm, I threw him into his companion. They crumpled into a heap against the stone column, covered in dirt.

I couldn't stop the grunt of pain that escaped me as I pushed to my feet again. Too many fights and too few hours of sleep had left me slow and sore. I rubbed my jaw, trying to ignore the headache that was throbbing in at the back of my skull. The two lycanthropes were slowly untangling themselves and getting to their feet.

The older of the two lycanthropes pulled a blade from where it had been held in a sheath attached to his belt. The silver knife flashed as it reflected a fragment of light from the car's headlights. I reached behind my back and drew my own knife from my lower back and smiled. I had been content to keep this limited to a brief scuffle in the dirt, but if they wanted blood, I'd give it to them.

To my surprise, the other lycanthrope pulled a small gun and held it trained on me. The sight of the gun wavered slightly as the young man's hand shook. My heartbeat picked up its pace and a cold sweat broke out on the back of my neck as I held my body perfectly still. This fight was taking a turn that I wasn't expecting.

"Shawn!" Nicolai snapped.

"I'm just making sure that this fight stays fair!" the young man shouted back with a tremble in his voice. "I've heard things. Heard he's got powers. It's the only way that he could possibly survive going up against Mira. I'm just making sure that he keeps things fair."

Fair? Two on one was fair? I kept my comments to myself as the older lycanthrope started to circle me to the right, stepping carefully over bits of broken rock and crushed beer cans. I moved within him, struggling to keep my attention fully on the man with the knife and not on the man with the gun.

He lunged at me first, using his amazing speed to his advantage. Instead of jerking backward, I slid to the side with ease, which allowed me to slash the blade along the man's rib cage. The blade cut though the man's coat, shirt, and skimmed his skin to give him a minor flesh wound, but it was enough to get his attention. With a growl, he pivoted on his left foot and stabbed at me again, but I was gone from the spot before he could make any kind of contact.

I had been fighting with blades for close to two millennia. They were an extension of my body. He hadn't a hope in the world of defeating me. I was just hoping that the other man didn't try to put a bullet in my temple when I finally brought his friend down. I inhaled slowly as the man made his attack and exhaled as my blade slashed across bare skin, taking my opponent down one notch at a time. As I flowed to my right, I stabbed the man in the side, sliding the blade through vital organs for a split second. The man cried out and tumbled to his knees. The blade fell out of his hand as he clutched his side in pain. I had no doubt that he would easily heal from this minor wound with a little time. However, I still had his companion to worry about. This dance of knives was over, quicker than I had anticipated, and now it was time to deal with the man with the gun.

In a flash, I darted behind downed werewolf. Grabbing his short brown hair in one hand, I placed my knife against his Adam's apple, pressing just deep enough to allow a trickle of blood to slip down his throat. Shawn held the gun with both hands, the weapon shaking violently as it was trained on us.

"Drop the gun or I'll slash his throat," I growled. "I haven't seen Mira. I don't know where she is."

"Are you looking for her?" Nicolai asked from his spot by the car. The blond lycanthrope hadn't moved more than two feet during the entire scuffle. I hadn't expected him to.

"No," I said, and then frowned. "I wasn't, but now it seems as if it is in the best interest of all those involved if I find the nightwalker."

"Then why are you here?"

"The dead girl."

"Put the gun away. This has gone too far already," Nicolai declared. "Go open the doors. Let's get out of here."

"Nicolai!" Shawn cried, but he was already lowering the gun. "We're not done."

"We're done," Nicolai snapped. "He hasn't seen her."

"How do you know he's not lying?"

"He's not. He had no reason to." A new wave of power brushed against my back for the first time, the smell of it darker and richer than the other two werewolves. I turned to see Nicolai's eyes glowing a deeper copper and I tensed. "He hunted Mira and survived. If he had killed her, he would have admitted to it and then killed the three of us for the trouble. We're done."

The standoff lasted for only a few heartbeats but it was long enough to tense every sore muscle in my tired body. At last, Shawn dropped the gun on the ground and took two steps backward away from it. I quickly pulled the knife away from the neck of the lycanthrope that I was holding and backpedaled toward the car, leaving the man holding his side and rubbing his neck while he sat on the ground.

There was no doubt in my mind now. Nicolai had been the alpha of his last pack and Mira had forced him into an existing pack. This was not good. No pack was strong enough to hold two alphas. It always resulted in the death of one.

"Get in." Nicolai's low voice jerked me from my thoughts. I walked around the car and fell into the front passenger seat as Nicolai slid behind the wheel. Shawn jogged down and opened the steel doors. The older were had yet to move.

Squinting and blinking against the morning light, we rode back toward the city, leaving Nicolai's fellow pack mates behind. The blond werewolf said nothing as we entered the city and he pulled the car back up to the curb where he had stopped me. By the clock on the dashboard, less than an hour had passed, but I still felt like I had been dragged behind a truck.

"If I find her, I'll have her call you," I offered as I grabbed the door handle.

"Just tell her to call Barrett," he said, his hand rubbing his forehead. His eyes were closed and lines of strain dug furrows in his young face. Hunted by an Ancient vampire and trapped in a pack that already had an alpha. In the end, he wouldn't be able to hide what he was. I didn't envy Nicolai.

Wordlessly, I climbed out of the car and started walking back toward the hotel I was staying in. My eyes lingered over the spot where I had seen the girl just before the werewolves had stopped me. She said that there had been nothing like this in Savannah before. Did she already know about the vampires and the lycans? A part of me wanted to go track her down and find out what she knew, but it would be nearly impossible. One small human in a city filled with humans and angry dark creatures.

Shoving my hands into my pockets, I lowered my head against the wind that whipped down the street as I headed back toward the hotel. I didn't need to look any further—the peace was starting to pull apart at the seams and Mira's disappearance wasn't helping. I needed to pry some more information out of James before I could continue.

FOUR

The little Themis weasel had his phone turned off, sending me directly into his voice mail. However, he left me a message stating that he and Ryan were already on their way to Savannah. My instructions were to stay put until they arrived later that afternoon.

This was not the news I had expected, nor was I relieved. Ryan didn't take little jaunts around the world on a whim. He had discovered that it was far easier to direct people if he remained in a single, central location—at Themis—and let everyone come to him. And they did.

It would be a few hours before they touched down and finally reached the city. I took advantage of the rare lull to shower and slip into bed. Despite all the chaos surrounding me, sleep came quickly, sucking me down into a swirling vortex of nothingness.

Not nearly enough time passed before I felt my thoughts surfacing again, pulling above the fog of sleep toward consciousness. Something or someone had wakened me. I lay there with my eyes closed, floating somewhere between sleep and consciousness, trying to remember where I was and why I needed to wake up. Someone was close. Where was I? Slowly I remembered that I was in the hotel. I paused. Had someone checked into the room beside me, the noise drawing me from sleep? That had to be it.

Exhaling, I let my mind drift back toward sleep. And then the bed moved. My breath caught in my lungs and my muscles stiffened, waiting for a sign that I had imagined it. I hadn't. The mattress dipped and shifted under the weight of someone crawling into bed next to me. Adrenaline raced through me.

Slowly I reached out with my powers just to get a feel for whom or what was now lying next to me. It didn't take much—the feel of the energy I brushed against was unmistakable. Vampire. Holding my breath, I stretched as if relaxing, reaching my right hand up under my pillow. My fingers closed around the hilt of a small knife. I wouldn't be able to kill the monster with it, but it might buy me enough time so that I could grab one of my swords on the other side of the room.

Had I been asleep so long that it was night again? Where the hell were Ryan and James?

A small, cool hand lightly touched my ribs and slid up my chest to settle over my heart.

My eyes flew open when I rolled over to plunge the dagger into the creature's chest. But the low growl lodged in my throat when I saw Mira lying beside me, an amused smile lifting her full lips while her red hair spilled across the white pillow beside me like a river of blood. In my surprise, she was able to easily grab my wrist and push me onto my back. She slithered on top of me so that she was straddling my hips, her luminous lavender eyes glowing faintly in the darkness. Holding my hand out over the edge of the bed, she gave it a little shake to get me to release it. I allowed the knife to fall. If Mira had wanted me dead, she would have killed me already.

Her powers flowed over me like a cool, summer rain. I fought the urge to let my eyes drift shut as the energy that poured from her washed away the last of my tension and anger. I knew she was a heartless killer, but there was something so clean and soothing about the caress of her powers. And to touch her was intoxicating.

"Oh, good," she purred. "You want to play. James said you'd be too tired."

"Get off," I snapped, lying still beneath her. I tried to ignore the way her dark red hair fell around her pale face and over her shoulders. I tried to ignore the feel of her thighs pressed against my hips. Anything to keep my body from hardening beneath her. Her playful mood didn't need to be provoked.

"I plan to. How about you?" she said with a wicked grin. She released her hold on my wrist and slid her fingers along the length of my arm back to my chest. Her other hand was splayed on my ribs and slowly moved higher to rest over my heart, pounding like a thing gone mad. Even without her keen hearing, I'm sure she could hear it.

With a gentle shove, I pushed Mira off of me and rolled to my feet, fighting the urge to shake my head. Mira couldn't use her power to fog my thoughts or coerce me into doing something I didn't want to do. Call it a natural immunity. Unfortunately, it didn't make me immune to Mira herself. After three months apart, I had forgotten what it was like to be around her, and now I was drowning. Somehow the memory of her smile, her smell, her touch had all faded with time, but now that I was faced with her again, I found myself aching to touch her.

I turned to face her, grateful that I had pulled on a pair of boxers before climbing into bed, not that they did much to hide the fact that the brief scuffle had left me rock hard. Mira smiled appreciatively up at me and stretched on my bed like a contented cat lounging in the sun. The lithe vampire lay on her side watching me, the white sheets tangled about her feet. She was dressed in a pair of tight-fitting, faded blue jeans and a plain back T-shirt.

"What vexes you, hunter?" she whispered when I frowned. I had forgotten how soothing her voice could be, like a cool balm over an angry wound.

"I've never seen you in jeans," I muttered, before I could catch the words. Leather, yes. Mira's closet had to be filled with leather. I'd even seen her in a business suit, but never in a pair of ordinary jeans and T-shirt. She looked so casual and relaxed, not like a killer who had witnessed more than six centuries of life.

For this rare spark of time, I could just see Mira as a young, vulnerable human woman lying in my bed with beckoning arms. How long had it been since I had fallen into a pair of soft arms like that? At this point, the face and name was lost to time itself, but the girl had managed to get me to forget about the bloody fight for my soul and to briefly escape the endless battle.

However, Mira wasn't a vulnerable woman, but a cold-blooded killer with more than six hundred years of experience under her belt. But then, I was no novice foot soldier either. Time had taught me that a pair of welcoming arms could be just as deadly as a man with a gun. I might want to escape the world for a time, but it always managed to find me.

"Don't you like them?" she mocked, rolling onto her back. "I can take them off." Digging her heels into the mattress, she lifted her slim hips and undid the button. I managed to clamp my eyes shut when her nimble fingertips picked up the zipper pull.

"Enough, Mira," I growled, earning a sultry chuckle from her. Her laugh was almost physical rubbing against me before dissipating into nothingness. "Where the hell have you been?"

"Come back to bed."

I opened my eyes to find her facing me once again. She rubbed her hand over the spot where I had lain just moments ago. "We can snuggle." Her nose wrinkled and her voice was teasing. "I'll behave."

"I thought you wanted to kill me."

"I'm sure we'll get back to that eventually." She flashed me a wicked grin just wide enough to reveal her fangs. "Come back to bed. You're tired."

I sighed, my eyes briefly flicking over to my alarm clock. It was almost 2:30. And then my eyes slammed back to the harsh red numerals as understanding clicked in my sluggish brain. It was almost 2:30 in the afternoon and Mira was awake. I turned around to my left and jerked open the heavy curtains that hung in front of the window. Beside me, I heard Mira hiss and launch herself off the bed. I looked away from the window to find her curled in the shadows of the far corner near the bathroom. Her eyes were wide and her teeth were clenched.

"What the hell are you doing?" she shouted at me. "Close the curtains!"

I glanced back out for a minute, just checking that I hadn't lost my mind and that it really was afternoon. The sun-drenched morning had given way to gray, overcast skies as a storm system moved into the area, leaving the heavens looking as if it would start raining at any moment. There was no sunlight to be seen, but Mira wasn't willing to take any chances.

I pulled the curtains closed, but she didn't visibly relax again until I took a couple steps away from the window. She slowly stood with her arms crossed over her stomach.

"How is it you're awake?" I demanded.

"A gift from a friend," she said, regaining her grin.

"Ryan." The warlock's name rumbled from somewhere in my chest and crawled up my throat, coated in frustration and anger.

"Your warlock is proving to be useful." She sounded indifferent, but I knew better.

"How? What has he done?"

"Nothing that concerns you."

I frowned at her, which only caused her smile to widen. I didn't trust either of them and it didn't bode well for anyone if they were suddenly working together. "You've been with Ryan all this time."

Mira chuckled, leaning against the corner of the wall.

She shoved her hands into the front pockets of her jeans and stared at me. "You make it sound so sordid. Jealous?"

"You've been missed. The lycans stopped me today in their search for you."

"Yes," Mira frowned. "Barrett was kind enough to leave a somewhat scathing voice mail on my phone today. Apparently, you've been busy. I spent the better part of an hour reassuring him that I hadn't been kidnapped or killed."

"You disappeared without a trace," I reminded her.

"I'm a nightwalker; it's what we do."

"Did you even bother to take Gabriel with you?" Previously she had not traveled without protection, but following the death of her other bodyguard, Michael, I sensed a hesitance to bring Gabriel along on her travels.

"I'm not helpless." Her narrowed eyes began to glow again, but this time it was from anger. I had no doubt Mira would tear out my throat if I pushed her too far. She wasn't known for her patience.

"But Tristan is. Did you even bother to tell him that you were skipping town?"

"He's not helpless!" she snarled. She pulled her hands out of her pockets and pushed off the wall toward me. "She just taught him to be that way." There was no question as to who "she" was. Sadira had made Tristan more than a century ago and Mira before that. She had kept Tristan weak and dependent upon her, as if to ensure that he never left her the way Mira had.

"I never asked for this," she continued, her eyes darting away from me for the first time as her hands balled into tight fists. She hadn't. Mira valued her independence, her lonely existence. She had told me once that she had never made another of her kind and that she never would. Yet, she was now saddled with another's child because she couldn't bear to see Tristan tormented by her peers. And to make matters worse, she had started a family with at least two other nightwalkers in an attempt to protect them and add some more security to the city.

"Doesn't matter. You're his mistress now."

"Who are you to lecture me about my duties, hunter? Tristan is mine and none shall harm him." Her powers suddenly filled the room like a cool wind sweeping in laced with the scent of lilacs. We stared at each other, the tension building to the point where the muscles in my jaw began to tic. I was waiting for her to twitch first. I wouldn't strike first.

And then just as suddenly, the energy flowed out of the room. Mira took a couple steps backward and shook her head, looking somewhat confused. I knew her thoughts had to be the same as my own. How had we pushed each other so quickly to the point of each nearly tearing the other's heart out? She looked up at me and her grin seemed sheepish. She had almost lost control. Mira had come in here to seduce me, not kill me.

"Why are we fighting?" she softly began, one corner of her mouth quirked in a playful smile. "Let's go back to bed. You're tired."

"Out, Mira!" I shouted, pointing toward the door. It was all just a game to her.

"Fine," she sighed. "I'll go play with James." Mira scooped up what looked like a cloak that had been draped over one of the chairs by the door. She wrapped it around her before she strolled out of the room, her hips swaying.

"Call Tristan!" I called after her before she shut the door.

I drew in a deep breath through my nose and slowly released it as I rolled my shoulders. I didn't completely relax until I felt Mira enter another room farther down the hall. By the thrum of power seeping from that direction, I was willing to bet it was Ryan's room. The warlock would keep her occupied while I caught a few hours of sleep.

Placing the knife back under my pillow, I lay back down on the bed and drew the sheet up to my stomach, but Mira's scent lingered on the pillow next to me. I closed my eyes, but her image danced there on the other side of my eyelids, her smile taunting me. I didn't want to think about her, much less about how the tightness in my chest had instantly unraveled when I saw her lying safe and smiling next to me.

I hadn't seen her in three months, but my body's reaction had been instantaneous. I loved the soft touch of her hands and her deep laugh when she was amused. It had been tempting to just slip back under the sheets and press her body to mine.

Mira could appear to be just a beautiful woman full of life and laughter, but she still held that exciting edge; that cold, crisp touch of power that followed her wherever she went, a barely concealed threat of danger and uncontrollable energy like a building thunderstorm. Around her, my blood pumped and the hair on my arms stood on end with the energy that crackled between us. For the first time in more centuries than I wanted to count, I felt alive when she was near. Before Mira, I had become a shell going through the motions of living, only getting a short brief burst of adrenaline when I was hunting. Yet, when Mira was around, it was an emotional roller coaster of anger, frustration, surprise, horror, and even joy.

But she was a vampire. A monster. A heartless killer.

At least that's what I tried to remind myself, but the longer I knew her—the more I saw of her world—the harder that was to believe. She didn't kill humans. She might have toyed with them and played her games, but she didn't kill. And regardless of whether she admitted it to herself, she cared about Tristan's safety.

In my head, I could easily imagine Bodhi shaking his head at me with his knowing little smile. I had traveled with the bald, bandy-legged gypsy for less than two decades, but he and his family had become my family for a time. He was first to try to get me to forgive myself for being born. He was also the first to point out that vampires were evil, following the loss of one of his sons. He would have reminded me that there is nothing wrong in appreciating the beauty and grace of a Bengal tiger, just never think you could take one in as a pet. It would only rip your heart out despite your admiration.

Staring up at the ceiling, I sighed and laced my fingers behind my head. Maybe Mira was right and I needed sex. It had been a long while since I had been with a woman. My attraction to Mira could just be a buildup of sexual tension, but I wasn't about to relieve that tension with her, no matter how tempting she was. I was tired of being a plaything for powerful creatures.

Five

My sleep was disturbed again less than four hours later. Lying on my back, I used my powers to discover James standing outside the door. I released the knife and shuffled across the room, wiping the sleep out of my eyes. I had managed to squeeze in close to seven hours of sleep. With both Ryan and Mira in town, I had a sick feeling that it was the best I was going to get for a while.

The young man smiled at me when I opened the door, easily ignoring my own sour expression as he stepped into the room. Early thirties, with brown hair and thin face, James had been assigned as my assistant less than a year ago and we were still adjusting to the arrangement. I always worked alone, but I depended on a specific contact within Themis to arrange for my travel, lodging, money, research information, and other odds and ends.

But for me, it was more than those basic necessities. James was my tie to the human world. He reminded me of what it meant to be human in the twenty-first century, which was not exactly the easiest thing for me to remember. I would turn 1,866 years old this year. After such a passage of time, things like polite conversation and mundane tasks tended to be forgotten under the relentless grind of life.

"You don't look as bad as she made it sound," James said, his sharp eyes skimming over my face.

I hit the light switch, bathing the room in warm, golden lamplight as I walked over to my bag. "She?" I asked, as I jerked the black cotton pants over my hips.

"Mira. She was worried."

I snorted. Mira's only concern was that someone would kill me before she had her shot. James also said nothing, but answered the door when another visitor knocked. A member of the hotel staff carried in a large tray with several covered plates, and the smell of coffee that caught my attention. The promise of warmth and caffeine wiped away the last of the fog from my brain. As James signed the bill, I started lifting covers to find a strange combination of breakfast and dinner. Scrambled eggs, sausage, steak with a baked potato, steamed legumes, lentil soup, whole-grain muffins, and a whole pot of black coffee. James was going to work out fine as my assistant.

"I wasn't sure what you'd want," James hedged as he came to stand on the other side of the table.

"This is fine," I muttered, falling into a seat as I dug into the food. Coffee and food would clear out the cobwebs and cure the aches. Then I would be able to tackle the growing mess that surrounded Mira.

"Any trouble with the vampires?" James asked, unable to keep the excitement out of his voice. He was still young and enthusiastic about this dark world in which I worked, wanting to know all the secrets and desperate to dive into it. However, after meeting Mira and some other vampires last summer, he had grown a little more cautious. Of course, he had also had to clean up the multiple naturi corpses Mira and her band had left behind following their last visit. Cleaning up that many dead bodies would have been a harsh wake-up call for anyone.

"Not with the vampires," I said with a shake of my head as I poured more coffee. "The naturi were another matter."

James slowly fell backward into the chair opposite me, his mouth falling open and his eyes widening behind his gold-rimmed glasses. "Naturi?" he nearly choked on the words. "I thought you said that these vampires were a part of Sadira's domain. Why would the naturi go to a known haven for a powerful nightwalker?"

"They might not have known," I said with a wave of my fork in between bites. "They might not have cared. After the doors opened, the naturi scattered everywhere. I have a feeling that they are going to go where they want to."

"I always assumed they would stick to wooded areas. I mean, they are nature-based creatures," James replied.

I stared down at my half-empty plate for a moment. He had just voiced the hope I had been harboring for the past three months: that the naturi would stick to the woods and leave mankind untouched while they worked out their own little political problems. With any luck, it would take years, enough time for us to come up with some solution to the problem of them even being in this world in the first place. But it wasn't to be.

During the past three months, I had destroyed more nightwalkers than I had naturi, but the number was steadily increasing. They were popping up on the outskirts of town, sometimes just seeming to watch me as I battled the vampires before they finally attacked. The trio in Spain had been the most I had encountered at once since leaving Mira's presence. But then the nightwalker had a special way about her that seemed to bring out the worst in the naturi. She reminded me of a young man I had trained with in the Legion. He had the same special knack. Every time we were sent ahead as scout, he would literally trip over the enemy. It's a wonder he lived through half as many battles as he did.

Pushing away those dark thoughts, I turned my attention back to the food that was growing cold before me and switched to a less tasteful topic. "Mira has been with Ryan for the past week?" I asked before shoving a piece of steak into my mouth. It was heaven. I tried to relax and just think about the taste, but I couldn't. I had to know what was going on before it rose up and bit me in the ass, literally.

"Yes."

"Why?"

James looked down at the white tablecloth, his hand jumping up to smooth his navy tie against his chest. "I can't say."

"And Ryan is here now?"

"Yes."

"Why?"

This time his eyes darted back up to my face and he frowned at me. "Danaus, I . . ."

I held up my right hand, my fork still pressed between my thumb and index finger. "Never mind. Forget I asked."

James slumped in his chair and pulled off his glasses so he could rub his eyes. "You know how he is," he grumbled.

Yeah, I knew how Ryan worked. He liked to be in control of the flow of information at all times. Ryan was from the school of thought that knowledge is power and he liked knowing more than everyone else.

I pushed aside my empty plate, cleaned of the steak and vegetables, moving on to the eggs. "How did they take Mira's presence at Themis?"

Resting his elbows on the arms of his chair, James stared at his glasses as he held them with both hands. "She's a great source of information, assuming she's telling the truth," he said slowly. One corner of his mouth lifted in a half smile. "But I think they're glad that she's gone." James looked up at me. I was surprised to find that his gaze was sharp, unlike the unfocused stare of someone suddenly caught without their glasses. Not for the first time I wondered if he actually needed his gold-rimmed spectacles.

"What did she do?"

"Not much." He shrugged as he slipped his glasses back on his nose. "Just her usual mischief, I imagine. But she stopped sleeping not long after her arrival and I think most people stopped sleeping as long as she was awake and wandering the halls."

It was on the tip of my tongue to ask how Ryan had managed that unique feat, but I swallowed the question. I doubted if James actually knew even though he doubled as Ryan's assistant when I was out of town. And even if he did know, I doubt he would be permitted to tell me.

Reaching for the coffeepot, I poured another cup, somewhat relieved to find that Mira hadn't caused too many problems. It was probably best that she had shaken things up back at Themis. I was learning that their understanding of vampires had little to do with reality, defying my entire reason for joining the society in the first place. "Is there anything else that I should know about?"

"Not much. Ryan has pulled back most of the hunters to Paris, London, or the Compound recently. He believes things have become too . . . tense at the moment and thought it best if we pulled back to guard our own for now. Last I saw, only Farkas and Collins were left in the field."

"Doing what?" I demanded, an uneasy feeling slipping down into the pit of my stomach. My right hand slipped from my coffee cup to rest on the arm of the chair.

"Farkas is on a quick scouting mission in Turkey. Something about a shake-up in the dominant werewolf pack in the area. Collins was sent to take care of a vampire hiding out in the Ukraine." James adjusted his glasses.

"When was Collins put on vampire duty?" I snapped, my right hand convulsively tightening on the chair so that the wood creaked softly.

James swallowed audibly and sat up straighter in his chair. "Last month."

"He doesn't have enough experience in the field and should never have been sent alone," I barked. "Who put him on vampire duty?"

"I think Ryan did." James scooted back in his chair so that he could put a little distance between him and myself. "Collins was told to only pursue the vampire during the day. If he can't locate its daytime resting spot, he is to call for assistance."

"Collins is going to end up dead," I grumbled. My grip on

the chair loosened and I reached for my coffee in an effort to wash the bad taste out of my mouth.

"I heard it was a young vampire," James countered, trying to soothe some of my anger. It wasn't working.

"That doesn't make them any less dangerous; just a little more careless. I have the ultimate authority over who is on vampire duty. Ryan knows that." I sat back in my chair, glaring at my empty coffee mug.

Why hadn't I been consulted? Derrick Collins had been with Themis for only a couple years and just served as backup on vampire hunts on a few occasions. He didn't have enough experience in the field to handle a nightwalker, even a fledgling. I had always had complete authority over those who served on vampire duty. I was the only one who hunted alone. I was also the only one with the skill, speed, and experience to hunt them at night.

Ryan had overstepped his bounds. The warlock had put an inexperienced hunter in an extremely dangerous situation and a part of me was reluctant to ask why. And this wasn't the first time. He had also brought James along to Crete, where the naturi were holding one of their sacrifice attempts. In this instance, I had to agree with Mira. The researcher had no business being anywhere near that dangerous situation, and Ryan had brought him along as potential bait.

Ryan was very wise and very careful, but I didn't always agree with his methods. His conscience had no problem withholding information or sacrificing a few lives here and there to accomplish his greater schemes. And while I wasn't a pawn, I had no doubt that I was still a chess piece for him to play with.

"When is my meeting with Ryan?" I demanded.

James pushed to his feet, shoving his hands into his trouser pockets. "He said to come down whenever you're ready. Room 705."

I needed a shower, shave, a fresh set of clothes, and then

I would be ready to deal with a warlock. "Tell him thirty minutes."

James nodded once and wordlessly left the room. I sat for a minute staring at the rumpled sheets on my bed. An uneasiness twisted in my chest. Themis was no longer the home that I needed it to be. When I had joined centuries ago, it was in the pursuit of more knowledge of the creatures that lurked in the darkness and fed off all that was good in humanity. Now I felt as if I were simply a foot soldier for Ryan in his quest for . . . whatever he was reaching for next. The information now flowed up to him instead of down through the entire collective. Not for the first time in the past few years I wondered if it was time to move on.

But for now, such thoughts had to be put aside. In thirty minutes, I would discover what had dragged Ryan away from his ivory tower and, hopefully, I would find out how and why he had given Mira the ability to walk around during the day.

Six

The sun had already set when I finally walked down the hall to Ryan's suite. Prior to his arrival in the United States, he had been meeting with various groups regarding the new naturi problem. A trio of warlocks from Quebec had made an unexpected appearance at the Compound during my last stay in the UK, demanding to speak with Ryan. There was no particular hierarchy among witches and warlocks. While small and large covens existed around the world, no single being ruled and set laws for the group. No king, president, or dictator.

But there was Ryan. In their small sect of the world, he was one of the oldest and strongest. He was also one of the only warlocks that were in contact with all the other creatures of the world. And as the head of Themis, he had near limitless amounts of information at his fingertips.

No, Ryan wasn't their king, but if he asked, their first thought was "How high?"

Outside Ryan's suite I paused for half a second. Mira was in there. I had hoped for a private meeting with the head of Themis, but I was beginning to see that was an impossibility. Still, the sight that greeted me when James let me into the room brought me up short. The entrance to the suite opened immediately to a large parlor of sorts with a sofa, chairs, and coffee table. To one side sat a large desk, stacked with several tomes that the warlock most likely brought with him from England. Ryan sat relaxed in a high-back leather chair, while Mira was perched on his desk before him, her bare feet resting on the edge of his chair on either side of his outstretched legs. There was a strange intimacy to the tableau that made me want to back out of the room, but I didn't move.

Both creatures looked up at me, their expressions unreadable. Had this been planned, and if so, by whom? Ryan had summoned me and both would have sensed my approach. There was no surprise in their eyes.

Mira moved first, placing her feet on the floor and sliding off the desk. As she walked around to the front of his desk, neither looked at the other, but I saw the fingers of Mira's right hand grasp Ryan's right hand for half a breath and then release it. Mira strolled past me, a strange smile on her lips. It wasn't her usual smug or teasing smile. It wasn't even seductive. A deep foreboding sank into my bones and I suddenly had the feeling that I had fallen in with a shark and a lion. It wasn't so much whether I was going to be eaten alive, but just a matter of how.

"It's good to see you again, Danaus," Ryan said, drawing my attention back to him. The warlock with the liquid gold eyes rose smoothly to his feet and shoved his hands into the pockets of his black trousers. A smile lifted his lips, making him look completely at ease.

Ryan had been with Themis for less than two centuries, joining several years after I had. While he didn't speak of it much, I had the impression that he had been a warlock for a long time before that—nice accomplishment for a human.

Of course, to look at him you wouldn't guess he had seen more than three centuries of life. His thin, angular face held an ageless quality, giving him the appearance of a man somewhere between the ages of twenty-five and fifty. His completely white hair hung loose just below his shoulders, casting shadows about his golden eyes. But in a few, unguarded moments, Ryan had spoken of being a young boy with brown curls and eyes in a small farm village. Heavy magic use had left its unmistakable mark on him, as it did with all powerful warlocks and witches.

"We need to speak," I said, still not moving from the doorway.

"Yes, we do," he replied, his smile slipping from his face. "Please come in." His eyes briefly drifted to James and then back to me. James left the room, closing the door behind him. I had no doubt that the researcher would be down at my room until the meeting was over.

My narrowed gaze fell on Mira, draped over the sofa against the back wall directly across from Ryan's desk. "Alone."

Her smile instantly changed from mysterious to smug; she had no intention of moving.

"I would prefer it if she remained," Ryan said. His voice was firm but not yet commanding. The warlock very rarely attempted to pull rank on me. "One of the matters we need to discuss involves her."

Clenching my teeth, I stiffly nodded and took a couple steps farther into the room, my feet sinking into the thick, caramel-colored carpet. "I don't see how she needs to be here to discuss Collins."

"Actually, Mira had a hand in Collins being in the Ukraine," Ryan said, his tone lightening a bit as he pulled his hands out of his pockets and sat back down. He motioned for me to take one of the chairs by the sofa, but I hesitated. The position would make it hard for me to look at both the warlock and the vampire at the same time. I took a few steps closer to his desk, folding my arms over my chest. The air was thick with magic, Ryan's almost electric power tingling with Mira's cool breeze. It fogged and jumbled my thoughts. I drew in a deep breath and closed my eyes for a second, trying to force my mind to clear.

"Danaus?" inquired Mira, her voice a gentle caress.

When I opened my eyes, she was standing directly in front of me, her soft hand pressed to my cheek. I stared into her lavender eyes, nearly drowning in their depth. She looked concerned, but I could feel other emotions bubbling just below the surface. When she touched me, it was like I had suddenly tapped into her thoughts and emotions whether I wanted them or not. The reluctant connection we had forged months ago was still there, waiting to be reactivated.

"Are you all right?" she whispered.

I hadn't even heard her move or felt her approach. She was just suddenly there. Had I blacked out? An anxious knot twisted in my gut and for a second I struggled to draw in a breath. What were these two plotting?

"I'm fine," I snapped, taking a step backward away from her touch. Mira nodded and walked back to the sofa.

Liar. The word whispered through my thoughts in Mira's seductive voice. I stilled and stared at her as she lounged across the sofa, her eyes never wavering from mine. I couldn't feel her in my brain. She had sent only the word into my thoughts, maybe just to prove that she could.

I jerked my gaze free of Mira and looked back over at Ryan. His own expression was guarded and completely unreadable as he watched us. Were they toying with me?

"What does Mira have to do with Collins being in the Ukraine alone? Or did I misunderstand James? He said that Collins was hunting a vampire," I demanded, pushing ahead once again despite my pounding heart. I might be able to pry information out of one of them later, but not while they were both together in the same room.

"No, he's hunting," Ryan confirmed. "A vampire by the name of Ivan has been causing a stir in one of the more remote cities. A number of police files have been accumulated regarding his killings and two people have gone missing. He has to be taken care of before he causes more problems with the humans."

"So why send Collins? And alone? Derrick Collins has been with Themis for two years and hasn't had enough training for dealing with vampires. He's going to get himself killed." I stepped closer to Ryan's desk, anger overriding my earlier caution. "You should have sent several of our more experienced hunters in. Patricks and Morrow are both at the Compound. They should have at least gone with him. You could have called me after I finished in Spain and I could have gone."

"I didn't mean to undermine your authority, Danaus," Ryan said calmly. "You've done a wonderful job with the hunters."

"Yes, just wonderful," Mira growled from behind me. I could feel a ripple of her rage brush against my back and then dissipate into nothingness as if she had turned off her emotions like flipping a switch. This wasn't a topic I wanted her around to hear.

Ryan sent her a quelling look, a frown pulling down the corners of his mouth. For a second, he looked older and a little tired. Ryan didn't frown often, and it was just a little reassuring that maybe this alliance between these two monsters was tentative at best and more than a little strained.

"I assigned Collins a new, temporary partner," Ryan continued, his eyes falling back on me.

"Who?"

"His name is Joseph," Mira interjected. A chill ran through me and the hair on the back of my neck stood on end as I looked at the vampire. The oh-so-smug smile had returned to her lovely face, causing my hands to ball into fists.

"Who's Joseph?" I demanded, forcing the words through my clenched teeth.

"Joseph belongs to me. He's been a nightwalker for roughly twenty years and is in desperate need of a little experience," Mira explained, sliding along the sofa so that she was now seated on the edge of the cushion.

"Are you insane?" I exploded, pinning Ryan with a dark gaze. "You sent in one of our inexperienced VAMPIRE

HUNTERS to hunt a vampire with another vampire as backup!" Usually I was a master at controlling my emotions, but this had pushed me screaming over the edge.

"Danaus—"

"What about Joseph?" Mira interrupted, drawing my eyes back to her face. "I'm trusting one of your damned hunters not to stake him as soon as the sun rises. I promised Joseph that he would be safe." Her narrowed eyes glowed in her growing rage, her hands tightly grasping the cushions.

"It'd be no less than he deserved," I growled.

I was ready when she launched herself off the sofa at me. I caught her thin wrists as her hands went for my throat, forcing me back a few steps to regain my balance. Her arms trembled and her teeth were clenched. Somewhere inside of her I could sense that she was struggling for control, battling the urge to set me on fire. Picking a fight with Mira was always extremely dangerous—she could just set you on fire and enjoy the blaze. I reached for the power that I could feel swirling about her, ready to take control of the nightwalker if necessary if she even attempted to set me on fire. At this moment, she was little more than a puppet to be used.

"Enough!" Ryan shouted. At the same time, a strong force slammed into my chest, throwing me backward. Mira's wrists were ripped from my grasp and she was tossed to the other side of the room. My back slammed into the wall, sending a shock of pain up my spine. I slumped to the floor, gasping for air. Mira skid across the floor and slowly rolled to her hands and knees. She tossed her hair out of her face and narrowed her glowing gaze on Ryan, who was now standing behind his desk. The warlock's dark expression was locked on Mira, waiting to see if she would now turn her anger on him.

"We don't have time for this," Ryan warned. I held my breath for a tense second and then another before Mira finally gave a curt nod. She pushed to her feet and returned to the sofa, brushing her long fiery locks out of her eyes. She never looked over at me. Ryan then turned his gaze on me, waiting. Still frowning, I pushed to my feet and turned to face Ryan, putting my back to Mira. I didn't trust her, but with her anger just shy of boiling, I knew I'd feel it if she moved closer.

"Both of your concerns are valid," Ryan continued. "However, I am confident that this new arrangement will work out. Collins was selected because he is so new to being a hunter. Anyone else on the squad would not have hesitated to stake Joseph at the first opportunity, regardless of my orders."

"That's their job," I said, crossing my arms over my chest.

"If so, then we were wrong. The hunters of Themis should never have been a roving band of mercenaries." Ryan sat back down in his chair and stared straight ahead, but I don't think he was seeing Mira. His expression was too distant and tired. "Nightwalkers are not the enemy we want them to be."

"The duty of the hunters is to protect mankind," I countered.

"Their duty is to protect the secret, which protects mankind," Ryan said stiffly, finally turning his golden gaze back to my face. "Whether we wish to acknowledge it or not, both the hunters of Themis and the nightwalker coven have adopted a similar goal. We both protect the secret. When a vampire threatens that secret, someone is dispatched to take care of that threat. To foster a new alliance, a nightwalker and a hunter have been assigned to work together to bring down a recent threat. They must protect and depend on each other in order to survive."

"So you've sold us out to the devil?" I demanded. I thrust my hands through my hair, pushing it back away from my face in frustration.

"If we're the devil, what do you call the naturi?" Mira asked.

I didn't have an answer for her. Was Mira the devil? No, I didn't think so. Was her kind evil? Yes. No. Maybe. I didn't know anymore. "This is wrong."

"Maybe," Ryan sighed, his shoulders slumping. "But we need them if we are to survive whatever the naturi are plotting. Right now, I'm just trying to buy us some time and a little more firepower."

"Have you spoken with the coven?"

"No. I have met with only Mira."

I chuckled, shaking my head. "So you've struck an alliance with the one vampire Elder that half the coven would like to see decapitated. How is that going to help us?"

"Let me worry about the coven," Mira interjected. "You have other concerns at the moment."

"Like what?" I asked, the muscles in my shoulders tensing.

"You're staying in Savannah." Ryan paused for half a breath. "With Mira." He watched me closely, trying to gauge my feelings. It was as if he was waiting to see if I was going to lose my temper again. I had a better handle on things now. I wasn't thrilled with the choice Ryan had made, but right now, there was nothing I could do about any of it. When the warlock was sure that I was calm, he continued. "Two nights ago, a young woman was murdered in her apartment. It looks like her attacker wasn't human."

"Vampire?" I demanded, resisting the urge to look over at Mira.

"Maybe," he conceded, "but some of the initial information that we have received makes it look doubtful."

Mira rose from the sofa and strolled over to Ryan's desk. She perched her hips on the front of it so that she was in my line of sight. Her hands were folded in front of her and she looked calm again. "Normally, my contacts would be able to hush this up, but the girl was the daughter of a senator. He's making too much noise and the press is digging in. We have to take care of the matter quickly and quietly."

"It's your city," I snapped. "If you were here, maybe this would not have happened. You should clean up the mess."

"First off, I requested Mira's presence, at the risk of both herself and her city," Ryan said, his voice growing strained.

"Secondly, with the recent increase in naturi activity, I thought it best if you two worked together. While the preliminary information does point to a vampire, I'd rather be cautious."

"And if it is a vampire, is she going to let me do my job?" I ground out.

"If it is a vampire causing all of this chaos and attention," Mira began, her voice a cold, hard wind, "you'd better stay out of my way so that I can take care of the matter. I'm not as neat and clean about the task as you are. I don't mind getting messy." Mira slipped off the desk and walked over until she was standing directly in front of me. She lifted up on the tips of her toes so that her nose was nearly brushing mine. The air around us chilled as her powers swelled, pushing against me. "Like you said, it's my city. You're here to back me up."

I stared into her eyes, the muscle tic in my jaw twitching as I struggled to keep control of my rising tension and anger. This was all too insane. I was once again working with Mira when I should be hunting her. At least she didn't look pleased by the prospect.

"Get your things. We leave in twenty minutes," she sneered then walked out of the room and into one of the two bedrooms in the suite, slamming the door shut behind her.

Beside me, I heard Ryan sigh heavily. The warlock leaned his head into his hand, his elbow resting on the arm of his chair. His eyes were closed and he looked very tired. I think the constant meetings were starting to wear on him, and to make matters worse, he had now formed an alliance with the nightwalkers.

"Did you have to anger her?" he asked, not looking up at me.

"An alliance with the vampires?" I demanded, ignoring his comment.

"We're out of options. If you can think of a better idea, I'd love to hear it. At the moment, it's all we have." Ryan opened his eyes and stared at me. The warlock waved his hand and Mira's door briefly glowed gold before fading away. A dampening spell. I had seen him use it several times since we had met. It ensured that no one could overhear what we were discussing. "Keep her alive, Danaus. This task will most likely be completed in a couple of days and we can discuss this more when you return."

"If this is such an easy mission, why am I being sent?" I asked, my brows knitting over the bridge of my nose.

"Just in case it's not. If it is the naturi, then they will want her dead. At the moment, she is our only ace." Ryan paused, a strange smile lifting his lips as he finally looked up at me. "I think Mira also trusts you. Well, maybe not you, but your sense of honor. I don't think she would let me send anyone else with her."

"Great," I grumbled, turning on my heel. I walked out of Ryan's suite and back down the hall to my room. I needed to pack my bag yet again.

Mira trusted me. Just great. While I was off staking vampires throughout Europe, Ryan had formed an alliance with the nightwalkers so that the hunters were now working together with their prey. And Mira "trusts me." I had seen entire nations rise and fall with less maneuvering than the schemes that Ryan and Mira were concocting, and I had no wish to be a part of another fallen nation.

SEVEN

James was gone, but my duffel bag had been repacked and the weapons bag sat open beside it. James knew that I had several weapons stashed in secret locations around the room in case I suddenly found myself under attack. He had obviously not attempted to search out all the hiding places, leaving me to the final task of gathering up my toys.

Within five minutes, I had the last of my weapons packed and the bag zipped. I shoved my hands through my hair as I stared down at the leather jacket that lay across the bed. It wasn't my usual duster, but a softer one that fell only to my thighs. James had left a note saying that he was having the duster mended after the attack in Spain and that he had replaced some of my worn clothes with fresh. So much for a break from the fighting.

But I had had my chance. After returning from Peru in September, Ryan had offered to let me rest and recover from the massacre at Machu Picchu, but I didn't take it. I couldn't sit still, had to keep moving, anything to push back the thoughts humming in my brain. So the warlock sent me out to hunt the naturi and vampires on the Continent, still moving, still hunting, but close at hand should he need me.

In Berne, Switzerland, I found an earth naturi wreaking havoc in one of the local hotels. The owner had initially blamed the chaos of broken dishes, upset furniture, and overgrown gardens on a poltergeist. I was there only two nights before I spotted the lithe creature. Standing barely above four feet and dressed in all red, it resembled a sapling willow tree with long, slender arms that ended with sharpened fingernails. It took me another week of stalking the spindly little monster through the quiet courtyard garden before I finally disposed of it.

In a lonely town south of Liege, Belgium, I encountered an animal clan naturi. In English mythology, the creatures are often referred to as will-o'-the-wisps or hinky punks. The creature was leaving a trail of corpses through the outskirts of the forests of Ardennes. The naturi would often take the form of a large black dog, pretending to be lost or wounded as it lured its prey deeper in the woods. I had initially thought it was a werewolf gone mad without its pack, but the naturi soon proved me wrong.

Then the South of France, to track down a creature that was leaving behind a number of bodies that had been drained of most of their blood. Most had been an assortment of animals like large cats and dogs, but then two children and one adult went missing on three separate occasions. I passed more than a month in the region searching for the vampire that continued to kill even though I was in its current hunting ground. But no matter how hard I tried, I couldn't sense the undead creature.

Dawn had just begun to creep over the horizon one cool morning when I felt the naturi lurking nearby. It was another week before I discovered that I was hunting a naturi from the wind clan. The four-foot, bony creature had bat-like wings that it wrapped around its thin frame when it walked on the ground. It was an odd mix of human and dog with its long, narrow snout and fangs poking just over its bottom lip. This strain of the wind clan had started the old popular fairy tale of the *streghe*, from the island of Corsica. This one either had moved farther north in search of better hunting grounds or had come through one of the doors that had opened in Europe and was on its way to Corsica. It never made it. I could only guess that it was trying to frame a nightwalker for its crimes against man by taking the blood, since it had no use for it. After two weeks of hunting, I finally destroyed the creature shortly after midnight near the Mediterranean shore.

I had forgotten about Mira until that moment. I had successfully pushed her to the furthest reaches of my mind, burying her under centuries of memories that I never wanted to recall again. Yet, after incinerating the body of the wind naturi, I wandered down to the rocky shore and washed my hands in the warm waters that clapped softly in darkness. Mira had once said that I smelled of the wind and the sea. I had been born in a small village near the sea and could only guess that some part of that beginning was imprinted on my being. And she could smell it, sense it when no one else could.

Up until my travels with Mira, my experiences with vampires had been extremely limited. In fact, they generally didn't extend much past a few dark threats of torture and death. None had told me about how my powers felt or that I smelled of the sun. For countless nightwalkers, I had been death.

But my relationship with Mira would always be different. More than three months ago, we had bonded in a way neither of us had thought possible. We joined powers and destroyed countless naturi across England. And while she managed to remain sarcastic and indifferent, I could taste her fear that night like stomach acid in the back of my throat.

Both our worlds had changed that night. She became a threat to her own kind and I now had a deep connection to a creature I had sworn to kill. Even now, I could sense her emotions with very little effort. While the emotional world of the vampires had always been open to me, it had been somewhat thin and hazy compared to Mira. Her emotions entwined with my thoughts and soul in such a way that it became difficult to distinguish hers from mine. If I wanted, I could let her wash over me until I was drowning in her.

Yet I fought the temptation, erecting mental walls to keep her out, but not before I took a small taste. She was walking down the hall toward my room. She was worried—worried and scared.

My only warning was a soft knock at the door before the lock clicked and Mira walked in. I guessed that she had gotten the room key from James. She had changed out of her blue jeans and into a pair of tight-fitting black pants and dark blue silk shirt that buttoned up the front. Mira paused beside me, looking down at my two bags before walking over to the windows and pulling open the curtains. The view was nothing spectacular, just the front of another building looking down on Bay Street, but for Mira, I don't think it mattered. She was home.

"I spoke to Ryan about Thorne's death," Mira suddenly announced. Her voice was just a pale ghost drifting through the room toward me, soft and ethereal. I jerked at her sullen tone, almost surprised that she had broken her silence.

Standing at the end of the bed, I could see only her profile. Mira leaned forward, touching her head to the glass as her eyes fell shut. I folded my arms over my chest and strengthened the walls around my own thoughts. It wasn't just that I didn't want her slipping into my brain, but there was something in her emotions, some chaotic quality that I didn't want leaking into me either. "What did he say?"

I was stunned she even wanted to discuss Thorne. We had been sent to protect Thorne so that he could replace his maker in the triad. Unfortunately, he was killed shortly after we found him, poisoned with naturi blood. By the tension in her shoulders, the failure continued to haunt her.

"Ryan located the witch coven that killed Thorne. A naturi had contacted them that night and had told them to kill me," she said, the words stumbling to me. "They hadn't even been hunting him. He was probably killed because that witch couldn't be sure which mug I would drink from, so she spiked them all."

The guilt lacing her tone was unmistakable. She had

blamed herself for not protecting him when she first met him and now she blamed herself because he just happened to be in the wrong place at the wrong time. Despite her general blasé attitude about life, she took each task assigned to her seriously.

On the other hand, I couldn't muster an ounce of guilt when it came to the death of the nightwalker. I hadn't known him beyond the fact that he was a vampire living "out in the open." In truth, if I had known about him prior to meeting Mira, I probably would have killed him for the danger he posed to the people of London.

"What happened to the witch coven?"

"Ryan said it looked like three of the original eight had been in the club that night and were killed by the fire. Two more were gutted, their hearts stolen," she said, counting off each one. She didn't need to go into any more detail than that. They had been killed by the naturi they served and their hearts harvested for spells.

"And the remaining three?" I prompted when she paused.

"Ryan says disbanded and scattered."

My arms loosened and my hands slipped into my pockets. "You're not hunting them?"

Mira cracked one eye open and turned her head slightly without lifting it from the glass to look at me, a grim smile quirking one corner of her mouth. "Why bother? The naturi will finish them. Let them die at the hand of those they serve."

What she wasn't saying was that she was confident that whatever death the naturi meted out, it would be slow and painful. What more could we ask for?

"Danaus?" The sound my name on her lips drew my narrowed gaze back to her face. For a moment, she sounded hesitant and even little lost. It was a foreign sound coming from her. Mira exuded strength and confidence in whatever she did, even when she hadn't a clue, and her weakness made me wish for a knife, to defend her against whatever threat had caused the slight tremor in her voice.

"James said that you've been out hunting naturi through-out Europe," she said then suddenly stopped, seeming to wait for me to comment. Placing her hand against the glass, she lifted her head and stared down at the city, her jaw tight.

"Since the door opened, they're everywhere and they're not limiting themselves to the woods," I replied. "They've been creeping into the cities, killing humans and vampires when they can do it quietly. They don't seem to want to be noticed at this point."

"Aurora is still plotting," Mira murmured. "She has her sisters to deal with now besides me."

The queen of the naturi did have more than a few prob-lems in her lap now that she was running free on Earth. Her younger sisters now stood opposed to her plans to destroy the human race, causing the naturi race to splinter into two factions. Where she had probably thought her only resis-tance would be the nightwalkers, Aurora now faced her own kind as well.

"It's only a matter of time before she makes her move," I said, but Mira shook her head.

"No, she'll want to solidify her claim as queen first, bring her people back together and crush her sisters. She's going to need as many of the naturi at her disposal as possible if she is going to destroy both the nightwalkers and the humans. We've got some time."

Mira let her eyes sweep over the room, her fists balled at her side, but I don't think she actually saw any of it. "Do you sense any more in the city?" she suddenly snapped, glaring at me.

"No. There are no more naturi in the immediate area," I said.

Mira gave me a jerky nod and directed her gaze back out the window. The anger and frustration seemed to slowly ooze from her body. Yet when she spoke again, a cold chill crept up my spine and coiled like a snake around my neck.

"We have to get rid of them, Danaus. You have to help me. You may hate my kind, but we are no great threat to the humans you protect. The naturi will wipe us all out if we don't act. You have to help me."

"Have you spoken to the coven?" I inquired. Mira's narrowed gazed darted back to my face and she took a small step backward so that her right shoulder touched the window behind her. The coven was the ruling body for all vampires under their liege, and last I heard, Mira ranked just behind the naturi, in their "least liked" category.

"What does that have to do with the naturi?" she demanded, her tone sharpening.

"I would like to know if I'm protecting you from just the naturi or if members of the coven are hunting you as well."

"Your job is not to protect me. Your job is to help me with the investigation. If we can kill some naturi along the way, all the better. The coven is my business."

"Is Jabari hunting you?" I pressed. Jabari was not only a member of the coven, but at one time the vampire Elder had been very close to Mira. The Egyptian vampire had been her savior more than five hundred years ago at Machu Picchu and then had tried to kill her just a few months ago in England.

"No, he needs me alive. He still has a use for me." Mira looked away from me for a moment then looked back, lifting her chin a little, her lavender eyes narrowed. "I don't know the coven's plans and I don't want to know. I have no doubt they would all rather see me dead, but the Elders have all seen more than a thousand years slip by them. Time means nothing to them. If they wish me dead, they will not rush it."

"Don't trust Ryan." The words slipped out, surprising me. I hadn't meant to say it. What did I care what she planned with the warlock? But I believed in a fair fight. I believed in knowing your enemy and honor and duty; things I knew that Mira believed in as well. She was being hunted by both the naturi and the coven because of her abilities. And for his own reasons, Ryan was aiming to use her for his own means. She at least should be aware of what she faced.

Mira pinned me with a surprised gaze, one corner of her

mouth quirking in a smile. She tilted her head slightly to the left, sending her hair falling over her shoulder like a cascade of liquid rubies.

"If he has to choose between the support of the rest of the coven and you, he will betray you in a heartbeat," I continued, when she refused to speak.

The nightwalker chuckled and took a couple steps closer to me. The scent of lilacs rose up around me as I sucked in a steadying breath. Her powers brushed against me in an almost nonexistent caress, leaving me wondering if I had actually felt something. "I have not lived this long trusting powerful creatures. I know Ryan will not hesitate to stab me in the back. It is how he learned to survive in my world."

"It's just that when I saw you in his office earlier tonight it looked like . . ." The words trailed off in the back of my throat. What was I supposed to say? That it looked like I interrupted a rather intimate moment between those two. That they looked like they were already lovers?

Mira just smiled a secretive little smile as she stared up at me. "Yes," she purred. "Well, that was something else. Don't worry, my handsome protector. I don't trust your fearless leader in the least." She extended her right hand toward me and I instinctively jerked backward out of her reach. She patiently waited until I had stopped moving and she slowly ran her fingers through my hair, moving it from my eyes.

"You've let your hair grow," she said in an almost absent manner. "I like it, but it hides your face. I can arrange for you to see my stylist when you're in town."

"Don't bother," I spit out between my clenched teeth, trying to ignore the pounding of my heart. She was mocking me now, her dark mood lightening. I jerked my head to the side, moving an inch out of her reach.

Mira shrugged, returning to her usual unflappable manner. "As you wish."

A knock at the door broke us apart, sending Mira back to her previous spot by the window, while I walked over to see who had interrupted us. James smiled at me when I jerked open the door. He was wearing a heavy wool coat, appearing for all the world as if he were preparing to go out for the evening. Stepping backward, I let the man enter and then followed behind him after shutting the door.

"Are we ready to go?" James inquired eagerly.

"We?" I demanded.

"Ryan wants me to tag along with you during the investigation. I will be able to provide you with valuable research information," James replied, his smile crumbling as he spoke. "I'm guessing that he didn't mention it to you."

"No, it must have slipped his mind," I said, frowning. My first reaction was to deny the researcher the opportunity to go hunting around the city with Mira and me for the killer, but I swallowed the words. The initial part of the investigation would be checking out the girl's apartment and the body—two things that were unlikely to present any kind of significant danger to the human. Besides, James was looking to get more experience in the field, and it was better if he was at my side than wandering around at night alone down vampire-infested streets.

"He must have been more concerned about the senator," James said, directing his gaze to Mira, who was standing with her back to us, staring out the window. "Ryan was wondering if you're going to take care of the girl's family personally or send someone."

"What does he mean 'take care of'?"

"The senator and his wife are making too much noise about the unfortunate death of their daughter. It's drawing too much attention to us," Mira said, crossing her arms over her stomach. She turned toward us, leaning one shoulder against the glass. "We can't do anything about the press, but we can adjust the memory of the senator and his wife, make them more . . . accepting of what the coroner has to tell them about their daughter. They will also be more effective in placating the press so that this all finally blows over." She looked out the window once more as she paused, chewing her bottom lip in thought for a second before directing her cold gaze back at James. "When you talk to Ryan again, tell him I'm sending someone I trust. I need to focus my attention on the investigation, and the nightwalker I send may need to stay with the family for a couple nights."

Someone she trusted. In Mira's world, those people were few and far between. I had a feeling that she intended to send Knox, her second-in-command within her domain. Not only was he old enough to handle some mental manipulation, but he was also one of the only ones that Mira trusted to get the job done to her satisfaction.

"I am assuming that since I'm packed, I'm being moved out of the hotel," I said, changing the subject.

"Oh, I guess he didn't mention that either," James said, a faint blush stealing up his cheeks as his eyes darted away from me to Mira.

"You're staying in my town house," Mira announced.

"Why?" I demanded.

Mira pushed off the window she had been leaning against and turned to completely face me. "Your presence in my domain tends to draw attention and cause problems. Staying at my town house will hopefully bypass some of those problems."

In other words, my presence in Savannah would have Mira's unspoken seal of approval if I were once again staying at her town house within the historic district. I didn't like it, but unfortunately, I could see the sense in it. The lycanthropes had already pulled me aside once in fear that I had done something to the keeper of the domain. If we were going to hunt down the killer of this young woman quickly, we couldn't afford more distractions.

"And James?" I inquired.

"I'm staying at the hotel for another night or two. I don't attract attention like you do," James said with a little smirk.

"Ryan?"

The smirk dissolved almost instantly and he shrugged. "I don't know his plans. He's given me no indication that he plans to stay. I'm sure others have begun to once again show up at the Compound looking for him."

I nodded and then grabbed my coat. Ryan wasn't one to tarry too long from the comfort of his perch at the Themis Compound. It was easier for him to collect information from all his various sources if he was sitting in his office back in England.

Mira silently stepped around me and stopped beside my two bags at the end of the bed. Grabbing the strap of one, she looped it over her shoulder and smiled at me. "Let's get out of here. The warlock says we've got work to do."

With a sigh, I grabbed the second bag and my jacket before following Mira out of the hotel room with James close behind us. For nearly two thousand years, I had hunted vampires, werewolves, and other dark creatures that threatened the safety of the lies humans told themselves. Up until a couple years ago, I knew without a doubt that all nightwalkers were evil killing machines. Before meeting Mira, I knew that all nightwalkers were agents of the devil. And now, for the second time in several months, I was walking beside Mira, protecting her because I knew that she was the only one who could protect us all.

Eight

Stepping out of the hotel, I was able to finally draw in a deep, semi-cleansing breath. For now, I was away from Ryan and Themis; I could handle this task on my own terms, or at least as much as Mira would allow me to. I had no doubt that she had her own set of plans and most of it would not include me, but the situation would be handled when it came to that particular impasse. We were in her domain, and for now, I was content to let her take the lead until we actually located the culprit behind the girl's death. I didn't trust her to properly mete out justice if the killer was a vampire.

"Where are we headed first?" James asked, as we paused just outside the hotel at the corner of Bay and Bull streets. The night air was cool, forcing me to partially zip up the front of the leather jacket.

"We need to see the girl's apartment," I stated. "Check to see if we can get any leads."

Mira smirked at me over her shoulder, her eyes seeming to dance with laughter. "I would have never guessed it."

"What?" I asked, though I really didn't want to know the answer.

"You watch those murder investigation shows." She snickered.

"Mira." I tried to sound dark and threatening, but it was impossible when she was grinning like an idiot up at me.

"Come on, Danaus. Tell me!" She continued to push, pinching my forearm as I came to stand beside her.

"All of them," I finally admitted, knowing she wouldn't stop until I told her. Mira threw her head back and laughed, falling sideways into me. I stood beside her, waiting for the light to change, having no idea where we were walking to since we were pointed away from River Street, where the girl had lived. Yet, at that moment, I didn't really care. I was standing, back in Savannah, with the creature that had saved my life more times than any other in my long existence. We had our differences, and they were substantial, but there were times when they seemed to melt away, like during the heat of battle or when she just smiled harmlessly at some ridiculous jest. Mira would always be my enemy because of what she was, but sadly, she was also the closest thing I had to a friend.

After nearly a minute, Mira's laughter subsided and she straightened. Then with an absolutely serious expression, she looked up at me. "Me too." The light turned and Mira crossed the street, heading down Bull Street toward Johnson Square.

I caught up with her as she stepped onto the sidewalk again, flashing me another mocking smile.

"You're a pain in the ass," I grumbled. "Where are we going? The girl's apartment is back there on River Street."

"Already scoped out the area?" she said, arching one brow at me. "My car is this way. We're going to dump off your bags and then walk back to the apartment." Mira suddenly froze, her gaze jumping around the shadowy square filled with enormous live oak trees that stretched their great arms out in all directions, creating a network of thick limbs. By the fountain to our left, I could sense a vampire; an extremely nervous one.

I reached behind me, palming the knife from the small of my back. The act, while smooth, jerked Mira back into motion. She tightly grasped my wrist in one hand while laying a second restraining hand on my chest. "Slow down." She carefully positioned herself in front of me. "She's in the square."

"So."

"Rule One for my domain: Johnson Square is the demilitarized zone," she said, pushing me back a step when I moved to cross the street to officially enter the square. James edged around me, trying to get a better look at what had Mira and me so excited. "Everyone knows there's no fighting, no spell casting, and no hunting in this square. Same goes for Forsyth Park, and Chippewa and Monterey Squares."

"So, she's hiding out in the open?" It didn't make any sense. Why would this frightened vampire be pacing Johnson Square? I knew for a fact that the naturi didn't abide by the rules that Mira had set down for her domain, considering the slaughter that had occurred in Forsyth Park just a couple of months ago.

A frown pulled at her full lips as her eyes darted over to the park. "She wants to meet with me."

"A meeting? This is how you schedule meetings?" I mocked, loving that I finally had the chance to rib her a little. "You know cell phones are a great, convenient way to communicate. I really didn't think you'd be so reluctant to accept this century's technology."

"Asshole," she snapped, releasing my hand. "Put the knife away before I give you a new place for you to store it." Mira darted through traffic using her gift of vampire speed, leaving James and me to catch up a minute later when there was a lull in the traffic.

When we got across the square to the small fountain on its eastern side, Mira was already standing next to the other vampire. She appeared to be a young woman, somewhere between the age of twenty-two and twenty-eight when she had been reborn, with long, dark brown hair that hung wild about her shoulders. She was talking quite animatedly until her wide eyes fell on me. Her mouth fell open and she attempted to step away until Mira grabbed her arm.

With the water cascading behind them, I couldn't make out their conversation despite my keen sense of hearing. The only thing I could make out was the frightened vampire saying "I'll tell them," before Mira released her. The vampire looked at me for a second and then ran.

By the time I reached Mira, she was cursing in Italian. The steady stream of water garbled some of her words, protecting the secrets that had been told at this spot over the years.

"Good news?" I asked when I finally came to stand beside Mira.

"No, I—" She stopped herself mid-sentence, shoving one hand through her hair as she paced a couple feet away from the fountain and back again. She stopped again and looked up at me before returning to her pacing. "Something has come up. You and James should go back to the hotel. I have to take care of this and then I'll come back for you."

"No." Dropping my bag on the ground, I grabbed her by the shoulders, holding her still so that she was forced to meet my gaze. "You're not going anywhere without me. What's going on?"

"Nightwalker business."

"We don't have time for this," I reminded her, releasing her shoulders.

"I know, but I can't put this off. They already know I'm here." She paced back toward the fountain and stared down at the dancing water that seemed to sparkle in the distant lamplight. The hand wrapped around the handle of one bag tightened, causing the leather to creak.

"What's going on? Does this have to do with the murder?" James inquired before I could. I had the sickening suspicion that she intended to work on the investigation without me. I didn't trust her to leave the evidence untouched or to take out the murderer with me there.

"No!" she snapped, turning sharply on her heel to face me. She was already frustrated by the sudden turn of events and pushing her wasn't helping her mood. And in truth, I wasn't feeling particularly patient either. The longer I stayed in Mira's domain, the more I felt like a perpetual outsider. I crossed my arms over my chest, balling my hands into fists.

The nightwalker ran her left hand through her hair again, pushing some errant strands from her eyes. She stared at me in silence, a slow smile slithering across her face. "Fine. You can come, too, but James has to remain behind. After this little meeting, we'll pick up James and then we can go to the woman's apartment."

"Where?" I inquired, the wary word becoming lodged temporarily in my throat. A knot of tension tightened in my stomach and I fought the urge to reach for my knife. I knew I wasn't going to like this at all.

Mira started to walk again, ignoring my question, but I could feel the laughter and amusement bubbling from her.

"Danaus?" James asked, looking more than a little lost and confused. He wasn't the only one.

"Go back to the hotel. I'll call you when we get back," I said before picking up my bag again and following her. "This isn't a game, Mira," I called after her. "I will defend myself if I am attacked."

Mira laughed deeply and spun around to face me. I didn't feel it like usual—it was just a sound. "We're in my city this time," she said, walking backward. "They won't touch you unless you strike first. It's all a matter of whether you can behave yourself."

From the square, we walked a couple of blocks to the east until we reached one of the city's few parking garages. At the back corner of the third floor, Mira stopped in front of a black car and sighed. There was an almost peaceful look on her face as she gazed down at the sleek vehicle.

"Isn't she beautiful?" she whispered, not even looking up at me when I came to stand beside her. "I got her a few days before James showed up. I ordered her months ago after Knox banged up my M5."

"You like cars?" I asked, unable to keep the skepticism out of my voice.

Mira snorted and looked up at me like I had lost my mind.

"This isn't just a car!" she cried. "This is a 2010 BMW M6 with a five-hundred-horsepower, V10 engine. This exquisite piece of steel, glass, and leather is a work of art." Then to my shock, she bent down and placed a gentle kiss on the hood of the car. "She's my baby." With another sigh, Mira walked around to the trunk, trailing her left hand over the car's sleek lines in a loving caress. She popped the trunk using a remote and dropped in the bag she had been carrying, then stepped aside so that I could place mine beside hers.

After thirty seconds on the road with her, I realized that it wasn't the supple leather seats, the impressive sound system, or the curvaceous lines that screamed of sin and seduction that drew Mira. No, it was the raw power that she had at her fingertips. With the tires squealing, we tore out of the parking garage and through a maze of streets to the interstate, pouring through all seven gears like water rushing down a narrow gully.

A smile lifted her lips and her eyes never wavered from the road as she weaved between the widely spaced cars on the expressway. Despite the breakneck speed, I felt safe. She wouldn't do anything to threaten the existence of her "baby." And she was right. The car was an impressive symphony of sex and power that fit Mira perfectly.

Nine

We followed the pale concrete ribbon winding north out of the city and along the interstate. As traffic picked up, Mira eased up on the gas and relaxed her grip on the black leather steering wheel. In the glow of the pale interior lights, I could see the tension creeping back into her face as the joy of being back in her car started to fade.

"Where are we going?" I asked, my deep voice rumbling in the silent car like a bit of thunder.

"A small gathering of nightwalkers," she stated.

"Why?"

Mira sucked her lower lip into her mouth, holding it with her teeth for a second. This couldn't possibly bode well for me. "First Communion," she finally volunteered.

"Why do I have a feeling that this has nothing to do with the Last Supper?" I said, sarcasm sharpening my tone. My right hand tightened on the armrest on the door. This was going to be bad.

"Last night, a nightwalker within the city brought over a companion," she began.

"Brought over? As in, made another of your kind?" I interrupted.

"Yes, and if you don't settle down, I'll lock you in the trunk," she threatened, her fingers tightening on the steering wheel. "I'm not too thrilled with this development myself, but it's too late. The deed is done." She pinned me with a warning gaze for a couple seconds, and I gritted my teeth and waited for her to proceed. This was an argument for another time. She was right, in that there was nothing to stop the fact that there was yet another vampire in the world.

"All right," she continued in a huff. "First Communion is the first time a new vampire feeds. For my kind, it's a big deal. There's no real ceremony, but if the sire and new nightwalker are hunting in another nightwalker's territory, it is customary for the keeper to be present at the First Communion."

"Why?"

"To begin the process of indoctrination into our culture. There is a lot a fledgling must learn if he or she is to survive. The new nightwalker must learn the full meaning of words like 'master' and 'slave.'"

Something cold and dead crawled into her voice. There were times when something dark uncoiled in Mira when she spoke of her kind. While she was a staunch defender of vampires against the naturi, there were moments that I don't think she really liked some of the aspects of her culture. And I think it was all from some dark corner of her past. I knew nothing of the years spent with her maker beyond the fact that Mira's hatred for Sadira was second only to her hatred of the naturi.

"Will other vampires be there?" I asked.

"I imagine it will be quite crowded. It has been a long time since we last had a First Communion and things have been dark since Machu Picchu. Besides, I have been somewhat inaccessible—when it spreads that I will be present, more will come."

"And you think it wise for me to be there? A vampire hunter? I hope you don't think to pass me off as a pet."

Mira laughed and there was something unexpectedly friendly in the sound. There was nothing in it to seduce or coerce like so many of her subtle little tricks. It was just the sound of pure amusement.

"You would never be considerate enough to play the

part," she chuckled, a soft smile lifting her full lips. "No, it's not wise for you to be there, but when have I ever been wise where you are concerned?"

"True," I conceded, fighting back a grin. Her good mood was almost infectious in the few moments that it blossomed into life.

"No one will attack as long as you don't attack them. However," she said, her smile slipping a notch, "the others will be feeding while we are there. Many of the nightwalkers will bring humans to feed from. All of these humans will be there willingly."

I snorted in disbelief and opened my mouth to comment, but Mira continued before I could speak. "First Communion is one of our most important rites of passage. For some, it's even an intimate moment. If a nightwalker brings a human, it won't be some random victim off the street. The human and nightwalker will have had a history; a relationship together for a length of time. No human will be harmed tonight . . . unless you start something."

It suddenly dawned on me that Mira's concern was not the nightwalkers' reaction to my appearance tonight. She was more concerned with me doing something that would embarrass her or endanger her kind. It was also strange that she was taking me to this ceremony when it was obviously very important to her kind. Now that I knew what was going on, I had no problem with Mira dropping me off to wait for her. Yet, now it seemed like she actually wanted me there and I couldn't even begin to guess as to why.

We slipped into a pregnant silence as Mira turned the car off the expressway, winding it along one of the exit ramps. We had entered a small suburb of Savannah, with its old houses and quaint shops. We were less than ten minutes from downtown. If we were lucky, the ceremony would go quickly and we could be downtown before 10 P.M. How long would it take for a fledgling to feed, for Mira to speak to her people, and then be gone? I couldn't imagine she would want to linger with me hanging on their every word.

As we headed deeper into the quiet neighborhoods with their barren flower beds and darkened windows, I could feel the vampires ahead of us. At first it was just a handful and then their numbers climbed. By the time we parked in the cracked and crumbling driveway of a two-story house with the peeling white paint, I could sense more than thirty vampires waiting inside. At a guess, I'd say that it was every vampire within a fifty-mile radius; maybe even farther. Savannah hadn't had thirty vampires even before I started cutting into their numbers months ago.

I looked over at Mira as she turned off the car. Even in the darkness, I could see her frown and furrowed brow. "Are you sure about this?" I asked, hesitant to even unbuckle my seat belt. I had never battled this many vampires at once, not even when we faced the coven.

"It's more than I expected, but everything will be fine," she said, pulling the key from the ignition. Mira opened her door and gracefully slid out. I followed behind her, distinctly lacking her confidence. Of course, Mira had walked into the coven's Main Hall with her head held high and oozing self-confidence. That was just her style.

As she shut her door, I saw her snap back around as something caught her attention at the last second. She lunged a couple of steps forward then stopped, her fists balled at her side. Her powers exploded from her body, nearly knocking me back a step. I grabbed my knife from its sheath at my side and stood beside her, stretching out my powers as well. I scanned the area, but I felt nothing but the vampires in the house behind us.

"What—?"

"Naturi. Do you sense any naturi?" she rasped in a low voice. Her whole body hummed with energy, ready to lash out.

"No. None anywhere near here." It had become second

nature at this point to search for them. The naturi seemed to be constantly at our heels, lurking around every corner. I've learned to search for them at every opportunity if I want to have any hope of staying alive much longer.

Mira stood in the middle of the empty street, her hands extended out from her body, bathed in blue flames. Confusion and rage rolled off her in equal parts, hitting me in the chest as I took a couple steps closer to her. My gaze swung from one end of the street to the other, praying that no one chose that moment to look out their window. Mira had always been very careful to be discreet about the use of her powers, doing nothing that would threaten the exposure of her world. Yet, I could feel the fear driving her to this desperate act. If anything moved at that moment, it was going to be burned to a crisp.

"Mira, you're drawing attention to us," I hissed. "Put the fire out."

"Are you sure?" she snapped, still not looking over at me as she ignored my warning.

"Yes."

"I want to search." She extended her hand toward me, her wide eyes still sweeping the empty streets. All the windows were darkened and doors shut. All the humans seemed to be settling in for the night, plopped down in front of the TVs, or snuggled in their beds. I could sense one man shuffling through the hall four houses down from us. Beyond that, there were only the vampires.

"Mira . . ."

"Please, Danaus," she said, jerking her head around to look up at me. "I have to be sure. Just like in Venice." It was the urgency in her voice that finally convinced me to wrap my fingers around her slender white hand. In Venice, we had bonded our powers so that she could search the home of the coven for a naturi; without my help, Mira could not sense the naturi. A web of vampire spells had blocked my senses, but Mira could peer through them. In

Venice, she had been right, so I was reluctant to second-guess her instincts now.

With her small, slightly chilled hand lost in my larger one, I drew in a deep breath, shoving it down to the soles of my feet. As I released it, I slowly pushed the energy perpetually balled in my chest through my arm and into Mira. Her hand jerked in my grasp as the power hit her and I could hear a small whimper escape her before she could stop it. At the same time, the wall that hid her thoughts and emotions from the world came crashing down. I sucked in a ragged, harsh breath, fighting for balance in the raging sea of her thoughts. Mira was confused and angry at what she saw, but somehow she managed to keep that thought hidden from me. I didn't fight for it when I tasted the slight tang of fear that lingered about the memory.

"Too much," she rasped, drawing my attention back to the task at hand. I turned my thoughts inward, focusing on the flow of energy I was directing into her. It was hard to control the flow. A deeper feeling of warmth filled my limbs and only intensified when I sent more power into her. There was also a sense of completion and peace that teased at the periphery of my senses, making me believe if I just let loose, the wonderful sensation would flood my brain and soul, finally making me feel whole.

Yet for all the peace and fulfillment I felt, Mira experienced equal parts pain. I could barely sense that gut-twisting agony, but I didn't need to. It was also written all over her trembling limbs and drawn expression. While this technique of combining powers was effective in killing opponents, I had a feeling that if I let loose, it would rip Mira in half. Particularly if she decided to fight me.

With the connection created and my thoughts firmly entrenched in Mira's mind, I reached out again. We scanned the area slowly, at first just a couple blocks, and then miles in all directions. There were no naturi in the region.

"Enough," I said gruffly, pulling my hand free of Mira's.

She stumbled a step forward but managed to catch herself before she fell to her knees. I reached for her arm to steady her, but then stopped myself. The connection was too fresh and I could feel the pain throbbing through Mira's trembling body.

The nightwalker straightened and shook her head as if to clear it. She was still frowning as her eyes swept the street one last time. "No one," she whispered, sounding confounded by the fact.

"What did you see?"

"I thought . . . I thought I saw a naturi," she said, struggling to say the word as if it would summon one by magic.

"Rowe?" I demanded, forcing the name past an unexpected knot in my throat. That one-eyed naturi had been the only one I had ever seen with the ability to pop in and out with magic. He had also tried to grab Mira on two separate occasions: once in Egypt and a second time in London. I had little doubt that the naturi was still alive somewhere and plotting ways to get his hands on Mira.

"No, not him," Mira said. Her voice was rough and uneven as she looked up and down the street. Her fingers flexed at her sides as if she were aching to once again light a fire to protect herself.

"Should we continue? If we're being watched, it might not be a wise idea to have everyone gathered in one place." A fight between vampires and the naturi in the middle of the night in a quiet suburb would not be a good thing. It would be splashed across every newspaper and news agency for days. It would also endanger the humans sleeping peacefully in their beds around us.

Mira shook her head and straightened her shoulders. "No, we continue." Her tone was strong and firm again despite the fear I could still feel hanging in the air around her. With her head up, Mira turned on her heel to walk up toward the house. "It was nothing. A trick of the light and shadow."

Her explanation sent a chill down my spine. A night-walker's eyesight was better than any nocturnal creature's regardless of his or her age. I was reluctant to dismiss Mira's partial glimpse, but there was nothing we could sense in the area. For now, a house full of vampires eagerly awaited our arrival.

Ten

The warped wooden boards creaked and groaned as we stepped onto the sagging porch. The sound echoed through the desolate neighborhood and a small woman with dark hair pulled open the door and quickly stepped aside to let Mira enter. She kept her head bowed when she saw the nightwalker and her smile was timid. Yet when her large, brown eyes fell on me, a soft hiss erupted from her throat and she leaped several feet backward. A flurry of Spanish escaped her, but I was unable to catch it all. It didn't matter what the words were, I understood the sentiment and there was no mistaking the fear in her eyes.

"He is my guest, Rosa," Mira proclaimed, her gaze never wavering from the terrified vampire's round face. However, her voice was loud enough to carry to everyone on the first floor. It was a general announcement to all those assembled.

"But . . . he is . . . the . . . the hunter," Rosa stammered, her mind struggling to wrap itself around the implications. Of course, so was mine. It was going to be an awkward night.

"He is my guest," Mira repeated. Her voice had hardened to the same steely consistency as her will. She was giving them an unspoken choice; accept my presence or face her.

"Of course, Keeper," Rosa said, bowing her head again. She pushed away from the wall she had pressed herself into to escape me and ushered us through the dimly lit narrow hall to the living room.

It was a small room made even smaller by the dozen vampires and their human companions strewn about the room like so much gothic decoration. It was a motley assembly ranging from the traditional Hollywood garb of black leather, dark makeup, and silver chains to the ultra-sophisticated in Armani, Valentino, and Dolce and Gabbana. These midnight predators were draped over the worn and faded furniture like pretty decoration. Some barely moved when we entered the room, nothing more than a quick flick of the eyes, while others shifted away from me.

Knox stood in the far corner with his arms folded over his chest. Mira's second-in-command gave me a brief nod, which was more than I had actually expected. The blond nightwalker named Amanda stood near him, her hands shoved in the front pockets of her jeans as she stood staring at the floor, avoiding my gaze. But then, most of the nightwalkers in the room refused to meet my eyes.

Mira barely looked at any of them, keeping her attention on the vampire who had opened the door. "Are we ready to begin?" she demanded.

"Yes, whenever you are ready," Rosa replied, wringing her hands.

"Then let's begin. I have other business tonight," Mira said. Around us, vampires rose to their feet like marionettes being pulled up by their strings. I barely managed to stop myself from pulling my knife at my side at the nightmarish sight. If I ever slept again, I knew this scene would be replaying for years to come in my mind. A few swept by us and back into the hall, but they never looked at me. For many, humans walked at their side, so silent one would think we were entering a cathedral for Mass.

Mira placed her hand in the crook of my left arm, drawing my eyes to her upturned face. It was only when she touched me that I realized that my heart was pounding and every muscle was tensed. The lavender-eyed nightwalker winked at me, one corner of her mouth quirked in a half smile as she guided me back to the hall. While she was teasing, I could still sense the underlying thread of worry running through her mind.

In the hall, we abruptly turned and marched single file down a set of wooden stairs into the basement. As Mira preceded me, she removed her hand from my arm, and placed my left hand on her slim shoulder. I didn't question this sudden need for physical contact. At the moment, I was in their world and would have to play by their rules. In the brief second that she touched my hand, she also took the opportunity to touch my mind.

Relax, she whispered in my thoughts. For once, I didn't mind the invasion. I needed the reassurance that we had not walked into a trap.

The basement was large and open with only an old cast-iron furnace resting in the far corner. A pair of bare lightbulbs dangled from the low ceiling, vainly attempting to push back the darkness. Vampires and their human companions alike stood and sat along the walls. They were all silent, but I could feel the faint pressure of the mental conversation among the vampires in my brain. These deadly creatures were completely still, standing like carefully arranged mannequins in the attempt to simulate life, but the air tingled with a strange mix of hunger and excitement.

In the center of the room sat a thin waif with stringy brown hair and sunken cheeks on a metal folding chair. Her skin had a sickly gray pallor. At a guess, this was the newborn, fresh from death. Behind her stood a man with blondish brown hair and clear blue eyes. When he had been reborn, he appeared to have been no more than eighteen or nineteen. While it was hard to pinpoint in a room with so many nightwalkers, he didn't feel very old. In fact, he felt a lot younger than I had expected.

Mira paused not far from the foot of the stairs and lifted

my hand from her shoulder. She looked up at me one last time and winked. *Stay here. Don't move unless I say to,* she silently directed. While I wasn't fond of the idea of following her commands, I had a feeling we would both live a lot longer if I did.

Yes, mistress, I hissed back.

Mira nearly choked on the bubble of laughter she fought back and failed. Shaking her head, she turned her back on me and walked over to stand in front of the fledgling and her maker.

"Welcome, Keeper," the male vampire said, his hand tightening on the back of his child's neck. There were lines of tension around his eyes and mouth.

"David," Mira replied stiffly, her hands resting on her hips. I couldn't see her expression any longer, but I could hear her draw in a long, deep breath. Expelling the unnecessary air, she made a sound of disgust in the back of her throat. "She smells more of death than life."

"She must feed," David quickly countered, looking a bit confused.

"Blood drawn tonight won't fix that," Mira snapped. "You made her too quickly." She placed her right hand under the girl's chin and lifted it so that the fledgling was forced to meet her gaze. "You both are too young."

"She will survive," David stated, as if by sheer will he could keep the newborn vampire alive. But I doubted it truly worked that way.

"Will she?" Mira shot back. The threat hung heavy in the air. Around the trio, the vampires seemed to lean in, intent on the conversation. When Mira continued, her voice had dropped to a whisper. "You didn't heed my advice. You sought me out; asked if you should turn her. I said no."

For the first time, David's strong voice wavered. "I don't need your permission to create a companion."

"No, but you went against my direct wishes," Mira hissed. David tried to take a step backward, but it was too late. Mira's hand flashed from the fledgling's chin to David's throat. With little strain she tossed him across the room and into the wall behind her. At the same time, the gathered vampires scattered, allowing David to slam into the cinderblock wall.

I tensed, waiting for the others to attack Mira, but no one moved. The excitement in the room doubled, thickening until I could nearly taste it like honey. Several vampires were now smiling, eagerly watching the display. The emotions pounded against my brain. And with it grew a red haze. They were hungry and the bloodlust was growing. The room suddenly grew hotter and there was a buzzing in my brain. The dark creature that seemed to live inside of me stirred to life, as if the potential for bloodshed had awakened it.

Coming here had been a very bad idea. Mira was aware that I could sense her emotions and thoughts, but she seemed to forget that I could also sense the emotions of other vampires. I had been around other vampires when their lust for blood filled them, but only a couple at a time, so I could fight off the feeling, suppress it so that it didn't overwhelm my own thoughts. But here in a small room with more than thirty vampires, it was swamping me.

The monster wrapped around my soul dug its claws deep and roared, demanding release. It demanded bloodshed and violence, and my hands ached to wrap around the handle of a blade. At the same time, the vampires' bloodlust beat against my brain, leaving my teeth throbbing, my tongue searching for nonexistent fangs.

With my jaw clenched, I drew in a slow, deep breath through my nose, and pushed the demon back down. I forced my attention back to David as he picked himself up off the ground. He kept one hand on the wall as if he was too scared to move away from it and closer to Mira.

"She didn't wish to grow any older," David said.

There was a gasp in the air at his admission and the vampire near him sidled away. The bloodlust ebbed under the weight of the shock and I was able to get a grip on myself again. Mira had been in the process of turning to look at me when David's words stopped her, allowing me to see a faint glow filling her eyes in the dim light.

"So you obey a human over me," she said in a deceivingly calm voice.

"No!" he cried. "Please, I love her."

"I have a remedy for your loyalty issues," Mira replied. For half a breath, David's eyes flitted over to me and then back to Mira. Enraged, she lunged at him, grabbing the front of his white button-up shirt. She threw David to the ground with a heavy thud and straddled him so that she could more easily wrap her hands around his neck. The vampires shifted; the excitement building, but I was ready for it this time, strengthening the walls around my mind. I couldn't read their thoughts without forcibly pushing my way into them, but a call for David's death hung ominously in the air.

I found myself leaning forward, my heart pounding in my chest as I waited to see if Mira would kill him. She had destroyed others of her kind as a test of power and skill. The Fire Starter was teetering on the edge as she battled her own bloodlust that was screaming in her mind. I could feel her frustration and her anger at David's choices, but there was something else gnawing at her thoughts that I couldn't quite define.

"Your problem lies with me," she growled through clenched teeth. "Not with the hunter. You are weak and you have created something less than chum. Neither of you will live long."

"No! David!" the fledgling cried, leaping from her small, metal folding chair. Mira launched herself off of David and into the young woman. Catching her by the shoulders, Mira slammed her into one of the metal columns supporting the main beam in the house.

"Who is your master?" Mira snarled.

"David," the girl cried, bloody tears streaming down her pale face.

"Wrong answer." Mira pulled the girl back and slammed

her into the column again, causing a deep, hollow bong to echo through the silent room. "One last try."

"I—I don't understand," the fledgling cried.

"Mira!" David shouted. He had rolled over onto his stomach, but froze in the act of pushing to his feet. "Mira is the keeper of the city and member of the coven. She is your master below our liege. I am your sire. Next to Mira, I am nothing."

"Very good," Mira murmured. She released the young vampire, letting her slide to her knees as tears poured down her cheeks. Turning on her heel, she gazed down at David, who remained lying on the dusty floor, afraid to move. His neck had been cut where Mira had grabbed him, staining the collar of his shirt red. "She has much to learn. I am going to be merciful, though I should kill you both. Teach her, David. Teach her everything you know." Mira lifted her eyes and slowly looked over the assembled group of vampires that surrounded her. "The naturi are here and we cannot afford to be weak."

The excitement drained out of the room to be replaced by a tremor of fear. Several vampires drew their human companions closer as if suddenly desperate for their warmth. The subterranean room grew cold and the air was stale. No one met another's eyes. Mira wasn't the only one haunted by the threat of the naturi. While I had a feeling that she was the only one who had experienced the dark threat of the naturi firsthand, the assembled mass could sense her fear and hatred when she spoke of them. That was enough.

Squatting down before him, Mira grabbed a handful of David's short hair and jerked his head up so that his wide eyes were locked on hers. "For now, you belong to me. You serve me and obey my wishes to the letter until I choose to release you."

Mira stood and walked back over to me, her face carefully blank. But the connection was still strong between us. I could sense her frustration and self-loathing burning away at her soul like acid. She hadn't enjoyed it like those hanging on her every movement. *Dirty* drifted through her mind for a brief second before she could catch it and hide it from me. The threats and violence had been a necessity. It was what her culture was built upon, what they responded to. She told me herself months ago that the most important thing in her world was power and the only way to express it was through fear and violence. While she might not like it, she was a master at the art.

Reaching up, I slipped my hand under her hair and touched the tips of my fingers to the back of her neck. It was easier to communicate using my thoughts when we were touching. It required less energy and I was trying not to draw the attention of the others to us as they watched David crawl over to his child. Mira flinched at my touch, surprised that I was reaching out to her.

You had no choice, I said firmly in her mind.

There is always a choice. Her emotions were solemn and dark, creeping into my brain like an icy fog.

You have to maintain control. It's like you said, you can't afford to be weak.

When her thoughts reached me again, they were weary. *I should have killed them both.*

Her statement made me pause. *True. But they do not think you are weak because you showed mercy.*

Mira's thoughts were blank for a long time as we watched David cradle the young vampire in his arms, soothingly brushing her hair from her face. Her sobbing had slowed to a soft whimper. Her initial fear had begun to subside and now the steady throb of hunger had begun to overwhelm her thoughts. I could feel it in my brain beside Mira, a burning need next to her cool, somber presence.

A quick death from me would be more merciful than one meted out by the naturi. Her haunted whisper crept back into my brain, surprising me.

You don't know that is their fate.

But it's mine, and the naturi will destroy everything in their path to get to me. Mira reached up with her left hand

and gently pulled my left hand away from her neck and drew
my arm around her slender waist. I tried to pull my arm free
without struggling, but she held tight to my wrist. She leaned
into me, pressing her back into my chest. Some of the tension eased from her shoulder and her mind was silent.

Mira. My tone had hardened and I tried to sound threatening, but her calm mood was leaking into mine. I had
wanted to ease her worries because any distractions could
put us both in danger, but for all intents and purposes, we
were still enemies. Right?

Hush. It's about to start.

We're going to watch her feed? I demanded, pulling at
my arm again.

And then some. I could feel the slight rumble of laughter
roll through her mind and into mine. My attention darted
back to the center of the room as a slender man in his late
twenties pushed off the wall to my right and walked toward
David and his child. He wore a pair of worn blue jeans and a
faded black T-shirt. The man's eyes never left the two vampires in the center of the room except to briefly flick over to
Mira. Kneeling beside the young woman, he ran his hand
over her head and down her back, smoothing her hair.

David leaned close and pressed a kiss to the man's temple
then whispered something in his ear that I couldn't quite
make out. The tension around the man's mouth eased and
he almost smiled.

Mira?

*He belongs to David. I think his name is Peter, but I'm
not sure. He will be Emma's first meal.*

I was about to question how she knew the fledgling's
name, but remembered that she had already spoken to David
about bringing the girl into the family. There was also the
chance that Mira had dipped into Emma's mind, inspecting
her.

The newborn nightwalker turned in David's arms so
that she was now facing Peter. I caught the faint glow of
her eyes before her back was to me and her hunger was now

pounding in my brain to the point where I could barely feel Mira's presence. I pulled against Mira's grip and tried to take a step away, but she held tight. I had to get out of there. I couldn't watch this. I couldn't watch another creature feed upon a human. I was drowning, my breath coming in shallow gasps between clenched teeth. The hunger was not just coming from the fledgling anymore, but from every vampire in the room. A cold sweat broke out across my arms and rolled down my back despite the chill that hung in the air.

Wait for it! Mira's voice sounded almost breathless in my mind, eager and a little desperate.

I never saw Emma place her mouth to Peter's throat, but I felt her sharp fangs piercing his flesh. I flinched, resisting the urge to touch my own throat to see if I was bleeding as well. And then the first wave hit.

Sensations exploded outward from Emma and Peter, slamming into my chest with enough force to push me back a step. The wave sucked me under, bathing me in a feeling of warm, liquid pleasure. I breathed deeply as the blissful sensation sank into my rigid frame, melting my bones. The air grew warm, drying the cold sweat that had formed just moments ago. Time slowed until I could crawl between the seconds and hold them apart. Tension drained from my limbs to pool at my feet.

As I grew accustomed to the feeling, I looked up in time to see the other gathered vampires pulling their human companions closer. It was like waves pounding on the shore during a violent storm, but this time there was no sensation of piercing fangs, just mindless, raw pleasure flooding my brain.

A deep moan slipped past my parted lips and I buried my face in Mira's neck as my eyes fell shut. I wrapped my right arm around her waist, pulling her tighter against me. My hand slipped under her untucked shirt, sliding across her smooth stomach. Her skin was like cool satin and I suddenly had the overwhelming desire to touch every inch of her. But even as the notion glided across my mind, I knew it wouldn't be enough. I wanted to know all of her; to be buried deep inside of her as her tongue grazed my feverish skin.

Mira arched against me, pressing her backside into my groin as I grew harder. Reaching up, she slid her hands along my shoulder into my hair. She held my face imprisoned against her neck.

My left hand tightened on her hip, keeping her pinned against me, while my right hand glided over her stomach, across the softest skin I had ever felt. Cool satin. I wanted to rip her clothes off and press her against me. Only the feel of her skin would cool the heat that continued to rise within me. My right hand closed over one breast and a soft moan escaped her as her hands tightened in two fistfuls of my hair. I breathed in her scent, letting my lips and teeth skim along her bare neck, nearly biting her.

Thoughts of our constant fighting were just a worn, faded memory. At that moment, there was only Mira and the need to possess her completely. I wanted to sink into this feeling that seemed to have been hiding in the shadows of my mind for months now and let the world slip away from us.

What felt like hours later, the waves lessened and my thoughts crept back to something that resembled logic. I drew a deep breath in through my nose, inhaling Mira's intoxicating lilac scent and a faint hint of her shampoo. I started to lift my head and my hand dropped from where it was still caressing her hard nipple through her lacy bra when her voice skipped through my mind.

Wait. The throb of need in her tone gave me pause. Her right hand slid from the back of my neck along my face, a gentle caress from my temple to my jaw. I got a deep sense of peace from the nightwalker; something I had never encountered in her.

With a heavy sigh, Mira dropped her hands back to her sides and I released my hold on her. Around the room, vampires and humans were entangled, locked in an embrace that was shifting from blood to sex. Peter lay in Emma's arms, considerably paler but still conscious. The fledgling was running her fingers through his hair while David trailed kisses up her neck to her ear.

David looked up at Mira suddenly. *I shall come when summoned.*

I jerked a half step backward at the invasive new voice. David locked surprised eyes on me then quickly looked away. He had not meant for me to hear that, only Mira. My connection with Mira was still strong and their thoughts were a low murmur in my mind. This was not something I wanted the others to know.

With a slight nod, Mira turned and walked back up the stairs. My heavy footsteps trudging behind her rumbled like thunder over the soft moans and sighs rising up from the basement occupants. I paused on the front porch and rolled my shoulders, welcoming the touch of the cold night air against my flushed cheeks.

Rational thought slammed through my mind once again, causing my hands to start shaking. What had I done? Mira was a vampire. She was my enemy, always would be. She and all of her kind were evil, and yet I had just wrapped my body around hers and wanted to bury myself so deeply within her that we could never be parted. I could blame the bori within me that made me susceptible to the blood-lust driving all of the nightwalkers in that basement, but if I was honest with myself, it was more than that. I was drawn to Mira. Her smile, her laugh, her irreverent sense of humor, and her compassion for those weaker than her-self all sucked me in, so that I felt as if I were sinking in quicksand. I was fighting a battle with myself to continue hating her, and tonight proved only one thing to me: I was losing.

"Why did you bring me here?" I demanded, still standing on the edge of the porch.

Mira continued to walk to the car, throwing a little smirk over her shoulder at me. She pulled the remote out of her pocket and the lights blinked once as the doors unlocked.

"Tell me why!" I commanded, hating the slight tremble in my voice.

She finally paused a couple feet from the car and turned to fully face me. So I could see a flash of fang pressing against her lower lip. "I need you to understand us," she replied. "And I need you to better understand yourself and your tie to my people. You're one of us."

"I am not a vampire," I said, descending the first couple steps.

"No, but you're closer to us than you are to being human." The wind picked up and pulled a strand of hair across her face, forcing her to thread it behind her ear. "The only way you will stop hunting us is if you understand that you are one of us. We're not the enemy."

"You're evil," I stubbornly said, but even that statement lacked its usual venom. I had had it beaten into my brain for centuries, but standing wrapped in the warm emotions of lust, passion, and even for some, love, I struggled with that belief. It was starting to crumble before my eyes.

"No more than the rest of mankind," she said with a shrug. "We were all human once. Becoming a nightwalker didn't change our souls."

"Just your instincts," I snapped.

To that, Mira simply shrugged as she turned back toward the car. "Come along, hunter," she said. "We don't have time to tarry here." With her hand on the door, she stopped and looked over her shoulder at me, a playful grin spreading across her face. "Besides, my restraint is fading."

Quickly descending the last of the creaking porch stairs, I jumped into the passenger seat, sinking into the soft leather. This battle would not be won or lost tonight. I needed to think more.

I glanced at the clock as Mira started the car. It wasn't yet

9 P.M. I stared at it, my mind unable to comprehend what I was seeing. We had been in there for only thirty minutes. I would have guessed hours had drifted by in mind-numbing bliss.

We were in the car for several minutes before my hard voice finally shattered the silence. "What was that?"

"First Communion."

"I've been around when vampires feed. I've never felt anything like that."

"What you felt is what we feel every time we feed. A nightwalker can control whether his or her victim or other nightwalkers can feel it. A fledgling cannot. The first time you feed, it's always the best. It's a rush of power and pleasure like nothing you've ever known. For the first time, you're connected to every living thing on the planet." Her voice had taken on a dreamy quality, caressing my mind. "It's why First Communion is so important. It's our chance to relive that one moment. And for some, it's a chance to remake that memory with someone important. Depending on the maker, First Communion doesn't always go well for a fledgling. Emma was very lucky."

"So now it has turned into an orgy."

"Yeah." Mira sighed. "You want to go back?"

I remained silent, watching out my window as we pulled back onto the expressway headed south toward downtown Savannah. Images and sensations were still strong in my mind and I was struggling to reconcile them. I had wanted Mira like nothing I had ever known before. Had she put those thoughts in my head? Were they the result of the feeding vampires? I had desired Mira before, but I had never touched her. She was a vampire; I was supposed to kill her, not want to have sex with her.

As the city rose up before us and we descended into the valley, I pushed those concerns away: but a new, grim thought dawned on me. "It looked like every vampire in the city was there."

Mira's hands tightened on the steering wheel and the car accelerated, gliding past ninety miles per hour. Her chin dipped to her chest, causing her hair to fall like a curtain along the side of her face, hiding her expression. "Almost."

Almost. Tristan, her precious ward and one of her few family members, had been missing from the gathering.

ElEVEN

On Bay Street, Mira pulled into an open parking spot just a few blocks from Bull Street and City Hall while I called James to tell him where to meet us. As she shut off the car, Mira reached down and pulled a lever that popped the trunk. I slid out of the car at the same time as she and walked to the back of the vehicle. Knowing Mira had an old-fashioned distaste for guns, I expected to see a variety of knives, daggers, and swords gleaming in the light from the overhead streetlamp. Yet, when Mira opened the black leather bag hidden in the back of the trunk, all I saw were clothes.

I threw her a puzzled look then reached down and lifted up a pile of clothes only to find more clothes. The night-walker smiled as she lightly smacked my hand away then returned to tucking in her shirt into her jeans.

"We can't all walk around looking like hired thugs for the Mafia," Mira teased. Rolling up her sleeves, Mira pulled a pair of wrist sheaths out of one pocket of the bag and strapped them on before pulling her sleeves back down. She also snapped a knife sheath to her belt, placing it down the back of her pants at her spine. All of her knives were small and lightweight, good for throwing or close fighting. With her clothes resettled, she pulled on a black suit jacket, but left it unbuttoned.

"A person will more willingly believe a thought you put in their head if it matches what they see," Mira explained. "And right now, I want them to believe we're detectives for the local police."

While Mira's clothes probably cost more than what most detectives made in a month, she did have a more professional air about her than usual. I, on the other hand, was dressed in my usual black cotton pants and turtleneck with worn black boots.

James appeared as she was shutting the trunk of her car, his cheeks flushed as he was slightly winded from the jog over from the nearby hotel. "Everything go okay?" he inquired as he brushed some hair out of his eyes.

"Fine," I replied sharply, at which Mira lightly chuckled. If I were lucky, what occurred at that house would never be spoken of. The implications were something I wasn't ready to contemplate while we were in the middle of a murder investigation, if ever.

With everything settled, we followed Mira down a dark set of stone stairs to the lower level, called Factors Walk. River Street was the next block over and was at the level of the river, while Bay Street was at least one story above River Street. This was where I had briefly encountered the young girl earlier in the day. A quick glance over the area revealed that she was currently nowhere to be found.

The wide alley was cloaked in darkness, as the main streetlamps on Bay Street didn't reach down into Factors Walk. A couple of the buildings had doorways on Factors Walk, but their dim lamps did little to cut into the thick darkness. Our footsteps echoed off the ballast stone street and along the surrounding walls and building fronts.

A man stood in one doorway, his back pressed to a wall, a position that allowed him to watch our approach. He pensively puffed on a cigarette, his dark eyes narrowed, deepening the crisscross of wrinkles that dug deep furrows in his face. His gray pants and white shirt were rumpled and half hidden beneath a dark brown trench coat. He reached up and twisted what appeared to be a blown-out lightbulb in a lamp by the doorway until it flickered on, blanketing the region in dirty yellow light.

"You're late," he announced, flicking away the cigarette. I sank back into the shadows, out of the reach of the light that hung outside the front door of the six-story redbrick building. My life had been spent perfecting the art of invisibility, slinking along the fringe of a person's memory. James, on the other hand, stood directly beside the nightwalker, blinking at the light as he stepped into it.

"Something came up," Mira replied, standing at the foot of the three stairs that led up to the building. She hovered along the edge of the light, her pale skin glowing like a grounded star. From her left jacket pocket, she withdrew a pair of sunglasses with blue-tinted lenses and settled them on the bridge of her nose.

The man shoved his right hand into his pocket and pulled out a creased pack of cigarettes. "I've been waiting for almost an hour, damn it. People are gonna start asking questions."

"You really should stop smoking," Mira calmly said, looking up at him.

"Smoking ain't gonna kill me. It's dealing with your kind that'll do me in," he grumbled, pulling out a cigarette. "You know of any city where your kind hasn't settled?"

"There's very few of us in the Dakotas," Mira supplied cheerfully, earning a derisive snort from the man as he flicked his lighter. Cupping his hands around the cigarette, the brief flash of light further illuminated his features and picked up the flecks of gray in his dark brown hair. He was older than I had initially thought, worn to an angry nub by his years.

"That's okay." His sarcastic sneer twisted his lips around

his cigarette as he took a long drag. "This is enough of a hole."

"Then move," Mira suggested.

"Can't," he sighed. "Annie's family is here and the girls are settled." For a brief moment, his expression softened and he exhaled deeply. With a shake of his head, he reached in his pocket. "Keys for the front door and apartment. Top floor. Can't miss it." Mira caught the pair of keys on a ring in one hand as he tossed them to her.

"The report?" She bounced the keys in her hand so that they jangled softly.

"I'm working on it. Probably won't have it all until morning," he said with another shake of his head.

"Leave it at the town house. He can look at it during the day," Mira directed, motioning with her head toward me. The man looked me over for a breath, his eyes sweeping over my features as if trying to memorize my appearance. I froze, my eyes locking with his, like I was a wolf sizing up an opponent.

"He's not one of yours?" he asked at last, his eyes still moving over my face as if he was internally weighing some thought that didn't match up with my appearance. There was something in his tone. I couldn't decide whether he was surprised that I wasn't a vampire, or surprised that I wasn't a vampire yet.

"No, just an associate," Mira replied.

"And this one?" he asked, nodding his head toward James.

James took a step forward and extended his hand toward the smoking man. "James Parker. I work as a researcher and I'm here to assist Mira in this matter."

Before the stranger could say anything, Mira took one step closer, and the man came down the stairs, careful not to brush against her. He gave a small grunt, ignoring James's extended hand as he took another puff off his cigarette. He paused a couple of feet away from me, looking up at Mira as she stood at the top of the stairs. "You've got to be quick about this one," he warned, his fingers nervously fiddling with his cigarette. "Too many people are watching." He then turned and quickly walked down the alley, a thin trail of smoke lifting into the air behind him as he turned a corner and headed down to River Street. I watched him for a brief moment then followed Mira and James up the three stairs and into the redbrick building.

Closing the door behind me, I blinked against the bright light that flooded the empty hallway. The walls were painted white and the doors and woodwork were all dark mahogany. The building was old, but very clean and well maintained. The floor was covered in tiny white and blue ceramic tiles arranged in an intricate design of flourishes and flowers. Someone had put a great deal of money into restoring this building.

Mira paused at the foot of the main staircase, sending her powers out around her. The cool brush lasted only a second and I found myself reaching out with her. It had become a habit now when she was near to search for the naturi.

"Anything?" she murmured, her left hand resting lightly on the banister.

"Only humans," I replied.

The nightwalker nodded and started up the stairs, her left hand sliding along the rail. I followed behind her, my footsteps loud and heavy in the silent apartment building. During my two previous trips to Savannah, I had spent very little time in this part of town. Here resided the young professionals that still liked to be close to all of the trendy clubs and bars in the city. The vampires were more than happy to hunt in this section of town, but it was dangerous for me to hunt them among so many humans. I would wait until they slunk back to the fringe of the city for their daytime slumber before I would attack.

And now one vampire had gone too far and killed a woman with connections. A careless or heartless moment had put everyone in danger of being outed. With the naturi lurking in the shadows, we were all walking along the edge of the knife, praying that the secret would last for just a few more years.

Of course, the coven would do what it had done for years and cover up this little mess. The vampires had their resources. Even Mira was not without her connections within the city.

"Who was the man out front?" I inquired, trying to keep my voice low as we reached the second-floor landing.

"Daniel Crowley," Mira replied, continuing up the stairs. "Homicide detective."

"And he helps you?"

"Sometimes. He gives me a call when something looks funny. He slows up the paperwork and gives me a look at what the police are seeing. He gives me a chance to take care of things before too many people start asking questions."

"Do you pay him for this inside information?"

Mira sharply turned on the stair to face me, her eyes narrowed. "Daniel isn't a dirty cop, if that's what you're implying. He's no different than you. He wants to protect the people of this city. Yes, I pay him a small consulting fee. He's got five daughters in private schools. That doesn't come cheap."

"I'm sorry," I said, breaking eye contact first. For a vampire that reveled in her independence, Mira was showing a surprising amount of protectiveness for a collection of creatures. But I had a feeling that Daniel had earned her respect. He was sticking his neck out to protect mankind and help Mira. What did I care if Mira compensated him for his troubles?

"Thanks," Mira said gruffly, then turned and continued up the stairs.

It wasn't until we had reached the third floor that James finally spoke up. "How did he find out . . . about everything?"

"His sister-in-law is a member of the local pack," she said, glancing over her shoulder. There was a somewhat wry smile teasing at her lips as she spoke. "Only Daniel and his brother know, but it opened his eyes to the rest of us."

That way was better than what I had been expecting. It probably hadn't been a comfortable moment for Daniel Crowley, but I doubted it caused him to wake up in a cold sweat with a scream lodged in his throat. Those few humans who knew that vampires, lycans, and all the other creatures existed were generally survivors with gruesome tales of blood and pain, and poorly healed scars.

I stopped at the top of the stairs on the top floor next to Mira. There were only two apartments on the sixth floor. The apartment on the left had its door close to the stairs. A woven mat with WELCOME in wide black letters beckoned all visitors. A fake potted palm also stood next to the dark wood door, adding to the warm atmosphere. The door to the apartment on the right was at the other end of the hall. Yellow police tape was stretched across the entrance, warning away the curious.

"What are the odds the neighbor heard or saw anything?" Mira said blandly, jerking her head toward the door on the left.

"We're not that lucky," I said with a frown. If the neighbor had seen the attacker, he or she wouldn't have lived to tell the tale. That, of course, is assuming the attacker didn't have the power to wipe a human's memory.

I walked ahead of Mira down the hall to the other apartment. I reached up to tear down the yellow tape, but my hand halted in midair as my eyes snagged on the streak of blood across the door. It wasn't drawn in any kind of symbol, but looked like someone had wiped the blood off his or her finger, smearing it across the lacquer surface.

Mira reached around me and tore down the yellow tape, making a noise of disgust in the back of her throat. Using the key Daniel had given her, she unlocked the door and shoved it open. I moved to follow her into the apartment, but she pressed her hand to my chest, stopping me.

"What?" I demanded, barely resisting the urge to take a step backward away from her touch. After what happened at the little vampire gathering, I thought it better if I maintained some physical distance from her. One of us was having restraint issues, and right now, distance could only be a good thing.

"Wait." Mira drew in a slow, deep breath through her nose and held it, her eyes closed. She didn't breathe, but vampirism did heighten her senses. Mira was smelling the air.

I quickly snapped my eyes from the way her breasts rose as her lungs expanded and stared blindly into the room, vainly attempting to concentrate on why we were at the apartment in the first place. "Anything?"

Mira shook her head, frowning. She exhaled and drew in another breath, holding it longer. "There's definitely something, but it's . . . hard to pick out. Lots of humans were through here, mucking everything up. There's something else, just a hint, but it's not anything I've ever encountered."

"So you're saying it can't be vampire," I said thickly.

"No," she growled, glaring at me over her shoulder. "But I can say that none of the nightwalkers we saw tonight have been in this apartment in the past few days. They would not be able to hide from me."

Leaning my left elbow against the doorjamb, I shoved my fingers through my hair, pushing it out of my eyes. "Let's get this over with," I muttered. I wasn't sure what Mira hoped to find that the police hadn't already found. On the other hand, our minds were open to the idea that the woman's attacker was not human.

The narrow hallway led into a large living room. The walls were made of the same redbrick and decorated with a collection of framed black-and-white photographs. One wall was filled with floor-to-ceiling windows looking out onto River Street and the Savannah River. The scent of apple-cinnamon potpourri hung in the warm apartment air.

However, the warm atmosphere suddenly chilled when my eyes dropped to the tape outline of where the woman's body had been found before the moss-colored sofa. The white area rug with an ivy design was stained a deep brownish red from her blood, and the taste of copper filled my mouth.

Slowly, I walked around the sofa to get a better view of the site of the woman's death. An odd tension twisted in my stomach as I quietly moved through the apartment. I had seen more than my fair share of corpses, but there was something strange about moving around the dead woman's apartment, as if her absence left the air feeling heavier. I rarely investigated human murders. It was usually my job to punish the murderer once he or she was identified.

Around me, Mira flicked on the lights. Her eyesight was extremely sharp, but she was obviously unwilling to miss anything. The nightwalker moved easily about the room as if she had no qualms over the fact that we were investigating the brutal murder of a young woman. Her feet were silent on the patches of carpet and only lightly clicked when she stepped onto the hardwood floor. I couldn't understand the vampire. Did she not care that the existence of one of her kind could possibly be hanging in the balance? Obviously not.

"Nothing looks disturbed. No sign of a struggle," James said in a soft voice, as he, too, was afraid to disturb the oppressive quiet of the apartment. Nothing was tipped over, shattered, or torn. Even the lamp shades were perfectly balanced.

"The door didn't look tampered with. So we can assume she let her attacker in," Mira said, walking over to stand beside me. She paused and then her head jerked up. "Unless the attacker was a magic user, cast a spell to unlock the door and walk in."

I shook my head, unable to tear my eyes away from the tape outline. "No residue."

"I beg your pardon," Mira demanded, her tone finally jerking my gaze back to her face.

"I have a . . ." I licked my lips, fumbling for the right word. " . . . sensitivity to magic. Spells tend to leave behind a residue. A spell to unlock the door would have left a residue behind in the wood. There was nothing."

Mira just arched one questioning brow at me then returned her gaze to the bloodstained carpet. "So, she probably let her attacker in. Could be a friend or lover."

The vampire squatted beside me, shaking her head as she looked over the scene. "It wasn't a nightwalker."

I couldn't stop the snort of disbelief at her comment, earning a dark frown from her. "You can't possibly know that by just smelling the air," I argued.

"Look at the blood," she said in a near growl. "There's too much blood." Standing, she walked across the floor and pushed the sofa off the edge of the area rug.

"Mira!" Her name escaped me in a harsh gasp. I pointed to the floor, showing her that she was standing in the outline of the body.

Mira looked up at me with a look of utter disbelief. "You're strange. You do know that?" she said blandly, narrowing her eyes at me.

I know it was a strange qualm, but you didn't walk on someone's grave if you could help it and you didn't stand in the place where a person died. Call it an old superstition. I did what I could to keep up with the changing times and ideas, but there were some notions that I struggled to shed.

Bending down, the vampire grabbed the edge of the carpet and pulled it toward me as she backed up. The sound of cracking filled the air as the crust of dried blood crumbled.

"Look. Not only did her blood saturate the rug, but it seeped through," she explained. I looked over the edge of the rug to find that small rivers of blood had dried in the ridges of the hardwood floor.

"So instead of killing her accidentally by draining too

much, the vamp came in with the sole purpose of killing her," I argued, stepping back and folding my arms across my chest.

With a growl, Mira released the rug and let it flop heavily back into place as she stood. "Even if a nightwalker had come in here with only the goal of killing her, he or she would not have passed up an opportunity to take a few pints from her," she argued, her anger causing her irises to flare slightly. "You never pass up a free lunch, especially if it's your enemy. This woman lost every ounce on the floor."

"So you're sure her attacker wasn't a vampire," I sarcastically said, fighting the desire to reach for the hilt of the knife resting along my left side. Anger started to bubble in my veins and roll in my stomach. Mira was sinking back into killer mode, donning the mantle of the ruthless hunter. I wasn't convinced that a vampire was guiltless of this woman's death.

"I'm saying fifty people could have been in the room watching her die, and I can guarantee not one of them was a nightwalker," she bit out through clenched teeth.

"Bold statement," I sneered.

"Yeah, it's why you love me." She laughed, reaching up and tweaking my nose. I blinked, staring at her for a breath. The anger had been washed from her eyes. There was a slight chill to the air from her powers, but it was quickly dissipating along with the scent of lilacs. And then, just as quickly, the fresh laughter in her eyes died and she turned serious. "But that still doesn't answer our question of who," she continued. "What are we left with?"

"Besides human and vampire?" James supplied.

"Yes," she hissed between clenched teeth, looking back down at the tape outline.

"Lycans," he suggested.

Mira shook her head. "Ryan said her throat was torn out. She wouldn't have stood here while a lycan changed.

She would have run. There would have been evidence of a struggle."

"Unless she knew this person was a Were," I stated, drawing Mira's thoughtful gaze back to my face.

"True," she slowly drawled. "Anything else?"

"Any shape-shifting naturi."

"That could be a long list. I imagine something from the animal clan would be able to shift." Mira shook her head, rubbing one hand over her face. "So we're still at square one. Do we know anything about this girl?"

James reached into his back pocket and pulled out a tiny notebook. He flipped through several pages before settling on the information that he was searching for. "Abigail Bradford," he read aloud. "Age twenty-six. Single. Daughter of Alabama senator John Bradford."

"Great," Mira muttered, drawing my gaze back to her. "That explains the media hysterics."

James paused in the middle of his recitation, partially closing the notebook as he looked up at her. "I don't understand."

"Bradford is one of those bible-thumping ultra-conservatives that will make the Great Awakening very painful. I have no doubt his family headed up the Inquisition and the Salem witch trials," she explained, pacing across the room. With a shake of her head, Mira turned back around to face the researcher. "Anything else?"

"Just that she worked as a curator for the Juliette Gordon Low house—"

"Oh, just stake me now!" she exclaimed sarcastically. "It can't possibly get any worse."

"Who was Juliette Gordon Low?" I demanded.

"She was the founder of the Girl Scouts," she grumbled. "Probably was a Girl Scout herself. Miss Abigail Bradford was raised by a squeaky-clean family and worked for a squeaky-clean museum. It's all too . . ."

"Clean," I interjected, crossing my arms over my chest. I

stepped away from the sofa and leaned my shoulder against the wall, turning my back to the tape outline and Abigail's gruesome death so I could think clearly.

"Ha." She glared at me. "Something feels off." Mira paced away from me toward the wall of windows, running one hand through her hair.

"You think it was all a setup to draw attention to the outsiders," I suggested. "Someone plotted her murder in order to shed light on the nightwalkers or lycans."

"Maybe." The single word escaped her in a soft, thoughtful whisper. "But that would indicate some long-term planning." She turned on her heel to look at me, her hands shoved into the pockets of her pants.

"Vampires are known for their patience and long-term schemes. You have all the time in the world," I reminded her.

"So do the naturi," she snapped. "We need to know how long she's lived in Savannah. Specifically, how long she lived in this apartment."

"I can look into that," James said. He reached into the interior pocket of his coat and pulled out an ink pen. Flipping to a new page in his notebook, he started to scratch out some notes. "Is there anything else you need to know?"

"Why she came to Savannah," I interjected.

"And if any family members or friends from her past are *outsiders*," Mira stated.

I sent her a questioning look as James continued to make notes. It seemed like an odd request. Yet James took it all in stride, never once betraying any doubts.

"Couldn't hurt to check." Mira shrugged before returning her gaze back out the window.

James was usually pretty good about getting random bits of information and would probably have our answers by late afternoon. Since acquiring him as an assistant, I was becoming accustomed to his strange quirks and rampant curiosity. But it was all temporary. I had outlasted more than two dozen assistants during my time at Themis. I outlived them all.

Mira's soft voice drew me back to our current dilemma. Her voice was so quiet, I think she was mostly speaking to herself. "Why here? Maybe we're making this too big."

"What do you mean?" I asked, walking over to the windows.

"What if we're looking for a conspiracy and there isn't one? What if it really is all about Abigail?"

"You think she's not as squeaky clean as her background?"

"She lived a block away from some of the hottest clubs and bars in the whole city. I doubt she moved here to visit the city library." Sarcasm dripped from her words.

"You have a theory?"

"A hypothesis," she said, pushing away from the window. "Let's test it. Go into the bathroom and check for pills. See what she was on."

I had a dark suspicion of what I was looking for, but I kept my thoughts to myself as I followed her down the hall off the living room. Mira turned left into the master bedroom while I took the first right into the bathroom, with James close on my heels.

It was a small room with tiny white tiles and pale blue walls. The large claw-foot porcelain tub dominated the far wall and matched the white porcelain wash stand. The room was softly lit with a pair of sconces with tulip-shaped frosted globes. It was all neat and tidy, with a scattering of female products that I didn't want to try to comprehend.

The mirror over the sink was a classic medicine cabinet. Pulling aside the mirror revealed the usual assortment of Band-Aids, ointments, creams, and pain relievers. What caught my attention were the vitamins. Eight bottles, including two that were over-the-counter iron supplements. Iron pills were a common with people who had heart problems or were anemic. At a guess, I had a feeling this was what Mira was looking for.

Grabbing one of the bottles of iron supplements, I closed the mirror and turned off the light before walking across the hall to the bedroom. Mira stood before an open drawer in the bureau, softly cursing in Italian. She was rather fluent and creative.

"Good news?" I inquired.

"Scarves," she muttered. "A whole drawer full." To emphasize her point, she reached in and grabbed a handful in her clenched fist. She let the sheer bits of fabric slip through her fingers and spill back into the drawer like a silken rainbow.

"A nightwalker can heal a wound caused by a bite," she began, closing the drawer. "But if you're keeping a pet, you leave the wound so everyone knows that she is already taken. Unfortunately, the human is left to conceal the bite during the daylight hours. Scarves are a popular remedy."

"She could just find them fashionable," James offered, drawing her dark gaze back to me.

"Do you believe that?"

"No," I replied, tossing her the bottle. She briefly looked at it, her fingers tightening around the plastic until it cracked and snapped.

"Somebody is going to fry," she snarled, stalking out of the bedroom. She slapped the switch, turning out the light as she walked past.

"Five minutes ago you were sure a vampire didn't kill her," I called, following her down the hall.

"I still don't think a vampire killed her," she snapped. In the living room, we began flicking off all of the lamps. "But if she was a pet, it means little Miss Abigail could have been involved in all kinds of nastiness."

Passing by the end table next to the sofa, I snatched up a four-by-five picture in a plain wooden black frame. It was of a pair of women with their arms around each other's shoulders. The large white fountain that dominated Forsyth Park rose up in the background. Both women looked to be in their early to mid-twenties, with bright smiles and a look of in-

nocence. Well, at least ignorant of the dark world that surrounded them.

"That her?" Mira asked, peering around my arm.

"One of them probably is," I said, taking the back of
the frame off. I removed the picture and shoved it into my
pocket before replacing the empty frame.

Mira looked up at me, a slight frown pulling at the corner
of her lips. "We'll find out when we get to the morgue."

Twelve

B ack on the street, I paused beneath the streetlamp next
to Mira, letting my gaze sweep up and down Factors
Walk. The whole area was thick with shadows and intermittently broken by dim lamplight. To my left, I saw
a small figure scurry down the alley before cutting down
between a pair of buildings. It was only a brief glimpse,
but my vision was keen enough to pick out what appeared
to have been a young girl with a ragged backpack. Could it
have been the same girl from earlier? I needed to find her
again, ask her what she saw. But it was too late to go chasing her now. I would have to do my searching by daylight
with James at my side.

"What if there was a witness?" I asked, staring at the
empty spot where I had seen the girl.

"Who?" Mira inquired. She moved out of the lamplight
and back into the shadows. I looked over in time to see her
putting her glasses back into her pocket, staring in the same
spot I had been just moments ago. Possibly she had seen the
girl too.

"What about a homeless person? This has got to be an
area where they occasionally gather," I suggested.

Mira frowned, crossing her arms over her stomach as she

looked up and down the alley. "It's definitely possible," she slowly conceded but then shook her head. "But the odds of finding that person are pretty slim. They're not likely to go to the police. I would need to meet the witness so I could pick the image of the killer out of his or her mind. The chances are pretty slim."

"True, but we don't have much to go on at the moment," I reminded her. "We haven't even narrowed it down to a particular race."

"I'll call Daniel later," Mira sighed. "See if I can get him to question some of the locals."

We silently walked to Mira's car, bogged down by our own thoughts. James lagged behind. In the silence of the night, I could hear his heart pounding in his chest. He was nervous about something.

"W—where do we go now?" he stammered.

"The morgue," I replied, turning to look at him. "We need to look at the body and talk to the coroner. The way she died may tell us more about our killer."

"Oh," he whispered.

"I want you to stay behind. Start doing some more digging into the girl's past. See what you can uncover," I said.

"Are you sure?" he asked, though the relief was already evident in his tone.

"Yeah, get out of here. I'll need you with me in the morning."

With a quick nod, he wished Mira good night and briskly walked down the street, back to the hotel.

I turned to find Mira watching me with a strange look on her face. "Should I ask what that was about?"

"After the attack on Themis last summer, I think he's seen enough of mangled dead bodies. He's more useful to me researching Abigail Bradford, not passing out at the sight of her dead body," I said.

To my surprise, Mira simply nodded and starting

walking back toward her car, passing up the opportunity to mock me and my decision to set the eager researcher free.

But in truth, I shouldn't have been surprised. We both had bigger issues on our minds. Was a new war brewing, and the catalyst the death of a human that happened to be in the wrong place at the wrong time? Had Abigail Bradford gotten in over her head? Or just ended up on the wrong side of a fight within the local pack? Lycans and nightwalkers were killed all the time. Heaven knows that I was more frequently than not the cause. Yet, no one digs into their deaths. The situation is quickly swept under the rug and the body disappears. Sometimes humans are caught in the middle regardless of whether they fully understand the situation or not.

Was this the case with the Bradford girl? Maybe, but there were other players lingering in the shadows. Creatures that would like nothing more than to see Mira's head roll because humans were enlightened in her city ahead of schedule. There were factors I was afraid Mira wasn't considering that could get us both killed.

"It seems doubtful a nightwalker killed her," I hedged when we reached the car.

Mira looked over the roof of the black BMW, her eyes narrowed. Her whole body seemed to have tensed in the pregnant silence that hung between us. "But . . ." she prompted.

"What if the order had come directly from the coven? Just kill the girl. No feeding," I suggested.

"No," she said with a shake of her head. Her answer had come so quickly that I thought it was more from fear of it being a distinct possibility than actual knowledge.

"Even an Ancient?"

Mira didn't reply, her eyes darting away from me to look at the side of the car. My heart did an odd little skip as I watched her expressive face turn over the implications. It was an angle she hadn't considered. Until now, I think we had both considered the woman's death to be accidental or an act of local revenge.

"I would have known if an Ancient had come into my territory," she stubbornly said at last, pulling open her car door.

I opened my door and slid into the leather interior at the same time. "Not if you were in London," I countered.

"If you're implying that Ryan—" she began, but I quickly cut her off. Was Ryan working with the coven? Maybe, but doubtful. From what I had seen, the warlock didn't play well with others. He liked being in control of a situation, and a herd of nightwalkers with their own agenda would not allow him to remain in control. Right now, I think he saw Mira as more malleable than trying to work with the whole coven.

"No. I think someone might have taken advantage of your brief absence," I ventured, trying to ignore the fact that if I was even slightly right, we were in serious trouble. "The Ancient could be in the city now. Jabari cloaked himself from you. I'm assuming this isn't a skill unique to him."

"Jabari was never in that room. I know his scent as well as my own," she argued. Mira shoved the key into the ignition, but didn't turn on the car, seeming content to sit in the darkness.

"It doesn't have to be Jabari. Any Ancient. Anyone with a grudge. What about the vampire from Machu Picchu?"

"Stefan." Her fingers tightened around the steering wheel.

Months ago, Stefan had been sent by the coven to aid us in our ascent to the ruins on the mountain where the naturi were attempting to open the door between our worlds. I didn't know how old he was, but judging by the power that rolled off him, he was fairly close to the thousand-year mark, if not already past it. He also didn't seem to be a very big fan of Mira's. Of course, neither were most of the vampires I had run across.

"My point is," I stressed, trying to bring Mira's dark thoughts away from whatever torture she was devising for Stefan. "Speeding along the Great Awakening meets with the desires of your liege and starting it in your city would give the coven yet another excuse to cut your heart out."

Mira growled in the back of her throat, balling her right hand into a fist. She raised her hand to pound on the steering wheel, but I caught her wrist in my hand. The nightwalker's glowing lavender eyes snapped to my face.

"You'll hurt your 'baby,' " I reminded her in a soft voice as I slowly released her wrist. The glow in her narrowed eyes instantly faded as a crooked smile lifted one corner of her mouth. Her skin was surprisingly cool to the touch with a somewhat waxy feel. I couldn't begin to guess how long it had been since she had last fed. A grudging respect for the vampire began to take hold when I realized she hadn't even made a move to bite me at the feeding earlier.

A new thought twisted in my gut, sending a wave of chills running up my flesh. Would I have stopped her if she had tried to bite me? Lost in one wave after another of mind-numbing pleasure, I couldn't imagine pushing her away if she had come offering to send me along that next wave. Hell, my own face had been buried in her neck and I could clearly remember the feel of my own teeth running along her skin. Even now, something dark and primal demanded I taste her flesh, to drink her in so that she would become a part of me.

"The coven doesn't need a fresh reason to confiscate my heart," she said, her grim voice bleeding into the darkness.

"They already have ample reason to cause problems here," I replied, forcibly pulling my thoughts back to the current quandary at hand.

"I know," she whispered, turning the key. The engine turned over with a feral growl then settled into a steady purr that would have been the envy of any large cat. "This is all great speculation, but that's still all it is. We need answers and I think we'll have a few more after we have a look at the body and autopsy report."

First, a rather posh apartment in the heart of the River Street club district, complete with body outline, and now the morgue. Traveling with Mira, I always got to see some of the more interesting sights within a city.

Thirteen

The Savannah morgue was a large, one-story building squatting like a fat toad just on the outskirts of town. Made of faded yellow brick, the building sagged and slumbered in a dreary neighborhood that seemed to be weighed down by the nearby hospital.

Mira deftly pulled into the small parking lot in the rear and settled her car next to a white Lexus with gold trim shining in the overhead parking light. There was only one other car in the lot; a beat-up Chevy Nova with fading gray paint and a sign announcing that it was for sale. At a guess, one car belonged to the coroner and the other to the night watchman.

As we slipped out of the car, the back door swung soundlessly open, revealing a short, balding man in a dark suit. His black-frame glasses were balanced on his large, bulbous nose, making his eyes enormous and almost owlish in appearance. He held the door open as we approached, the stubby fingers of his left hand fiddling nervously with the buttons on his blazer.

"We're in trouble," he announced in a low voice as Mira stepped into the brightly lit interior. Her pale skin took on a strange iridescent glow under the harsh fluorescent light. It explained why I had never run across a vampire in the aisles of an all-night mega-store.

Mira's shoes scraped along the battered white linoleum as she turned to look at the man. "What do you mean? Lose the body?" She looked over the rim of her pale blue sunglasses at him.

"Of course not!" he huffed, puffing up his chest a bit at the affront. He lifted his chin and hurried around me, the top of his head not quite reaching my shoulders.

Mira shrugged, throwing me a mischievous smile over her shoulder. "So much for hoping."

"Who is he?" the man asked with a jerk of his head before continuing down the hall.

"Forgive my lack of manners," Mira said. "Archie, this is an associate of mine, Danaus. Danaus, this is the Chatham County coroner, Dr. Archibald Deacon." Her introduction oozed with irritation.

An associate. I didn't like the sound of it. It made me sound like a business partner, or in the mind of a human, one of her kind. But I wasn't a nightwalker. Of course, I wasn't quite human either. Even though I might not like the phrase, it's not like she had a lot of options. *This is Danaus, the vampire hunter.* Just trying to wrap his mind around all the ramifications would probably cause his brains to slide out of his ears.

However, the coroner said nothing. He briefly paused as he pushed open a door leading to a stairwell and nodded to me before leading us down the stairs.

"So what's the problem?" Mira asked, her voice echoing slightly off the concrete walls.

"This body is the problem," he said sharply. "I didn't know it was one of yours."

"Mira—" I began, a fresh knot of anger twisting in my gut. What kind of an arrangement did she have with the city coroner? Did I not know about all of her kills because she had a deal with the coroner to keep everything nicely hidden?

"He means death by an *outsider* or death of an *outsider*," she grumbled over her shoulder at me then turned her attention back to Archie. "What's been done?"

"Everything," he said, throwing up his hands in a helpless gesture. "I wasn't called to the scene of the crime because it was drawing too much attention. You can't have a senator's daughter killed in her River Street apartment and not expect a press circus to set up camp outside. I didn't see the body until it was brought in." Yanking open the door with a soft grunt, he led us down a narrow hall to a pair of steel double doors. "I had been told that it looked like she died from an animal attack. I ordered the usual autopsy and thought nothing of it. It wasn't until later that afternoon that I saw the digital pictures the police took of the crime scene. By then, both my toxicologist and serologist had been all over the body. A pair of zoologists had even been through, trying to make a guess at what made the teeth marks."

In the center of the cool room crowded with shiny stainless-steel operating tables was a large table under a bright light. A body lay on the table covered with a white sheet. Archie walked around to the far side while Mira and I stayed on the side closest to the door.

The chill in the air seeped through my leather jacket and crept up my spine. I had seen more than my share of death over the years, and been around plenty of dead bodies (not to mention a few dead bodies that sat up and talked when you had been quite sure moments earlier that it was completely impossible). Yet being surrounded by all the shining silver instruments and the rows of stainless-steel refrigerators used for housing the bodies caused the illogical wave of dread to sweep through me. The dead were supposed to be burned or buried when the soul left, not dug into and examined.

"Cause of death?" I asked, shoving my hands into my pockets.

"It's a tough call. Either blood loss or asphyxiation," he said blandly as he pulled back the sheet.

Abigail Bradford lay cold and dead under the harsh overhead light. Her skin was a stomach-turning gray now that
all the blood had been drained from her body. Her shoulder-
length blond hair was slightly fanned out beneath her head.
She almost looked like she was sleeping. The analysts had
not made a single cut on her body. There was no need. The
source of her demise was rather obvious: more than half of
her throat was missing.

Unfortunately, the throat wasn't neatly cut up. A chunk
of flesh had been torn out using sharp fangs, leaving behind ragged bits of skin and muscle. Could a human have
done this? No. Impossible. I doubted a normal human
had the strength, and the damage left by the teeth was
all wrong.

Could a vampire? Possibly, but a vampire would have
spit out the chunk of flesh and no one had yet to mention
finding it.

Could a lycan? Definitely.

Archie took out a small penknife and pulled open the
wound slightly. My stomach lurched and I fought the urge
to step backward. I had spent ample time around dead
bodies and caused the deaths of others. I had been surrounded by men mangled by the viciousness of war, but
this felt like desecrating the remains, even though pursuing
a murderer.

"If you'll look closer, you can see where one of the lower
canines of her attacker scored one of the vertebrae of the
spinal cord," Archie explained. "All wrong for human canines. Definitely animal of some sort."

"I'll take your word for it," Mira growled, pacing away
from the body. She ran one hand through her hair, but I
couldn't tell if she was shaken or just irritated. "Why can't
you just say she was attacked by an animal?"

"Other than the fact that the apartment was completely
undisturbed?" he demanded incredulously, shoving the penknife into an interior pocket of his blazer.

"Leave that to the cops. Your job is to give a cause of death. You have it. Her throat was ripped out by a very large dog," Mira countered. She walked back over to the table, her heels angrily clicking on the pale yellow linoleum.

"What about the bruises?" Archie snapped.

"What bruises?" I asked.

The coroner pointed out a pair of small, circular bruises under her collarbone near her shoulders.

"Could be anything," Mira shrugged.

"Look at her back," Archie directed.

Frowning, I grabbed Abigail's right shoulder and pushed her up so that she was balanced on her side. A chill swept through me as I realized the flesh of the dead body felt sickeningly similar to Mira's when I had touched her wrist earlier in the evening.

With considerable effort, I turned my head to look at the corpse's back. Near the shoulders were a set of four circular bruises marring her white skin like fingerprints. Someone had held her still, or held her down.

"Can you date the bruises?" I demanded, carefully laying the body back down.

"I'd say same night as her death," Archie replied.

"Backdate the bruises in your report by a couple of days," Mira said with a slight shake of her head. "It will look like she had a fight with her boyfriend."

"Mira. . . ." He sighed.

"We can do this," Mira said, her voice firm and strong. She was back to exuding her usual confidence, taking control of the situation. "Backdate the bruises. Put down she was killed by a large dog. It'll be another five weeks before the blood test comes back and the report is ready, right?"

"Yes."

"I doubt anything will show up, but if it does, fudge the report. I don't want anything showing up in her blood but a couple shots of tequila at most."

"What about the police? They won't believe—"

"I'll take care of the police. We've got to give the press and this girl's parents something nice and neat to cling to before this mess gets any nastier."

"Are you sure?"

"Yes. Now get out of here," she commanded. Her tone hardened to the same consistency as granite and the room grew colder, as if the air conditioner had been kicked into high.

"But—"

"Get out," she bit out through clenched teeth, her hands gripping the edge of the table. I stood still, the palm of my right hand itching slightly from the overwhelming desire to grab one of my knives. "Go take the elevator up to your office. Check your e-mail. Talk to the guard for five minutes and then leave. We'll be gone before you reach your car."

Wisely, Archie just nodded and slipped around the table. His sharp, clipped footsteps echoed through the silent room as he beat a hasty retreat. Mira waited until the double doors were once again closed before she released her hold on the table and walked around to stand where the coroner had been moments before.

Leaning close to what remained of Abigail's neck, she took a deep breath through her nose. I could only guess she was checking to see if she could pick up the same scent she got a hint of at the apartment. The vampire suddenly lurched away, taking a few stumbling steps deeper into the room, hunched over and gagging. I froze. I had never seen a vampire gag on anything, especially the scent of a decaying body. I honestly didn't think anything bothered them. Mira finally dropped to her knees, with one hand pressed to the cool floor while the other was pressed to her chest. A fresh round of dry heaves wracked her thin frame, keeping her partially doubled over.

"Mira?"

"I'm okay," she whispered, her voice hoarse and rough. She held up one hand, warding me off. After another minute, her whole body stilled, her eyes closed in a look of peace. Whatever it was, it had finally passed.

"How's your sense of smell?" she asked, slowly pushing off the floor. I was surprised that she didn't use her power like usual to lift herself to her feet, but the nightwalker had been acting strangely since I first saw her at the hotel. Why should this be any different?

"Human," I replied. I had the same sense of smell as a normal human being. Being part bori enhanced only a few aspects of my life.

"Figures," she grumbled, walking back over to the corpse.

"What happened?"

"I've never smelled anything like that before," she said. Her upper lip curled in disgust. She was now keeping a bit of a distance from the body, as if trying to keep from getting another whiff of whatever she had smelled. "It's worse than rotting meat left in the noonday sun. It's more than just the smell of death. And it's not coming from her. It's whatever attacked her."

"The same as what you smelled in the apartment?"

"Maybe . . ." she said slowly, her eyes narrowing on the girl's throat. "It was just so faint . . . I don't know."

"Does that rule out vampires then?"

A frown tugged at Mira's full lips and creased her brow. For a second, she looked very sad and weighed down by her thoughts. "Unfortunately, no." The two lonely words were a faint whisper as they tripped from her lips to me. I think she had come here confident that she would find her answers, but ended up with only more questions.

"We have to go," I reminded her.

"Just a minute," she said, picking up Abigail's left arm. She turned it, looking at the inside of the bend in her arm. Mira then reached across the body and picked up the right arm, inspecting the interior of the arm. "Look," she said, running her thumb across a pair of faint white scars. Vampire bites.

"I thought you preferred the neck," I said.

"Her owner would have. It's the first place we look to see if the human has been tagged," Mira said, putting the arm down and turning her attention back to the side of the girl's neck that was untouched. "Someone not her owner must have taken a nibble. Look. Here's another set."

I walked around the table so that I could see the girl's neck more clearly. There was another set of bite marks on her neck. These looked like they were a week or two old at most, compared to the set on her arm. "So she was bitten on the arm weeks or even a month ago, and her owner bit her a week or so ago. Two vampires fighting over the same piece of flesh. One decides to kill her so the other can't have her?"

"Part of that is probably right. The neck wound is only two weeks old and was probably made by her owner, but the wound on her arm is only a few nights old," Mira began. She lifted up the girl's arm to the light so that I could clearly see the two marks left by vampire fangs. "The nightwalker tried to heal it but didn't finish, or botched the job. The wound is closed, but the bruising is still there. For such an aged-looking scar, there shouldn't be any bruising."

"So who are the two vampires?" I inquired.

Mira leaned close to the girl's arm. I didn't even see her take in a breath. She jerked back with a hiss, dropping Abigail's arm back to the operating table. "We have to go," she said, her words sharp and crisp as she quickly walked around the table.

"What?" I demanded, jogging after her. "Who is it? What about the neck wound?"

Throwing open the double doors, Mira hurried down the hall to the staircase. "I'll never pick up the scent of the other vampire over the scent coming off the neck wound. It doesn't matter. I know how to get the information."

I followed after her as we silently climbed the stairs and slipped out the back door into the parking lot. Things were exactly as we left them. Mira's BMW sat all sleek and black next to the white Lexus under the single parking-lot lamp. The Chevy Nova hunkered in one of the far corners, hoping to go unnoticed.

The second her feet hit the blacktop of the parking lot, a wave of power exploded from Mira. The tidal wave swept out from her body, washing over the city. I nearly stumbled under its unexpected weight. She was searching the city for her prey. And I had no doubt that whoever the culprit was, he or she knew we were coming.

Fourteen

Anger radiated off the nightwalker as her hand slid along the steering wheel. Mira remained silent, as if words couldn't squeeze between her clenched teeth. The air in the car had chilled to the point where I expected to see my breath fog if I sighed. Yet this cold would not be cut by a blast of warm air from the heater. She had erected a barrier around her thoughts, keeping me out. But I didn't need to be in her mind to know that whoever had been involved with Abigail Bradford was toast, literally.

We had returned to the historic district of the city, quickly stopping at a lonely square near the edge. I had expected us to return to the club district of River Street, where most nightwalkers were known to congregate while in the process of hunting down their prey. Mira whipped the sleek, black BMW into an open parking spot on the street and was out of the car before the engine was completely shut off.

In the far corner of the square rose an ornate gazebo. Constructed of stone, the architecture had an Old World feel to it, with its odd bits of ironwork. In one of the windows looking out at the small fountain in the center of the square sat a vampire.

The air was silent except for the crunch of stray gravel beneath our feet. I followed behind her, a knife tightly gripped in my right hand as I searched the area for other vampires. There were a few lurking about a mile off, but after Mira's brief display of power at the morgue, I doubted any other vampire was going to risk coming close enough to catch her attention.

I reached the gazebo just a couple seconds behind Mira, who was now standing in the center of the structure. My heart lurched in my chest as my eyes settled on the creature resting on the ledge of the gazebo and I fought the urge to scan the park again for another vampire. I couldn't stop from blinking twice, convinced that my eyes were lying to me in the darkness.

"How is it that I find you involved in this?" Mira snarled. The heavy shadows within the gazebo hugged her body, making her little more than a threatening voice in the cool winter night.

Tristan sat with his back against one of the columns that formed the window. His right leg was bent before him with his foot resting on the ledge and his right wrist balanced on his knee. His left leg hung limp in the air, swaying slightly. The vampire appeared relaxed, and he had yet to look directly at Mira. His gaze was straight ahead as if he was intently watching the fountain in the center of the square. "I didn't kill her." His normally soft voice held an underlying edge to it that I had never heard from him before, causing my muscles to clench defensively. It was a warning for Mira to back off.

"Did you know who she was?" I asked. My deep voice broke between the two in an attempt to put a little distance between them before Mira set him on fire. There was still a good chance that he had some valuable information as to who Abigail Bradford was and with whom she associated. I would prefer to acquire that information before Mira finally lost her tenuous hold on her temper.

"Yes," he hissed. Tristan slowly turned his head to look at me over his shoulder, his pale blue eyes seeming to pick up the distant lamplight like a cat's. "I had seen her around town during the past month. She was the daughter of a prominent official and a fan of our kind."

"Why didn't you contact me immediately when it happened?" Mira snapped, her temper still bubbling to the top.

The younger vampire's icy gaze finally reached Mira's
face. "Contact you?" he repeated with a slight tilt of his
head. "And how would I have done this? I reached for you,
but as far as I could tell, you were as dead as Sadira."

"My cell ph—"

"Cell phone!" he shrieked. In one fluid movement, he
unfolded his body and poured to his feet before his mistress.
"Call you like a common servant, like Charlotte or Gabriel?
Contact you like a human would? You're my mistress and
yet I am to be without your presence."

To my surprise, Mira broke eye contact first, pacing away
from him. "I'll not have you mucking around in my mind
at all hours." She slowly circled to her right, moving with
the grace of a panther edging closer for the kill. "I'm not
Sadira."

Tristan moved as well, his hands out at his sides and open
like a gunslinger waiting for the first opportunity to reach
for his guns. The two vampires were sizing each other up.
The younger vampire was greatly outmatched by Mira. Any
scuffle between the two would prove to be brief, but even
with the odds against him, it didn't seem to be enough to
deter Tristan from wanting her blood.

"It's more than that!" he shouted, his voice echoing across
the empty park. "You're not in my thoughts either. Since my
arrival in your domain, you have not once dipped into my
thoughts, not reached out to make your presence known."

"Forgive me. I didn't realize you needed a babysitter,"
she sneered, with a mocking bow. "More than a century of
time has slipped before your eyes. You don't need me there
watching over you at all times."

Mira's only warning was a low growl in the back of his
throat. The younger vampire lunged at her, knocking her
onto her back. He gripped her shoulders tightly, his legs
straddling her slim hips. His shoulder-length hair fell like a
curtain around his face, making it impossible to determine

if he had bared his fangs to his mistress. As a reflex, I took a step forward, trying to decide how to best separate them without getting my own throat ripped open in the process.

"This has nothing to do with you, hunter," Mira said with a grunt, pushing Tristan off of her. The young vampire quickly rolled to his feet but remained squatted low, waiting for his mistress to attack. Mira remained seated on the ground, but she had pulled her feet up underneath her body so that she could quickly rise if she needed to.

"It's not about needing a caretaker," Tristan began. His hands were clenched so tight into fists they trembled. "As I'm sure you remember, Sadira provided ample restriction. It's about compassion. About having a familiar voice in the darkness."

"So when I was unavailable, you chose to pursue a girl that could make our lives unbearable? You know the rules. Avoid those that can't disappear," Mira argued, but I could feel the anger in her subsiding as her taut shoulders started to slump.

"The girl was nothing. Just a meal. She belonged to others and was offered to me in a gesture of hospitality." Tristan straightened, shoving both of his hands through his hair in a frustrated motion.

Mira stood as well, a soft sigh escaping her parted lips. "I don't know if I can be what you want, Tristan," she whispered. "I'm your protector. That is all."

"This family might be just the four of us, but it is still a family. You neither seek nor give comfort when we both need it so much. Particularly now, when hunters wait for us to slip." Tristan's eyes lifted to settle on my face. Mira turned her head to look at me as well, her hair slipped like a waterfall off of her shoulder. I had thought they had forgotten I was even there, but now the spotlight had shifted to me.

Standing in the thick darkness with two vampires was not a strange occurrence for me. What was strange was that now I felt like the outsider in a dark world I had inhabited for most of my life. I was the foreign creature that had invaded their domain. I didn't like the feeling. Clenching my fist, I was surprised to discover that I was still holding my dagger. My eyes fell on the silver blade glinting in the distant lamplight. And maybe I was the only threat standing in that small, circular building. Neither had attacked me or even made a move toward me, and yet I stood ready to cut out the heart of the first creature to look my way.

Mira walked over and wrapped her arms around Tristan's shoulders, pulling his left shoulder against her sternum. "No," Mira murmured with a shake of her head. Her left hand drifted across his face, her thumb grazing his cheek in a caress that drew his eyes from me to her face.

"But he's still a hunter," Tristan said. I could barely make out his expression, but the words sounded like more of a question than a statement. I had a feeling that Mira had said something to him telepathically, but I didn't pick it up.

Leaning in, she pressed a gentle kiss to his temple. "Always." The word had been so soft that it sounded like she had breathed it rather than whispered it. Her gaze returned to me, her glowing lavender eyes coldly weighing me. When she looked at me, I no longer had the feeling that she saw me as the enemy. Like she had said earlier, she saw me as one of them and was determined that I see myself the same way.

"Enough," I gruffly said, sliding the dagger back into its sheath. The conversation was starting to grow uncomfortable and it would only result in my grabbing a second dagger. "What about the girl?"

"I don't know much." Tristan shrugged as Mira released her hold on him. "I stopped in the Dark Room more than a month ago. She was there with a group of others. They offered her and I accepted."

"What do you mean 'offered her'?" I was already feeling on edge. After the confusion of the First Communion, then the apartment, the morgue, and now this scene, I was ready to call it a night and start fresh tomorrow. Exhaustion was starting to coil in my shoulders, causing the muscles to throb and ache. The night was still young, but I felt the need to sit down and think about what was happening instead of just getting sucked deeper into the chaos that was Mira's existence.

"Like a host offering you a bit of wine and cheese upon your arrival at their house," Mira said lightly, as she strolled over to the far side of the gazebo. She turned and leaned her back against the ledge, crossing her left ankle over her right as she shoved her hands into her jean pockets. "The locals are curious about Tristan, I'm sure. They invited him over for a bit of light conversation. Sharing a pet is a polite gesture."

"And she came to you willingly?" I asked, tearing my eyes from Mira to Tristan.

"Of course."

"But that wasn't the last time you saw her," Mira prompted. There was no thread of anger or threat in her voice. "The mark on her arm was from you, but it wasn't a month old."

"Four nights ago," he softly said. His eyes fell to his shoes as his right foot slid along the rough concrete. "I was passing through the club district. It was early and I hadn't fed. She saw me. We talked for a while and she offered." Tristan looked up, locking his wide eyes on Mira. "I tried to heal the wound, but she wouldn't let me."

"Who did she belong to?" I demanded, taking a step into the gazebo.

"Gregor. She was with Gregor's group," Tristan said. He shoved his hands into his pockets and walked over to lean back against one of the window arches near Mira.

"Gregor!" Mira cried, running one hand through her hair to push it back from her face. The nightwalker lurched to her feet, pacing toward me. "What possessed you to associate with that pack of mongrels?"

"Mira . . ." I sighed.

"Yeah, yeah," she grumbled, waving me off as she turned and paced back to the opposite side of the gazebo. "New to town. Doesn't know any better."

"Can this vampire still be found at the Dark Room?" I asked, trying to get us back on track. I didn't care about her personal opinion about the various vampire cliques within the area.

"Yes, but we can't go there tonight," Mira replied as she folded her arms over her middle.

"Why not?" I snapped. I felt like we weren't getting anywhere, but Gregor might finally be able to give us some background information on this dead girl, and yet Mira was unwilling to track him down.

"He was at the gathering," Mira said, pointedly frowning at Tristan for a second before looking back at me. "After that, I doubt he would go back to the Dark Room and I would rather handle this matter there. Besides, there are other matters that need to be taken care of before we approach him."

The question was on the tip of my tongue, but I swallowed it. I truly doubted that she would give me a direct answer. "Then where to now?"

"The town house." She sighed, her shoulders slumping. She put her hand in her jacket pocket, causing her keys to jangle softly. "I've had enough of you." Mira turned to Tristan, who had moved deeper into the shadows. "Return home. We'll talk more later."

Mira swept past me, her keys jingling in her left hand as she walked toward the car. I looked back into the gazebo to find that Tristan had already soundlessly disappeared. I could only guess that he had gone through one of the large windows and was cutting across the shadowy plaza. Taking a deep breath, I reached out with my powers, stretching out across the square. Tristan was easy to spot, already on the other side of the plaza, deep within the shadows that lounged in the far corners of the park. The vampires I had sensed just a mile away had already departed.

Sunrise was still several hours away, but it seemed like Mira was calling a halt to tonight's investigation. Was she tired? By her extreme paleness and the cold, waxy feel of her skin, I knew it had been a while since she had last fed. There was also the slight feeling of her hunger beating against me, but the feeling was still weak and thin, as if it had yet to gain any real strength. I knew she wouldn't feed with me at hand, a fact that I was extremely grateful for. It was something I didn't want to see or feel. But even if she did drop me off so she could feed, there were still too many hours left until she had to seek shelter. I didn't trust her not to continue the investigation without me. Was she trying to protect her own kind from me, or maybe just Tristan?

I shifted my scan to the opposite edge of the park and froze, my breath becoming lodged behind an anxious knot in my throat.

"Mira!" I shouted, turning on my heel to look back at the Fire Starter. She paused and turned to face me, still playing with her keys. The light metallic jingle was the only noise in the air. "What's up that hill?" I pointed toward the dark, winding road that disappeared around a sharp corner.

"The conservatory. Why?"

"Naturi."

Fifteen

The Telfair Conservatory was a large structure made almost entirely of glass and steel, housing some of the rarest flowers and plants in the world. Except for a couple of streetlamps at the top and bottom of the block, the area was completely black. Large trees and palms rose up around the conservatory like prehistoric beasts in the night, guarding the structure and its secrets.

Mira parked her car in front of the enormous greenhouse and stuffed her keys deep into her pants pocket so they wouldn't jingle as she walked. For the first time in Savannah tonight, she looked tense. Her hands were balled into tight fists at her side and her face was carefully wiped of all expression.

Of course, I wasn't feeling much better. There were six members of the naturi somewhere in the large structure, and I couldn't begin to guess why. Could it have something to do with Abigail? Or had they been sent by their queen, Aurora, to collect a specific flower or plant for a spell? If so, why here? The Telfair Conservatory couldn't be the only hothouse to have what Aurora needed. Why willingly go into Mira's known domain unless it was with the sole purpose of taking on the Fire Starter?

Unfortunately, I hadn't a clue as to what we were facing. I

could only sense the naturi; I couldn't tell exactly which clan we were dealing with.

"Open the trunk," I said when Mira started to walk away from the car. With brow furrowed, the vampire pulled her keys out of her pocket and pushed a button on the remote. The latch gave a muffled click and the trunk popped open.

Lifting the lid higher, I dug through my duffel bag. In the faint yellow illumination cast by the tiny trunk lights, I quickly inspected my Browning, checking to see that the magazine was still full. Slipping it back into the holster, I clipped it to my belt at the small of my back. I shed my jacket, tossing it in the trunk. The cold night air bit through my cotton turtleneck.

"Need anything?" I asked, looking up at Mira. The nightwalker glanced over her shoulder for a second at the looming glass building then moved to stand beside me at the trunk, a dark frown pulling at her lips. She opened her own bag and withdrew what looked to be the Glock I gave her months ago when we flew to Venice. With more ease than I had expected, she slipped the magazine from her gun, briefly glanced at the bullets, and then easily replaced it. When I first gave her the weapon, she had held it like a piece of rotting garbage. Apparently, her view of guns had changed. While I had never been overly fond of guns, they were very effective when attempting to dispatch the naturi. For that reason, I adapted.

Mira shoved the gun into her jacket pocket and softly shut the trunk. The vampire led me around the side of the conservatory to a side entrance. I pulled my wallet out of my back pocket and withdrew a pair of tools to pick the lock, a skill I had picked up during my travels to the Far East and refined upon my arrival in London, though I was still struggling with some of the more sophisticated burglar alarm systems. I was about to kneel down before the door, with its curved steel handle, when Mira put a hand on my shoulder stopping me. Stepping in front of me, she pulled her wallet from her back pocket. I snorted derisively when she withdrew a credit card and returned the wallet back to her pocket.

"You're kidding, right?" I whispered.

"Nope," she murmured. She carefully worked the credit card into the slim crevice between the door and the door-jamb. "The conservatory is run and funded heavily by the local pack. Only idiots with a serious death wish break in."

Yeah, idiots like us. I thought it, but didn't say it. With Mira, it was always something.

After only a few seconds of shimmying the card, Mira had the door unlocked.

"You've done this before," I said as she slipped the credit card back into her pocket.

"This is one of my favorite spots in the city, but it closes at five. I have no choice," she hissed.

"I'm not judging you." And I wasn't. There were many things that Mira missed out on due to her extreme allergy to sunlight.

"Sounds like it," she grumbled, releasing the door as she stepped inside. I barely managed to catch the heavy metal door before it could bang closed.

"Why don't they just give you a key?" I whispered.

Mira looked over her shoulder at me, her brow furrowed in confusion. "Why? My method works just fine."

I followed behind her, soundlessly closing the door as I inwardly cursed her grouchiness. Her sharp mood shift could be understood, though. The naturi put her on edge. Neither of us knew what we were facing. We could be entering a battle with anything from the five different clans, or even Aurora herself, though I found it doubtful that the queen of the naturi would come after Mira. After the nightwalker nearly carved out her heart, I was willing to bet that Aurora was going to give the Fire Starter a little room for now.

All moonlight was instantly blotted out by the thick overhead foliage. The air was warm and dense with the scent of plants. The faint sound of trickling water tripped from deep in the room. A dozen different floral scents assailed me, mixing with the lilac scent drifting off of the nightwalker standing before me.

Mira stopped just inside the doorway, her tense body and still as a statue. She reached back with her left hand until her fingertips brushed my arm.

Are they close? She shoved the question within my brain. With those three words came a tumble of emotions, some feelings I struggled to even put names to. But mostly, it was anger. The naturi were not only in her home, but also in the one place she regarded as a private sanctuary.

"No," I whispered, batting her hand away. I didn't want her in my head, cluttering up my thoughts. "Feels like at the other end of the building, larger room."

"How many?"

"Six."

"Can you see?"

"A little," I hedged. I blinked my eyes a couple of times, waiting for my night vision to improve. It was better than most humans', but from what I could tell, I still lagged behind vampires and most lycans.

Ahead of me, trees and large plants began to take shape. A break in the leaves revealed a glimpse of the windows that comprised the opposite wall. The room we were standing in wasn't more than twenty feet across.

"The path is narrow and wraps around the room. Stick to your right or you'll fall in the water in the center of the room," Mira instructed.

"What room is this?" I asked, following behind her as she headed deeper into the darkness.

"Rain forest."

That explained the overwhelming humidity. I half expected the ceiling to open up in a brief downpour. Ducking my head to miss a low-hanging palm leaf, I stumbled into Mira, who had halted in the middle of the path.

"Do you hear that?" she demanded in a harsh whisper. I paused, straining to hear anything, but there was nothing beyond the high-pitched laughter of running water and the faint brush of leaves.

"What?"

Mira gave her head a hard shake before slowly moving forward. "Nothing." Yet even as she spoke the word, I felt her send out a wave of energy from her body. The cool pulse passed through me and rippled through the rest of the building. She was searching for something or someone, which was strange because she could not sense the naturi without me. The nightwalker had briefly gained the ability while in Peru, but from what I had gathered during our recent association, she had lost the power. The ability seemed dependent upon her having access to large amounts of energy from the earth.

"Anyone?" I inquired after a couple of seconds.

"No." She sounded puzzled, which did not fill me with an abundance of confidence. Mira was a vampire with more than six centuries of experience. The only thing she couldn't sense was the naturi, and the occasional Ancient vampire. I didn't like that she sounded puzzled.

"But . . . ?"

Mira paused before a set of doors, her hand resting on the pale silver handle. "I thought . . . I thought I heard a baby crying," she hesitantly confessed, then shook her head. "But it was extremely faint. It could have been a car or something else."

"Do you think . . . ?" I started, but the words seemed to die in my throat. The stealing of human babies was one of the few tales that the old mythology actually got right about the naturi. Unfortunately, they weren't grabbing the infants because they preferred them to their own sickly children. Theories ranged from ingredients for complex spells to attempting to weaken a generation of humans.

"Maybe, but . . . I don't know. The sound is gone now. Let's keep moving," Mira said, jerking open one of the doors.

We entered the main lobby of the conservatory, with its ceiling now standing a good two stories above us. Moonlight poured down, glinting off the polished marble floors. In one closed-off room to our right stood a gift shop, while a small office rested on the opposite side of the lobby. The doors to both rooms were closed and they were dark.

Laying a hand on her shoulder, I dipped into Mira's thoughts. *The naturi are close. Do you know the layout?*

Yes. Exactly across from us is the exhibit room, which leads to the bonsai exhibit and desert garden. To the left is another rain forest exhibit. There's a set of stairs leading down to it.

They're in the other rain forest. Beneath my hand, I felt Mira reach in her jacket pocket where she had her gun hidden. I pulled my own gun from its hiding place in the small of my back.

There are two entrances into the room. If we split up—

Her words were suddenly lost under a surge of fear that threatened to swallow us both. My hand tightened on her shoulder as I sucked in a sharp breath between my clenched teeth. Her fear started to pump through my veins, winding a sinuous course through my body until its claws dug into my muscles.

I lowered my head so that my lips were right next to her ear. "What?" I whispered. Her mind was still open to me, but I had no desire to dip into her thoughts just yet. I was still struggling to surface from the last tidal wave.

"Can't you hear it?" Her words escaped her in a fractured breath. "The crying . . ."

"A baby? No." This wasn't good. My hearing was good, very good. In fact, I was willing to bet that I could give most lycans a run for their money, but I couldn't hear anything beyond the sound of falling water. Was Mira's hearing that much sharper than my own?

"It's across the lobby. In the exhibit room or maybe the desert."

"I don't sense any naturi in that direction," I whispered after another quick scan of the conservatory. Of course, the only other creatures that I could sense in the conservatory besides the naturi were Mira and I. I didn't sense a human in the area. "You go check it out. I'll take care of the naturi."

Mira nodded and darted forward, slipping out of my grasp. I watched her for a moment, moving like she was just another shadow within a house of shadows. Silently, she pulled open a set of doors and disappeared into another room.

I remained in the thick shadows by the door, staring toward the deep, black pit in which the naturi were hiding. Trees stretched up to the ceiling, their leaves brushing against the windows, but all their color and detail was lost to the night. The only sound breaking the perfect silence was a torrent of rushing water coming from deep within the blackness. This was no little fountain. The water roared out of the darkness like a set of rapids in a narrow gully. I could only hope I would be able to use it to mask any sounds I made as I moved closer, because heaven knew I wouldn't be able to see where I was going.

With my Browning cradled in both hands before me, I edged away from the door to the entrance into the open rain forest room on my left. My heart had begun to thud faster in my ears and a bead of sweat trickled down my spine. I needed this—to violently lash out at the world, proclaiming to all who could hear me that I lived and I would take back my soul. Even if it meant saving humanity by destroying one monster at a time.

In a rare stroke of luck, the left-hand entrance was a gently sloping ramp for wheelchairs. I easily sidled down it, my back pressed against the metal railing while I faced the center of the room. I kept the gun pointed up toward the tops of the trees. The naturi were up in the thick foliage somewhere deeper in the room. Shafts of moonlight intermittently broke through the leaves, giving the darkness shape and depth.

Reaching the path at the bottom of the ramp, I caught a flash of moonlight glinting off a shimmer of water. The cen-

ter of the room contained a narrow pool that ran the length
from the lobby to the source of the roaring water. Around
me, trees and bushes rose up, hugging the little path in a
warm, humid embrace. I edged down the smooth track, my
back brushing against the rough rocks that comprised the
wall, which hemmed in the man-made rain forest.

I paused when I was just a dozen feet away from where
the naturi were hiding above me. Nothing moved. The sound
of rushing water had grown louder and a cool breeze drifted
toward me from the rear of the room. The leaves were still,
refusing to reveal my prey. The six naturi were clustered
tightly together at the top of a couple of large palm trees. I
ransacked my brain for anything that could have been able
to huddle tightly together at such a height.

With Mira hidden somewhere else within the conservatory, I was on my own and wasting moonlight. I had to
get these things taken care of before my nightwalker escort
needed to find sanctuary from the rising sun, or worse,
feed.

Lifting my gun, I aimed at the spot where it felt like the
little buggers were clustered and squeezed off a single round.
Leaves fluttered as the bullet ripped through a thick layer of
foliage and eventually buried itself in a tree trunk. Nothing
moved. Nothing made a sound but the roar of water.

Moving the sight slightly to the left, I squeezed off another around. The bullet tore through a clump of leaves at
the top of a tree before pinging off the metal window frame.
There was a single, high-pitched scream, like a mouse might
make if it were run over by a steamroller. Something larger
and denser than a palm leaf fell from the top of the tree and
splashed into the water below.

I couldn't identify the little corpse as it fell, but I didn't
need to. Its companions had taken to the air and I could
clearly identify them. The naturi were from the wind clan,
similar to the ones we had seen in the forest outside of London, with their butterfly-like wings and small, lithe bodies.

Sure, they weren't a pack of angry air guardians with talons ready to disembowel me, but their poison-tipped darts were painful and frequently deadly. It also didn't help that they had me outnumbered by five to one. Where the hell was Mira?

As they zipped through the air above my head, the wind naturi took on a slight glow in the overwhelming darkness like little balls of Christmas lights. Three were a brilliant blue while the other two were a bright orange. Two different families within the wind clan, I wondered. What the devil were they doing here in the conservatory? Hiding? Or nesting?

"Be gone from here," ordered one of the naturi as it hovered overhead. "You've no business here."

"And you're not welcome in the Fire Starter's domain," I called back, lining up the gun's sight with the creature's heart.

"The Fire Starter does not know we are here. She does not need to know. We've killed none of her humans," the naturi countered.

"She knows now."

Another naturi zipped over to the one that was speaking to me, laying a hand on her slim shoulder. "He's that hunter that travels with the Fire Starter," she proclaimed. "He would have brought the Fire Starter here. She knows." At once, the wind clan naturi started darting around the area, searching the immediate area for the nightwalker, causing me to lose my shot as they moved in and out of the trees.

"Where is she?" one demanded, pausing on the side of a tree. I took the opportunity to bury a bullet deep in the chest of a naturi with an orange glow.

"She's busy looking into what other mischief you've been up to within her domain," I said over the scream of the naturi as it plummeted from the tree to the hard cement sidewalk.

A dart whizzed by my head and thunked into a tree just behind me. It was a warning shot. "Why are you killing us?

We've done nothing to you. We've harmed no one within the Fire Starter's domain. We simply wish to exist here."

"Coexist peacefully with humans? I doubt that," I said, moving slightly to my left down the sidewalk, trying to get a better shot at the naturi that also had a wrist crossbow trained on me.

"True," she admitted with a wide, evil grin. "It's only a temporary arrangement, but for now we are willing to coexist in harmony with the earth killers. Can you not leave us in peace as well?"

"No," I replied just before firing off two shots. The naturi dodged the bullets, dipping low as she also fired off another poison-tipped dart.

"So be it. We'll kill you off first and then go looking for the nightwalker," the naturi murmured as she flew back up into the thick, black foliage near the ceiling of the hothouse. I fired off another blind round, hoping to at least clip her wing, but I heard only the unmistakable sound of breaking glass. I cringed as a bullet broke through the window, shattering it. The large plate of glass flashed and almost seemed to chime as it crashed to the floor. I was trying to avoid creating any damage that might be difficult for the authorities to later explain. The broken window also provided the remaining four wind naturi with a quick exit. However, they seemed content to fire their little arrows at me for the time being.

I continued down the path toward the sound of the raging water as the three blue naturi darted in and out of the heavy swath of trees. Thick leaves made it difficult to get off another shot. The breeze intensified so that I could now feel it like a cool hand brushing against my face. Sweeping the gun around, scanning for my missing prey, I found that I was standing a few feet away from a two-story waterfall. The rushing water reflected the moonlight that poured down through a break in the trees, revealing a small, wooden bridge that crossed over the stream in the middle of the room.

A flicker of blue caught the corner of my eye, drawing

my aim to my right. I was too slow. The tiny dart plunged
into my shoulder, digging deep into the muscle. The stab
of pain was instantly followed by an intense burning that
slithered down my right arm and under my shoulder blade.
The liquid fire stole through my limb, sapping my strength
so that I was forced to slip the Browning into my left hand. I
squeezed the trigger, but the naturi darted away just in time.
Sucking in a sharp breath, I jerked to the left as I sighted the
naturi again, ignoring the faint breeze created by the dart
that just missed my neck.

I fired the gun again. The naturi didn't even have a
chance to scream, as the nine millimeter bullet tore through
its throat, nearly severing its head. The creature flopped
down in a bed of ferns and didn't regain the air.

With my back pressed against the rock wall, I scanned
the area, the gun raised in my left hand. My right arm hung
limp at my side, fire pumping through my veins. The poison's darkness closed in around me, crowding my vision.
The naturi had disappeared, possibly hoping that the poison
would work its magic and allow them to pick me apart when
I finally fell unconscious at their feet.

Fighting the urge to lower my gun in frustration and rub
my aching eyes, I reached out with my powers to search the
room. I didn't expect to locate the last three. A window was
broken. They had an easy escape route.

I definitely didn't expect to sense one directly behind me.
Swinging around, I took a step backward toward the bridge.
My heart pounded in my chest, increasing the throbbing in
my arm, but also washing away some of the lethargy that
had crept into my frame. For now, I just needed some time
to fight this poison that was burning through my system.
My own supernatural healing would fight it off and finally
overcome its effects. It just needed a little time.

Something large and dark suddenly flew at my head. As
I ducked, I fired off a shot at the blue monster. My aim was
off and I heard the bullet tear through wood. The local pack
wasn't going to be pleased in the morning. Out of the corner

of my eye, I saw something flop and slap against the floor in a pale strip of moonlight. Looking down, I discovered what looked to be a gold and white koi. Great. The bastards were now throwing fish at me.

Gritting my teeth, I resumed my search of the room. I stepped toward the bridge, carefully avoiding the fish. The wood creaked and groaned under my weight. Another flash of blue darted out from behind a thick grouping of leaves. I lifted my gun, my finger putting pressure on the trigger as I tried to lead my target. Yet before I could squeeze the trigger, another fish was pitched at me in the darkness. This one looked to be the size of a large trout instead of the fist-sized koi I had encountered just moments ago. I tried to lift my right arm to block it, but it was slow to respond. Twisting, I felt a sharp stabbing pain biting into my left calf muscle.

With a curse on the tip of my tongue, I fell backward over the railing of the bridge into the water. The only positive was that I had the presence of mind to fire back at the naturi to my right before I hit the icy water. My back slammed into the rock floor, knocking the air from my lungs as my head went under the water. Despite being in a representation of the rain forest, the water that flowed through the room was ice cold. It seeped into my clothes and dug its sharp talons into my skin.

I shoved myself back to my feet, only to discover that the pool of water barely reached my knees. The falling water pounded the floor behind me, sending up a cool mist. My teeth were clenched in a desperate attempt to keep them from chattering as I scanned the area with both my eyes and my powers. There were only two naturi left. Apparently I had managed to get off a lucky shot before hitting the water.

Enough games. I was cold and wet. The pain in my arm and leg was throbbing, sending angry waves through my body. It was becoming a struggle to remain conscious as the poison flooded my systems and leaked into my brain. I had had less trouble with the damn naturi in Spain. Shoving the gun back in the holster at the small of my back, I stepped

forward. With both hands on the railing, I slowly hauled myself over it and back onto the bridge.

The naturi chose that moment to attack, believing that
I was helpless. Blue and orange glows shot from behind a
tree and flew straight at me. Expelling a slow breath, I lifted
my empty left hand and concentrated on the creatures about
the size of a young child. At the same time, I reached down
into the black shadowy core that existed deep in my chest.
The hard ball of power roared with hellish joy as I touched
it with my thoughts, summoning it. It flowed out, faster than
the water falling behind me until it filled my entire frame. It
blotted out the pain in my limbs and the chill that was eating
away at my skin.

Suddenly, I could hear the naturi's heartbeats, thudding
faster than a hummingbird's. I could hear the blood pumping through their nimble little bodies. I concentrated, struggling to control the rush of power that was swamping my
brain. It wanted more than just these little naturi. The tiny
creatures came to a sudden halt in midair, their voices raised
in an ear-piercing scream before they fell back to the earth
with a soft thud.

Lowering my hand, I reluctantly pushed the swell of
power back down to the dark core. It shoved back with a
frustrated roar in my head, demanding to be set free. It was
intoxicating. A rush unlike any I had ever felt. But I would
never let it rule me. Power such as that had only one purpose: to kill.

Slowly, the power drained from my limbs and I discovered I was trembling in my cold, wet clothes. I drew in a
couple breaths through my nose, expelling them through my
clenched teeth. Pushing away from the railing of the bridge,
I walked over to where the last naturi had fallen. I couldn't
see it, but I could hear a faint pop and hiss of bubbling flesh.
I had caused its blood to boil within its skin. I imagine its
little heart had exploded or melted under the sudden intense
heat.

A bori owned half of my soul. I could heal faster than normal humans, sense other creatures, and I didn't age. But my true "gift" was my ability to cause another creature's blood to boil. I was a bigger monster than Mira ever could be.

Leaning against the nearby wall, I drew in a steadying breath. My legs were like jelly and my arms were trembling. I was cold and exhausted. And I wasn't alone. My only warning was the snapping of a branch. I didn't have enough time before the naturi was on me. Slamming her small body into mine, she shoved a small blade deep into my stomach. I groaned as she pulled the knife free and held it to my throat, cutting through the thick fabric of the turtleneck to slice the tender flesh beneath there. I could smell her blood on the air and her arms trembled as she fought me.

I was a fool. I had managed to wound the naturi I shot before falling into the water, but I didn't complete another scan of the area to be sure that I had actually killed her. She had been hiding in the shadows, waiting for me to relax so that she could finally strike.

"You may have killed my people, but you won't leave here either," she snarled. One of her hands bit into my shoulder, her nails digging through my shirt, while the other held the knife pressed against my throat. I gripped one wrist with both hands, fighting to keep the blade from digging deeper into my throat. She wasn't that strong, but between the poison and the use of my powers, I was exhausted.

Gritting my teeth, I let my eyes fall shut as the knife edged another millimeter deeper into my flesh, hitting veins that released a fresh flow of blood. It didn't take much to tap in to the powers that lingered just below the surface, demanding the life of this naturi. The release was like an explosion from my chest, causing me to cry out in surprise. I was too tired to keep it under tight control as usual. The naturi jerked as the energy swept through her in a flash, bringing her blood to an almost instant boil. She died so quickly she didn't even have enough time to scream in pain.

I shoved her corpse off of me and collapsed to my knees, my breathing labored as stars spun before my eyes. The energy continued to flow from my soul, searching for other creatures to destroy. It was only a second before I sensed Mira close by. The monster within me chuckled with glee as it reached for her own energy. But instead of destroying her, I could feel it wanting to combine the two powers, creating an even bigger threat to the world.

"No!" I groaned, pressing both hands to the cold concrete walkway as I centered all of my attention on the powers that were running rampant from my body. I had never lost complete control like this. I was a danger to every living creature around me—human, nightwalker, or naturi. Race didn't matter, only that the creature had a soul that I could possess.

Summoning up the last of the energy that I had within my trembling frame, I mentally wrapped my fingers around the power that was searching for its next victim and pulled it back into my body. I could feel it fighting me, jerking against my grasp. Muscles ached and my lungs burned as I stopped breathing for fear of losing my grip on the monster. After what felt like an eternity, I pulled the powers back into my body, tapping them back down into the core of my soul where none could reach it. For now, the world was a little safer from me.

Sixteen

I clung to the sound of the rushing water as I lay on the ground in the darkness. My throat had stopped bleeding for the most part, as the thick cotton sweater had staunched most of the bleeding. The pain in my arm and leg had faded to a dull ache, falling behind the low roar in my chest. The monster inside me wanted out—demanded more blood than just one measly naturi. It wanted larger prey and more of them. I should never have tapped that power balled inside me. Leaning on my forearms with my head pressed against the walkway, my thoughts raced through a dozen scenarios that would have allowed me to safely dodge the naturi and draw my gun. But I hadn't. Seconds earlier, not a single one of those options had been present in my thoughts.

But then again, there had been no conscious thought seconds ago. I'd given in to my anger and fear. Tapping that ready source of energy had been quick and easy. It also felt good, like unclenching a tensed muscle. The pain-melting warmth spread through my limbs and seemed to heat my very soul.

Of course, it all came with a price. I lay there now struggling to push it all back down and safely replace the lid. All

the aches and pains were creeping back into my awareness.
My cold, wet clothes stuck to my frame, making my teeth
chatter. But I welcomed it. Anything to remind me that I was
still human. Anything to separate me from the demon that
had its claws in my soul.

With a shudder, I rose slowly to my feet and continued
the rest of the way around the room, my left hand held out
to my side so that it skimmed the rock wall. At the marble
stairs that led back up to the main entrance of the conservatory, I paused. I scanned the rest of the building for naturi.
Reaching out with this power was different from touching
the one that seemed to be wrapped around my soul. This
one was outside of me, alive in the air. It felt like I was temporarily removing a blindfold so I could look around. At
one time, I had tried to maintain this awareness constantly,
but it proved to be too exhausting and distracting.

A quick scan of the glass building revealed that I was
alone except for Mira's shadowy presence. I frowned as it
suddenly dawned on me that she had never returned. She
was not one to miss out on a chance to destroy some naturi. Something must have kept her, but I sensed no one else.
Of course, that didn't necessarily mean that she was alone.
Older vampires could cloak their presence for a limited
amount of time.

Pulling my knife from its sheath on my hip, I silently hurried up the stairs and across the main lobby to the other exhibit room. I peered through the screen door to find a large
open area bathed in silver moonlight. There were no large
trees in this room to cover the windows. Along the walls
were undulating hills of flowers, and the soft trickle of water
filled the air, indicating another small fountain. The center
of the room was empty.

Slipping inside the room, my eye caught on a flicker of
light off to my left, like dancing firelight. That was not a
particularly good sign. Had she been threatened? I reached
out mentally for Mira to tell her that I was coming, but was

met with a brick wall. Mira had shut me out of her thoughts before, but it had always left an emotional imprint, an impression of her state of mind. This was just cold, unforgiving oblivion.

Dread knotted in my stomach and my hand tightened around the grip of my knife as I hurried toward the door of another room. Reaching for the handle, I froze, my heart giving a strange little lurch as I gazed through the window of the door. Mira sat on her knees in the middle of the room. She was doubled over with her forehead pressed to her legs and her hands covering her ears. A ring of yellow and orange flames rose up from the stone floor surrounding her. She was completely alone.

Jerking open the door, I stepped inside. I was hesitant to put up my knife even though I could neither see nor sense another creature. Had her attacker left just seconds before my arrival? My eyes carefully scanned the large, narrow room. Shadows lunged and danced in the firelight, but I could still easily pick out the nearly two dozen bonsai plants on wooden pedestals lining either wall.

I reached out again to touch her mind, but was met with the same impenetrable wall.

"Mira!" I shouted above the pop and crackle of the chest-high flames. Their heat cut into the chill that held my frame, stopping my teeth from chattering.

The vampire's head suddenly jerked up. Her lavender eyes glowed with their own light. The flames jumped and roared, while several of the bonsai trees exploded into flames as if they were merely kindling in the face of a rampaging forest fire. Flowing to her feet with a surge of power, she reached down and quickly snatched up a pair of knives that were resting at her sides.

"Where did he go?" she demanded in a rough voice. Her hand clenched the knives so tightly they trembled.

"Who? Who was here?" I asked. The flames kept me backed toward the entrance into the tiny room, which was growing unbearably hot. Sweat trickled down from my forehead along my jaw, while my palms grew damp.

"They're stealing children. I can hear them crying but I can't find them," she said, her eyes sweeping over the entire room as she turned in a circle. The barrier she had erected between her emotions and me was beginning to crumble, and I could feel her rage and overwhelming sorrow.

I've failed. Oh, god, he's got her! I've failed, repeated across her brain.

"Who?" I demanded again when she didn't seem to notice me. "Who are you talking about? The naturi? They're not here." Mira didn't reply to me. In fact, she stared straight ahead and yet I got the feeling that she didn't actually see me.

Unsure of what to do to finally capture her attention, I reached out mentally, hoping to snap her from her growing inner turmoil. *Has Rowe been here?*

Nerian! She mentally screamed before her gaze snapped over on my face. Mira blinked twice and she slowly lowered her shaking hands to her hips. She looked more than a little lost and confused, as if she couldn't understand how she came to be standing there encircled with crackling flames. A part of me wondered if she was even aware she had conjured up the flames. Such a skill had been with her even during her human years. I imagined it was now as much a reflex as breathing was for us.

"Danaus." My name drifted from her lips in a thready whisper. She wiped her cheeks roughly with the heels of her palms before placing the blades back in their individual sheaths at her sides. The flames went out with an audible whoosh, plunging the room back into nearly complete darkness. For a brief moment, she seemed weak and frail, as if the weight of the world were resting on her shoulders and her will were beginning to break.

"What happened?" I demanded, forcefully shoving my thoughts back to the matter at hand. Such a line of thought would lead me nowhere safe. I returned my knife to its sheath and crossed my arms over my chest in an effort to hold in what little heat I had gained from Mira's brief fire show.

"I—" she began, then suddenly halted as if the words had become lodged in her throat. "I heard crying. A baby crying. I followed it in here. It was so loud, but . . . no one was here. I don't . . ." She trailed off again. I didn't want her to finish the thought. We let the silence and the night sink back in between us.

"You said Nerian's name just a second ago," I said slowly, hating to even mention the creature. The mere sound of his name had the power to send a chill through Mira, as memories of her time with her tormentor rose up to eat away at the remains of her sanity.

"I couldn't have," she said with a sharp shake of her head. "It—it doesn't make any sense." Mira shoved both her hands through her hair, moving it away from her face as she looked around the room. A soft whimper escaped her as she caught sight of the decades-old bonsai trees that had been reduced to fragile cinders. She clenched her eyes closed and sucked in a steadying breath. She was still, but her emotions were bleeding back into my thoughts. There was nothing calm about Mira. She opened her eyes wide, locking them on my face, as she seemed to beg me for an answer. "The naturi?"

"There are none close by." I hesitated, but I had to ask. "Can they . . . can they get in your head?" While it was relatively rare, from my understanding, there were some naturi that could create hallucinations.

"No."

"Are you sure?"

"Yes. They tried years ago, when they tortured me. They were rather pissed that they couldn't screw with my thoughts," she admitted. Her voice suddenly sounded weary, matching her slumped shoulders. "They shouldn't be able to now. I'm older now, stronger. Nothing's changed."

"Except for Aurora."

Mira looked down at the floor. A shiver of fear ran

through her thoughts before she could hide it from me. The queen of the naturi was now free in our world and no one could even begin to guess how it was going to affect how the game was played. Would the naturi grow stronger, more powerful because their queen was finally with them? Maybe. Could the conservatory have been a trap for Mira? Possibly.

Was I grasping at straws? Definitely.

"We should go," I said at last. Nothing would be gained in sitting around here. We already had a murder to solve. The quandary of a handful of naturi hiding in a greenhouse would have to wait.

Mira nodded, and slowly crossed the distance between us. She was turning toward the door when her eyes suddenly snapped to me. Even in the shadows, I could still make out her furrowed brows and frown.

"What the hell have you been doing?" she demanded.

"I was killing wind clan naturi while you were busy searching for a nonexistent baby," I growled. I really didn't need her drawing attention to the fact that I was still wet and half frozen. My only thought at the moment was getting somewhere so I could change into some warm, dry clothes.

"And you found it necessary to swim in the pond?" she continued.

Biting back a snide comment, I stepped around her and left the bonsai exhibit, heading back toward the lobby. My feet squished uncomfortably in my shoes and the rubber soles squeaked across the marble floor now that I was making no effort to be quiet.

I paused in the main lobby and looked over my shoulder at Mira as she stepped through the door. "Should we do something with the naturi?"

"I thought you killed them," she snapped. Her left hand darted into her jacket pocket and she quickly pulled out her gun.

"They're dead. I meant the bodies," I corrected. The nightwalker's frame instantly relaxed, her arms falling limp at her side. Her face smoothed to placid, unreadable calm.

"I'll leave a message with the pack leader when I get home. They can clean up the mess before the place opens," she said, waving off my concern.

I followed her back out the same side door we had come in and to the car. Yet instead of pushing a button to unlock the doors, she popped the trunk. Mira reached in and picked up my bag. I easily caught it when she threw it at me, the steel weapons inside clanging softly.

"Go change," she commanded.

"What?" I said dully. I thought she was going to tell me to go find a place to spend the daylight hours on my own.

"You're wet and smell like fish," she announced, leaning against the side of her car. She folded her arms over her chest and crossed her ankles. "You're not getting in my car like that. Go change clothes behind a tree. Unless, of course, you want to ride naked." An evil grin spread across her face and faintly lit her eyes. Yeah, she was bouncing back just fine.

Teeth clenched, I turned on my heel and strode back down the walk, disappearing around the corner behind a large pine tree. I didn't know if Mira could see me and at the moment I didn't care. Quickly digging through my duffel bag, I pulled out the first shirt I came across. In a couple quick movements, I peeled off my sodden clothes and pulled on what turned out to be a short-sleeved black shirt, boxers, and jeans. Still barefoot, I shouldered my bag. With my boots in one hand and wet clothes wadded up in the other, I walked back to the car. I was still cold, but it was no longer biting down into my bones. As I appeared, Mira pretended to look down at a nonexistent watch on her bare wrist.

"My, that was quick," she teased.

"Let's go," I grumbled, dropping the wet clothes and bag

into the trunk with a heavy thud. I picked up my leather jacket and shrugged into it.

"You could have ridden naked, you know. I wouldn't mind," she continued, shutting the trunk. She pulled the remote out of her jacket pocket and unlocked the doors. I tried to ignore Mira's comments, but it wasn't the easiest thing. It had been too many years since a woman had last made a pass at me. Most took one look at me and quickly scampered away in fear. I bit back the urge to smile as I pulled open the passenger-side door. Sliding into the car, I pulled on my boots over my bare feet.

Jumping into the car, Mira made a tight U-turn and headed back into downtown. I remained silent, content to watch the lights blur past my window and think about what had occurred since I had landed in the vampire's domain. I had been accosted by the lycans, attended a First Communion, searched for clues in a dead girl's apartment before looking over her corpse, interrogated a vampire, and then killed some naturi hiding out in a conservatory. It had been a full night. And the worst of it all was that I still didn't have a clue as to what was going on. It also didn't help that Mira was acting strange. Despite her occasional quip and sarcastic remark, she was more reserved than usual.

Mira parked her car on the street in front of the three-story town house I had stayed in the last time I had been in town. Popping open the trunk, she grabbed one of my bags and tossed me my ball of wet clothes before handing me my second bag of weapons. I followed her up the stairs and onto the porch where she unlocked the door and gave it a little shove open with her foot.

"You can stay here while you're in town," she said.

"I can just as easily maintain my room at the hotel with James," I reminded her.

"We discussed this," Mira said with an irritated sigh. "You're likely to run across fewer problems while you're staying in town if you're at my residence." Any comment I would have made was cut off by her slamming the door behind me. My only concern was that maybe I didn't like the signal it was sending to everyone within her domain. It certainly didn't help my reputation as a ruthless vampire hunter.

The town house was still the same elegant yet functional place that I remembered, with its mix of marble and dark hardwoods. On the right side of the hall was the parlor with a comfortable leather sofa and a mix of older high-backed chairs settled around a dark wood coffee table. The walls were lined with paintings. They were all modern pieces, realistic paintings of people. Nearly all of the paintings were of women alone. Their faces were mostly hidden or limited to just a glimpse of their profile. Yet there was something in the way those women held their sinuous frames that implied that the artist had caught them in a moment of deep contemplation, a second in time where their individual futures hung by a slender thread.

Frowning, I followed Mira through the adjoining dining room, with its large table, into the kitchen. It was decorated in various shades of dark blue, steel gray, and black, from the marble countertops to the appliances, which I seriously doubted had ever been used. Everything about this room was dark and cold, threatening to swamp anyone who dared to enter the room.

The nightwalker paused for a moment as if in thought, then jerked open one of the drawers by the sink. Grabbing a set of keys, she tossed them to me and motioned for me to precede her back into the living room.

"Those keys are to the town house and to the red Lexus parked around the block," she said, leading me back to the only hallway off the living room. Tromping up the stairs, she stopped in the first bedroom off to the right and dropped my duffel bag at the foot of the king-sized sleigh bed made of dark cherry. In here, the colors were a combination of deep burgundy and dark gray, except for the carpet, which was as black as night. Even the various lamps that were scattered about failed to pierce the darkness that pervaded the room.

"I expect that you'll find this place comfortable enough again," she announced to the air. Her eyes skimmed the room for a moment, as if taking in her surroundings for the first time. All the paintings in the bedroom were abstracts with the same color scheme as the room. "If you make a mess, you have to clean it up. I don't currently have a cleaning service."

"Yes, it must be difficult to find someone who can get out the bloodstains," I muttered.

Mira chuckled softly. "First rule of being a vampire: never eat where you sleep," she said lightly. "If something were to happen that prevented you from wiping your prey's memory, he or she would know your resting place."

"But you've never slept here, have you?" I guessed. The question wiped the smile from Mira's face and she stared at me silently for a couple of seconds. The only sound that could be heard was the soft hum of the heater pumping warm air into the town house.

"No," she admitted at last. "I don't sleep here. Never have." Mira stepped around me and walked back down into the living room. I shed my jacket and tossed it onto the bed before I followed her. She stood in front of the large windows that looked out onto the nearby square with its enormous live oak trees, their arms stretched out to encompass the entire park. The streets were nearly barren of people, leaving the traffic lights to go vainly through their cycles without anyone to pay them heed.

I stood behind the sofa, watching Mira for a minute. Her arms were folded under her breasts, and her shoulder was propped against the glass. I could see only her profile, but her expression was blank of emotion. In that moment, she was human to me. There was nothing other about her, nothing to expose her for the dark threat that she was. For the single breath, she was just a woman weighed down by the world that she existed in.

It was when I was precariously balanced in that moment of forgetfulness that I hated her the most. I loathed the fact that she could lull me into sympathizing with her. It was locked in those silent seconds of weakness that all my hopes of regaining possession of my soul were threatened.

"Have you always lived like this?" I suddenly demanded, trying to redirect my thoughts from the way the light from one of the nearby lamps fell across her cheek, highlighting her high cheekbones. Her gaze drifted back to me. Her expression remained carefully blank and the current of concern running through her seemed to quiet, as if she was battening down ahead of a storm.

"Like what?"

"This," I repeated, throwing out my arms to encompass the opulent town house. "Do you have any concept of what it means to be poor?"

One corner of Mira's mouth quirked in a surprised grin. She pushed off the window and turned to fully face me, her hands slipping into her jean pockets. "I was born in a two-room house with a leaky thatched roof. In the summer, I slept in the stable with our one horse and sheep. In the winter, I slept on the floor in front of the fireplace or snuggled with my parents in our one bed. I never expected to have any better than that."

"But . . ." I prodded. As I leaned forward, my hands sank into the back of the sofa. The cool leather crackled and grumbled in the quiet.

"Sadira demanded luxury." She shrugged. It was one of the rare times she managed to mention her maker without oozing animosity. "One becomes accustomed to it. What about you? Always been a wandering sword for hire?"

Frowning, I looked away from her toward the sofa before me. My life had begun at the opposite end of the spectrum. The only child of a successful politician, I had lived with my mother in a lavish estate a couple of days' ride

outside of Rome. I had every luxury at my fingertips until I
entered the military, and even then I would never describe
my situation as dire. It wasn't until I left the military and
started to wander that my situation grew grim. Then food
was a matter of what I could catch and money came from
what random odd jobs I could find. Vast expanses of time
were lost to one-room hovels and tiny monastic cells with
little more than a straw pallet and a washbasin.

"No," I found myself saying. "I was the only son of a
senator. We were quite wealthy."

"What happened?"

"My mother was killed," I lied. Mira didn't need to know
that I had been the one to kill my mother. She didn't need
to know that I still felt no regret or remorse about the act. It
was enough that she knew that my mother had been the one
to sell me out to the bori for more power. The nightwalker
knew too much about me already.

"So you left, turned your back on it all," she said with an
all-too-understanding nod. "It's late," she continued before I
could comment. "Get some sleep. I'll call later."

"Mira, it's just after midnight," I needlessly reminded
her. It was still early by her standards. There was ample time
left to get things accomplished.

She shook her head, her gaze drifting back to the scene
on the city streets below her. "Not tonight. I need to think.
There are naturi in my city, Danaus. I need to think."

"We'll figure this out."

Mira's eyes jerked back to my face and she forced a stiff
smile onto her lips. "I won't do anything else regarding this
investigation tonight. I promise. Tomorrow night, we'll pay
Gregor a visit."

"I'm looking forward to it," I replied, earning a smirk. I
followed Mira to the front door. It was on the tip of my tongue
to ask if she knew what was going on, but I bit back the question. I tightly held the edge of the door as she walked past
to the porch. The wall was back up between us and the lack

of contact with her emotions left me feeling as if she was no longer real. Resisting the urge to shake my head, I closed the door and locked it. I had my own work that needed to get done and I had only so many hours to accomplish my goal before Mira called upon me again.

Seventeen

The sun had just begun to peek over the horizon when I pulled the car up to an empty parking spot along Bay Street. After Mira had dropped me off at the town house, I quickly jumped into the shower, washing off the remains of my encounter with the naturi in the Telfair Conservatory. A brief call to James had the researcher locating Barrett Rainer's private telephone number for me while I solidified my defenses at Mira's town house. The place had its own security system, but I had a habit of stashing weapons at strategic locations around any place that I stayed for an extended period of time. More than once, such planning had saved my hide from unexpected intruders. In my line of work, daylight didn't automatically equate to safety. A vampire's human associates were just as happy to bring about my death when I was in town threatening their master.

By 2 A.M., I had the number for the Savannah pack alpha. While he was less than enthusiastic to be receiving a call from me so late in the evening, he was willing to set up a meeting with Mira and me for the following evening. After what I had seen at the morgue, I was less inclined to believe that a nightwalker had caused the woman's death. And while I had my doubts about a lycanthrope being the ultimate culprit, if anyone else saw the body, fingers were going to start pointing in their direction. Barrett needed to be brought up to speed on this matter.

Unfortunately, I wasn't exactly looking forward to the meeting. The last time I had seen the shapeshifter, I had slammed him into Mira's refrigerator. I had lost my temper, but then we had all been on edge as we prepared to leave for Machu Picchu and what we all were sure was going to be the end of days for each of us.

Parking the red Lexus, I walked the half block down to the hotel where James was still staying and met the young man in the lobby. He stood staring off into space as he gave a jaw-cracking yawn. I doubted he had grabbed more than three hours of sleep last night because that was about all I had managed to grab between phone calls and the drive back downtown. There was one errand that I wanted to run with James at my side, but I had a feeling that we would have better luck during the daylight hours.

"Wake up," I growled as I approached him.

James gave a startled little jump and then sheepishly smiled at me. "Sorry about that. Haven't slept much recently," he said.

"You can catch up on your sleep tonight," I said, motioning for us to cut through the hotel to the back entrance that led to River Street.

"I know. Ryan is sending me back," James replied.

"Really?" I asked before I could stop myself. The warlock had given me the impression that he wanted the researcher at my side, but now he was pulling him back to London. It didn't make any sense.

James shrugged as we stepped onto the elevator. He pushed the button that would take us down to the ground floor. "You know Ryan."

I did know Ryan. The warlock never did anything unless he had a very good reason. For some reason, he didn't want James helping me any longer, and I didn't like it.

"Is he going back as well?" I asked.

I caught James's furrowed brow reflected in the silver

doors of the elevator just before they slid open. "I thought he had already left. He hasn't contacted me since I returned to the hotel."

Shaking my head, I stepped out of the elevator and walked toward the doors that led out to River Street. "I don't know what Ryan is up to. Can you tell me what he was doing with Mira?" I held the door open for him, forcing him to meet my gaze for a moment as he walked past me. The young man glared at me, knowing that I was ultimately catching him between his two masters.

A long silence stretched between us as we walked down the block in the cold morning air. The sidewalk was empty of tourists and most of the shops were still closed at this hour. We had the riverfront area almost completely to ourselves with the exception of the occasional homeless person settled in a shelter alcove or along the boardwalk.

"They were hunting naturi up in Scotland," James said at last when I had become sure that he wasn't going to answer me at all. "I was sent a couple weeks ago to pick her up. I wasn't there, but I booked the flight. They went up to Edinburgh, hunting an earth clan naturi. Afterward, she returned to the Compound. She was in a series of meetings with Ryan, but she also met with me. She told me things." He hesitated a moment, licking his lips as he thought about his next comment. "She told me things about nightwalkers and lycanthropes and the naturi. But I—I don't know how much I should believe."

Pausing at a corner, I shoved my hands in my pockets and gazed up the alleyway that led to Factors Walk. "Believe her," I said grudgingly. Mira wasn't one to sugarcoat the truth. If anything, she had a tendency to take a bleak look at the world around her.

"But it means that so much of what I've studied is wrong," James said, frustration eating away at his voice. "So much of the world that I thought I understood has been wrong. I can't believe that Ryan has the same misunderstanding and yet he's done nothing to set us on the right path. If Themis is wallowing in centuries of untruths, then I can't in good conscience remain there. It doesn't make any sense. We're not helping anyone. If anything, we're perpetuating more untruths."

With a frown, I stared out at the river as it wound its way past the city and down toward the massive shipping docks that were just around the bend. These were the same thoughts that had begun to plague me. I knew my time was growing short with Themis, but standing here with James, I knew that it was time to let the research group go. I had already seen and experienced more things during my time with Mira than James ever would, and if I honestly faced the facts of those events, I knew that many of the things I had learned with Themis were painfully wrong, resulting in the deaths of people who had done nothing to deserve their execution.

"And if we leave Themis, where do we find a place in this world?" I asked.

James heaved a heavy sigh and shook his head. "I don't think there is a place for us yet."

Those with knowledge of the others didn't find an easy home within this world. The everyday world in which most people existed seemed like a pale, gray-shaded lie that left a nasty taste in the back of your throat. We had to maintain some kind of link to the others if we were to remain sane, if we were to find some way to sleep at night, even if it was with a knife under our pillow.

"Not yet, but after the Great Awakening, the world will make a place for us," I commented, starting up the hill toward Factors Walk.

"After hearing Mira's thoughts on that auspicious event, I have to admit that I'm not particularly looking forward to it. I can't imagine that it's going to go smoothly, no matter when it happens," James said, walking just a couple steps behind me. "I mean, people just don't like being lied to. They don't like secrets."

I stopped when we reached Factors Walk and looked up

and down the wide alley. We were only a few dozen feet away from the apartment building where Abigail Bradford had been killed. The area was still blanketed with heavy shadows, but my keen eyesight could easily pierce the darkest corners. From what I could see, we were alone.

"What are we doing back here?" James finally asked after nearly a minute of silence.

"I was down here yesterday morning and a girl stopped me from walking up here," I replied, slowly turning back to face the alley that linked Factors Walk and River Street. "She made it sound like she had seen the killer."

"Really?" James demanded, coming alive and awake for the first time since meeting me that morning. His doubts about Themis and Ryan were temporarily forgotten as he turned his mind back to the mystery currently at his fingertips. "What's her name? Can we speak with her again? Did you get any kind of description?"

"No, no name. She ran off before I could catch her name or any additional details." I shook my head and walked back down toward River Street. "She called Factors Walk the Dark Walk."

"Fitting," James mumbled as he walked beside me.

"She said that the thing that killed the girl has been lingering around the region and that it's unlike anything that's been here before."

"But—" James started, but abruptly stopped as if the thought caused him enough of a problem to halt his feet. "But that makes it sound like she knows about creatures like nightwalkers and shifters. Could she know about . . . the others?" he asked, lowering his voice to a whisper.

"Why not? You do," I said with a smirk that finally got him walking again.

"Yes, but who is she?"

"Another homeless soul. This city has more than a few of them," I said, crossing the street to walk along the boardwalk. "She looks to be around twelve to fourteen years old.

Brown hair. Brown eyes. A little over five feet tall. Slender, with a worn backpack and dirty jeans."

"Is that why we're out this morning? Looking for her?"

I weaved around a park bench and regained the sidewalk near the cobblestone street. "Yes," I admitted. "She was scared of me that last time. I thought maybe if I brought you along, she might be more willing to talk."

"You think two strange men are better than one?" he inquired incredulously.

"You don't have a very threatening manner," I said.

James fell silent after my less-than-flattering assessment of his person and we continued down the walk until it finally wound away from River Street and followed the river into a park-like setting. I was about to give up and head back to Factors Walk when we finally spotted her sitting against the bronze Waving Girl statue, weaving Savannah roses with dried palm leaves.

Her head snapped up at the sound of James's footsteps as we turned the corner. She placed one hand on the ground and was preparing to surge to her feet and bolt out of the area at the first sight of me.

"Wait!" I commanded. "We're not going to hurt you."

"Please!" James called after me. "We've got questions."

The girl paused, standing, clutching a half-finished rose in her left hand and a pair of scissors in the other. Her bag was still on the ground along with a half dozen finished palm-leaf roses. If she ran now, she would be forced to leave all of her stuff behind if she had any hope of escaping both of us.

"What do you want?" she demanded belligerently, pointing the scissors at me like a knife.

"My name is James and this is Danaus," James calmly said, with his smooth British accent and impeccable manners. "We're looking into the murder of that poor woman who lived over on River Street. Danaus indicated to me that you might have seen the person who killed her. We are simply looking for a little information."

The girl directed her gaze over at me, arching one eyebrow and crinkling her nose. "Is he serious?"

"Very," I replied around a half smile. Sometimes James could be a bit stuffy, but I had a feeling that that was half the reason that Mira liked him as much as she did. He was easy to tease.

The girl frowned, as she squinted her eyes at James, carefully looking him over before turning her gaze to me, weighing me with the same heavy stare. "Just hang around River Street or even any one of the churches. It'll show up eventually," she said at last, as she plopped back on the ground next to her things and resumed the task of weaving another rose.

"What is it?" James inquired, slowly edging closer one step.

The girl shook her head, not bothering to look up at him. "Don't know. Like I told him, I've never seen anything like it before and there's more than enough strange things hiding in this city."

"Strange things?" James repeated.

"Yeah, like him," she stated, jerking her chin toward me. "Or that woman you were with last night. Vampire, ain't she?"

"So you do know," I stated, earning a grim smile from the girl. She gazed up at me with old eyes that bespoke too many years lived on the streets.

"Vampires? Yeah, I've seen them. Werewolves, too. In the past few months, there's something else lurking around the area, fighting with the vampires," she said. With nimble fingers, she wrapped a thin strip of gold thread around the throat of the rose, tying the leaf in place and finishing yet another flower. She laid it down with the others and pulled up another long palm leaf.

"Naturi," I said.

"What?" she asked, her head popping up, her hands finally freezing.

"Those other creatures you've been noticing are called naturi," I explained. "They're earth creatures out to destroy both mankind and vampires. I'd keep my distance from them."

She gave a little snort and returned to the leaf between her fingers. "Thanks for the advice," she said sarcastically. "I've learned that it's best to stay away from all of them. All those damn things are always looking for a bite and you don't want to be their next snack. They might be strong, but you can't count on them to watch your back, particularly during the daylight hours."

"But this creature that killed the woman, it's not any of these creatures?" I said, turning the conversation back to the reason we went looking for her.

"Yeah, nothing like them. Its look is closest to the vampires, but this thing is stronger. It just feels . . . evil," she said. A shiver wracked her too-thin body for a moment, causing her to edge a little to her left so that she was sitting more in the sunlight.

James squatted down near her, and picked up one of the roses she had made, twirling it between two fingers. "Have you seen it during the day?"

"Day. Night. It's always around," she said with a shrug.

"How long ago did you last see it?" I asked.

"Last night."

"Will you take us to where you last saw it?"

The girl's head fell back as she loosed a high-pitched laugh. "Are you crazy? There ain't no fucking way I'm gonna go anywhere near that thing if I can help it."

"We can't get rid of it if we can't find it," James said when her chuckles died down.

"Get rid of it? You think you can actually get rid of it?" she asked, her eyes jumping from James to me.

"Well, actually, that's more of Danaus's thing. But he's had a lot of experience getting rid of unwanted creatures. This will be no different for him," James said.

She stared at me for a long time in silence, her hands falling limp into her lap. "You're really old, aren't you?" she said at last.

"Yes."

A frown slipped across her face as she looked down at her hands. She was at least thinking about our request, which was a start. I had no doubt that she knew she'd be considerably safer if I relieved the city of Savannah of this creature that was starting to kill people. Like she said, this city had more than enough creatures running around. There wasn't room for another.

"Fifty dollars. We'll give you fifty dollars if you take us to where you last saw it," I offered.

Her head immediately snapped up, her brow furrowed in thought. "A hundred dollars."

"Fifty dollars if you take us to the spot. Another hundred if we actually find it," I countered.

Another laugh escaped her, but this one was a little more muted than her earlier one, as if the suggestion wasn't quite as ludicrous as the first one. I knew she had to be thinking about it. It was a lot of money. It would take care of her problems for a while if she was conservative.

"We can't stop it if we can't find it," James reminded her.

"I won't let it come near you," I promised.

"Fine," she said at last. Dropping the flower she was making on the ground, she shoved her scissors into her worn backpack and pulled it over her shoulders before she picked up her roses and remaining palm leaves. "But I can't promise that we'll find it. It comes and goes wherever it wants to."

We followed the young girl back down the boardwalk toward River Street. At the first opportunity, she hurried across the street to the sidewalk opposite the river and then cut back up to Factors Walk. She paused just at the edge of the building and slowly peered around. Her breathing had grown a little heavier as she stood there and the palm leaves crackled softly in her hands as they tightened.

"I'll go first," I stated. "Which way?"

"Right," she murmured.

I stepped forward into the wide alley, looking up and down the area. The region was completely empty of people, both through the alleyway and on the walkways above that connected Bay Street with the second-floor entrances into the buildings. Drawing in a deep breath, I slowly released it through my nose as I reached out with my powers. I didn't sense anything in the immediate area, neither nightwalker nor naturi. There weren't even any lycans in the immediate vicinity. Yet, as I was pulling my powers back into my body, I felt a spike of energy at the far end of Factors Walk. It was approaching quickly, and unfortunately, it felt extremely familiar.

"It's here," the girl said in a shaky voice.

"Stay behind me," I commanded. My hand slipped down and I palmed a knife that I kept at my side.

"Danaus!" said a bodiless voice not far from where I stood. "You've brought me my newest little friend. I've been trying to win her over, but she's been most stubborn. But you'll help me, won't you?"

I knew that voice. It was the same creature that I had encountered in Spain. The same creature that had possessed the nightwalker and killed the naturi. From what I could tell, it was pure energy and seemed to struggle to take a solid form.

"No!" the girl screamed. Dropping her roses, she darted out from behind James and me, running for the nearest set of stairs that led out of Factors Walk and up to Bay Street. The energy surged away from me and beat her to the staircase. It finally appeared once again in the form of a transparent angel with broad white wings and a silver glow. It smiled kindly at her, but there was something dark and menacing that glowed within its black eyes.

"Come now, child," it purred. "I won't harm you. I can help you. You can be stronger, so much stronger than the dark creatures that hound you each night."

"No! J—just leave me alone," she cried. She pressed her

back against the stone wall, holding her hand up as if she could ward it off. To my surprise, James leaped between the angelic form and the girl.

"Back off," he snarled.

The angel smiled and quickly shifted form to a slender woman with dark hair and bright blue eyes. Regardless of its form, it remained translucent, like a ghost. "James," it sweetly said. "Please, help me. I can't survive without your help."

I opened my mouth to shout at the creature, aiming to draw its attention back to me, but James spoke before I could. "You're not welcome here."

"I need the girl," she said. "Give me the girl, and no one else will be harmed. The girl is in danger out here alone on the streets. I can protect her. You can't."

To my surprise, a copperish glow lit the researcher's eyes as he pushed the young girl farther behind him. A deep growl rattled from his chest and he pulled back his lips in a snarl, revealing a growing set of sharp canines. Apparently, there was more to James's heritage than we had originally believed. Unfortunately, this wasn't the best time or place for it to present itself. I had to take control of the situation before James finished shifting in a place where someone could easily see him.

"Gaizka!" I shouted. The creature's head snapped around, a wide grin spreading across his face.

"I warned you, Danaus." It laughed.

Before I could say anything else, the sound of heavy footsteps echoed off the ballast stone street. We all turned to look at an older black man as he entered the alleyway, his brow furrowed as he took in the scene of me holding a knife pointed toward James and the girl, who were backed against the wall.

Gaizka instantly disappeared and reappeared directly before the man in the form of an elderly woman. "Please, Owen!" it cried in a trembling voice. "These men are trying to harm me, trying to destroy me. Please, help me."

"Mom?" the stranger gasped in strangled tones as he looked on what appeared to be a ghost.

"Please, my boy. Please, help me."

"Yes, anything!" he cried.

"No!" I shouted at the same time, but it was too late. The ghost flowed directly into the man's chest, causing him to jerk for a half second. And then he started at me with glowing red eyes. Gaizka had found a new puppet he could use to fight me and kill others if it wanted to.

I rushed forward, slashing with my knife, hoping that a slight flesh wound might force the creature out or at least wake the man out of his possession. However, Gaizka's presence made the man both faster and stronger than a normal human. He easily caught my wrist and tossed me across the alley. The creature then turned toward James and the girl. She let out a bloodcurdling scream, her hands tightly fisted in James's coat.

Still sitting on the ground, I raised my hand and unleashed my powers from where they were curled around my soul. I could feel Gaizka's laughter within my head as I instantly brought the poor man's blood to a boil. He kept moving as Gaizka worked to heal the wound, but it was only when I knew the man's organs were reduced to useless mush that the bori finally fled his puppet. The man was dead before he hit the ground.

The sound of footsteps echoing off the stone pavement jerked my head up in time to see the girl racing up the stairs, her backpack swinging back and forth on her back. She never looked back and I had a feeling that I wouldn't be able to find her again, which was a shame since it seemed that Gaizka had taken an interest in her.

James slid down the wall and sat on the ground. He looked down at his shaking hands, a tortured look on his face. I knew his thoughts without asking. He had thought he had escaped the fate of his parents. We all had. He had shown no signs in all his years, but now he had to face a new fate and he wasn't ready for it. For the first time in his life, I thought he actually needed the sanctuary Themis offered.

With a sigh, I looked down at the body of the poor man who simply walked back into an alley to check on a man and girl who looked like they were in trouble. A good Samaritan, and I had been forced to kill him before he killed someone else against his will. I closed my eyes for a minute and forced the bile back down my throat along with the scream of frustration. Gaizka could easily read minds and take any form it wanted in an effort to win over its prey. I couldn't find it unless it wanted to be found and I had no idea if it could even be killed. A bori had found its way into Mira's domain and it was my fault.

"James," I called. The researcher's head jerked up, his eyes wide and terrified. "Go back to the hotel. I'll take care of this."

"I-I-I can't do this," he said, shaking his hands at me. "I-I can't be this way. I thought I was s-safe."

"We'll get through this. I'll talk to some people who can help you. Go back to the hotel and get some rest. It will help," I said, knowing full well that it would be a long time before the young man had another good night's sleep. But to my surprise, he nodded as he pushed to his feet. Blindly, he trudged down Factors Walk and headed back to the hotel.

I stood as well and walked over to the dead body. I pulled it over to the shadows, where it was out of the direct line of sight of anyone who might be passing by. Taking a small bottle of accelerant from the interior pocket of my jacket, I sprayed it on the body. I kept it with me in case I had to quickly dispose of a vampire or naturi body. I piled a couple empty boxes on top of it to make it look like someone had lit some trash on fire. With a heavy heart, I threw a lit match on the pile. I waited only long enough to make sure the accelerant caught on fire before I jogged up the same stairs the girl had disappeared up just minutes earlier.

A sigh escaped me as I drove back to Mira's town house. I had little doubt that Gaizka was behind Abigail Brad-

ford's murder, but I just wasn't sure of the creature's motives for killing her. If it wanted to start killing humans
and causing chaos, it could have easily taken control of
Mira and torched all of Savannah. Of course, that could
just be the next stage in its master plan. If that was the case,
then no one was safe and I would finally be forced to kill
the nightwalker. Unfortunately, I was no longer sure that I
wanted to.

Eighteen

A heavy pounding dragged me from the deep abyss of sleep. Twisted in the soft cotton sheets, I lay on my back rubbing my eyes. Sleep had come faster than I had anticipated, pulling me under the moment my head had hit the pillow. Twice in too few hours had I used my powers, with too little sleep and food. I needed to sleep for at least a few hours before trying to butt heads with Gaizka yet again. As I stared up at the white ceiling, my thoughts were finally starting to congeal in a semi-coherent fashion when the pounding started again. Someone was at the front door.

Throwing back the black covers, I swung my feet to the floor and pulled on the pants I had worn the night before. I had left them crumpled on the floor next to the bed in case I needed to be dressed quickly. Grabbing the knife from under my pillow, I silently walked down the stairs. Late-day sunlight was entering the room at an angle, creating long shadows.

"Who is it?" I called before reaching the door. My voice was still heavy and rough from sleep.

"Peter Teague," a male voice replied from the other side of the door, soft and muffled. "We sort of met last night at the party."

I had opened my mouth to say that he had the wrong address when it dawned on me that he could be referring to the First Communion gathering. Frowning, I gazed through the slender window beside the door to find last night's main course standing on the front porch.

With the knife still tightly clenched in my right hand, I unlocked the door and jerked it open. I stood in the opening, blocking his entrance. "What do you want?"

"Welcoming committee," he said, his thin lips twisting into a sneer. Peter wore a white button-up shirt that was wrinkled and left untucked from his faded blue jeans. His brown hair was damp as if he had just recently gotten out of the shower. Dark shadows underlined his brown eyes and his skin was pale. Rough night, no doubt.

"Go away."

Peter caught the door as I tried to shut it. "They just want a little information," he interjected before I could completely shut the door in his face. "You would too if your mother had welcomed a serial killer into your home." I paused with the door half open, staring at the man. His mouth moved again, some of the sneer leaking away. "Think of me as a diplomat, smoothing the waves."

The nightwalkers were nervous about my appearance at Mira's side. Not that I was surprised by the fact. Unfortunately, that anxiety could prove to be a distraction for Mira, and I needed the Fire Starter focused as much as possible on our current problem. I couldn't afford to have her running off to deal with her fellow vampires when I needed her with me.

Frowning, I stepped aside and opened the door so Peter could enter the town house. He walked in, his gaze sweeping over the grand hall, eyes glimpsing the giant library to the left and the living room on the right. His hands were shoved deep into his pockets and his shoulders were slumped.

He wandered into the living room and stopped before the picture windows. "She has one of the best views in the whole city," he muttered softly under his breath as he shook his head. He then turned on his heel to face me. His lean face twisted and wrinkled as he took in my dirty hair, bare chest, wrinkled pants, and bare feet. "You just get up?"

"Late night," I grumbled, following behind him. "What time is it?"

Peter pulled his left hand out of his pocket and glanced down at his watch. "Couple hours before sunset."

Turning my back on my unexpected guest, I stumbled into the kitchen, stretching my arms over my head in an effort to wake up. I had slept later than I had meant to. Peter's reply also surprised me. He measured time the same way nightwalkers did, in relation to the rising and setting sun. I was willing to bet he had been among their kind for more than a year or two.

I heard his soft footsteps on the carpet as he followed me into the kitchen. I tried to ignore him as I opened the black cabinets. There was a small coffeemaker sitting on the counter beside the sink. I was hoping to find some coffee and maybe a filter or two. The last time I was here I had stayed only a couple days and the food in the house had been takeout, including the coffee.

"Left of the fridge, top shelf," Peter said from where he was leaning against the doorway.

Following his directions, I found a bag of ground coffee and some filters on the top shelf. I pulled them down and then looked at my guest, waiting for an explanation of how he knew.

Peter shrugged his slim shoulders, his eyes darting away from mine. "Mira threw a party here a couple months ago. There were a few humans. I made some coffee."

I walked over to the coffeemaker and started prepping it. "How long have you known Mira?"

"Mira threw a party here a couple months ago," he repeated, sarcasm lacing each of his words. "There were a few humans. I made some coffee." I looked back over at him as I poured water from the carafe into the top of the coffeemaker. "I don't," he admitted, into the growing silence. "I've seen her only twice, including last night."

"How long have you . . . ?" My voice drifted off, unsure of how to ask what was for some a delicate and awkward question.

"Been a pet? A plaything for the undead? A warm meal?" The sneer returned to his lips and I suddenly realized that Peter wasn't mocking me; he was mocking himself.

"Yeah."

"I met my first nightwalker when I was fifteen. I stumbled across him while I was running from some kids who were threatening me. The vamp took care of them. After that, nightwalkers always seemed to be in my life in one way or another. I came to Savannah about five years ago."

He paused in his story, bringing my gaze back to his face. Peter was staring at the floor, his brows bunched together over his nose in concentration. "The nightwalkers I knew at the time were . . . well, it was getting rough. I came to Savannah because of Mira's reputation. I knew I wouldn't be followed here. After a couple of weeks, I ran into David."

I leaned my hip against the counter, crossing my arms over my chest as I faced him. "You've lived here for five years and been involved with vampires all this time, yet you've met Mira only twice."

"Mira doesn't spend much time with her own kind," he said. "And honestly, I think they're glad she doesn't."

I couldn't blame them. Mira was a law unto herself, with the ability to take out her own kind with just a thought. She was a lethal protector of both her own kind and, as I was learning, humanity. Her powers and strength had earned her the fear and respect of her own kind.

"Yet, she threw a party?"

"Just one of the things they are anxious about. Five months ago, you sweep into town, hacking down any vampire to cross your path. And then both you and she disappear," he said, pushing off the wall to stand with this hands in his pockets and his legs spread wide as if waiting for an attack. "She returns a couple weeks later with a new nightwalker. As if that wasn't a big enough surprise, Mira appears at every nightwalker hot spot for six straight nights with this new nightwalker in tow."

Mira was sending out the message loud and clear, Tristan was under her protection. I have no doubt that she never used the word "family," but she didn't have to. Mira loved her independence, and yet she was suddenly making public appearances with another vampire.

Peter stared at me, as if waiting for me to confirm or deny any of his story. I turned my back on him and started hunting for a coffee mug. The smell of brewing coffee was starting to fill the air and I could feel the last of the fog lifting from my thoughts. I found a set of dark blue mugs in the cabinet over the sink and pulled one down. I didn't grab one for Peter. I didn't want him to get the impression that he was welcome or that he was staying long.

"And now you're back," he said heavily when he finally caught on that I wasn't going to provide him with any information. "A known vampire hunter. They don't think you're her pet."

The very thought made me clench my teeth until my jaw ached. The idea of being a plaything for vampires was repugnant. I had spent most of my life hunting down the evil creatures and the idea that I had to work with Mira was grating on my nerves, but I reminded myself that it was for a greater good. It was also temporary.

"But they've also seen Mira's power. They think it's unlikely that you are somehow forcing her to obey your wishes," Peter continued, into my silence.

"And this is where I tell you what?" I said, looking over at the young man. "That I'm not here to hunt the vampires? That the bloodsuckers are safe?"

Peter clenched his fists at his sides as he finally raised his voice in obvious frustration. "I don't know! Anything? Why are you here? Has Mira lost her mind?"

"Mira and I have business together. That is all."

Peter stared at me for a long time, his clenched fingers going slack at his sides. He closed his eyes and leaned against the doorway. "I've known a few nightwalkers that I wouldn't mind you hunting." His words drifting across the kitchen soft and slow. "But from what I've heard and seen, Mira is different. She makes this city safe for people like me. She maintains a good relationship with the local pack and she had tight control over the nightwalkers. From what I hear, there aren't too many cities like this one."

He lifted his eyes to meet my hard gaze and I realized he was pleading for Mira's life. "Most of the nightwalkers that hunt in this city have been here for a long time. Mira offers stability, the promise of something that resembles a normal life."

What he wasn't saying was that if Mira were killed, the city would almost instantly disintegrate into chaos and fighting as the large number of older vampires fought for control of the city. Unfortunately, there was no one near as strong as Mira in the area. The power vacuum would almost certainly draw the attention of vampires from other cities, luring them with the promise of chaos and blood.

Mira claimed dominion over a single city, but her reach was felt all across the continent. She kept the peace and all those weaker bowed to her will. While Mira kept herself blissfully blind to her influence, it was well known not only to those in the United States, but also those across the ocean. She was a thorn in the side of the coven, especially now that she had taken the open seat on the ruling party, and it was only a matter of time before someone in the coven decided to pluck out that thorn.

As much as it galled me, I was not the greatest threat to Mira. The coven was. And now there was Gaizka.

"I am here to deal with the naturi," I said, finally unclenching my jaw. "Right now, vampires are not my main concern."

"That's the best I'm going to get, isn't it?" Peter said.

"You're lucky you got that."

"Thought so. Good luck." Peter shoved off the wall and pushed one hand through his damp hair. I followed him to the front door and locked it behind him. Turning back to the kitchen, my footsteps were halted by an odd sound that trickled through the silence of the town house. It took me a moment to realize it was coming from my cell phone. I jogged back up the stairs into the bedroom and picked up the slender phone from the nightstand, but I didn't recognize the caller, and only James knew this number.

"Mornin', Sunshine," Mira's voice cheerfully replied when I finally answered the phone.

I lumbered back down the stairs to the coffee that was waiting for me, shoving my left hand into my hair to push it from my eyes. I stopped when I encountered more than one knot and dropped my hand back to my side. "How did you get this number?"

"James."

"Did you threaten him?" My Themis assistant knew better than to give out my cell phone number to anyone. He was lucky I answered it when he called. Hell, I doubted that even Ryan had this number.

Mira's sultry laugh rippled through the phone, but lacked its usual feel. It was nice to see that her powers had some limitations. "Of course not. James loves me," she replied, almost purring.

I snorted, turning to gaze out the bank of windows that looked down on the city. The streets were clogged with cars, their windshields reflecting the last tendrils of sunlight. Men in suits carrying briefcases crossed the square, hurrying to one of the many parking lots that dotted the terrain.

"We have some business to attend to tonight," Mira said, but I was no longer paying attention. It had suddenly dawned on me that there was a lot of sunlight left, way too much for the sun to have set already.

"Mira, the sun is still up," I said, unable to keep my voice from hardening to a brutal edge.

"Danaus, not every nightwalker sleeps until sunset," Mira replied. There was no missing the mockery in her voice.

"You do," I snapped. "You sleep late."

The nightwalker laughed again, but this time the sound was darker, colder. There was none of the carefree joy that seemed to accompany Mira wherever she went. This was the other side of Mira, the one I saw when she was dealing with the coven in Venice and when she spoke of the naturi. It was the laugh of a ruthless, calculating killer.

"I'll pick you up in an hour and a half. Be ready." The phone went dead before I could demand more answers from her. I stared down at the phone in my hand, my thoughts speeding through my brain at a reckless pace.

Mira had the ability to be awake before the setting sun. I had run across some Ancients that could awaken an hour or two before sunset, but Mira wasn't an Ancient. Had she somehow escaped the boundaries set on her by the sun? James had said that she had been walking around during the daylight hours at Themis and I had seen her during the day in my hotel room. While she loathed it, being trapped and helpless during the daylight hours gave humans the only edge they had against vampires. What kind of deal had she struck with Ryan?

But I had no answers and I had no doubt that Mira wouldn't volunteer any for me. Overall, it didn't matter. Judging by her behavior at the hotel, she was still vulnerable to the sunlight. She was conscious, but she couldn't leave the protection of her home until after the sun completely set. I had a feeling getting here in an hour and a half might even be pushing it unless some thick cloud cover moved in.

Slipping the phone in my front pocket, I returned to the kitchen where I sipped a cup of coffee before grabbing a shower. The reason behind Mira's new ability would be revealed in time. After living for more than one thousand years, patience I had in abundance, which proved to be the key to hunting nightwalkers. The long-lived creatures learned to move slowly when it was necessary, limited only by the hours in a night. What was one night when eternity stretched out before you? Hunting vampires had taught me to move as slowly and cautiously as my prey.

Yet Mira continued to elude me. First, as my prey, she seemed to remain one step ahead of me, just beyond my grasp. Her behavior was erratic, bouncing from killer to protector in the same breath.

And now as allies, I struggled to keep pace with her. I hated to admit it, but I didn't think she was the evil creature I had once believed. Even in her coldest moments, she still clung to a tattered sense of honor. She protected those whom she believed needed her protection, even at the risk of her own neck. But I would catch her in time.

Nineteen

Less than two hours after Mira's call, I stretched out my powers, allowing my extra sense to crawl over the city like a spider dragging its web behind it. The sun had set just twenty minutes earlier and I could feel no vampires in the immediate vicinity. It brought up the interesting question of whether any of them actually kept a lair in the downtown area. Of course, Mira's admonishment came ringing back in my head. *Never eat where you sleep.* And the downtown region was a massive feeding ground for nightwalkers.

I caught my first faint touch of Mira several blocks away, but steadily drawing closer. Judging by her speed, she was in her car. Something inside of me seemed to relax when I was suddenly aware of her presence, as if a hidden ball of tension began to unwind. I couldn't read her thoughts, but brief touches of her emotions brushed against my mind. She was calm, but neither happy nor sad. Beneath it, there was a red haze clouding everything. For a moment, I thought it was a deep, simmering anger, possibly her hatred for the naturi or Jabari, but it didn't fit.

When she was only a couple blocks away, the feeling grew more intense and clear—she was hungry. No, Mira was starving. Her hunger was clawing away at her insides. She needed to feed.

I pulled my powers back into myself and drew in a deep, cleansing breath. Thick walls went up around my thoughts, blocking out all outside influences, but it was another full minute before the same red haze faded from my mind. I looked down to find my hands were shaking.

It had been like that when I had seen my first vampire so many centuries ago. It was several hours before sunrise, and I had walked into an empty square that was quiet except for the splash of water from a nearby fountain. A pale man in deep burgundy robes had stepped from an alley, and I was immediately hit with this red wave of hunger. My knees nearly buckled beneath me and I stumbled backward a couple steps. Stretching out his hand, he beckoned to a woman, who approached him as if she were in a trance. Her face held no expressions, her eyes wide and vacant. Before taking her back into the dark shadows of the alley he had stepped out of, he turned and smiled at me.

I knew when he bit into her neck. I knew when he drew blood from her body, filling his own cold frame because I could feel it. It was the same liquid warmth that swept over my frame when I was at the First Communion with Mira. However, this heat held no seductive allure, but a horror as I came to realize that such a creature existed and that I was somehow linked to them. I could sense them, feel their differentness. In a crowded room, I could locate the one night-walker with my eyes closed. Their emotions drifted to me like a woman's perfume on the breeze.

But their hunger came through the clearest. I could feel the pain, the driving need, the unrelenting fixation that could force out all other thought. I could drown in that feeling until it became my own. It was a dual-edged blade. I could not only feel the mindless pain, but also the overwhelming feeling of satisfaction when the starved creature finally fed. Yet, it wasn't until the First Communion that I began to understand how deep that feeling ran.

Getting a grip on reality once again, I shrugged into my jacket and quickly locked the door to the town house. I was standing on the edge of the porch when Mira pulled up to the curb in front of the house.

"Aren't you full of tricks?" she teased as I slid into the passenger seat. "You were watching for me."

I had purposefully met Mira on the street. She would have picked up Peter's scent in the town house, and I wasn't sure how she would react. My gut said she would be upset, but then again, I had seen her laugh off bigger problems. Regardless, it was a distraction we didn't have time for.

"I've got a few tricks," I said as I pulled on the seat belt.

I looked over to find Mira's full lips quirked in a small smile as she turned the car back away from the town house. "I know you do," she whispered. "I underestimated you once. Never again."

"Only once?"

Mira's smile widened so that her right fang poked slightly against her lower lip. "How did you sleep?"

"Fine. You?"

"My day was just fine," she replied, now secretive and close-lipped.

I let the silence sink in as we wove our way around the square and through the historic district. Mira deftly drove us along a road that followed the Savannah River like a lover's hand in a long, slow caress. Night sank in, the darkness filling the car so that we were bathed in the pale blue glow of the interior lights.

"Where are we going?" I asked.

"Dark Room. It's the best place to find Gregor."

"We've got another meeting first," I said, inwardly cringing at her reaction to this unexpected development. "I scheduled an appointment with Barrett Rainer at Bella Luna."

"You spoke with the alpha?" she demanded, coming to an abrupt stop at a red light.

"The lycans need to know what's going on. Fingers are

going to start pointing in their direction if it gets out how the Bradford girl died," I explained.

Mira stiffly nodded, her hands tightening slightly on the steering wheel. "I agree. Does Barrett know why we are coming?"

"I told him that it's in relation to our investigation."

When the light turned green, Mira swiftly changed lanes and abruptly turned left, heading around another square. "I wish you would have told me a little sooner," she said, sounding a little irritated, but nowhere near as angry as I had expected her to be. The nightwalker was long used to being in control of every situation, particularly within her domain. However, I was afraid she would put off or completely avoid the meeting due to their strained relationship. Ever since the naturi had come to Savannah, tension had been running high between the shifters and the vampires.

"Why? So you could skip the meeting?"

"No, you ass," she said with a surprising chuckle. "I wish you would have told me sooner because I already drove past the restaurant."

My eyes immediately jerked back to my window and the Savannah River several yards away. We were still in downtown Savannah and nowhere near any bridges to cross out of the city proper. "The head of the local pack? On this side of the river at night?"

Mira gave a little laugh in the back of her throat and shook her head. "I guess I was wrong."

"How?"

"I have underestimated you yet again."

I couldn't stop from smiling. Surprising Mira was not the easiest of tasks, but I had succeeded yet again by knowing more about her domain than she expected.

"How much time have you actually spent in my domain?" she asked, one brow arched, though her eyes remained on the road.

I hesitated, but I could hear no malice or hostility in

her tone. She seemed honestly curious. "Less than two months."

"James keeps you well informed."

And I was very observant. The ongoing peace between the lycanthropes and the vampires in the city was no great secret. Nor was it any secret that Mira worked very hard to maintain that peace. The lack of animosity between the two species made Savannah peculiar.

But then again, the Savannah pack was peculiar in itself. Barrett Rainer was the alpha male of the pack and head of the Rainer family, who had ruled the pack for more than a century. In fact, more than seventy-five percent of the local pack was also a member of the Rainer family. Before any lycanthrope could move within a twenty-five-mile radius of Savannah, he or she had to petition the pack. Not an out-of-the-ordinary procedure, but it was also very difficult to be accepted.

The other peculiarity of the area was the agreed-upon "living" arrangement. No lycanthrope was permitted to live within ten miles of downtown Savannah unless they set up residence across the river on the north side. A werewolf could work anywhere he or she wanted in Savannah, but when night fell, they knew they were in nightwalker territory.

On the other hand, no vampire was permitted to hunt on the other side of the river. And on the night of the full moon, no vampire was permitted in lycanthrope territory at all. While strict, the rules worked to protect both sides from stupid mistakes.

Most of the information was known by only the locals, but careful watching of both sides had revealed most of the details, which James later confirmed for me.

"Barrett's family has operated Bella Luna on this side of the river for decades. It seemed silly to ask him to move it," Mira said when we stopped for a red light. "Everyone knows where it's located and they steer clear."

A few minutes later, we were entering a small building

with two walls of windows. The front was ringed with a low, black iron fence. The area looked like it was large enough to hold several tables for outdoor dining in nice weather, but it was now empty except for a few dried leaves.

Without a thought, I reached around Mira and grasped the old, brass handle, pulling the worn wooden door open for her. Some habits never die. When I realized what I had done, I expected a snicker or a snide remark, but Mira simply said, "Thank you."

A young woman with short brown hair looked up when we entered and she smiled stiffly. "It's good to see you again, Mira. He's expecting you. Let me show you to your table." The woman then turned her gaze to me, but this time her smile reached her brown eyes. "I'll be with you in just a moment, sir."

"He's with me," Mira deftly interjected.

The young woman blinked, her smile slipping completely from her face as she looked from me to Mira. With a little effort, her stiff smile returned. "Of course. Please, follow me."

Grabbing two menus from behind the maître d' stand, she smoothly wove her way around the tables to a secluded spot near the back of the restaurant. It was hardly the best table in the place considering it was close to the kitchen. However, I realized after sitting in the circular booth that we had an unobstructed view of the whole restaurant, and the noise from the kitchen would hinder any attempts to eavesdrop on our conversation.

As soon as the young woman stepped away from the table, a man in a pristine white shirt and black slacks set a glass of red wine before Mira. He then soundlessly put an entire place setting before me. Apparently, Barrett had informed his people that he was meeting with Mira, but he forgot to mention that she would have a companion.

"What can I get you to drink, sir?" the sandy blond server inquired.

"Nothing, I—"

"He'll have a glass of ice water, no lemon, and a cup of Earl Grey with honey, if you have it," Mira quickly said.

"Very good." The server disappeared into the kitchen and I looked over at Mira. She had removed her black leather gloves and she was fiddling with her salad fork, refusing to meet my gaze.

"You would never relax around me to actually drink a glass of wine and you don't seem the type to enjoy a Coke with dinner," she said, her words coming out rushed and defensive.

It was the start of an explanation, but I was curious as to how she knew I liked Earl Grey tea with honey. Was it something James or Ryan had told her? It didn't seem like it should have been a topic of conversation that would have come up. "How did you—?"

"You had it in Venice," she interrupted before I could finish the question that we both knew was hanging in the air.

Her words were like the caress of butterfly wings. My gaze had drifted around the restaurant and I was now fighting the urge to look at her again. My breath was trapped in my lungs as I waited to see if she would continue, threatening to pull me deeper into the spell she seemed to be weaving.

"I awoke one night and I could smell it faintly in the air." As she spoke, her eyes drifted shut as she became lost in the memory. "Earl Grey and honey. You had had seafood that night for dinner with fresh bread. I had forgotten what it was like to awaken to the smell of food."

"I can't imagine that it's happened recently," I whispered, letting myself get pulled deeper into the moment. The flickering light from the candle in the middle of the table danced across her features, caressing them, reminding me of the way the lights reflected off the Venice canal waters had danced across her body.

"You wore a short-sleeved linen shirt," she said, a smile tweaking the corners of her mouth. She drew in a deep breath and shook her head as if to brush away the last of the memory. "It's the only good memory I have of Venice."

I stared toward one wall of windows. The growing night had made them mostly mirrors, reflecting back the numerous diners that filled the cozy restaurant, but for a brief moment I was back in Venice with Mira. We had been surrounded at all times by creatures that wanted us dead. Yet, with a self-mocking smile, Mira swore to protect me. At great risk to herself, she kept her word.

But it was more than that. While in Venice, she had not only guarded me with an unexpected vehemence, but she also drew Tristan and Nicolai under her protective wing. I had seen Mira fight and kill. I had seen her bask in the power she could wield over her chosen victim, but those poor creatures had always struck at her first. Mira didn't kill without reason or purpose. A code I lived by as well.

It was the protective side of her that I struggled to understand. For so long, I had had it pounded into my brain that vampires were mindless killing, feeding machines. I had never expected to find a vampire that not only cared about other creatures, but that also had a deep sense of honor and responsibility. It just ran contrary to everything I believed about them, making me more frustrated the longer I knew her.

Desperate to distract my brain from the contrary signals I was getting from Mira, I scanned the restaurant until my eyes finally settled on something else that I could talk about. "Are they all part of the Rainer family?" I asked as another server came out of the kitchen carrying a pair of plates and headed toward an old couple.

"Most are, but less than half are also part of the pack," she replied, her voice lifting to its usual volume. "Can't close the place because it's a full moon."

Our server returned with my water and tea, and then asked for our order. When I hesitated, Mira made several suggestions, indicating that we were at least staying for dinner. I had assumed that Barrett would prefer to get Mira out of his restaurant and on her way as quickly as possible.

Either Barrett was not opposed to our presence, or he was more concerned with keeping up the façade that we were a normal couple in for a quiet meal.

Until the food arrived, our conversation stayed light, with Mira spinning one story after another about her time in Savannah. Her love for the city and its people was evident in every word she spoke. This was her home, and it was as much a part of her as the heart that lay still in her chest. It was a little surprising considering her carefree, cavalier attitude about everything else in her life.

When our plates had been cleared, Barrett Rainer finally appeared, wearing a dark suit and hunter-green tie. He stood close to six foot, with a stocky build. His hair was dark burnished gold and he had narrow copper eyes. An air of authority surrounded him. There was no mistaking that he was the Alpha of the Savannah Pack.

"It's good to see you again, Mira, he said, his deep voice rumbling in his barrel chest. There was a tension in his voice and running through his taut shoulders that made me doubt if he was truly happy to see the nightwalker. A few months ago, a number of lycanthropes had been killed when the naturi had been in town searching for Mira. Barrett had lost two brothers in the struggle and most likely held Mira personally responsible.

"Hello, Barrett," Mira purred, smiling up at him. "May I introduce a friend of mine? Danaus, this is Barrett Rainer, proprietor of this wonderful establishment."

Sliding to my feet, I took Barrett's hand and shook it. His rough hand was warm and I felt a faint ripple of power surround him. He was strong, and powerful for a lycanthrope. The species wasn't generally known as magic users, but there was no question he had a strong connection to the earth.

"Yes, we've met," Barrett said grimly.

"Really? When?" Mira demanded, her brow furrowing. An unexpected tension crept into her voice.

"He briefly stopped by the town house a couple months ago just before we left for Peru," I replied.

Mira frowned, the memory undoubtedly slipping back to the forefront. "Oh. Yes."

"I'm relieved to see that your prediction proved to be false," Barrett said, releasing my hand.

"So am I," I said. Just after throwing him into the refrigerator, I had informed him that Mira was going to die in Peru in order to protect everyone from the naturi. She nearly proved me right.

"Regardless, it's good to officially meet you, Danaus. Mira has never introduced me to her friends," Barrett said.

"That is because I am very cautious about the friends I make," Mira interjected.

"And Danaus is an interesting choice for a friend, from what I hear."

Mira shrugged her slim shoulders. "I am drawn to men of honor."

"Would you join us, Mr. Rainer?" I asked, hoping to redirect this conversation away from me. I was growing extremely uncomfortable with the trend I was seeing. First, the gathering last night and now a formal introduction to the alpha male of the local pack. It felt as if Mira was carefully weaving an intricate web about me, but I couldn't see to what end she was working.

"Call me Barrett, please."

"I wish to thank you for agreeing to meet with us," I said.

"It's not a problem. I'm always happy to make time for Mira." The smile that crossed his lips as he looked down at Mira didn't reach his eyes, and it looked stiff and forced on his face.

Barrett slid into the booth across from me so that Mira sat between us. I returned to my seat and tried to appear relaxed. Beside me sat a vampire and across from me was an extremely powerful lycanthrope. And both knew I was a hunter. I had definitely been in more dangerous situations, and oddly enough, most involving Mira, but neither creature could do much while we were surrounded by unsuspecting humans.

"How is the family?" Mira opened. Her hands were settled in her lap, just beneath the white tablecloth. I was beginning to realize they easily gave away her anxiety as she struggled to still her nervous fingers.

"We are still adjusting to our recent loss. My mother and sisters have returned to town and are happy to be home again. We are still adjusting to our newest arrival as well." Lines crept into Barrett's face, stretching from his eyes and around his mouth in tension. "I hope you are not planning to give me a new bundle."

"Nicolai is strong and intelligent," Mira swiftly said. "Has he caused you problems?"

"No."

"Has he questioned your authority?"

"No."

"If he had applied to the family, would you have accepted him?" Mira pushed, sitting forward as her voice dropped closer to a whisper. After Mira had staked her claim on Nicolai in Venice, she immediately shipped him here along with Tristan in an attempt to protect both their lives. While she could force the resident vampires to accept Tristan, Nicolai Gromenko had been another matter. He had to take his place in the local pack, which meant getting past Barrett. Apparently, Mira had called in a favor. A big one.

"I might have, but I don't recall being given much of a choice," Barrett said in a low, deep voice that seemed to rumble across the table.

"Nor was I," Mira softly said, sitting back in the booth again so that her back rested against the supple leather. The table fell silent as our server brought over a glass of wine and set it before Barrett.

"Nicolai Gromenko is a good, compassionate man," I said, drawing the lycan's hard stare back to me. Mira placed her cool hand on my wrist. Her thumb brushed across the inside of my wrist across my pulse in a caress.

Thank you. The two words whispered across my brain.

Barrett nodded to me, some of the tension easing from around his mouth and eyes. "I have no complaints regarding Nicolai beyond the means of his arrival. I am cautious."

I could not blame Barrett for his caution. Regardless of whether Mira realized it, I had no doubt that Barrett knew that Nicolai had either been the alpha of his last pack or had been born to be an alpha. You couldn't have two in the same pack. Either one had to leave soon or die.

The lycan's gaze drifted back to Mira, who pulled her wandering hand back to her lap. "But you did not come to discuss Nicolai, did you?" Rainer continued.

"No."

"The girl?" The question slipped past his thin lips in a weary sigh. "A few members of the pack work at the zoo. I've been hearing bits and pieces of rumors."

"Someone from the pack was called to examine the bite marks," I said, talking mostly to myself as I shook my head. I hadn't expected Barrett to be so well informed on what was happening with the investigation. But then, was it any surprise that Mira had contacts in the morgue and Barrett had people on the inside at the zoo? It shouldn't have been.

"Nearly. Our man was out that day and another went to examine the wound. He heard about the findings later that night and reported to me."

"What are your thoughts on the matter?" Mira inquired, her tone even and neutral.

Barrett paused in the act of lifting his glass to his lips and both of his eyebrows rose at the nightwalker in obvious surprise. "That's it?" he said returning his glass to the table without taking a drink. "I thought you were here to claim the head of the wolf responsible for this mess."

"Are you saying it was a wolf?" I demanded. This meeting was taking a turn I hadn't expected, particularly since

I already knew who the culprit was, but just couldn't find the right words to tell either of them. Having a bori running loose in the area was just as much of a nightmare situation as it was when the animal clan naturi were searching for Mira months ago.

"No," Barrett sharply said, holding up both hands. "But I saw the pictures and the report of the zoologist. Animal bites turn all eyes away from vamps and over to my people."

"Have you spoken to your people?" Mira asked. Her left hand slipped back onto the table so that her long fingers now caressed the slender stem of her wineglass.

"Yes, only a couple knew of the woman and those that did knew she preferred to run with your kind. I can vouch for all of my people, even Gromenko."

I shook my head, a wry smile pulling at the corners of my mouth no matter how hard I tried to hold it in. "Why do I feel like there is a 'but' hanging off the edge of that sentence?"

"Because there is," Barrett grumbled. He took a deep drink of his wine and placed the glass back on the table before he continued. "Just because I can vouch for my pack does not clear my people. It looks like an animal bite. A rogue could have moved into the area, and I don't know it yet. I can't be sure for another couple weeks."

A quick count in my head left me with the full moon in two weeks. Barrett's powers would be at their peak. I could only guess that he would be able to more accurately scan the region for a rogue, or possibly even call the outsider to him. I wasn't sure. My experiences with werewolves and other shapeshifters had been limited. And after discovering that many of the things I had been told about nightwalkers were wrong, I wasn't too willing to risk my life on the information I did have regarding lycanthropes.

"If the killer was a lycan, you've got more to worry about than just a rogue," Mira said, her eyes falling to the table where she traced the tip of her fingernail over the tablecloth.

"I've been to the apartment and to see the body. There's an odor clinging to both I don't think I've ever encountered before."

"Is that why you are here?" Barrett said, his voice hardening to stone as he looked over at me. "To find the killer?"

"I'm here to get this question answered as quickly and quietly as possible, regardless of who the culprit is." My right hand slipped to the edge of the table and it was a struggle to keep from balling it into a fist. I didn't think it was prudent at that moment to reveal that the head of Themis also charged me with the task of protecting Mira. I doubted the nightwalker was even aware of Ryan's wishes on that front.

"He is right," Mira conceded when Barrett looked at her. "However, I think there is more at work here."

"The naturi," Barrett said.

I watched Mira as she nodded, her gaze falling back to her wineglass. Her long red hair fell forward to create a curtain around her face, as if trying to shield her from the curious as she sank into her own dark thoughts. But there was no missing the movement of her jaw as she clenched her teeth or how her full lips flattened into a hard, thin line.

"Possibly," I said when she seemed unwilling to continue. "I am willing to bet that members of the animal clan can shape-shift."

"Yes." The single word escaped Barrett in a hiss. "I have felt them in the area. We enjoyed the break in September when you wiped them from the region, but little by little since your return from Peru, we have felt their presence creep back into the area." Barrett paused and directed his piercing gaze at me as if he meant to pin me to the spot. "I heard you hunted them in the city. Animal clan?"

"No," I sharply replied. "Six wind clan naturi at the conservatory."

"Are there . . . ?" Barrett paused and licked his lips before trying again. "Have you seen any animal clan here?"

I understood his caution, his fear. In the world of the naturi, the animal clan held the biggest threat to the lycanthropes. They had the ability to call and control the shapeshifters.

In September, more than a dozen werewolves had been slaughtered at Machu Picchu when the naturi sent them against the nightwalkers ascending the mountain in an attempt to stop the sacrifice that would open the doorway for the naturi. And still more were missing from their packs.

"I've seen no member of the animal clan in this area," I said. "Last night's encounter was with a group of wind clan members of the naturi."

"Keep your people close to you at all times." Mira's voice was low and seemed to slowly creep across the table toward us. "Hold them together. Stay in their minds. The naturi will wear us down and build their army by picking us off one at a time."

"I will," Barrett said with a stiff nod.

Mira blinked a couple times and lifted her head, straightening her shoulders, as if she were waking up from a bad dream. I resisted the urge to lay my hand on her arm. She was fighting back a swell of emotions that were attempting to overwhelm her. I could feel the chaos swirling in her when she thought of the naturi. They had tortured her, killed her people, and killed a human that was very close to her. So much of her world had been ripped apart by the naturi.

When I started on this journey, the naturi were little more than a job for me. I had heard the stories of their evil, the way they killed humans with no thought, no remorse. To them, humans were a blight on the Earth that needed to be expunged.

But that changed when I captured a half-mad naturi called Nerian. During his captivity, he told me more about Mira than any other had been able to tell me. Nerian had been her personal tormentor during the nightwalker's two-week captivity centuries ago. He told me in gruesome detail the physical and mental torture she had endured. Nerian could relate the intensity of her pain to the tone and style of her begging. And she had managed to survive only because they could not reach her mind during the daylight hours.

When Mira saw the naturi or even spoke of them, her body seemed to relive the pain over again until it nearly consumed her. I had seen the pain reflected in her wide violet eyes and touched the scars on her back where they had carved symbols from their language so deeply she could never heal them.

Mira's pain gave me cause to hate them. The nightwalker and I seemed to be forever on opposite sides of our own personal war, but I respected her sense of honor and justice. She was loyal to those who earned her respect and kept her word regardless of the danger to herself.

With a blink and a smile that attempted to cloak deeper emotions, Mira looked up at Barrett and extended her hand. "We should be going. We have other matters to look into tonight."

Barrett took her hand and squeezed it briefly before releasing it. "I understand. Good luck."

"Before you go," I said quickly, stopping the shifter before he could slide to his feet, "I wish to ask a favor. It's for a friend."

Barrett frowned at me as he folded his hands on the table before him. "I hope you're not looking to extend my family any further."

"No, but he does need help," I said, and then hesitated. I didn't know how to continue. James couldn't go through this alone and Themis wasn't equipped to help him. They didn't have the knowledge and experience that Barrett possessed. "We thought he was in the clear. He hadn't shown any signs, but something happened recently . . ."

Barrett's expression eased to one of concern. "And you're sure he's going to change?"

"He went through a partial shift when we didn't think he

could at all," I explained. To my left, Mira remained surprisingly silent, though I had a feeling that she was simply waiting until we were alone so that she could pound me with questions.

"Then he'll have no choice. When the full moon arrives, he'll have to shift completely," Barrett confirmed with a solemn nod of his head. "He'll need help. Fighting the change will only make it more painful the first time. He'll also need guidance back. His family?"

"No family. No pack," I said firmly. Barrett had to understand that James had nowhere else to turn.

His brow crinkled as he looked at me and a fresh frown formed on his face. "Is he searching for a pack?"

"No, I doubt he will ever be a part of one. He just needs someone to help him get his feet under him again. Get him through the first full moon. A little advice and guidance. That's all I'm asking for."

To my surprise, the lycanthrope only thought about it for a couple of seconds. "Send him to me a couple days before the full moon. The pack will help him."

"I'll do what I can," I replied, feeling as if a weight had been lifted from my shoulders.

"You're not sure he will come?" Barrett asked, his tone jumping in surprise.

"This has all come as a surprise to him," I admitted. "He may be resistant at first."

"How old is he?"

"I—I don't know. Mid-twenties, maybe." I honestly hadn't a clue as to how old James was.

"He's twenty-eight," Mira interjected, drawing my gaze back to her. For a moment, I wondered how she knew I was talking about James and then I felt it, a shift in power. She was a ghost in my thoughts, listening in undetected when I didn't think such a thing was possible. I had been so focused on getting James help from Barrett that I had dropped my guard.

"It will be hard on him, but the pack can help. Get him here," Barrett said and then rose to his feet. "We'll do what we can."

I slid to my feet at the same time as Barrett and shook his hand. "Thank you for meeting with us and for your assistance."

"My pleasure, and please, dinner is on me tonight."

"Barrett!" Mira started, but the lycanthrope held up his hand, stopping her.

"Accept it as an apology," he quickly said, forestalling any further comment from the vampire. "I had some of my people speak with your friend recently." His dark copper eyes returned to my face and he gave a brief bow of his head. "For the trouble. I did not understand the nature of your relationship with Mira."

It was on the tip of my tongue to argue that I had no relationship with Mira. That our preferred arrangement was one of hunter and prey. That this "friend" status Mira was bestowing on me was complete bullshit. But I kept my mouth shut and tried not to glare. This wasn't his fault. It was Mira's.

While I was standing, Mira slid out of the booth and I silently followed her out of the restaurant. It was only when we were both out on the street again in the cool fall air that I felt as if I could relax. I rolled my shoulders and leaned my head toward either shoulder, loosening up the muscles. I hadn't realized I had grown so tense while talking with Barrett until we were away from the restaurant.

Mira walked beside me, jiggling her keys in her hand. "At least that is out of the way," she muttered.

"Not exactly informative."

"I didn't expect it to be," she replied, walking around to the driver's side of the car. She hit the button on the remote, and the lights briefly flashed as the doors unlocked. "I took this meeting as just a kind of warning that you and I are looking into the murder."

I paused in the act of lifting the car door handle and tilted my head slightly to the side as if I was trying to hear something, but I was actually reaching out with my other sense. My powers flowed out from me, covering the area. The dozen or so lycanthropes in the nearby restaurants muddied up my senses, but as I reached past them, it cleared.

"We have to go now," I said, looking at Mira over the roof of the car.

"How many?"

"Four and they're approaching fast."

Mira looked up at the black night sky as she jerked the door open, as if she expected them to swoop down on us at any moment.

"No," I said, jumping into the car as she did and slamming my door shut. "By land. I think they're in a car."

"Damned naturi."

Twenty

It was only after the tires finished squealing, launching us out of the parking lot and back onto the street, that Mira tried to speak. Battling any member of the naturi was a tricky matter at best.

"What do you mean you think they're in a car?" Mira snarled, as both of her hands gripped the wheel. "Naturi? Is there something else with them?"

"No," I said, twisting in my seat to look behind us while struggling to hold onto the armrest on the door. Mira was whipping us down a winding street, continuously keeping me off balance. I had yet to actually see the car, but I could feel them following. They weren't gaining ground on us, but they weren't losing any either.

"Naturi are driving the car? Are you serious?"

"Damn it, Mira! You're a vampire and you're driving a car." For a brief moment, I wondered which one of us had actually lost their mind; Mira for her shortsighted bias or me for even participating in this argument. Of course, the thought was shoved from my mind as Mira made a sharp left turn in front of a semi, causing its tires to screech as the driver slammed on his brakes.

"I know! I know! I'm still getting used to the idea," she shouted, waving one hand in the air.

"Where are you going?" I demanded when I learned to breathe again.

"Highway. I've got to get them away from the lycans," she said as she finally grabbed an on-ramp to the highway, leading us north.

I sat back in my seat, staring forward as I shoved both hands through my hair, pushing it away from my eyes as I tried to think. Mira was still weaving through traffic like a madwoman, but I had faith in her quick reflexes not to plow us into a concrete divider or crush us under the tires of a tractor trailer.

"How the hell did they find us? Naturi can't sense vampires. At least, they never could before," Mira ranted, her voice dying off at the end.

"Shit," I hissed, barely resisting the urge to smash my fist into the car door on my right. "I bet they can track humans."

"Yeah, but you're . . ."

"I'm still at least half human."

Mira stared at me with wide eyes. The few times the naturi had managed to locate her, I had been at her side. They had learned to locate me and were potentially following me or at least watching me from a distance, waiting for me to join Mira. They were using me as a homing beacon to locate her.

"We can separate," I suggested.

"No!"

I sat back and released my seat belt, causing a little bell to start chiming in the car. "Let me out, and I can draw them away from you."

"I said no," she repeated, punctuating her remark with an ominous *thunk* that echoed all around me. She had locked the doors with the switch at her side. "I didn't save your sorry ass in Venice to hand you over to the naturi now. If I just randomly drop you off, they might guess that we're on to their little trick. They will have no use for you, and will simply kill you. "

"I can take care of myself."

"Maybe you can and maybe you can't. We're stronger as a team and you know it. So why don't you stop arguing with me and help me think of a plan." Mira glanced at me for a second before looking back at the road long enough to cut between two cars to get to an open lane. "And put your goddamn seat belt back on."

I didn't take my eyes off her as I drew my seat belt back on and latched it with a soft click. There were lines of strain cutting across her forehead and pulling at the corners of her eyes. Her fingers continued to tighten and loosen on the steering wheel. She was fighting to stay in control while fear of the naturi beat at her.

In truth, I wasn't feeling much better. And worse, this was my fault. The longer I remained with her, the easier it was for them to track her down. But Mira was right. We were stronger when we worked together. While I acted as a beacon, bringing them to her side, I was also her only warning that they were even in the area. Vampires couldn't sense the naturi and the naturi couldn't sense vampires. Up until now, it had been an arrangement that seemed to work for both sides.

"Can you see them?" she asked, her voice sounding somewhat calmer.

Twisting around to look out the rear window, I let my eyes dance over the cars that were keeping pace behind us. No one seemed to be in any great hurry to catch up to us. "No, but they're still coming." I could sense them, four naturi approaching fast.

"Do you need to see them to boil their blood?" Mira inquired.

"What?" I demanded, jerking around so that I was sitting back in my seat again.

"I have to see the naturi to burn them," she explained. "Do you have to see them to boil their blood? Or is it enough that you can sense them?"

"I—I don't know," I admitted. "Anytime I've used that

power I've been able to look my enemy in the eye. It's a last resort."

"Well, I think we've reached that point," Mira snapped. "Unless you really want to pull over and fight them hand to hand."

"I can try it, but they're in a car. If it works, they're going to crash," I pointed out. "Innocent people could die."

"There would be another investigation, more memories to wipe, bodies to dispose of . . ." she softly listed under her breath with a shake of her head. "I can't do it."

"What's wrong?"

"I—I can't do it," she whispered then shook her head violently as if to wake herself up from a trance. "It won't work. We need another plan and I think I've got one," she announced with renewed vigor. "Are they still following us?"

I reached out with my powers briefly, touching on the naturi that were still speeding along behind us. They seemed a little closer than they had been only a couple moments ago, but they weren't quite breathing down our necks. "They're still there."

"Good." To my surprise, Mira jerked the car across three lanes of traffic and grabbed the first exit. I didn't say anything, but held on as she jumped off the expressway and then grabbed the first on-ramp to the highway, heading back south.

"Where the hell are we going?" I demanded once we were comfortably settled in front of a semi.

"Back to Savannah," she informed me, as she actually slowed the car down to the legal speed limit.

"I thought you wanted to keep them away from the lycans," I said, flinching when she abruptly changed lanes a little closer to a Toyota Prius than I thought was sensible.

"They're not animal clan," she replied. "If they were, they would have called up the shifters when we were at the restaurant. I think these are from the wind clan."

"Why do you say that?"

"Because the only thing that's been in my domain since you showed up was from the wind clan. The group in the conservatory."

"So it's somebody out for a little revenge," I said, frowning.

"But why only the wind clan?" Mira asked as she glanced up into the rearview mirror.

"Who do we know from the wind clan?"

"Rowe, Cynnia, and her sister Nyx," Mira quickly replied. "I don't think they're with the pirate. He was banished. Besides, if Rowe wanted my head, I have no doubt that he'd come here to get it personally, after his falling out with Aurora."

"Do you think they were sent by Cynnia? Trying to extend an olive branch?" I asked. I barely resisted the urge to turn the heat on in the car. The later the night grew, the more the temperature dropped, so that now my fingers were growing stiff from the cold.

"Then I guess we might get to see if these naturi want to talk or fight," Mira said, taking an exit into Savannah. "Are they still following?"

"Yes," I said, glancing over my shoulder as I continued searching for the car that I knew held the naturi.

Beside me, I could feel a slight chill enter the air. It reached through my clothes and brushed against my skin. I jerked and looked back over at my companion. The unexpected touch of cool energy was coming from Mira. She was using her powers, but I couldn't begin to guess at what she was doing. The energy was very slight and I might not have noticed it if I hadn't been sitting so close to her.

"What are you doing?" I demanded.

"Saw this in a movie once," she said, flashing me a somewhat strained grin.

"You know movies aren't real life," I reminded her.

"Yeah, well this movie didn't also have a wily nightwalker as the lead, so this may just work," she joked, then abruptly turned serious as she headed toward the riverfront area. "Open the glove compartment. You'll find a garage door opener inside."

Leaning forward, I popped open the glove compartment. Inside lay only a 9mm automatic and a small remote control for a garage door opener. I pulled out the remote, but didn't close the glove compartment door. I wasn't carrying a gun and I felt safer with the weapon just a matter of inches from my fingertips.

"When we turn the corner, hit the button," Mira directed.

Mira headed into what appeared to be a somewhat dodgy part of town, full of old warehouses and worn houses. She suddenly took a left turn and I hit the button. I looked around, trying to discern what I had opened when I heard a low, metallic creak and grumble just down the street from us. A large metal doorway was rolling up to a warehouse. Mira quickly jerked the car into the opening, the roof of the car barely missing the bottom of the doorway as we squeaked through the opening.

"Don't close the door!" she quickly ordered before I could push the button again. "If they're close behind, they could see it going down." Mira hit the brakes and turned off the car before we came to a complete stop, plunging the warehouse back into total darkness.

"Now what?" I asked.

"We wait," she whispered. Mira sat back, letting her hands slip from the steering wheel and into her lap. "How close are they?"

I closed my eyes and stretched out with my power, letting it run through the entire city. I could feel nightwalkers leisurely strolling all over the place, or seated in close quarters with other warm bodies. I could sense a scattering of naturi all over the city, but the set of four moving fast enough to be in a car were a distance off; maybe a half mile away. "They're not close. Actually . . . I think they're moving away from us."

"Did they ever get close enough to get a good look at my car?"

"I don't think so."

"Good," Mira said with a soft sigh. "Then we'll just wait a little while and make sure that they aren't getting any closer."

"How?" I asked. Releasing the seat belt, I turned in my seat so that I was partially facing the nightwalker. My eyes were slowly adjusting to the darkness, picking up the small chunks of dirty light that was filtering in through the window on the second floor and through the roof skylight. I could pick out the outline of broken wooden pallets and the occasional crate. Mira remained a faint outline in the dark car.

"When we entered the city, I started cloaking you. I wanted to see if I could cloak you against the naturi. If they're headed away from us, it would seem that the answer to my question is yes."

"And if the answer is no?"

"Then we fight them in here, away from anyone else that might be hurt."

I sat back in my seat again and stared off into the darkness. One thought kept repeating through my head. This choice didn't fit her usual actions. When I arrived in Savannah in September, she had been in a car chase with the naturi. She had caused them to wreck and then continued the fight on the side of the road. This time we were hiding. Something had changed.

"Why are we hiding?" I demanded.

Mira turned her head and looked out the window to her left. "It's for the best. No one gets hurt."

"And it leaves naturi running free within your domain."

"I never said that I was happy with the decision!" she snapped, her temper briefly flaring. "I just said that it was for the best."

"What's going on? Normally, you would have set the four on fire by now and we'd be merrily on our way," I pressed.

" 'Merrily on our way,' " she repeated, a grin spreading across her face as she looked back at me. "I don't recall us ever doing anything merrily. You'll have to remind me."

"Drop it! I'm being serious. What's going on?"

The grin fell off of her full lips and she looked down at the steering wheel. "I can't start fires."

I stared dumbfounded at the nightwalker for nearly a minute, my brain seeming to shut down under that unexpected pronouncement. The Fire Starter could no longer start fires. How could such a thing happen? What was going to happen to her and her standing within the domain once the other nightwalkers discovered her ugly little secret? Fire had always been Mira's edge.

"How did it happen? When? Is it because of what Cynnia did to you? But that can't be, because you used fire at Machu Picchu and at the conservatory. Is the ability completely gone?" I started, the questions pouring out of me before actual thought seemed to kick in once again.

"I haven't lost the ability," she said, sounding painfully defensive. "I could still burn you to a crispy critter if I wanted to, so stop celebrating." Mira drew in a cleansing breath that she didn't need and gripped the steering wheel tightly. "I haven't been feeding enough."

"I've noticed," I growled. When I let my guard down, the world around me was washed in a red haze when I was with Mira. Her hunger beat at me until I thought I would go mad. I couldn't imagine how she managed to focus through it.

"I haven't been feeding enough," she repeated stiffly, ignoring my interruption. "I don't have the energy to create and manipulate fire. It would be too exhausting. If I'm pressed and desperate, I could, but it would leave me . . ."

"Vulnerable," I finished.

"Yes."

For a heartbeat, I thought about it. She was weak. She was little more than a normal nightwalker now. She wouldn't have the power to set me on fire. She wouldn't have the strength to fight me if I tried to kill her now. The fight would be over in a matter of minutes and the world would at last be rid of one of the most dangerous creatures to ever walk its face.

And yet, in the very next heartbeat, I knew I couldn't do it. I couldn't kill Mira. Maybe one day when we were finally standing on opposite sides and not drawn together by some common foe, I would be able to finally strike her down. But not tonight. For now, she was my ally, the one person in this world I had been charged to protect. Not only was she safe from me, but she also needed my help.

Leaning my right elbow on the door, I rested my head in my hand. I honestly couldn't believe I was about to say this. "Then feed, Mira. We can't afford to have you weak or possibly distracted. The naturi are running around your domain again and we've got something else chewing up young girls."

"You don't think this thing is naturi?"

I sighed, somewhat surprised to see that my breath was visible in the cold. I wasn't ready to tell her. I needed more time to think, to figure out how we could possibly deal with this threat before setting the truth lose into the air. "I don't know. You said there was a strange smell that you could identify. You've been around all the naturi, you know their smells."

"So maybe the attacker isn't naturi. Could be lycan or . . . warlock?"

"Or bori?" I said, mentioning the one creature I knew that she wouldn't give voice to. The suggestion had to be thrown out there. She had to at least consider it.

"Highly unlikely."

"And I'm sure you would have said that it was highly unlikely that I would have been affected by the Stain in Peru, but I was," I said, turning my head to look at her. The spell had awoken the bori that held a part of my soul and the results had nearly been disastrous.

"Are the naturi close?" she demanded, ignoring my comment.

"No. Far end of the city and getting farther away."

"Good. Then we continue this investigation by trying to find out why the attacker might have chosen Abigail Bradford for his victim when he could have chosen anyone else." Mira reached for the key and started the car, causing its animal-like rumbling to echo through the empty warehouse.

"Where are we going?" I asked as she slowly backed the car into the street.

"The one place a nightwalker goes to get gossip: the Dark Room."

Twenty-One

I hesitated in the entrance to the Dark Room, my eyes growing accustomed to the low lighting. One thought kept repeating in my head: I shouldn't be here. The floor was black marble, too closely resembling the throne-room floor of the coven's headquarters in Venice. The small antechamber was lit overhead by a single lamp that cast down a red glow, while coat-check rooms rested on my left and right.

Mira led the way into the nightclub for the damned, a sway in her hips as if she was already moving to the beat of the music that was throbbing from the main room. We paused on the threshold, our eyes slipping over the gathered crowd. I could sense a somber apprehension emanating from Mira, though it never outwardly showed. I, on the other hand, was fighting back a growing sense of dread. A quick count revealed that more than two dozen nightwalkers filled the club, accompanied by almost as many human companions. A small knot of lycanthropes was clustered at the bar off to my left, trying to maintain a distance from the nightwalkers while still claiming their right to be there.

Why am I here? I sent the thought winging into her brain, not wishing to be overhead by any other vampire.

We're conducting an investigation. Gregor will provide us with more information about Abigail, she replied, but there was no missing the mocking in her tone.

This meeting could have been held anywhere but here.

Mira simply looked over her shoulder at me, arching one fine red eyebrow.

First Communion, the formal introduction to Barrett, and now the Dark Room. I'm no idiot—What are you up to? I demanded.

Mira's smile widened as the fingers of her left hand slipped through the fingers of my right hand, allowing her to pull me a few steps into the club. Her touch was cool, while the scent of lilacs wafted to my nose. *How else will be you ever understand my world unless you're a part of it?*

I'm not a part of your world, I mentally snapped, but her smile only grew before she turned to look straight ahead again.

It's a little late for that.

Before I could come up with a reply, Mira released my hand and roughly grabbed the shoulder of a nightwalker who was trying to edge past her.

"Has Knox been here tonight?" she demanded.

"Came and left about an hour ago," the nightwalker replied, his dark brown gaze jumping back and forth between me and Mira.

With a nod, Mira released the nightwalker. I would have preferred to have Knox and his calming presence at the Dark Room while I was present. I had encountered Mira's second-in-command only a handful of times, but he seemed to be very rational and levelheaded, something that would be appreciated right now.

Since my arrival, the tension had increased in the crowded nightclub. Many of the nightwalkers had moved from the dance floor to the shadowy confines of the booths that lined the right and back walls of the large room. Only human whispers could be heard as an undercurrent to the hypnotic music that filled the air. The nightwalkers had slipped into telepathic communication for a more private conversation about the nightwalker hunter in their midst.

Should we wait for Knox to return? I telepathically inquired. I wanted this meeting to go as smoothly as possible and Knox would help greatly toward that end.

He's gone with Amanda to meet with Abigail Bradford's parents, Mira explained. *He's helping to deliver the bad news of the animal attack and hopefully quiet the press circus.*

In other words, Mira's trusted second-in-command had been sent with Amanda to tweak the memory of the senator and his wife, making both more pliable and agreeable. The investigation would continue on, but the dangerous human element would be removed for now. It had been a close call and we could only hope that the press would back off. I wasn't banking on everyone believing the nonsense that Abigail Bradford had been attacked by a dog, but it was the only plausible answer that didn't include vampires, lycanthropes, naturi, or the bori.

"Let's get this over with," I said under my breath, trying not to worry about how many nightwalkers actually heard me.

"Agreed," Mira said, beginning to sound a little worried herself.

I followed Mira as she wove her way through the maze of tables to the back corner of the club. I could feel dozens of eyes watching my steady progress through the room. Nobody moved, the clubgoers becoming pale statues in the dim light.

The corner booth was larger than the rest, allowing six nightwalkers and humans to lounge in comfort, partially obscured by a dark red curtain that hung on the sides of the entrance to the booth. In the back corner sat a nightwalker in classical Victorian garb, with his ornately embroidered waistcoat over a pristine white shirt and neckcloth. His eyes briefly skimmed over Mira before settling on me with a wide grin.

"Mira," he seemed to purr. "You've brought us a guest."

"Everyone out," Mira ordered, ignoring the nightwalker. "I need to speak with Gregor alone."

The nightwalkers and two humans in the booth slowly pushed to their feet and slunk away, all of them careful to not walk past me. I slid into the booth next to Mira, while a low table separated us from the nightwalker called Gregor. I recalled seeing him at the First Communion with a conservatively dressed brunette.

"To what do I owe this unique honor?" Gregor asked, oozing a wicked kind of glee as his eyes failed to waver from my face.

"Abigail Bradford," I said in a stark cold voice, finally causing the smile to fade from his mouth.

"Oh, that business," Gregor mumbled. The nightwalker slouched in his seat, laying his hands limply in his lap. "It is a shame about her, but I can't tell you who killed her. Heard it was quite messy, but again, I don't know the 'who' behind the act."

"I'd be shocked if you did know who killed her," Mira said with a shake of her head. "I didn't come here for that."

"What else could you want to know with your new beau in tow, looking to scare us all into submission?"

I gritted my teeth, but otherwise kept my comments to myself. It wouldn't help our cause and certainly wouldn't make Gregor any more cooperative.

"I want to know if there could be a specific reason as to why she was chosen," Mira said, easily brushing aside his comment.

"You mean it's not enough that she was the only daughter of a United States senator?" Gregor inquired. One thick eyebrow arched as he turned his full attention to Mira.

"Speaking of which, who was the idiot that brought her in? It's not like she could easily disappear if there was some kind of unfortunate accident," Mira demanded caustically.

"I believe it was Everett who officially welcomed her into

the fold," Gregor said, then shrugged his narrow shoulders. "At least, that's who I saw her with first."

"That's convenient," Mira muttered. She flopped backward against the back of her seat and slouched slightly as well, nearly matching Gregor's posture as she grumbled to herself about the ironic whim of the fates.

"I don't understand," I said, drawing Mira's gaze back to my face, but it was Gregor who spoke up first.

"Mira is unable to punish our dear Everett for bringing in the wrong type of human because you already took the trouble of killing him this past summer." Gregor's smile darkened to something more twisted and evil.

In return, I sat back, crossing my arms over my chest as I frowned back at him. I wasn't going to apologize if that was what either of them were looking for. I was a hunter. Killing nightwalkers was what I did. When I came looking for Mira in July, I had slaughtered several vampires in an effort to locate her. Everett was just one in a long list of deaths that had occurred at my hand.

"And after Everett disappeared, you welcomed Abigail into your little group?" Mira pressed, ignoring the staring contest that was building between Gregor and me.

Gregor blinked first, jerking his attention back to the Fire Starter. It was clear within her voice that she was growing more irritated with both of us. "She was a sweet girl," Gregor commented. "Funny, charming, and adventurous. She already knew about us so I saw no problem in allowing her to continue her association with our kind through me and my friends."

"You could have wiped her memory," I snapped.

The nightwalker sat up a little straighter, his smile dimming into a slight frown as he looked at me. "Yes, I could have, but in truth it never occurred to me. I didn't discover that she was the daughter of a senator until after she died. All I knew was that she kept an apartment on River Walk, was a sweet little curator at one of the local museums, and enjoyed club hopping. Abigail was just another one of the crowd."

"And she knew Tristan?" Mira inquired.

Gregor's smile returned as he looked over at Mira. "Yes, Abigail was with us the night that Tristan happened in the Dark Room. I invited him over to sit with us, to have a bite to eat. Abigail was more than willing. I thought it would please you that I made the effort to welcome your young one into the area."

This time it was Mira's turn to frown at Gregor. She leaned forward, her nails digging into the seat cushion beneath her. "Have a care with Tristan. I don't always approve of your games with the fledglings, but I have been lenient and allowed you to have your fun. I will not be so forgiving when it comes to my family."

"I have in no way threatened Tristan," Gregor quickly argued, holding both of his hands up and open toward us in surrender.

"You never threaten," Mira countered. "You offer up little games, escapades of chance and risk, and fledglings end up dead."

"Your warning has been noted, but again, I must state that I have not threatened Tristan in any way," Gregor amicably said. "I only offered him a hand of friendship, a sip from my cup."

"A cup that happened to be Abigail," I said.

The nightwalker shrugged, folding his hands in his lap. "She was willing and it certainly wasn't the first time. She knew what she was doing. Again, as far as I know, none of us were aware of the young woman's parentage. I like to think that we would have taken care of her memory should it been known."

"Besides your little group, was there anyone else that she was known to associate with?" Mira inquired, dragging us back to the topic at hand. The reason we had come here was not to draw lines in the sand where Tristan was concerned, nor had we come here to discuss my disgust for their habits.

"Not anyone that I noticed," Gregor replied.

"What about the lycans?" I asked.

Gregor frowned as he looked out toward the dance floor, seeming to be lost in thought for a moment. "Back before the naturi, back when there was peace with the shifters, she spoke with them here at the club," Gregor said, his voice taking a somewhat wistful tone. "I never noted a particular preference for any one lycan. She was just friendly, striking up a conversation with someone who happened to be standing next to her at the bar as she waited for a drink. Abigail was a free spirit."

Shoving my right hand through my hair, pushing it away from my eyes, I gazed down at Mira, who seemed to be staring at the table, lost in thought. "It doesn't sound like she was chosen because she was involved with any particular nightwalker, but because she was involved in this world," I said. "It's not enough that she was a senator's daughter who died under suspicious circumstances. That could be covered up."

"But a little digging into her habits, her friends, the people that she was known to associate with could reveal our entire world," Mira continued, picking up the thread of my thought. She looked up at me, a frown pulling at the corners of her mouth. "It would at the very least start pointing fingers at the Dark Room. Nightwalkers can do without the publicity."

Gregor suddenly sat forward, his hands coming to rest on his knees. "You're not going to shut down the Dark Room again, are you?"

Mira shook her head, looking down at the table again. "So far, it's been quiet. The media haven't gotten past her squeaky clean background as an honor student and museum curator for the Girl Scouts. Unless we close this case soon, they're going to start digging deeper and it's only a matter of time before people start pointing out where she spent her nights."

"She frequented a number of the bars around the city," Gregor argued. "The Dark Room is just one of the many."

"The Dark Room is also the only exclusive, members-only club in the city. It's going to raise some eyebrows and put this place in the spotlight," I said, drawing Gregor's ire. When I was hunting for Mira, I quickly learned to keep my distance from the club, as the concentration of nightwalkers would easily overwhelm me. The temptation had been to linger not far away and watch for someone of Mira's description to appear, but the risk had been too great.

"I'm content to leave things as they are for now," Mira said with a heavy sigh. "Since you are so partial to the Dark Room, I put it in your hands to keep an eye on the media and see to it that they don't go looking into our little establishment."

Gregor jerked in surprise at this pronouncement. "Really? Isn't such a thing within Knox's domain?"

"He's got enough to worry about," Mira snapped. "Maybe you'll prove to be useful to me at long last instead of a pain in my ass."

"As you wish," he said, with a nod. The nightwalker then looked over at me and waved absently. "Watch yourself."

My would-be attacker's footsteps were nearly silent under the loud music that now blasted through the nightclub. As I turned, a young woman carrying a blade rushed me. Her teeth were clenched and bared so that I could hear the low rumble of a growl coming from her as she lunged. I hesitated, my brain struggling to understand why this complete stranger had decided to attack me unprovoked. At the last second, I caught her wrists with both hands, but not before she managed to bury the tip of her knife in the meaty part of my shoulder, slicing through muscle.

A hiss slipped from between my clenched teeth as I shifted my weight to my left foot so that I could shove the woman away from me. She kept her tight grip on the blade, pulling it out of my arm as she stumbled backward.

The scent of my blood hit the chilled air and I was immediately swamped by the wave of hunger that washed red through the club. I blinked a couple times, struggling to focus on the world around me, the pain in my arm, anything but the swarm of nightwalkers that suddenly felt the urge to drain me dry. Suppressing a growl, I closed up my mind as much as possible, dampening the hunger pangs echoing through my brain. Mira was the only creature that I couldn't completely block out. I could feel her as a slim shadow in my thoughts, simply watching while hunger gnawed at her insides.

The enraged woman shoved away a chair that had become entangled with her feet and tightened her grip on the bloody blade in her right hand. She took another swipe at me, but I easily slipped out of her reach as I sidled away from the booth. Unfortunately, my back was now turned toward a growing throng of nightwalkers who were intently watching the scuffle. I needed to end this as quickly as possible before anyone else decided to join in the fray. In Mira's weakened state, I wasn't so sure she would be able to control this mob and I wasn't about to put it to the test.

"A fan of your work?" Mira inquired from behind me. She sounded as if she were still lounging in the booth with Gregor.

"You fucking bastard!" the woman snarled, looking as if she was searching for an opening.

"Guess so," Gregor muttered, but I ignored them both. My focus was on the woman. A quick scan revealed that she truly was just human. Not a vampire. Not a lycanthrope. Not even a witch. I killed nightwalkers by the light of the moon. How could she possibly hope to kill me? Unless she didn't. Maybe she was the distraction. I couldn't take any chances surrounded by this many nightwalkers. I had to end the confrontation as quickly as possible, and preferably without any additional bloodshed.

"What do you want with me?" I asked, taking a step away from the woman in an effort to establish a little breathing room.

"I want you to die!" she screamed. As she swung the blade at me, a swath of brown hair fell across her face, momentarily blocking her vision. I snatched up the opportunity, ripping the knife from her grip. She shrieked at me in rage, lurching toward me with her fingernail aimed to remove a layer of flesh from my face. Placing my hand on her bony shoulder, I shoved her backward. Nightwalkers scattered as the woman stumbled away from me until she finally fell to her butt in the middle of the dance floor. The grinding music had been stopped and the silence was broken only by the woman's jagged breathing.

"I don't know you," I said in a firm voice. "Why do you want me dead?"

The first of her tears started slipping down her pale face as she stared up at me from where she continued to sit on the dirty floor. "You killed him," she started in a low, haunting voice. "They told me that you hunted him down and killed him."

A new darker sense of dread took hold in the pit of my stomach. I didn't like the direction this was headed and my only hope was that someone had lied to this poor woman.

"Who?" I asked, my voice losing some of its former strength.

"Mark! His name was Mark and you killed him," she shouted. Her hands balled into fists at her sides and shook with her anger and her obvious pain.

I turned so that I could look at Mira, while still being able to watch the woman out of the corner of my eye. "Mira?" I prompted. She was the keeper of this domain; she would know what had happened to this lost soul.

"She's right," Mira said in a weary voice. "Mark was the third one you killed when you came into my territory in July.

My shoulders stiffened and my fingers tightened around the handle of the knife as I turned back to face the woman, who was now gasping for air amid her sobbing. Her slim shoulders jerked as tears streaked down her cheeks to splatter on the floor.

"You don't remember him?" the woman demanded in a

ragged voice. "You fucking bastard. His name was Mark and he had soft brown hair and gentle brown eyes. Would never have hurt anyone! You killed him and he never did anything to hurt anyone!"

I had killed someone important to her—a friend, a lover. And I couldn't remember his face. He was lost to the overwhelming tide of blood and death that had followed me for endless centuries.

In July, I came into Mira's domain searching for the Fire Starter. I killed any nightwalker that attacked me and any that refused to answer my questions. Five died in all, but I couldn't recall the faces of any of them. They were just nightwalkers; dark creatures that fed upon the life of humans.

And yet I had succeeded in wounding the very creatures I had sworn to protect. The poor human weeping at my feet had been hurt by my decision to kill her lover.

Clenching my fists at my sides, I turned my head and glared at Mira. I wouldn't apologize for what I had done. I couldn't do it. I still believed in what I was doing. Someone had to protect the humans from the nightwalkers.

Yes, but some humans don't want or need your protection, Mira mentally said to me, proving that she had been listening to my thoughts. *Your actions have more severe repercussions than you sometimes realize.*

I save lives.

And sometimes you destroy them. A sad look filled Mira's lavender eyes as she met my gaze. For a moment, it felt as if she pitied me and I wondered if she was right. But I crushed the thought as quickly as it appeared. Someone had to protect humanity from vampires. Right?

I won't apologize, I sent the stubborn thought to her, though it felt more than a little tired and worn.

I never asked you to, Mira replied. She slid out of the booth and flowed to her feet like liquid. I could feel all the eyes in the room suddenly shift from me to the keeper. She was finally going to take control of the situation and everyone knew that someone was going to finish the night in pain.

"Who does this woman belong to?" Mira demanded, raising her voice so that it easily reached all the dark corners of the club.

When no one immediately spoke up, Gregor ventured a guess. "Mark?" I resisted the urge to look over my shoulder at the nightwalker, suddenly understanding why Mira found him to be such a nuisance. Instead, I let my gaze travel around the room. No one was willing to meet Mira's direct gaze.

"All right. Let me try this again. Who brought this woman into the Dark Room?" Mira demanded, her tone growing sharper with each word. The Dark Room was a membership-only club and members had to be either nightwalkers or lycanthropes. Humans were only allowed into the club under a lycan or vampire escort.

"I brought her in," said a blond nightwalker. She held her hand slightly above her head as she stepped forward from a knot of nightwalkers. "We're friends. I didn't know you were going to bring the hunter here. If I'd known, I would never have let her in."

"But I'm sure you were kind enough to inform her exactly who Danaus was when he did appear," Mira sneered.

"She asked," the vampire said with a shrug. "I didn't know she would react like this."

Neither Mira nor I believed her. The nightwalker could have easily read my attacker's mind and seen what she planned to do. Of course, there wasn't a nightwalker in the place that I would have expected to stop the woman before she brandished her knife. Mira might be the possible exception to that, but even that was doubtful, depending on her mood. The only thing about this whole mess that I did find surprising was that Gregor had seen fit to warn me that she was about to strike. He could have easily allowed her to stab me and no one would have thought less of him.

In a flash, Mira palmed a knife that had been at her side and threw it at the blond. The knife hit her with enough force to throw her back a few steps as it buried itself in the vampire's shoulder. The blond cried out in pain and surprise as she wrapped her hand around the knife. The scent of fresh blood once again hit the air and the haze of bloodlust grew thicker, but this time there was a new feeling in the air. It was the same demand for death and pain that I felt when Mira was punishing David at the First Communion. When it came to a struggle between two nightwalkers, there was little loyalty to be found, only a thirst for destruction and violence.

"Your lack of discretion could have created chaos and deaths we cannot afford among our ranks. You are not welcome at the Dark Room until you are back in my good graces," Mira pronounced. "I will not abide attacks on my guests and on members of my family."

A second later, a bouncer that had been hovering at the front door of the Dark Room when I walked in with Mira swooped down and grabbed the blond by the arm and ushered her out of the club before she could even pull the knife free from her arm.

A heavy silence settled over the club except for the loud sobbing of the woman still seated on the floor. She had not moved during the brief scuffle between Mira and the blond nightwalker that had been her friend.

"What do we do?" I asked, dragging Mira's gaze back to me.

She frowned at me, creating little lines between her thin brows as she gave a little shrug. "That's actually up to you. She attacked you. You beat her. By our laws, her life belongs to you now. You can kill her if you like."

The woman let out a soft whimper and pushed a little away from me before I could even speak.

"Absolutely not!" I snapped. "Just let her go and let's forget about it all."

"Unfortunately, that's not a possibility either," Mira said. She turned and looked down at the young woman with the red, tear-streaked face. "She broke our rules. She attacked my guest, insulting me and shaming her host. She's proven that she can't be trusted. How do we know she won't turn us in to the Daylight Coalition next because she didn't get her proper vengeance?" The Daylight Coalition was a group of human vampire hunters, and they would love to get information from an insider.

"What do you suggest?" I inquired, a part of me dreading her answer.

Mira turned her gaze on Gregor, who was still lounging in the booth, watching the drama unfold like a movie on the big screen. "Wipe her memory," Mira ordered.

"How much?" he inquired, slowly pushing out of his slouch to the edge his seat.

"All of it. Everything associated with our kind and lycans."

Gregor frowned, but nodded at the direct order from the keeper of the domain. Rising to his feet with the natural, fluid ease of a nightwalker, he walked over and knelt before the woman, who was still sitting on the floor. My attacker tried to push backward, putting some distance between herself and Gregor, but the nightwalker grabbed her wrist, holding her in place.

"No! Wait! You can't—"

"It's okay," Gregor said in a low, soothing voice. "This won't hurt a bit. In fact, it'll take the pain away," he promised. The nightwalker pressed his hand against the woman's head and temple before his eyes fell shut. A couple seconds later, the woman went completely limp, her eyes falling shut as well. The two stayed like that for a moment before Gregor lowered his hand and lifted his head.

"It's done," he announced. He slowly pushed back to his feet. As he wobbled slightly, one nightwalker caught him by the elbow and held him steady.

"Someone take her home," Mira ordered. "I never want to see her here again."

I watched as a tall male nightwalker bent down and put the unconscious human over his shoulder before carrying her out of the nightclub. The rest of the nightwalkers returned to their booths or dancing on the dance floor, the event of the evening seemingly forgotten. I walked back over to Gregor's booth and stood next to Mira as she gazed down at the annoying nightwalker.

"It's always interesting when you're around." Gregor chuckled when he looked up at Mira.

"Do you have any other information you can provide me about Abigail Bradford?" Mira stiffly said, ignoring his comment.

"Nothing that I can think of," Gregor said with a shrug. "I believe that she was chosen simply because her death could cause the most trouble in our world."

"But that means that the killer had to know something of our world in the first place," Mira replied.

"Chilling thought, isn't it?" Gregor said, his carefree demeanor finally slipping away. His gaze drifted up to me as he continued, "It's as if our world is changing around us and not for the better."

"Our world changed forever when the naturi returned," I said.

To my surprise, Mira threaded her fingers through mine and we walked out of the Dark Room side by side. I had a grim suspicion that my appearance and obvious guest status in the nightclub had shaken up more than one nightwalker in Savannah and I knew the repercussions would be felt for many nights to come. I didn't know what Mira was planning, but I truly doubted that I would like it. I rarely did.

Twenty-Two

"That could have gone better," I said after several minutes of silence in the car. Mira was driving back toward the waterfront, weaving through the quiet elegance of the historical district.

"It could have been a lot worse," she replied, as she parked the car in an empty spot on Bay Street.

Unfastening my seat belt, I put my hand on the door handle. "I don't want to imagine how that could have gone worse."

Mira reached across and placed a restraining hand on my left arm as I started to exit the car. "Oh, please do," she pressed. "I do love a good horror story."

"You're a walking horror story," I grumbled, pulling out of her grasp as I got out of the car. Her low laughter followed behind me. Looking over the hood of the car at her, I frowned, though her light mood felt like an infection slowly defeating my immune system. "Did we accomplish anything by going there?" I demanded, trying to hold on to my anger and frustration.

"More than you realize," she said in mysterious tones.

"Anything regarding the murder?"

"A little bit," she admitted as she shut her door. "I think someone is trying to expose nightwalkers by killing the Bradford girl. And considering the method and gruesome manner of her death, I'm willing to put my money on the naturi. They stand to gain the most from our exposure."

"Yes, but there haven't been that many naturi in your domain," I said as I followed her down a flight of uneven stone steps to Factors Walk. I needed to tell her. I had put it off long enough. There was nothing to be gained from keeping Mira in the dark about the bori in her domain. While I doubted that she would be able to fight it at all, she may know something about the race that would finally give me an edge should I be suddenly faced with Gaizka again.

"Regardless, they are here." Mira led the way down the shadowy alleyway that slipped between River Street and Bay Street, the heels of her shoes clicking on the stones. "You killed a horde of them at the conservatory. And then there was the bunch that followed us in the car. They're here."

Cutting down a short street between Factors Walk and River Street, we headed toward the river and the most crowded section of the riverfront district, with its bars, restaurants, and gift shops. There was a sharp bite of cold to the air, keeping most of the tourists that had stumbled into Savannah during December back in their hotel rooms. It was also starting to get late and the shops were closing up for the night. We were nearly alone on the street.

"If you're convinced it's the naturi, what are we doing here?" I asked, shoving my hands deep into the pockets of my leather jacket in an effort to stay warm. "Are you making another pass by the apartment?"

"Nope," Mira replied with a shake of her head. She threaded her left arm through my right and snuggled close as if she were trying to stay warm. "I've got one more resource that I want to check. The nightwalkers don't know anything. The lycans don't know anything. But this guy's got a different connection. He might know something. I'm just hoping that we can catch him."

"Who is this guy?"

"A very interesting human," she said, flashing me an evil grin before stopping in front of an opening in a build-

ing with an orange-and-green awning that advertised "Old
Town Trolley Tours." A scattering of people were gathered
around the opening, buying tickets and making reservations
with a young woman behind the counter. When the woman
finally looked up, Mira waved at her. "Hi, Emmy!" Mira
cried in a genuinely happy, excited voice that I had never
actually heard her use before. It was surprising.

"Mira!" Emmy cried back, her expression instantly
brightening. "Let me get these people settled and then
I'll get to you." With a new vigor, I watched as the young
woman whipped through the crowd, taking money, checking off names, and handing out tickets for what I could only
assume was an evening tour of the city. Though I was confused as to why anyone would want to take a nighttime tour
of the city since so much of the amazing architecture would
be obscured by the darkness.

When the line had finally dwindled to nothing, Mira
stepped over to the booth, pulling me along when I seemed
to hesitate. However, the nightwalker released me long
enough to lean across the counter and grip the young black
woman in a tight hug.

"Danaus," Mira said the moment she released the woman.
"This is a dear friend of mine, Emma Rose. She handles the
ticket sales for the Old Town Trolley Tours Company here
in Savannah."

"It's a pleasure to meet you, Danaus," Emma Rose said,
extending her hand to me.

"Likewise," I said gruffly, quickly taking her hand for
a single shake before releasing it again and taking a step
backward from the booth. I felt ill at ease with the situation.
Nightwalkers, lycanthropes, warlocks, and even the naturi,
I could handle with little problem. Humans, on the other
hand, were something that I had lost touch with. I didn't feel
as if I belonged with them any longer, and hadn't since I was
young, so long as I could barely remember.

However, Mira refused to let me remove myself from
the little meeting of friends. She quickly threaded her arm

through mine, holding me in place, as she plunged into some idle chitchat about health and other random gossip about who was seeing who within the city. As a new line started to form, I loudly cleared my throat in an effort to prod Mira back to the whole reason we had come to this part of the city in the first place.

Mira threw me a dark look and then returned her attention to Emma Rose. "I won't keep you any longer. I was just looking for Nate. Is he working tonight?"

"Yeah, he should actually be arriving any minute now," Emma Rose said, glancing briefly down at the sheet of paper in front of her.

"You have any openings on the next tour? I need to talk to him about something important for a few minutes."

"Oh, sure! We haven't been full all night. It's the time of year. Just way too cold," Emma Rose replied with a casual wave of her hand.

Mira reached into her back pocket and pulled out her little black leather wallet, but Emma Rose quickly waved her off. "Don't worry about it. I have no doubt you'll jump off halfway through, like you always do."

"Thanks, Emmy," Mira said, pulling her into another tight hug. "I'll catch you later."

Mira and I walked over to the side where a group of people were waiting for the next tour bus to arrive. Mira cuddled close and I stared down at the top of her head.

"You don't like humans very much, do you?" she inquired softly, surprising me with her question. She turned her face up to look at me; her lavender eyes seemed to pierce me to my core.

"Humans . . . are . . . are fine." I stumbled, unsure of how to answer the question. "Why would you ask a question like that?"

"It's how you act around them. Emmy, James, Daniel. When you're around all of them, you're distant and cold. You don't look them in the eye and you rarely speak. What do you have against humans?"

"I don't have anything against them," I said, inwardly cringing at the defensive tone that had crept into my voice against my will.

"Is it because you're not really one of them? Are you envious?"

"I'm not envious!" I said sharply, then regretted it as several people looked around at us. I leaned closer, dropping my voice back to a whisper. "I don't have anything against humans. I just don't spend a lot of time dealing with them."

"But Themis?"

"I'm rarely there, and when I am I encounter only James and Ryan." I hesitated a moment, frowning down at her. "It's just that I don't feel like I . . . I understand them any longer. They're fragile and their lives are so short. I—I haven't been one of them for so long. I'm not one of them."

My eyes fell shut as I slowly drew in a deep breath. I wasn't human. I technically never was a human, though I had believed I was for at least the first couple decades of my existence. But now, I wasn't like anything else that existed. I wasn't human, vampire, lycanthrope, or warlock. I wasn't truly a bori, but some kind of half-breed that was too dangerous to be left alive, and yet Mira protected me at the risk of her life and her people.

Mira laid her cold hand against my cheek, letting her thumb run across my cheekbone in a gentle caress. "You're not alone," she whispered. She was close enough that I could feel the breath from each word skim across my lips. "You're never alone."

"It's better than I am," I murmured, afraid to move or open my eyes because it would shatter this moment.

"You're not alone. I won't allow it," she said before pressing her lips to the tip of my nose in a quick kiss. I opened my eyes and stared into her, locked frozen in a moment that I thought would never happen again. The world had slipped away and there was only Mira's hand on my cheek and her parted lips inches from mine. She stood before me like a bundle of unspoken promises; promises of compassion, affection, laughter, and unwavering strength and loyalty. I just needed to lean in those few final inches . . .

Behind us, a car rumbled down the cobblestone street, snapping Mira's head around and shattering the moment. I stood a little straighter, while her hand slid down my face to rest on my chest over my heart. Reaching up, I covered her hand with mine and gave it a little squeeze, needing to hold on to that moment just another second longer. If anyone knew what it meant to be alone and an outcast, it was Mira. She was my enemy. She was my friend. She was the only one who would understand that chasm of emptiness that threatened to consume me each night when I awoke. Hunting her kind was all that I had to keep me sane through the endless years. But standing there, holding her hand, I knew that those days were slipping from my grasp. The time was coming when I would have to choose between killing her or facing the life that she was offering me.

I could feel the excitement rolling off her in massive waves as she stared down the empty street. She was up to something and I knew that I wasn't going to like it. I released her hand and shoved mine back into my jacket pocket. Mira rubbed her hand over my chest one last time as she smiled up at me before threading her arm back through mine.

"What have you done?" I asked in a low voice, trying not to attract the attention of anyone else standing near us.

"I have no idea what you're talking about," she said, looking up at me with what I'm sure she meant to be an innocent expression, but she couldn't even manage that as she quickly broke into a smile.

"We're going on an evening tour of the city?" I pressed, arching one eyebrow at her, which only sent her into a soft fit of giggles.

"Nate is a tour guide."

"How are we going to talk to him if he's giving a tour?"

Mira shook her head at me, her smile slipping a little bit. "Part of the tour goes through this house, but that section of the tour is given by the actual homeowner, so Nate will have a fifteen- to twenty-minute break. We can grab him then."

"I don't understand why a nighttime tour of the city is so popular," I grumbled. "You can hardly make out all the amazing architecture that blankets this city. It makes more sense to do this during the day."

Mira's hand tightened on my arm and her smile had completely disappeared when she looked up at me again. "Is the city that much more beautiful during the day?"

For a moment, I had forgotten that Mira had never seen her city bathed in sunlight. She had never seen Forsyth Fountain glistening in the summer sun or the way the light cut through the thick leaves of the live oak trees that filled each of the squares. She had never seen the bustle of tourists through the city market as they prepared to grab one of the carriages that crisscrossed the historic district of Savannah.

"You have a very beautiful city," I found myself saying, one corner of my mouth quirking in a smile. "Both in sunlight and by the moon."

"Thank you," she whispered as she looked back down the street. "Oh, look! Here he comes!"

I turned my attention from the nightwalker that was clinging to my arm as if we were out on a date to the vehicle that was rumbling down the street we had walked down just a few minutes earlier to reach River Street. It was not a tour bus like I was expecting. No, it was a trolley. A black trolley with a black light glowing from its undercarriage. Tattered lace and fake spider-webs hung in the rounded windows. And across the side in white letters was written GHOSTS & GRAVESTONES. That explained the nighttime tour; it was a ghost tour.

Laying my hand over Mira's, I pulled her a couple steps away from the rest of the crowd and hunched down so that I could growl in her ear. "A ghost tour? Is that what this is?"

"Of course! Why else would you see the city at night?" she asked, looking up at me as if I were the one who had lost his mind. "Savannah has a reputation of being the most haunted city in America. Of course we've got ghost tours."

"Yes, but I didn't expect you to want to do this! I mean, this is ridiculous. There are no such things as—"

"Finish that thought and I will drain you, Danaus," she said in a low, dark voice. "You of all people should know better."

Yes, I knew better. There were such things as ghosts. I couldn't see them or talk to them, but there had been a few occasions where I had felt them. However, it was nearly impossible for most humans to detect the presence of a ghost. It just didn't work that way. In most cases, sightings could be explained away as an overactive imagination, while pictures were generally nothing more than dust on a lens.

"I do, but this . . ." I said, motioning toward the black trolley, which people were now boarding. "They can't possibly expect to see a ghost."

Mira lifted her chin at me and gave a little sniff. "You'd be surprised," she said, then turned back to the trolley. "Besides, we're not here to see a ghost. We're here to talk to Nate. And there he is."

At that moment, a man in baggy brown pants and white shirt stepped off the trolley. In his hands were an old-fashioned lantern and a shovel that clanged when he set the tip on the sidewalk. He was dressed as a gravedigger, which seemed only fitting, since I was sure that I was going to put Mira in her grave if she tried to pull me onto this trolley.

"Nate!" Mira cried, pulling me along as she walked over to him.

"Mira?" The gravedigger spun around at the sound of his name. When he turned, I found a youthful face covered in a white and gray theatrical makeup to give the effect that he had spent more time with the dead than the living. Mira released her hold on me when Nate scooped her up in a bear hug. I jerked out of the way just in time as the spade of the shovel came close to taking off my nose.

"What are you doing here?" he asked, holding her at arm's length.

"I was hoping to talk to you about a couple things," she said, then motioned toward the trolley. "Couple work-related items."

Nate set his lamp down on the sidewalk and scratched his chin. "Yeah, I guess I should have been expecting you. I think a part of me was hoping that I was overreacting."

"Has it been that bad?"

"No, not like you would think," he said, then shook his head as he shoved one hand through an unruly crop of brown curls. "Actually, can we talk more later? I've got another tour to start in a few minutes."

"We're actually on this tour. Already cleared it with Emmy. Can we talk at Sorrel-Weed?"

"Yeah, sure," he said. "Who's with you?"

To my surprise, Mira actually blushed, though it was almost impossible to make out in the faint lamplight. She reached over and pulled me back to her side. "Danaus, this is a friend of mine, Nathaniel Mercer. No relation to Johnny Mercer. He's a grad student over at SCAD, specializing in historical preservation. By night, he's a gravedigger tour guide for Ghosts and Gravestones."

"Good to meet you," Nate said, shaking my hand.

"Likewise. What's SCAD?" I asked as I released his hand and took a step backward.

"Savannah College of Art and Design. A place Mira has been a big supporter of. We wouldn't be able to accomplish half the things we have without her assistance," Nate said.

"You're helping to preserve and restore a city I love. How could I not?" Mira said with a slight shrug of her shoulders.

Nate just shook his head as he bent down and picked up his lantern again. "Go ahead and get on the trolley. We've got to get this tour rolling before we get behind schedule."

Mira stepped onto the black trolley and I followed behind her, trying to keep from frowning. I was going on a ghost tour through Savannah. Not exactly how I anticipated my evening would go. But then again, nothing had gone how I might have expected since our brief appearance at the Dark Room. Mira was just full of surprises this evening.

At the back of the trolley, Mira paused and allowed me to sit next to the window while she sat as close as possible to me. The trolley soon filled up with somewhat hushed tourists as they took in the pseudo-creepy décor of fake cobwebs, skeletons, and tattered antique lace. After a brief introduction by Nate warning that the trolley was going to be traveling into the dark, grim past of Savannah and that passengers should be forewarned that the dead were eager to reach out and make new friends, we pulled away from the sidewalk and rumbled down the uneven stone street.

As we traveled down River Street, Nate wove tales of despair and woe. Once-prosperous shops from ages ago were filled with tales of suicide and fires, murder and disease. When we turned off River Street, I looked over at Mira to find that she was watching Nate with rapt attention.

How can you buy into this stuff? I asked, touching her mind so that I wouldn't disturb the other passengers who were listening to Nate with a mixture of mild interest and vague boredom.

It's not the ghosts, she mentally scoffed. *It's about the history of Savannah. Some of these stories I was actually here to witness firsthand. I remember reading about some in the paper. For me, it's about reminiscing about events that I lived through. Don't you ever like to look back at your past? Take another look at what you survived?*

In truth, I tried to never look back. I had survived more than a millennium of world events. Wars, famine, natural disasters, the rise and fall of entire civilizations, the discovery of new worlds, the deaths of people I viewed as friends. My memories were colored by a bleak landscape of death, blood, and struggles against an evil that I was now seated cozily against in a black trolley. But most of all, my past was covered in a seemingly vast emptiness that could never be filled up.

No.

To my surprise, Mira wrapped her arm around mine again and laid her head against my shoulder. I could feel her relax against me as if some secret weight had slipped from her shoulders. I tried not to think about her soft body pressed against mine, nor listen to Nate's monologue of death and despair, but I wasn't having much luck. Tonight, Mira had gone out of her way to touch me and remain close. When I was surrounded by nightwalkers, I had taken it as a way of signaling to them that I belonged to her and that I was not to be molested. However, seated in the dark trolley, surrounded by human tourists as we wove our way through the old city, there was no reason that I could think of for her to be touching me. And yet, I could not bring myself to disentangle her from my frame. In fact, I sat back against the seat and felt some of the tension ease from my own shoulders. For a moment in time, we weren't running, hiding, or fighting. We were just two people on a ghost tour of Savannah. I had forgotten what it was like to do something normal and mundane.

It had been more than seven decades since I had last touched a woman like this. I had been hunting vampires in Paris for more than a week, and had finally succeeded in eliminating the strongest of them. The remaining few had left the city, from what I could tell, and I was prepared to do the same. Yet, I lingered one last night in the City of Light, wandering through the winding streets and past the crowded restaurants and cafes. Pausing briefly in the doorway of one bar, I looked up to find a woman smiling at me, a cigarette between her pursed lips. Her name was Cherise and she had green eyes.

We talked of nothing and laughed and kissed over a bottle of cheap wine. We walked down the rain-slicked streets, arm in arm. And then we were attacked by four nightwalkers. I had been distracted by Cherise, wasn't watching my back. They killed her in an instant, leaving the blood on my hands as they escaped before the sun could rise.

Time had left a gaping void of loneliness within my chest, haunted by a pair of green eyes and an enigmatic smile. There had been no other women since Cherise and too few before her. I couldn't protect them. Just fragile flowers waiting to be crushed under the heel of the world I lived in. Too many years of fighting had piled up to leave me with nothing more than a memory of green eyes.

Mira shifted in her seat beside me, leaning forward to look around my chest and out the window as we passed by an old hotel. She squeezed my arm as she looked up at me, flashing me another excited smile. The woman that sat beside me now wasn't fragile or weak. She was strong, a powerful force within our world. And while I was under orders to protect her, Mira had been protecting me along the way as well.

After passing a couple of old hotels and some locally famous houses, we pulled up to a two-story burnt-orange house with palm trees surrounded by a brick wall. It was the infamous Sorrel-Weed House; supposedly one of the most haunted homes in all of Savannah. The occupants of the trolley quickly pushed to their feet and exited the trolley for what Nate said would be a brief tour of some of the rooms of the Sorrel-Weed House. We held back until everyone had gotten off the trolley before we exited.

Nate laid down the shovel he had been holding in the trolley and leaned against a tree, shoving his hands in his pockets.

"So, what do you think of the tour?" Nate asked as I stepped to the sidewalk. "Cheesy, right?"

"It's interesting," I said slowly, bringing a smile to his lips.

"It's one of the most popular in Savannah because we're the only ones that get you into Sorrel-Weed," he said proudly.

"It's fun, too. You know, just to pretend that some of it might be real."

"You don't believe in ghosts?" I asked while Mira snorted behind me.

"No, I believe," Nate said with a wry grin.

"Nate can see them and talk to them," Mira volunteered. I turned to look at her, confusion undoubtedly filling my face. I had never heard of a human being able to do such a thing.

"Talk to them? Necromancer?"

"Dear God, no!" he cried, pushing off of the tree that he had been leaning against. "Who would want to look at a decaying corpse? Besides, from what I hear, they don't come back all that intelligent. I just talk to the spirits."

"Speaking of which . . ." Mira said, trailing off as she finally got around to the actual topic at hand.

"Yeah," Nate sighed, leaning up against the tree again. "Things haven't been too good lately. Well, actually that's not exactly right." He hesitated, running one hand through his curls, sending them into disarray. "Things have been oddly quiet. A number of the locals that I'm used to seeing have disappeared and the few that have remained rarely come out. I've talked to a number of the hotel owners along the route and they say that activity has dropped to almost nothing. Mira, this isn't good. We're a city known for being haunted. If things go quiet, the tourists might stop coming."

"The tourists aren't going to stop coming," Mira said, waving off his genuine concern. "What about Sorrel-Weed?"

Nate made a noise in the back of his throat like a laugh, while one corner of his mouth pulled into a frown as he looked up on the looming structure. "The ghosts in that house are too angry to ever go completely silent. However, Scott, the owner, says things have recently been limited to the carriage house."

"Should you try talking to them, considering they're still active?" I suggested.

"Nah," he replied, turning his gaze back to me. "It's like I said. Too angry. You go up there, you're just going to get something thrown at your head."

"What about over at Colonial Park?" Mira asked. Nate hesitated, looking down at the ground as a frown deepened on his young face. "It's still on the tour and it would only take a few seconds," Mira continued. "We just want to see if anyone will tell you what's got them so upset."

"I'll see what I can do," Nate replied in a low voice, his gaze drifting back over toward Sorrel-Weed at the sound of approaching footsteps. "Why are you so interested anyway?"

"A girl was recently murdered and we're looking into it," I said, causing Nate's gaze to snap back to me.

"And you think a ghost did it?" he demanded in hushed tones.

"No, but they may know who did," Mira said, grabbing my arm and pulling me back onto the trolley. We resumed our seats as the rest of the tourists jumped onto the trolley.

Watch what you say! Mira said in my brain as soon as we were settled. *He doesn't know what I am, doesn't know my place within Savannah. You may find this hard to believe, but there are some people who still think I'm a normal human being.*

You're right. I snickered. *I do find it hard to believe. A human that believes another human can see and talk to ghosts?*

Okay, so maybe he thinks I'm a slightly eccentric human, but still human.

I laughed softly as the trolley pulled away from the curb and Nate resumed his dark monologue about the city. Mira settled against me. Her hunger was still evident as it beat against me, but underlying that red haze was a feeling of contentment.

We trundled along for another few blocks before the trolley driver stopped next to the Colonial Park Cemetery. We got off the trolley and followed the rest of the tourist herd down the ornate brick sidewalk to the side of the cemetery so that everyone could stare through the iron bars at the thick blackness that blanketed the graves. Out of habit, I completed a quick scan of the region, sending my powers out from my body to sweep over the tombstones until they reached the opposite wall.

"Anything?" Mira whispered, undoubtedly feeling the wave of energy wash from me.

"Nothing." And that's what had me concerned. While it made perfect sense for the naturi to be trying to sabotage the nightwalkers through the murder of Abigail Bradford, it didn't make any sense for the ghosts of Savannah to be upset by their presence.

We waited until Nate finished with his tale of duels and Civil War soldiers bunking down with the dead in the middle of winter before we approached him. Most of the tourists had begun to head back to the trolley while Nate stood at the fence, one hand gripping a black cast-iron bar.

"Nate?" Mira asked, laying a hand on his shoulder.

"There's a couple out there. Slowly coming over to me. They're . . . scared. Something has been hanging around the cemetery. Ghosts have disappeared."

"Can they tell you what it is?"

"What's happening?" Nate asked the darkness. "Who's with you?"

We all waited in silence for nearly a minute before Nate finally frowned and shook his head as he turned away from the bars. "They don't know. Something they've never seen before. It's killing them, which doesn't make any sense. I don't know how you can kill a ghost, but they're upset and keeping low."

"Were they upset like this back in September?" I asked as we followed him back to the trolley.

"Nope," he said, looking over his shoulder at me. "This only started in the past week or so."

I turned to find Mira standing a few feet away from me, staring through the bars into the cemetery. Her voice was low, just above a whisper. I stared at her a moment, straining to hear what she was saying, when I realized she was singing. Walking over, I discovered that she was singing what sounded like a lullaby in Greek. Her right hand was continuously moving through the empty air as if she were petting something.

"Mira," I said, trying to grab her attention.

The nightwalker looked down at the swath of air that her hand was moving through and she smiled before starting the lullaby over again, oblivious to the world around her.

"Mira!" I said a little louder as I grabbed her left arm. She jumped, her head snapping up as she stopped singing. She blinked and looked around as if she was seeing the cemetery for the first time. She then looked down at the open air where her right hand hovered, a look of confusion crossing her face.

"Where did she go?" she asked, looking around her.

"Who?"

"I—" Mira started, and then shook her head. I released her arm and took a step backward, giving her some room as I could once again feel a wave of cold energy washing off of her. She was using her powers as she possibly searched for something or worked some other kind of nightwalker magic. Pressing the fingers of her right hand to her forehead, Mira clenched her eyes shut and drew in a sharp intake of air through her nose. "It's nothing. It was nothing."

Mira turned and started to board the trolley, but I grabbed her arm, stopping her. "Do we need to talk to Nate anymore?"

"No," she replied, arching one brow at me.

"Then let's walk back to the car. I need to think," I suggested. Mira simply nodded and took her foot off the first step of the trolley. She gave Nate a brief hug and then turned back toward the cemetery while I shook the ghost talker's hand. He hadn't provided us with much information, but it was enough to confirm a dark idea already implanted in my head.

Mira waited until the trolley had rumbled away and we had walked more than a block in silence before she finally spoke up. "You don't think it's the naturi, do you?" she ventured.

"If it was the naturi, the ghosts would have been upset back in September when the city was crawling with them. There are fewer naturi in the city now and yet the ghosts are upset. Something else has moved into the region." I zipped my jacket up a little higher and shoved my hands into my pockets as we walked along the dark street back toward the riverfront.

"Do you also have a theory as to what?" Mira inquired.

I stared down at my companion in silence, knowing she wasn't going to like what I had to say. I wasn't particularly pleased with it myself. "Ghosts are nothing more than bodiless spirits. Souls," I said slowly, but it was more than enough. Mira came to an abrupt halt just as we were about to cross an empty street and jerked her head up to look at me with wide, horror-filled eyes.

"You can't possibly think . . . ?" she gasped. "It's impossible. How could a . . . a . . . a bori escape?" she said, whispering the last two words as if the mention of the creature would summon it to our side. A bori was the only creature dependent upon soul energy. It was using the ghosts in the city somehow.

"I don't know. The naturi escaped," I replied, taking a step to cross the street, which helped to jolt Mira from her own paralysis.

"But some naturi were already out, working to free the others. There are no other bori here. They were all caged centuries ago."

I frowned at that bit of logic. "You can't be sure of that," I grumbled. "My mother found a way to make a deal with one of them after they had already been exiled."

Mira plopped down on one of the benches near the center of Oglethorpe Square and put her head in her hands as she rested her elbows on her knees. "I can't keep doing this, Danaus," she moaned. "First it was you, then Jabari with the coven, and then it was Rowe and the rest of the naturi. Now, a bori? I can't do this. I came to Savannah to escape the insanity that seemed to follow me throughout Europe. Now it seems to have followed me here."

I stopped and knelt in front of Mira, wishing I could tell her that I thought I was wrong and that it was something less frightening. The bori were called the guardians of the soul, while the naturi were the guardians of the earth. The two races had been born to create a balance on the Earth, but from what I understood, the two seemed to be locked in a permanent power struggle over who truly ruled the Earth. Centuries ago, long before I was even born, the bori and the naturi were imprisoned in separate, alternate realities. For the most part, the naturi had succeeded in escaping from their cage this past fall and their now-queen Aurora was free. Though at least she had her own problems in the form of a younger sister who was attempting to wrest the crown from her.

A bori running loose in the world was an entirely darker matter that neither Mira nor I truly wanted to face. The bori were the creators of the nightwalker race, from what I understood, and had the same ability to control the nightwalkers the way the naturi could control the lycanthropes. Mira already had had to suffer the indignity of being controlled like a puppet by Jabari and me. She didn't need to have a bori free in her domain as well.

Putting one hand on her knee, I placed my other hand under her chin and forced her to look up at me. "We'll get through this," I said firmly. "We've survived the naturi. We can survive a rogue bori."

"You say rogue bori, but you don't know," Mira said grimly. "How do we fight a creature that can control us both?"

I flinched—the bori that had a hold on my soul had

managed to take control of me when we were in Peru. Mira and another nightwalker named Stefan had cast a spell that killed a horde of naturi and captured their souls. The bori that held me reacted to the souls and appeared to feed off the energy, controlling me and forcing me to attack Mira.

"We'll find a way."

Mira frowned at me. She wrapped the fingers of her left hand around my hand, which was still beneath her chin. "I would never have expected you to be such an optimist."

I smirked at my companion in this nightmare that never seemed to end. "Do we really have any other choice?"

"Not really," she admitted.

Mira looked up over my right shoulder, squinting as she tried to focus on something. Then she suddenly lurched to her feet, nearly knocking me over in her haste. She took a couple steps forward as I rose to my feet. Her emotions pushed unbidden through me, filling me with fear and rage.

"Scan the area," she ordered in a gruff voice. Her hands were held out to her sides, her fingers curled slightly as if she meant to summon up balls of fire at the first sign of trouble.

I sent my powers out from my body so that they flooded the park, and then farther away, covering several blocks. There was nothing out there. A scattering of nightwalkers and a couple of lycanthropes, but not the naturi I knew that she had me searching for. I reached out farther, covering the entire city, and to my surprise, there wasn't a single naturi in the region.

"There's nothing here," I said, drawing my powers back into my body. They swept over Mira, pulling with them an unexpected cold chill, as if a part of her energy had mingled with my own.

"That's impossible," she replied, twisting around to pin me with a confused glare. She pointed toward a tree more than a hundred yards away, but I saw nothing there. "I saw one right there!"

"Was it Rowe?" I inquired, taking a couple steps toward her so that I was standing beside her. My eyes covered the entire region surrounding the tree, but nothing moved. The one-eyed naturi was the only one we had encountered that could magically pop in and out of an area. He had nearly captured Mira that way in London.

"No," she whispered, turning her back on the tree and walking back over to the empty park bench she had been seated on only moments ago. I watched her shake her head as if to clear it while her slim shoulders slumped. Her fear had dissipated with the wind, but now a growing confusion ate away at her thoughts.

"Who was it? A naturi you've seen before?" I pressed. We needed to know if there was another naturi like Rowe, that could use magic to appear and disappear at will. This added a new element of danger to the naturi if there were more that could potentially grab the Fire Starter.

"It was nothing," she muttered. "Just a trick of the shadows and the night."

An uneasiness grew in the pit of my stomach and a frown pulled at the corners of my mouth. Nightwalkers had the best night vision possible, as far as I knew, and between the lamp and moonlight, the park wasn't that particularly dark. How could Mira have mistaken a shadow for a naturi? Was this the same shadow she had seen outside the house of the First Communion? Or similar to the crying baby that she had heard at the conservatory? Something had potentially found a way to play with the nightwalker's mind, making her more dangerous to those around her.

"Mira . . ." I started, but my voice trailed off. How was I supposed to tell her that I thought something was intentionally driving her crazy?

"It's nothing, Danaus," Mira said, turning to face me again. She resumed her walk through the park and I fell into step beside her, unable to tap down my growing concern for the nightwalker. "Our focus needs to be on finding a way to locate our killer," Mira continued after we had walked a couple of blocks.

Between the Fire Starter and a nightwalker hunter with a bori-owned soul wandering around Savannah, I had little doubt that the bori would eventually come looking for us.

Twenty-Three

There were still a few more hours before sunrise when Mira dropped me off at the town house. She had muttered something about wanting to do some research. I said nothing as I got out of the car. The nightwalker had been through enough for one night. So had I. As I reached the top stair leading to the front porch, I turned and watched her drive off in her sleek car, disappearing into the thick shadows cast by the trees.

Instead of going into the house, I trudged back down the stairs. While it was late, I knew I wouldn't be able to fall asleep anytime soon. Images of the naturi and the threat of the bori were dancing through my brain. In fact, that combination left me wondering if I would ever sleep again.

The naturi had become a threat bigger than I had ever anticipated. They had slaughtered dozens of humans since Rowe began his campaign last summer to free his wife-queen. From so many bodies, the chests had been ripped open and organs stolen for blood-magic spells woven to give the one-eyed naturi an edge when it came down to hunting Mira. At Machu Picchu, thirteen humans had been slaughtered to open the door between worlds—hearts stolen from innocent people.

And now that Aurora was free, the killing would only grow worse. Her only desire was to wipe humanity from the face of the Earth, freeing the planet from a deadly parasite. The queen of the naturi had yet to make her move, but it was only a matter of time. She would strike, and I feared that the nightwalkers would not be strong enough to combat whatever she threw at them. We had underestimated their determination at Machu Picchu. Now they were more numerous and more powerful with Aurora at their side.

Gaizka was an entirely different matter. I hadn't expected to ever be faced with the bori that held a chunk of my soul. It had allowed me to slaughter a nightwalker and an innocent human he was using as puppets. One woman had her throat torn out simply because she associated with nightwalkers in what was possibly a scheme to expose the nightwalkers to the rest of the world. And now it was chasing after a young girl simply because she had the unique ability to spot the creature.

The girl. She had slipped from my mind in the chaos that was swirling around me whenever I was near Mira. I needed to find the girl. It was only a matter of time before the bori either possessed her or finally killed her out of frustration. She was running out of time. We all seemed to be running out of time.

Upon reaching the sidewalk, I shoved my hands into my pockets and crossed the street into the small square in the center of the small neighborhood. A plaque at the entrance to the park revealed that it was Monterey Square. The park was veiled by a mix of live oaks and magnolia trees. A large white temple flanked the park to my left, while the infamous Mercer House lay on my right. In the center of the square was the Pulaski monument.

The night was quiet except for the scrape of dried leaves across the sidewalk as a breeze began to stir. The night was growing colder, so that my breath fogged when I exhaled. In the distance, the steady hum of cars rushing down some of the main streets could be heard. It felt as if the world had fallen asleep around me, and yet I didn't feel as if I was alone.

Standing with my back to the monument, I slowly turned,

my eyes scanning the area for the being that I knew had to be close. I was summoning my powers to complete a more thorough search of the area when a creature rose to its feet from where it had been sitting at the base of an oak tree. The thin figure seemed to rise out of the shadows themselves as if it were made of them.

I took a step backward and palmed the knife I kept at my lower back, allowing the silver blade to catch some of the light thrown down by a nearby streetlamp. It failed to deter the figure as it continued to approach.

After a couple feet, he finally stepped through a shaft of light and I clenched my teeth. It was a naturi. He had brownish-blond hair and green eyes that shone like gems in the bit of light. The naturi gripped a small blade in his right hand and grinned at me, his smile stretching over his sharp, angular face like a mad jester.

"You can't keep her safe," he called when we were separated by only eight feet of open air. He stopped walking and stood with his hands out to his sides as if encouraging me to finally attack him.

I said nothing as I stood watching for him to make the first move. He wouldn't leave this square alive, but I wasn't about to be the one who started this fight, not when he might first feel the need to talk.

"We'll have the Fire Starter eventually," he proclaimed a couple seconds later, when I had yet to speak. "She'll not escape us again."

"You'll not have her so long as I am in the city," I replied in a low, even voice.

"You?" The naturi snorted. "How could you possibly hope to stop us, hunter? Far from killing her, you've become her lapdog as she leads you about the city."

It took a moment for me to unclench my jaw so that I could reply. This naturi was well informed, which was more than a little surprising since I hadn't been able to sense a single naturi within the city all evening.

"How have you gotten into Mira's thoughts?" I demanded, struggling to ignore his far-too-astute comments.

In response, the naturi's smile widened even further, reminding me of Nerian's. It was the same exact smile the insane naturi wore when he laid eyes on Mira for the last time. The smile sent a chill down my spine and seemed to cool the blood in my veins.

"Seeing things, is she?" the nameless naturi taunted. "Feeling somewhat haunted? What a pity!" The naturi let out a laugh that seemed to skip about the small park before dancing off among the trees. However, the smile seemed to slip off his face like a flash of lightning, leaving me staring at a grim mask. "But we're not the only ones messing with the Fire Starter's mind. Oh, no! She's found herself a new plaything," he continued. "You should never have allowed it."

"It doesn't matter," I said, lifting my empty left hand as if I were reaching for him. "You're done tormenting her with shadows."

Reaching deep within my chest, I tapped into the power that was coiled around my soul. The beast inside awakened and roared with joy in my mind. It was far too rare that I used my unique ability, the danger was too high and the risk to my own soul was too great. But tonight, I was willing to make an exception. This dark creature had found a way to torture Mira with images of naturi, leaving her fearful and uncertain within her own domain. He was part of a race that had taken joy in torturing the nightwalker, leaving her scarred on the inside and out. He was part of a race that sought the extermination of the entire human race. I needed no more excuse.

A deep cold breath filled my lungs as I sent my powers out from my body. But nothing happened. I reached deeper and sent more energy out from my body until my fingers began to tremble and beads of sweat traced lines down my face from my temples. Nothing happened. Finally, I scanned the park and came up with nothing. Despite the fact that the naturi was standing just eight feet away from me, I couldn't sense him.

A dark, evil laugh rose up from the naturi as he took a step closer to me. I dropped my left hand back to my side and raised my knife as I took a step backward. My heart hammered in my chest and thundered in my ears.

"You can't kill me, hunter," he mocked. "And you can't save her unless I allow it. You have until tomorrow night. Then I will be back and you will do as I say or I will destroy the Fire Starter and her lovely domain."

"What are you?" I demanded, tightening my grip on the blade in my hand. It was neither human nor nightwalker, lycanthrope nor warlock. I couldn't sense the creature and yet there was a heavy weight of magic in the air.

"Just think of me as an old friend of the family," the creature mocked.

"Gaizka!" I snarled, which only caused the creature's smile to return to its sharp, angular face.

"I'm the least of your worries, Danaus. There are naturi within Mira's domain and you need to use your powers combined with the Fire Starter to destroy them all. Rid the world of their kind and save humanity," Gaizka said smoothly, starting to circle me. The creature finally stepped into a block of light, showing that he was still translucent. The bori couldn't take a solid form unless he was possessing someone, and I had a dark suspicion that it couldn't possess a naturi even if it managed to convince one to allow it.

"Why are you so anxious for Mira and me to combine our powers?" I demanded.

"Because it's the only effective way to destroy the naturi. Surely you've discovered that for yourselves. You both were quite efficient while you were in England last summer," he purred.

"No."

"I don't recall giving you a choice in this matter," Gaizka said. At the same time, I felt a force wrap around my chest and pick me up. My arms were pinned to my sides and I struggled to free myself. The energy picked me up and flung me through the air, slamming me into the trunk of a massive tree. Pain exploded through my frame, knocking the wind out of my lungs as I heard the cracking of at least three ribs. I fell to the ground in a heap, but laid there for only a second before the energy wrapped around me again. It dragged me across the ground, knocking me headfirst through a park bench before slamming me into another tree.

My vision blurred and doubled until I could barely see the faint outline of the bori in naturi guise. My skull was cracked and my left shoulder had been dislocated. Pain wracked my body in sickening waves. I lay limp on the ground, struggling to breathe. I had but two powers at my disposal—the ability to sense other creatures and the ability to boil blood. Both were useless against this creature. I couldn't kill it because it had no body for me to wound. I was trapped, hanging at the mercy of a creature that could easily snap me in half. My only hope was that it still needed me alive to complete whatever task it wanted. However, that didn't mean it couldn't spend the rest of the night torturing me.

The sound of my heart pounding in my head, throbbing at the same rate as the wound in my skull managed to cloud my thoughts, making it hard to focus. A low moan escaped me as the energy once again wrapped around me and pulled me up so that my toes were scraping against the cold ground. My head lolled to the side and it was a struggle to draw a lungful of air. Gaizka walked over to where I hovered helpless in the air.

"I did not spend your lifetime preparing you to fight me in this moment," Gaizka calmly stated. "Don't fight me on this matter, and I won't be forced to destroy you and everything that you care about."

With a wave of its hand, the creature tossed me aside. I slammed into the pavement and rolled several feet before my back crashed into the Pulaski monument in the middle of the square. A cry escaped me as fresh pain exploded in my frame.

With a grin, the naturi turned and walked back toward

the shadows he had risen out of. With a shaky hand and a soft grunt, I threw the knife as hard as I could. The blade flew straight and true, glinting faintly in the moonlight. It passed straight through the back of the naturi and hit the ground with a heavy thud just before he completely disappeared from sight. Gaizka was right. I couldn't kill it, which left me with no way of protecting Mira or the humans of Savannah.

I lay on the ground for several minutes, blood oozing from my skull, waiting for the worst of the pain to subside so that I could drag myself back to Mira's town house. Yet, as the pain slowly slipped from my fractured frame, it was replaced with a deeper sense of hopelessness that I couldn't push aside. We weren't going to win this battle.

Twenty-Four

Stifling a yawn, I rubbed my left eye with the heel of my palm as I slowly trudged up the stairs to the police station. The sun had been up for only a few hours and I was running on less than five hours of sleep. It had taken me the better part of an hour to drag myself through the streets the previous night and into bed in Mira's town house. My body was healed, but still somewhat tender.

But a slim shred of hope lingered as I slowly mounted the concrete stairs to the police station. Daniel Crowley had woken me from a dead, healing sleep to inform me that he had a potential witness; someone who actually saw the murderer leave Abigail Bradford's apartment building. So far, all the detective had been willing to tell me was that I had to hurry if I wanted the chance to talk to her.

Still bleary-eyed, I was shuffled through the building until I landed before Daniel's desk. The detective looked exhausted, having already worked past the end of his shift. The sleeves of his wrinkled white shirt had been rolled up past his elbows and his tie dangled like a worn noose around his neck. Papers, files, and used paper coffee cups cluttered his desk in a growing pile, until it appeared the mountain would soon spill off the edge.

"I guess it's a good thing you're around, or Mira would

have missed this opportunity," Daniel said by way of a greeting. "I've got to take her over to Family Services before I clock out for the night."

"Family Services?" I repeated dumbly, my brain still trying to function without that first cup of coffee.

"Yeah. She can't be more than thirteen, though you can hardly get a straight answer out of her." Daniel paused and ran one hand over his face as if to clear his thoughts. "She lives on the streets—runaway. We've picked her up a couple times before. She won't stay in any of the homes that she's placed with."

"How did you get her?"

"She came to us. Scared out of her mind. Don't think she's slept in days," Daniel said with a heavy sigh as he pushed himself out of his chair.

"Did you get a description of the killer?" I asked, following him down the hall past a series of interrogation rooms.

"She spent most of the morning with a sketch artist," he confirmed, and then paused, his hand on the doorknob. "I was just going to send a copy of the picture over to Mira, until she said that the guy's eyes glowed red. It could have been a trick of the light, but I thought it best if one of you people talk to her first."

I flinched at the "one of you people" comment and gave a soft affirmative grunt. I wasn't a vampire or lycanthrope, and Daniel knew that. However, I doubted that he was aware that I wasn't fully human. He simply lumped me with them because I associated with Mira.

"We had one other strange development," Daniel admitted as he took his hand off the interrogation-room doorknob. "We had a floater turn up this morning."

"A floater?" I inquired, my brain struggling to keep up.

"Dead body in the river, down by the shipyards," Daniel replied.

"And you think it's linked?" I was surprised that there was no mention of the man who had been cremated on Factors Walk. Of course, the body might not have been found yet or it wasn't being listed as a strange death similar to what Daniel was accustomed to seeing with Mira's crowd.

"Possibly. Archie already called. Says the teeth aren't human, but animal fangs. The jawbone has been completely shattered. And from a rough description, it appears this guy matches the kid's description," Daniel explained.

"So the killer has been found," I said. I should have felt overwhelming relief, but instead all I felt was growing fear. "What did the man die of?"

"According to Archie, all of his internal organs were reduced to black goo. His body completely shut down," Daniel said. "What could do that to someone?"

"I have no idea," I admitted, but I was beginning to wonder if the dead man had simply been a carrier for something darker. "Let me talk to the girl," I said, nodding toward the door. My hopes weren't high that she might know something useful, but at this point, I would take whatever information I could get.

Following Daniel into the interrogation room, I found the young girl from Factors Walk seated at the table, cleaning the dirt out from underneath her fingernails. She looked up at Daniel and frowned, then her eyes traveled over to me. In a flash, the girl launched herself out of her chair and jumped to the other side of the room.

"What the hell are you doing here?" she demanded, pressing herself into the far corner.

Daniel looked at me strangely, while a frown pulled at the corners of my mouth. I'd hoped to find the young girl that James and I had spoken to, but I wasn't expecting to find her this way. I also hadn't been expecting this kind of welcome, but after our run-in with the bori, I guess I should have.

"We've met before. Can you give me a moment alone with her?" I asked Daniel, while my eyes remained on the young girl.

"No! Don't!" the girl cried, holding up her hand to ward me off.

"I won't harm you," I said, taking a single step forward. "I just came to talk to you about what you saw outside the apartment building."

"Why are you here? You're the reason I'm being hunted!" she demanded again.

"Hunted?" Daniel asked, and then he quickly held up his hands to stop us from answering his question. "I think it's best I leave before I hear anything else. I know more than I want to already." Before the girl could argue, Daniel stepped behind me and jerked open the door, making a hasty retreat.

"How am I the reason you're being hunted?" I asked, remaining where I was near the door.

"I don't know. That thing knows I know you and it wants you, doesn't it? Or maybe it just wants me because of what I know? I don't know anymore," she cried, slamming her fist into the wall to her right.

"What you know? What is it that you know that no one else does?"

"I don't know," she shrugged, staring down at the ground. Her hands remained balled into fists and her lips were pressed into a hard line as if she were fighting to hold her secret deep within her.

"What do you see that makes me different?"

"Nothing," she mumbled, crossing her arms over her middle.

Frowning, I pulled out one of the chairs from the table and sat down, remaining near the door so that she had nowhere to go. "We both know that's a lie. You apparently know a lot more than anyone is willing to give you credit for. You know that vampires are real. What else is real?"

She gave a soft snort, glancing up at me for only a second. "The fucking tooth fairy."

"Watch your language," I grumbled. "You know about

the vampires and the werewolves. You can tell one just by sight, can't you? I've seen you squinting at both me and my friend James. You squinted just before you spotted that creature that killed Abigail Bradford. You can see something no one else can."

The girl continued to stare at me, but some of the tension seemed to have left her skinny frame. She cocked her head at me as she looked at me, but for some reason it didn't seem as if she was looking directly at me but at something just past my left shoulder.

"You see something when you look at me, too," I said, leaning forward a little to rest both my arms on the top of the table. "What is it? Do you think I look like a vampire? I can show you now that I'm missing the necessary fangs." I flashed her a broad smile, revealing a set of normal-looking teeth.

"No, it's your look, really. You . . . your aura is similar to a vampire," she finally admitted in a low voice.

"Really? You can see auras. That's interesting. I've never met anyone who could read auras. At least, not with any accuracy," I said, folding my hands together.

"You believe me?" she said, surprising filling her voice. She leaned back into the corner, her shoulders resting against the two walls. She slipped her hands into the front pockets of her jeans, striking a pose that reminded me far too much of Mira.

"Of course. I've met creatures far stranger than you in my time. Why shouldn't I believe you?"

"I'm not some creature! I'm a human being!" she suddenly shouted, pushing away from the wall.

"So am I."

"No, you're not," she snapped. "There's a black shadow that streaks across part of your aura. It's exactly the same kind of shadow that I've seen on those vampires. You may not be one of them, but you're definitely not human."

"My name is Danaus. And you're right. I'm not completely human. I'm nearly two thousand years old and I have many of the same abilities as a vampire, but I don't drink blood and I don't burn up in the sunlight."

"Whoa!" she said, stepping back to lean against the wall again.

"What's your name?" I asked, trying not to think about what had her so impressed. I didn't like it being pointed out that I was a freak of nature. I liked it even less that my aura had such a similar marking as a vampire. It was just another similarity to the race that I could do without.

"Runt," she said, putting her hands behind her back.

"Your real name?"

"No one ever uses it," she hedged.

"I would like to. I'm not going to call you Runt."

The young girl huffed softly, her dark brown hair falling in front of her eyes. "Lily."

"It's nice to meet you, Lily. Would you like to sit down? You look exhausted."

"I'm not tired," she snapped, forcing herself to stand up straight.

"That's a lie. I can feel your fatigue from here. Your knees are about to give out. You've got nothing to gain by forcing yourself to stand when you can sit at the table with me," I said, motioning toward the chair she had been sitting in when we came in at the opposite end of the table. "I just want to ask you about the person you saw at the apartment building."

"He wasn't a person," she said.

"I didn't think so," I replied. "It wasn't human, was it?" Lily remained leaning against the wall, staring down at her dirty and worn sneakers. "Something about it scared you; enough to convince you to come to the police. They told me that you live on the streets. I imagine you already know how to take care of yourself pretty well, but this thing scared you enough to want some protection."

Lily pushed off from the wall and slowly walked over to the table. Without looking up at me, she slid into the chair and put her hands on the table. She picked at her fingernails for nearly a minute before she finally spoke again. "I don't know what it was. I've never seen anything like it. Its aura wasn't like anything I had ever seen before. It was like a black, endless shadow, one that could hold the whole world within it."

"Besides the black aura, what did the creature look like?" I asked.

She shook her head and sat up as she finally came to look me in the eye. "Its aura wasn't black. It was a shadow like the one across your aura. I can see color and depth beneath your shadow, the rest of your aura. This thing's aura was a bottomless pit."

"Okay, I'm sorry. Besides its shadow aura, what did it look like?"

"A regular man," she said with a shrug. "Thin, about six feet tall, with blond hair. The only thing strange about him was that his eyes glowed when he looked up."

"And he saw you, didn't he?" I asked softly, though by the way her hands trembled when she spoke of the creature I had no doubt that he did.

"Yeah."

"The shadow creature possessed the blond man the same way it possessed that other man that morning when we were all on Factors Walk," I said, and she nodded, dropping her head into both of her hands as she rested her elbows on the table. "Has it come after you since that morning?"

"Not exactly, but I've seen it from a distance like it's stalking me," she said in a low, shaky voice. "I've tried hiding in churches and in crowds in broad daylight, but it doesn't go away. It keeps finding me. I didn't have any choice. I had to come here. I keep saying no, but it's not listening to me. It doesn't care. I think it wants to take me over like it did those men."

"It's only natural that you came to the police for protection. It's their job," I said, trying to ease her fears and her obvious dislike for what she saw as weakness for turning to someone else for help. She had lasted out on the streets a few nights, but her fears finally got the better of her, or worse, she had actually been cornered in a lonely alley by the creature. She wouldn't last but a couple seconds in a fight with Gaizka.

"So much for protection," she scoffed. "They're planning to send me off to Family Services again. No one is going to be able to protect me if that thing comes looking for me."

"I can help you," I offered before I could stop myself. She was a young child, lost in this world, and surrounded by monsters at all times. It was only a matter of time before one of them finally swallowed her up.

"How?" she asked skeptically.

"Like I've said, I've been around for a long time. You don't live that long without learning a few things. I also have some friends that could be of help as well," I replied.

"And you'll help me stay alive?" she asked, still sounding doubtful. And I honestly couldn't blame her. A total stranger who wasn't quite human, offering to help protect her against something dark and evil. Why would she believe me?

"I'll do everything within my power, but that also means trusting a few vampires," I said. I knew that I would have to introduce her to Mira, which would most likely include Tristan and possibly Knox as well. Hell, if she could point us in the direction of Abigail's murderer, I was willing to call together all the nightwalkers of Savannah in order to protect this young girl.

"Not all vampires are bad," she quickly said, surprising me.

"Yeah, they're just misunderstood," I retorted, earning a soft giggle from my young companion.

"Well, I wouldn't go that far," she said, a small grin starting to show on her pale, dirt-smudged face.

"Are you willing to come with me? Let me protect you?"

"You won't dump me with Family Services?" she demanded, her smile instantly fading.

"As long as you agree to help me as well. I need as much

information as you can give me. This creature has killed a few people, and my friend and I have to stop it before it hurts anyone else. It could be dangerous, but I will do everything I can to keep you safe," I promised.

She looked at me again, squinting slightly. I was willing to guess that she was reading my aura again, gauging my sincerity. I remained sitting quietly while she stared at me. Lily was trapped between a rock and a very hard place. She could either take her chances with me, which would potentially put her in danger, or she could take her chances with Family Services, which offered little to no protection whatsoever.

"Can we stop and get something to eat first? I'm starving," she said at last, earning a surprised chuckle from me. I honestly couldn't remember the last time I had spent this much time with a child, and Lily was undoubtedly different from anything I might have expected. Much like Mira, I was sure that she was going to keep me on my toes until this creature was taken care of at last. The only plus was that I finally felt as if we had taken a step forward in this investigation. Lily had seen the mark of the creature's aura. While it might be forced to switch bodies, with the girl's help we might be able to find the creature. We might still be searching for a needle in a haystack, but at least we had acquired a metal detector to help with the process. I just hoped we could finally catch this thing without putting Lily in any more unnecessary danger.

Twenty-Five

My stomach tightened as anxiety pumped in my veins the closer we drew into Mira's house. After grabbing some fast food for Lily we had returned to the town house, where she could finally clean up, eat, and sleep. I kept her up on the third floor in hopes of slowing any attempts to sneak away. But for now she seemed content to curl up like a cat in the middle of the queen-sized bed and sleep.

However, a phone call from Gabriel quickly destroyed our cozy atmosphere. Mira's bodyguard sounded more than a little harried when he demanded that I immediately come to Mira's house and help him make the nightwalker see reason. He would give me no more information other than the fact that Tristan's life was on the line.

Considering that the naturi could seemingly sense and track me, I was more than a little hesitant to go trotting off to the Fire Starter's secret lair. I was also nervous about dragging Lily into a particularly dangerous situation, but I had no choice. I couldn't leave her alone, and with Gaizka hunting her, I thought she was better off at my side than left alone in the town house. Besides, Mira would need to meet the kid soon enough, and the two of us, along with Gabriel, could provide better protection for Lily than if she were on her own.

With a frown, I parked the car in front of Mira's garage

and turned it off. But I didn't get out of the car. Instead, I looked down at the young girl seated next to me. Was I putting a child's life in danger by bringing her to this house? Just a few months ago, my answer would have been an unwavering yes. Now, I couldn't imagine Tristan or Mira doing anything to harm her. Had I finally spent so much time surrounded by nightwalkers that my sense of reality had been severely compromised?

"Whose house is this?" Lily inquired when it became obvious that I was reluctant to go inside.

"A friend," I replied then frowned. I couldn't think of any other description that would make Lily feel comfortable, and "an enemy" was neither accurate nor comforting. "She's the one helping me to catch the killer."

"Is she human?"

"No," I drew in a deep breath and slowly released it. "Mira is a nightwalker. Both she and Tristan live here and are nightwalkers."

"Are they dangerous?"

My frown finally eased into a half smile and my hand dropped to the door handle. "Not with me here," I said, earning a grin out of Lily as well.

We had started to walk toward the front of the house when Gabriel opened the back door and motioned for us to come that way. The brooding figure stared down at Lily from the patio, his large arms crossed over his chest. Dark circles underlined his eyes and his shoulders seemed to slump under some unknown weight.

"This really isn't a good time for visitors," Gabriel said, pulling his confused gaze from Lily to me.

"She needs to meet with Mira," I said firmly when Lily's step faltered and slowed so that she was now a couple paces behind me.

Gabriel frowned as he pulled the back door completely shut and stepped out onto the patio. "Like I said, this really isn't a good time," he repeated in a low voice. "Mira's not doing so great."

"What do you mean?" I snapped, resisting the urge to lower my voice as well. "Vampires don't get sick."

"Mira is," Gabriel said, causing me to pause before I made a grab for the backdoor knob. "She's had me running around the city all day and when I get back, she's completely forgotten that she sent me out. I've caught her shouting at the open air, seeming to argue with someone called Nerian—"

"Nerian?" I demanded, my stomach twisting into a tight knot again.

"Yeah, shouting at nothing. Pointing and creating fires while addressing someone called Nerian. Who is that?"

"A dead naturi," I said under my breath as I grabbed the doorknob. Something was seriously wrong. Nerian was dead. There was no question about it—she had ripped out his throat and incinerated him months ago. This didn't make any sense. Unless the naturi had found a way to mess with Mira's mind.

I pushed open the door, but Gabriel put a restraining hand on my shoulder, stopping me. "She's in there with Tristan now. She's been on his case for more than an hour. She's upset. I'm afraid she's going to . . . I can't go in . . ." he trailed off in frustration.

Gabriel didn't need to say it. He was afraid that Mira was going to kill Tristan, and he knew that he didn't have a chance at stopping the powerful nightwalker without getting himself killed in the process. I, on the other hand, had a chance of getting Tristan out alive.

"I've got it," I said.

"Danaus?" Lily said, capturing my attention. Her voice was soft and unsure, not that I could blame her at all. I had brought her to a strange place that was now more dangerous than I had anticipated.

"Everything is going to be fine," I reassured her, though I wasn't sure how I was going to help Mira if the naturi were attacking her mind. "You stay with Gabriel. Order some pizza. We're going to be here for a while."

As I stepped over the threshold, I was immediately

swamped by the overwhelming hunger radiating from Mira. The world was washed in a red haze and there was a strange roaring in my ears, as if I were next to a rushing torrent of water. My vision swam and everything seemed off kilter. I laid my hand on the kitchen counter as I tried to get my bearings. Closing my eyes, I sucked in a deep breath and raised as many mental shields as possible, trying to block Mira's presence. It wasn't easy. The Fire Starter filled the air like smoke in a tiny nightclub.

Getting my sense of balance back, I walked through the kitchen, briefly nodding to a strange Asian man hovering in the doorway between the kitchen and the hallway to the rest of the house. Mira had mentioned hiring someone to replace Michael, her fallen bodyguard, but I had yet to actually meet the man. Of course, now wasn't the time.

"Do it again!" Mira shouted, her voice carrying down the hall. She sounded positively angry, making this a potentially explosive situation. I peered in the open door to find books floating around the room as if they had grown invisible wings and decided to take flight. Mira stood in the center of the room with her hand wrapped around Tristan's neck. The younger nightwalker was looking up at the books, his hands extended and shaking.

"Rearranging your books?" I asked as I took a step into the room.

Mira briefly glanced over her shoulder at me, and then turned her attention back to Tristan. "He's been holding out on me," she snarled. "He's come here to kill me, take over my domain."

"I would never do such a thing," Tristan said in a rough, strangled voice.

"Lies!"

"Mira, what's going on?" I asked in a low, soothing voice.

"He can move objects telepathically. He's older than he claims to be," Mira replied, her gaze once again slipping over her shoulder at me. There were dark circles under her eyes and a gray pallor to her skin. She looked nearly dead, as if she had neither eaten nor slept for days.

"I'm barely over one hundred years old," Tristan pressed. The trembling in his hands had increased as we talked. He was growing tired and wouldn't be able to hold the books up in the air much longer.

"Then how is it you can use psychokinesis?" she demanded, giving him a little shake. Her nails dug deeper into his throat, causing a small stream of blood to trickle down his pale flesh.

"I don't know! I've been able to do it from almost the moment I was reborn."

"Lies! I can't! You're lying about your age. Are you an Ancient?"

"No!" Tristan shrieked, jerking backward at what I knew was an absurd suggestion. I couldn't read nightwalkers as well as Mira could, but I was willing to bet my life on the fact that Tristan was no Ancient. I believed him when he said that he was barely over one hundred years old.

"Mira, I believe him," I calmly said. I walked into the room and placed my hand on her shoulder. "And you know that there has to be another explanation to all of this. Tristan is loyal to you. He would never do anything to threaten you."

Mira's face twisted in thought, as if she were fighting something. I let my eyes slip nearly shut as I reached out and subtly tried to slip into her mind. I had to know if the naturi had found a way to influence her. Again, I was hit with an overwhelming red haze of hunger. Her mind was a swirling whirlwind of broken and shattered thoughts. I caught glimpses of horrific images and heard screaming voices, until I felt a shudder skitter through my own frame. I pulled away reluctantly. I couldn't sense any naturi in the area or within her mind. There was only Mira and her memories.

"Let him go, Mira," I said, squeezing her shoulder.

"But . . ." she said in a soft, unsure voice as her wide

eyes stared up at me. I could suddenly feel her terror cutting through the hunger, filling her to the point that it was blocking out all rational thought.

"Tristan won't hurt you, I promise. I won't allow it."

She turned her gaze back to the young nightwalker before finally releasing her hold on his throat. His pale skin had cuts from where her nails had dug into his flesh. Tristan lowered his arms, allowing the books to slowly float down to the floor. He looked up at me, gratitude in his eyes, but he didn't speak. We both knew that we were still walking on eggshells around the Fire Starter.

"Go to the kitchen and help Gabriel," I said, giving him the opportunity to escape the room. "I'll stay with Mira."

Tristan nodded and quickly slipped out of the room, but the motion seemed to snap Mira from her brief moment of calm. Her head snapped up and she jerked away from my grasp. She trained her angry gaze on me as she backed to the other side of the room.

"Why? You want to try to kill me now?" she demanded, but before I could deny it, she whipped around to face an empty corner of the room. "Shut up! You don't know what you're talking about. Danaus would never touch her! He's not like you."

"Who's here with us?" I asked warily, wishing I could pull a knife from my side, but I was afraid that the appearance of a weapon would set her off.

"Nerian," she said in a low growl. At the same time, she did something very strange. She took a couple steps backward, with her hand behind her as if she was keeping someone behind her as a form of protection. Nerian wasn't the only one that she claimed to see in the room.

"Mira, Nerian's dead," I said firmly.

"I thought so too, but he's standing right over there," she said, pointing with the hand that wasn't still holding the imaginary figure behind her back. "He's been with me all fucking day."

"What do you mean all day? Another dream?"

"It's not a dream! He's standing right there!" she shouted, pointing at the open air again.

Frowning, I walked over to where she was pointing and stood in the exact spot. "He's not here, Mira. You killed him. In July, you came to my house. You ripped out his throat and you burned his dead body to white ash. Nerian is dead and gone."

The finger pointing at me began to violently shake as a single bloody tear slipped down her pale cheek. "But I can hear him. I can hear him laughing and mocking me. He's convinced the others to kill me. To kill . . ."

"Who else is here with you?"

Mira looked down at the floor for a second, taking a step backward, as if to shield the invisible figure a little better. Her head suddenly snapped back to face me while her free hand pulled a long knife from a sheath at her lower back. "And you've come to kill us both as well!"

"No, I haven't! Mira, you're talking nonsense."

"Of course you have. You're a hunter. It's what you do," Mira sneered. With a scream, she lunged at me with her knife, preparing to separate my head from my shoulders. The only reason I survived the slash was that she was exhausted and not moving as fast as usual. I dove out of the way and rolled back to my feet, struggling not to draw a blade as well. I knew it would only make the situation worse.

A faint glow lit the nightwalker's eyes as she stalked me in the small room. There wasn't anywhere for me to go, between the chairs and the large desk that dominated the room. I stood my ground, trying to think of some way of snapping Mira out of her delusion. She came at me again, blade singing in the air as it sliced downward. I dodged it again, but this time she came back with a stabbing motion for my stomach. I barely managed to capture her wrist with both of my hands, stopping the tip of the blade just before it punctured skin. She pressed forward with all her remaining strength, and slowly started to win.

Clenching my eyes shut, I reached out with my powers

and grabbed ahold of her. My energy flowed into her body, taking control of her. Mira let out another tortured scream that echoed through the house. She fought me, trying to push me out, but she was too weak. I hadn't wanted to do this, but she had left me with no choice. Slowly, I got her to inch the blade away from my stomach before I was able to rip it out of her hands.

To my surprise, she rallied enough strength to grab the front of my jacket and toss me across the room, where I slammed into the bookshelves. A cascade of books fell on my head and shoulders as I pushed myself up into a sitting position.

"No!" she screamed, her face twisted in rage and fear. I looked down to find that I was sitting in the exact same spot she had been standing in only moments earlier. "You'll not touch her." Mira lifted both of her hands and massive balls of fire popped into existence. They spun around her body fast enough to make her hands dance slightly in the growing breeze. Her eyes glowed with a brighter light, but she seemed to grow even paler. She was going to collapse from exhaustion soon, but I was willing to bet that she had enough strength left to destroy me first if she wanted to. I could take possession of her again, but it would not get rid of the rage that was burning in her. It would not rid her of these enemies.

"Mira, we're alone in this room. Who do you think I'm threatening?"

The glow dimmed slightly from her eyes, and she looked as if I had unexpectedly slapped her. "Calla's here," she whispered in a shaky voice. "He's going to hurt Calla."

I had never heard the name before, but for some reason it caused my heart to stutter. Mira's fear filled the room, pushing out the hunger for a moment. Whoever Calla was, she dominated Mira's concerns. Her fear for Calla was enough to make her threaten the very people she trusted the most in the world, including myself.

"Who's Calla?"

Mira lifted one hand to her head, which she shook as if trying to finally clear the clutter surrounding her thoughts. A couple more tears streaked down her cheeks and her other hand began to tremble. The balls of fire slowed in their course around her body.

"Who's Calla, Mira?"

"She's my daughter," she whispered in a broken voice. "Please, Danaus, don't hurt my daughter."

I stared at the nightwalker, afraid to speak. Mira had once told me that she had had a life before she had been reborn as a nightwalker. It had never occurred to me that she might have actually had a daughter. And right now, I didn't want to be the one to tell her that her daughter had died centuries ago.

Slowly, I crossed the room and stood before the nightwalker who had fought and protected me. Reaching above the fireballs that had stopped moving, I cupped her face with both my hands, wiping away her tears with my thumbs. She trembled at my touch, but didn't try to move away as I forced her to look up at me. I could see the pain in her wide lavender eyes. I had to wonder if the hunger was driving her mad. It didn't make sense that she refused to feed. My presence had never stopped her from feeding in the past. Why should it now? Unless there was some darker reason for her reluctance.

"Mira, she's gone," I murmured, trying to put it as gently as possible. "Calla passed on centuries ago. She was your human daughter and she has already died. She's safely away from Nerian and the reach of any other naturi."

"But . . ."

"She's not here," I continued. My left hand swept up and pushed some red hair from her face. "I'm sorry. It's just you and me, alone in this room. No naturi. No Calla."

"I saw them!"

"No, you didn't. They were just hallucinations. You haven't fed for days. I can feel it. You need to feed before you hurt someone or yourself."

Mira blinked and confusion filled her gaze. The fear that had filled her seemed to be washed away and the hunger swam to the forefront again. She flinched at its sudden return, but I could feel her pushing it back. At one time, she had sworn that she would never feed off me and strangely enough I believed her when she made that vow. She was starving now, but I knew that she wouldn't bite me if it was within her power not to. However, I think that decision was slowly slipping out of her grasp.

"Danaus?" she whispered. "What's happening to me?"

"You need to feed. Gabriel's here. Or you can go into the city and hunt. You have to do something before you kill someone."

"I—I can't," she said before jerking out of my grasp. The fireballs were instantly extinguished, seeming to plunge the dimly lit room into darkness.

"This can't go on," I said, unable to believe that I was arguing for her to actually feed off of someone. However, the alternative was worse. A starved Mira was infinitely worse for this city and the world. She was hallucinating, her mind spiraling into paranoia and madness.

I took a step toward her as she stumbled over to her desk. She picked up her cell phone from the top of the desk and quickly dialed a number.

"I need you," she said in a low voice. "I can't wait any longer." It didn't seem as if she waited for a response before she hung up the phone.

I started to walk toward the nightwalker, desperate to convince her that she needed to feed when there was a soft pop in the air near the doorway. I looked up to find Ryan standing there in his usual gray suit, while his pure white hair brushed his shoulders. His gold eyes lit on me before he looked over at Mira.

"What are you doing here?" I demanded, suddenly angry at his presence in Mira's house. The warlock was supposed to be in England already, not still lingering in Savannah. This couldn't possibly be a good sign.

"I'm here to help Mira," he said with a smile.

"Leave, Danaus," Mira ordered in a firm, cold voice.

"I'm not leaving," I replied, starting to raise my voice. "What's going on here?"

"I believe the lady said leave," Ryan said, his smile widening. With a slight wave of his hand, Ryan magically lifted me off my feet and threw me into the open hallway. Behind me, the double doors to the library slammed shut, sending the noise echoing through the entire house. Mira was alone with Ryan, and there was no way I could stop whatever the warlock had planned for her.

Twenty-Six

I paced like a caged tiger, my footsteps muffled by the Persian rug that ran the length of the hallway. Upon regaining my feet, I had tried to open the doors and barge back into the room, but they had been magically sealed. I was not getting back into the room until Ryan was done with Mira.

The warlock had a way of using people without their knowledge. Charismatic and deeply manipulative, Ryan always seemed to get exactly what he wanted with as little compromise on his part as possible. When he swept into Themis centuries ago, I had been content to let the researchers follow his lead. They were searching for information on the occult and nothing appeared to be more opportune than a powerful warlock offering to provide them with the inside information they sought.

In the end, what did I care who they picked as their leader? So long as I was able to hunt nightwalkers and purge the earth of their evil, I didn't care who was running Themis. But I should have cared. For two centuries, I watched Ryan use and manipulate creatures for his own benefit, seeming to suck them dry until they were nothing more than hollowed-out shells of hate and fear. The warlock fed my own hatred for nightwalkers, never seeing fit to disillusion me of some of my more erroneous beliefs about the species. My own burning hatred only served to blind me and tighten Ryan's hold over me. His own personal executioner.

And now the gold-eyed warlock had set his sights on the Fire Starter, one of the most powerful nightwalkers in existence. He couldn't have her. I wouldn't allow Ryan to use Mira in the same way he had used me. He was powerful enough alone. He didn't need Mira fighting at his side.

Turning back to the doors, I gritted my teeth and prepared to put my shoulder into the thick wood when I heard the soft metallic click of a lock being unlatched. One of the doors swung silently open and stopped. I lurched forward and shoved both doors open. Ryan was slumped in one of the chairs, his skin a sickly shade of white. His tie had been loosened and the left side of his neck lay bare. Mira leaned against the front of the desk, a flush to her pale face. The red haze that had filled the house had finally abated, with Mira's hunger satisfied at long last. And yet, the circles under her eyes seemed darker now, with color in her face, and her fingers were still trembling.

With a low snarl, I grabbed the lapels of Ryan's coat and lifted him out of the chair to his feet. "Whatever you're doing has to stop!" I shouted, giving him a hard shake.

"He's helping me," Mira said, placing a hand on my shoulder.

"He's not helping you," I snapped, my gaze never wavering from the warlock. While he was not openly smiling at me, I could see the laughter in his eyes. "Ryan doesn't help anyone but himself."

"Maybe helping Mira is in my best interest," Ryan purred.

I snorted in response, my fists tightening in the material of his jacket. I was ready to pitch Ryan through the nearest window if I thought for a second I could.

"I need his help," Mira said. Her hand squeezed my shoulder, and it was a fight to not shrug her off.

"He's made you dependent on him," I argued. "You won't drink from anyone else and you're willing to starve yourself until you can finally get back to his side. What happens when he returns to Themis? You trail after him like the lap-dog he wants you to be?"

"It's not like that," Mira replied, releasing me suddenly.

"No, not yet, but it will be," I said. I threw Ryan back into the chair, sending it skidding loudly backward several inches. "Get out of here. Don't ever come back."

Ryan smiled up at me, his eyes jumping with laughter. "As you wish," he replied, and then disappeared.

"No!" Mira screamed. She pushed past me, reaching for the warlock, but came up with only open air. "What have you done?" she cried, turning her horror-filled gaze on me. "You don't understand. I need him."

"You don't need his help," I firmly said, helping Mira back to her feet from where she was kneeling before the empty chair.

"Yes, I do. He's given me my only edge over Aurora," she adamantly argued as tears filled her eyes.

"What are you talking about?" I said. Mira only looked away from me as she tried to walk back toward the desk. I grabbed both of her arms and held her in front of me. "How? What kind of an edge was he giving you?"

But the nightwalker refused to answer me. She refused to even meet my gaze, causing my chest to tighten as if it were suddenly caught in a vise. "Mira, he's not helping you," I continued when she refused to speak. "Whatever he's doing is destroying your mind. Ever since I came to town, you've been seeing and hearing things. You attacked Tristan, ac-cusing him of betrayal when there is no one who could pos-sibly be more loyal to you."

"There are risks with everything in this world," she said, staring over my shoulder. "It's worth the risk."

"It's not!" I shouted. "It's destroying you. You're going to hurt someone important to you or yourself if this doesn't stop. You also can't risk being under Ryan's control. Isn't it enough that both Jabari and I have that power over you? Do you really want to have another holding your leash?"

"No! I don't want this!" she screamed, her composure splintering before me. "But it's only temporary. Once we kill Aurora, it will be over. Ryan and I will go our separate ways."

"And how long will that take? We haven't seen any sign of Aurora since Machu Picchu and it's likely she will remain in hiding while she tries to find a way to deal with both you and Cynnia. This arrangement with Ryan can't go on that long."

"I have to," Mira whispered.

"Danaus?" asked a soft voice off to my left. Mira and I both looked over at the same time to find Lily standing in the doorway. I felt Mira flinch at the sight of the girl and seem to draw into herself in pain.

"Calla?" Mira murmured in a breathless voice. The nightwalker lurched to her side, trying to get at the girl. Luckily, I was still holding Mira's arms and I managed to stop her before she could get more than a step toward the young girl. "Calla!" she cried again in a louder voice, as she desperately tried to twist out of my grasp. My only saving grace was the fact that Mira still wasn't up to her full strength or I never would have been able to hold her back.

"It's not Calla," I firmly said, forcing Mira to look up at me as I turned my back on Lily.

"But it is!" Mira said, jerking in my grasp in an attempt to look around me and at the girl again. "Look at her, Danaus! It's Calla."

"It's not Calla! Calla is dead. You know this." Tightening my grip on Mira to the point of bruising, I finally got her to look up at me. "Think about it, Mira. You know that Calla is gone from this world. I'm sorry, but it's the truth."

"But . . ." she whimpered.

"That's Lily. She's agreed to help us."

"Danaus?" Lily repeated, her voice growing more unsure.

"It's okay, Lily. This is Mira, a friend of mine. She's very sick right now," I explained as I watched the confidence slowly flow from Mira's expression only to be replaced by pain and a growing confusion. Her mind was coming back to me for the moment. Ryan's blood may have satiated her hunger, but it failed to heal whatever damage was being done to her mind.

"Can I help you?" Lily asked.

"Not right now," I said. "Go back in the kitchen with Gabriel and the others. I'll join you there soon."

"I was wondering if it would be okay if I went upstairs with Tristan. He was going to show me this computer game he's having trouble with. Can I?" she hesitantly asked.

I frowned, not at all liking the idea of Lily being alone with Tristan. She was a young, vulnerable girl who had been through enough. I didn't bring her here to be a light snack for a nightwalker.

"She's safe with me," Tristan said to my surprise. I hadn't even heard him approach. My mind was too full of Mira and her deteriorating condition. "She's a guest in this house. Besides, I know what you're capable of."

"It's fine, Lily. Go with Tristan," I said, some of the tension flowing from my shoulders.

I knew the moment that Tristan and Lily disappeared from the doorway because Mira relaxed in my hands. She directed her tortured eyes up to my face at last. I dipped into her mind to find it a mess of fractured thoughts. Yet, the nightwalker was standing in the middle of it all, clearheaded for the moment.

"I don't understand. What's happening to me? Why do I keep seeing these . . . images? Are they ghosts?" Mira asked.

"I don't think so." I sighed. Ghosts were a more appealing idea than the threat of insanity that I offered her. "Ryan's blood is doing something to your mind or something has found a way to affect your thoughts. Either way, feeding off of the warlock has to stop."

"I can't!" she argued, pulling out of my loosened grasp. "It's my only edge against Aurora." Mira clasped her head in both of her hands and let out a low moan as she battled whatever demons were fighting for control of her now.

"This can't continue."

"But Aurora . . ."

Taking one step forward, I swept Mira up into my arms. "I think I might have another solution," I said. The nightwalker didn't try to push out of my arms. To my surprise, she actually curled up against me, still clutching her head. I could feel her warm body starting to cool, as if whatever warmth she had gained from Ryan was quickly dissipating.

Marching through the house, I gave Gabriel only a glance at where he was seated at the table in the breakfast nook. The other man was gone, possibly off to get pizza.

"Where are you going?" Gabriel demanded as I jerked open the back door.

"To see someone who might be able to help Mira. Keep an eye on Lily for me," I replied before walking out of the house, leaving Gabriel to shut the door behind me.

Unfortunately, I didn't get far. I had just deposited Mira in the backseat of the car and shut the door when the kitchen door opened and Lily came running across the backyard to the car. She must have heard the door close or looked out the window.

"Wait! Wait for me!" she cried.

"I want you to stay here with Gabriel and Tristan," I said calmly, placing a restraining hand on her slim shoulder. "I need to take Mira to see someone who might be able to help her."

Lily jerked out of my grasp, taking one step backward from the car. "You said that you would protect me."

"Gabriel and Tristan will keep you safe. I won't be gone long," I countered, feeling guiltier by the minute. I had promised her that I would keep her safe and now I was ditching her with a human bodyguard and a nightwalker.

"You think I haven't heard that one before?" she scoffed, plopping her hands on her hips. "Leave me here and I won't be here when you get back."

I frowned down at the teenager and she glared back up at me. I couldn't take the risk of her running when Mira and I still needed her. She was also risking her own life by potentially falling into Gaizka's hands. Furthermore, she wasn't the responsibility of Tristan and Gabriel. She was mine.

"You do exactly as I say or I will put you in the trunk for your own protection," I threatened, but Lily paid me no heed. She gave a little excited skip and ran around to the front door on the passenger side.

Reaching into my back pocket, I pulled out my cell phone just before sliding behind the steering wheel. After my initial arrival in Savannah, I had stumbled across a local witch who provided me with some valuable information on the workings of Mira's domain. She hadn't been too thrilled to help me months ago and I didn't get the feeling she believed I'd actually survive when I went head-to-head with the Fire Starter.

"LaVina, this is Danaus," I blurted out as soon as she answered the phone. "I'm bringing you someone that needs your help." I hung up the phone before she could reply and started the car. I just hoped that she could help. Mira wasn't going to last much longer as she was.

Twenty-Seven

The small white two-story house sat out in the middle of a field nearly a mile from the road. Oak trees surrounded the house, shrouding it from view with their thick leafy limbs. Lily shifted in her seat, growing more uneasy the closer we drew to the house. The night was overcast, blocking any moonlight, leaving the area cloaked in thick darkness.

"Whose house is this?" Lily asked as I put the car in park.

"Her name is LaVina and she's a witch of sorts," I replied as I unlatched my seat belt.

"What's that mean?" Lily demanded as she slowly released her seat belt as well.

"LaVina specializes in voodoo, but has expanded her practices to various forms of earth and blood magic. Several months ago, she helped me to locate Mira," I explained, and then got out of the car before she could ask her next question.

Lily followed behind me as I picked up a silent Mira from the backseat and carried her up the front steps. The old wood planks of the porch creaked under our combined weight, announcing our arrival.

The front door opened, revealing an old black woman as

thin as a skeleton with her gray hair drawn back into a tight bun. Her bony hand wrapped around the door handle of the screen door, holding it shut.

"You shouldn't have hung up so quickly," she criticized in a heavy Southern accent. "I would have told you not to bother to come."

"Just take a look at her," I said, ignoring her comment. I wouldn't be turned away.

"What am I supposed to do with a sick vampire?"

"She's been drinking from a warlock," I said quickly, hoping to pique her curiosity. "She's been hearing and seeing things. Ghosts from her past. Savannah needs Mira. You know that. She's not going to last much longer as she is."

"Bah!" she scoffed, a frown drawing down the corners of her mouth. "Who's the young one?"

"Lily. A friend."

LaVina stared at us for another few seconds before she finally released the door handle and shuffled into the house, leaving us to follow.

"Danaus, are you sure about this?" Lily asked in a low voice as she took a step backward.

"Everything will be fine," I said, raising one corner of my mouth in what I hoped looked like a reassuring smile. "What's wrong? See something?"

"No, and that's the problem. She doesn't have an aura," Lily whispered.

It was strange enough to give me pause, but not enough to stop me from opening the door. Mira needed help and LaVina was my only option at this point. I could only hope that maybe the child was tired and possibly mistaken. Or maybe LaVina was powerful enough to cloak her aura from others. Either way, it really didn't matter. I was desperate.

"Just stick close to me," I said as I entered the house. Lily was quick to obey, as she followed close enough to bump into me when I suddenly stopped outside the living room.

With her hands on her narrow hips, LaVina stared down at Lily, clucking her tongue at the girl. "You're a bit of a ragamuffin. Need something to eat? Let me get you some-thing fixed up."

"That's okay. Gabriel's getting some pizza. I'll just have that when we get back to Mira's," Lily quickly said.

"That's no meal for a girl your age. You need some real home cooking and you're not going to get that with some vampire," LaVina argued with a dismissive wave at Mira, who lay limp in my arms.

"It's okay, LaVina. We can't stay long. We just need you to look at Mira," I interrupted.

"Fine. Fine. Have it your way," the old woman said, throwing her arms up. "Follow me."

Suppressing a sigh of relief, we followed LaVina down a narrow set of wooden stairs into her basement. The old witch waved her hand as she descended the stairs, causing dozens of candles to flicker to life. To my surprise, a low giggle escaped Mira as she raised her hand. All the candles went out again, plunging the basement back into complete darkness.

"Oh, so the corpse is awake," LaVina said as she lit the candles again.

"Sorry, LaVina," I said, descending the last few stairs to the dirt floor. "Mira hasn't been thinking clearly the past few days."

"Bite me, Danaus," Mira said as she finally started to stir in my arms.

"Just set the bloodsucker on the floor over there," LaVina directed, waving one hand toward the far wall as she fiddled around on a workbench covered with all sorts of strange odds and ends.

I sat Mira on the floor so that her back was against the concrete wall and she was facing the bench where LaVina was busy pulling together whatever she needed. I remained closer to Mira while Lily sat down on the stairs, refusing to come any farther into the tiny, claustrophobic basement. There were no windows and the walls were covered in all manner of symbols, none of which I could identify. The air was musty, filled with the rich scent of dirt, dried flowers, and a hint of incense. Beneath it all was also the faint odor of dried blood. Creatures had been sacrificed in this small cloistered refuge from the modern world.

LaVina hummed a nameless melody to herself as she went about lighting a bit of incense and pulling down little bottles of unknown liquids and fragments of plants. Jerking open the door of an old wooden birdcage, the old witch plunged her hand inside and quickly pulled it out again, holding a small bird in her grasp. With a speed and ease that bespoke of years of experience, she picked up a small blade from the table and chopped off the creature's head before it could make a single chirp. I quickly looked over at Lily and was instantly relieved to find that she was looking at Mira and me rather than the witch. She didn't need to be exposed to any more violence and death than she already had been.

I was beginning to think that bringing her here had been a serious mistake. LaVina was eccentric at best. When I had seen her the last time, she had stood naked in a ring of fire in her backyard, her body smeared with the blood of a dead dog, demanding the spirits of the dead tell her where I should go to hunt the Fire Starter. I might not be a believer in her methods, but the next night, I finally encountered Mira and our journey together began.

"Good dirt," Mira suddenly murmured, shattering the silence that had dominated, other than LaVina's soft humming. I looked down at the nightwalker to find her digging furrows in the dirt with the fingers of her right hand. She picked up a handful and let it fall through her parted fingers. Her head popped up and she looked at LaVina for the first time. "This isn't Savannah dirt," she ventured. "Peruvian?"

LaVina took a couple slow steps toward the nightwalker, her brow wrinkled with surprise and her fingers stained red. "Good guess," she replied softly. "Some of the dirt was shipped in from the Sacred Valley in Peru. I also had some brought in from the Black Forest in Germany and from the Blue Mountains in Jamaica. Strong bits of earth for spell casting. But I'm surprised you could tell such a thing."

Mira shrugged her shoulders as she dropped the last of the dirt back to the ground. "Like I said, it's good dirt. I've slept covered in Peruvian dirt."

"But still," LaVina pressed as she edged closer. "No nightwalker should be able to sense such a thing. All night-walkers lose their connection with the earth upon rebirth."

"Yes, well, I'm special," Mira said, curling her lips in such a way that she briefly flashed her fangs. There was also no missing the sarcasm that laced every syllable of that statement.

To my surprise, LaVina knelt on the ground next to Mira and clasped the nightwalker's chin between two thin fingers. She tilted Mira's head up, looking into her lavender eyes as she once again clucked her tongue. "You, my child, should never have been reborn as a nightwalker."

"No kidding," Mira replied snidely as she tried to turn her head away, but LaVina jerked Mira's head back to face her.

"You were destined for many great things," LaVina continued. "Being a nightwalker may have delayed, if not completely deterred those things. So sad."

"What are you talking about?" I asked when Mira just stared mutely at the old witch.

"Nothing specific," LaVina quickly said, releasing Mira's face. "Just idle dreams and broken nightmares."

Using the blood that was still on her fingers, she traced a symbol on Mira's forehead that caused a knot to form in my stomach. I knew a few old symbols from my travels, and this one felt positively ancient. Older than the pagans, older than Mesopotamians, older than most civilizations that had crawled across the Earth. The monster that lived wrapped around the remains of my soul recoiled at the sight of it and my skin crawled. While I couldn't name the source of the symbol, something told me that I was looking at the original marking for chaos.

Energy sizzled in the air around LaVina and Mira, as the old witch started speaking in a tongue I had never heard before. My ears started ringing and the air started to grow too thick to draw into my lungs. I thought I would soon begin choking. Mira lay as still as death while LaVina worked her magic, her eyes closed, but a glimmer of lavender light still shined beneath her eyelashes. I didn't like this.

"LaVina?" I pressed, touching the woman's arm. The witch immediately stopped what she was doing and smiled at me. She placed her hand in mine and I helped her to stand again. She walked back over to the bench where she fiddled around with some unseen objects.

"So, you were saying that this nightwalker has been drinking from a warlock," she said, changing the subject to the real reason we had come to her in the first place. I was tempted to pull her back to our previous topic, but decided to drop it. It was more important that we got Mira well and sane again.

"Yes." I sighed.

"Powerful one?" she asked, glancing over her bony shoulder at me.

"Very powerful."

"Hmmm . . ." she said as she slowly turned around again. She leaned up against the bench and crossed her arms over her middle. "Did you know different types of blood affect nightwalkers in different ways?"

"I'm not surprised," I said, shoving my hands into my back pockets. "Naturi blood is poisonous to nightwalkers."

"In that same vein, some nightwalkers can't drink shapeshifter blood. They're too close to that nature tie, and it makes them sick for several nights on end."

"Mira can drink shifter blood," I countered, recalling Mira's special meal with the lycanthrope Nicolai in Venice.

"Hmmm," she said again with a nod. "I'm not surprised by that. For some, shifter blood can temporarily make a nightwalker stronger, heighten senses, and satisfy the thirst for longer. However, blood from a powerful witch or warlock does none of those things."

"Then why drink it?" Lily inquired. I looked over my shoulder to find her rising and walking down to the stand on the last stair.

"Because it can have special side effects," LaVina said, smiling up at the girl.

"Like what?" Lily asked.

"I don't know. Why don't you tell us, Mira?" I asked, turning my attention back to the nightwalker. Mira had dropped her head and was once again running her fingers through the dirt. She refused to look up at us, but there was a new stiffness to her shoulders.

"Go to hell, Danaus," she muttered.

"Oh, think about it," LaVina chided. "Weakness, trembling hands, circles under her eyes, hallucinations. At the root, Mira's still human."

"She's not sleeping," Lily murmured. My gaze jerked from the teenager to the nightwalker. Her shoulders were now slumped as if she were cowering away from me. Could it be something as simple as not sleeping?

"That's not possible," I said, pinning my gaze on Mira. "You can't be awake during the day. Nightwalkers can't be awake during the day."

"Ryan's blood is special," Mira admitted in a low voice. "I drink it and I can stay awake during the day."

"How long has it been since you last slept?" I demanded.

"I need this," Mira said, clenching her fists in the dirt. "It's my only edge against Aurora. What if she sends someone for me during the daylight hours?"

"How long?" I repeated.

Mira pushed to her knees so that she was now facing me, her fists clenched at her side. "She's going to come for me during the day! I won't be helpless against them."

"How long has it been?" I shouted back at her, taking a step toward her.

"Ten days!" she shouted back, tears slipping down her cheeks. "I've not slept in ten days!"

Pacing away from Mira, I shoved my hands through my hair, but managed to hold my tongue as I caught sight of Lily intently watching me. Ten days. Humans were known to hallucinate after just a few days without sleep. Vampires were resilient creatures, but even their minds couldn't possibly withstand such an extended period of deprivation. James had mentioned that Mira was up during the day, but it never occurred to me that she was never sleeping. I had just thought that she was waking earlier in the evening or maybe staying up a couple hours past sunrise—not staying awake the entire day.

"How long did you think you could keep this up?" I demanded, losing my tenuous grip on my temper.

"Months, if I had to. Whatever it takes!" she shouted at me.

"Leaving you at Ryan's mercy."

"Better at the mercy of a warlock that is just trying to help me defeat the naturi than at the mercy of an entire race that wants to see me dead."

"You think Ryan is a better option than the naturi?"

"Of course he is."

"Ryan doesn't care about you," I snarled, taking a step closer. "He only cares about how he can use you. You're a member of the coven. You're one of the most powerful vampires in all the world. How could you think something so stupid as this notion that he cares about protecting you?"

"Fine, maybe he doesn't care about me, but he at least doesn't want the naturi to succeed in wiping out humanity. At least we have that in common! Keeping me alive helps that goal. We can't let the naturi win."

"I don't want the naturi to succeed either, but this isn't the best way to beat them."

"They're going to come after me again."

"I know," I murmured. I knew it like I knew the sun was going to rise in a few hours and that Gaizka would come hunting for the rest of my soul. Little inevitabilities that we couldn't escape. Once Aurora had her forces pulled together, she was going to come after Mira again and she wouldn't stop until the nightwalker had suffered a gruesome, excruciating end. If the naturi won, Mira faced a horrible death.

"I won't let Aurora have me without a fight. She'll come during the daylight hours when I am vulnerable. They'll steal me away again and no one will be able to find me. Not even you and all your magic tricks. I swear I won't sleep again until Aurora is dead," Mira vowed.

I turned to look at LaVina, who was watching Mira intently. I had no way of winning this argument with Mira. She was being completely irrational, and in truth, I couldn't completely fault her. The naturi had grabbed her once already in her long lifetime and subjected her to two weeks of endless torture in an effort to break her will and use her as a weapon. But her plan was flawed. "How do we get her to sleep again?" I demanded, looking up at LaVina.

"No! I can't!" Mira argued, but I kept my eyes locked on the old witch.

After a moment, she shrugged. "Just get her to drink from someone other than this warlock. The fresh infusion of blood should dilute the power of the warlock's, forcing her to sleep again when the sun rises," LaVina replied.

"I won't do it, Danaus."

I looked back down at Mira to find her sitting on her heels, her arms folded over her stomach as if she were trying to guard herself against me. She was frowning at me, but there was no missing the desperation in her eyes. I felt trapped.

"Ryan is using you," I said, trying to find the best way to build my argument. "He's locking you to his side. Soon, he will be force you to do horrible things in order to get at his blood. You're stronger than this."

"Do you think I don't know this?" she snapped, lowering her eyes to the dirt floor. "My leash has enough owners. I don't need another. At least, not one of my own making. But I'll also do whatever it takes to survive. I'll not let the naturi have me again."

"This route risks the lives of others," I said. Taking a step forward, I knelt before Mira, cupping her face in my hands. Her skin was cool and almost waxy to the touch, as if the life had already seeped out of her. "You could have killed Tristan tonight if I had not arrived when I did. If you go much longer without sleep, someone will die at your hands. Are you willing to risk Tristan's life? Or Gabriel's? Or mine for that matter?" I had thrown in the last as a joke, hoping to bring a smile to her lips. Instead, she raised her right hand and laid it against mine as she shook her head.

"No," she whispered.

Her fear was a palpable thing in the room, seeming to form a cocoon around us. Lily and LaVina slipped away, and for a brief period of time, it felt as if I were finally alone in the world with Mira. The naturi were gone. The bori were a distant memory. The coven was just a bad dream. I rubbed my thumbs over her high cheekbones, wiping away a stray tear.

What am I to do? she asked, using the mental path we had trod so many times before it had begun to feel like a lover's familiar caress.

Tonight, you're going to hunt and then you will sleep safely through the day with me watching over you, I replied, using the same mental touch.

Mira's head snapped up so that she could look me in the eye, surprise and hope filling her expression. I stared at her pale parted lips, wishing I could see another wry smile dance there. *You will?* she demanded.

I will protect you until you can protect yourself, I confirmed.

Tonight?

For as long as you need me.

Mira turned her face and pressed a kiss into the palm of my left hand, then looked back at me. "All right. I'll feed from a human and sleep tonight," she said.

"It's about time." I sighed. A part of me was stunned that I was advocating for a nightwalker to feed. But then, I had seen and felt the chaos that ensued when she did not. It was safer for all those involved if Mira remained on her diet of human blood.

Pushing to my feet, I took Mira's hand and helped her up as well. I turned to find LaVina leaning against the bench, watching us with a thoughtful frown. "Thank you for your help," I said.

The old witch snorted and waved off my comment. "Didn't need me. I wasn't of much help. You just needed to know how to put some sense into that one," she said, jerking her head toward Mira.

"Why have I never met you?" Mira inquired as I started to walk toward the stairs. It seemed as if every muscle in my body tensed at that exact moment. Mira was having one of her moments of clarity and it was not exactly the best time. I was hoping to escape LaVina's place before she started thinking about it too deeply.

"I don't come into the city much and that is where your domain is," LaVina replied.

"Mira, we should be going. It's getting late and Lily's tired," I interjected, but the nightwalker didn't even look over at me. She just continued to stare at the witch.

"And yet, Danaus knows you. Are you a part of Themis?"

"His silly organization of so-called researchers? Bah! Bunch of utter nonsense," LaVina replied, leaving me straining not to roll my eyes. "The boy came into town last summer looking for you. I pointed him in the right direction."

I moved to grab Mira's shoulder to stop her from lunging at the old witch, but I stopped sharp when Mira simply smiled at LaVina. A broad grin grew across her face and laughter seemed to twinkle in her eyes. She was actually amused by the witch's bold honesty.

"You wanted him to kill me?" Mira inquired.

LaVina gave an unlady-like snort and pushed away from the bench, but didn't take a step toward us. "As if I thought for a second that he would do such a thing."

Mira gave a soft chuckle and shook her head as she turned back toward the stairs. "Watch yourself, witch," Mira said under her breath.

"You too, vampire," LaVina replied.

The car ride back into the city was quiet, with Mira seated in the front seat beside me, while Lily sat in the back. We returned to Mira's house to find Gabriel and his silent companion waiting for us to return.

"Danaus, this is my new bodyguard, Matsui." Mira introduced the Asian man from earlier as we paused in the kitchen beside the breakfast nook.

I nodded to the Asian man and then turned my attention back to the nightwalker. I was going to hold her to her promise to feed tonight, even if it meant that I had to accompany her on her hunt. "What's your plan? Do you need me to go with you?" I demanded.

"No," Mira said, shaking her head. "Gabriel will help me tonight. It's the safest option. I would never do anything to harm him."

"Mira?" Gabriel said, placing his hand on the nightwalker's arm. "What's going on?"

"I need to feed. I need to finally sleep and I can only do that if I drink from a human," Mira said, placing her hand on his. "Will you help me?"

"Happily."

"Mira, what about Lily? I promised that I would protect her as well," I said before the nightwalker could leave the room with her warm meal.

"I guess we're having a sleepover then," Mira said, cock-

ing her head slightly to the side as she looked down at Lily.
The teenager looked skeptical, but wisely kept her comments
to herself. "This is the safest place in the city. Danaus will be
with me during the day, but Gabriel and Matsui will be there
to protect you. They will get you whatever you need during
the day. Tomorrow night, we'll see about getting you some
new clothes and settled in the town house with Danaus."

"What do you mean, 'settled'?" she asked.

Mira arched one eyebrow at the young girl and crossed
her arms over her chest. "Daniel left a message for me. Said
a runaway saw the killer. I'm assuming that you're the runaway. You've now fallen in with us, which means you're here
to stay for a while. As such, you're going to need clothes
and some other basic necessities of life. We'll see to that
tomorrow."

"I'm staying with you and Danaus?" Lily asked, her
mouth falling open in shock.

"You are if you can tolerate being around a pompous
vampire hunter and a bunch of vampires," Mira said.

"That's so awesome!" Lily cried, launching herself at the
nightwalker. I made a grab for her but missed. Lily wrapped
her arms around Mira in a quick hug that caught the nightwalker completely off guard. "You guys are great. I'd love to
stay with you. You're the only ones that don't make me feel
like some freak."

"You're not a freak," I said, putting my hand on her shoulder as she came to stand beside me again.

"Why would we think you're a freak?" Mira asked, her
brow furrowing as she looked from Lily to me.

"I can see auras. Didn't he tell you?" Lily suddenly
seemed to shrink in on herself. She took a step backward,
starting to partially hide herself behind me.

"No, that only makes you more valuable," Mira said, with
a shrug of her shoulders. "Go upstairs and find a room to
sleep in. Danaus will inspect it while I grab a bite."

Frowning, I followed Lily up the stairs. We peeked into

five different bedrooms before she finally chose one with soft yellow paint and a striped comforter on the queen-sized bed. I didn't like where this was going. Mira was making the assumption that we would be keeping Lily indefinitely. While I had to admit that I hadn't made any specific plans for the child after we finally managed to catch Abigail Bradford's killer, I didn't see how it would be possible for us to raise her. I had to return to London and Mira . . . Mira was a nightwalker. She couldn't properly raise a child. In the end, Lily needed to be turned over to the authorities once we were sure that she was safe.

While Lily kicked off her shoes and hopped onto the bed, I walked over and quickly checked the windows, making sure they were shut and properly sealed. All the security measures that lined the interior of this house were properly in place. Mira was right. This house had to be one of the safest places in all of the city.

I shoved my hands into my pockets as I walked back over to the bedroom door. "It looks like there's some pizza down in the kitchen if you're hungry," I said, turning and leaning my shoulder against the wooden doorjamb. "Gabriel will make sure that you have something for breakfast and lunch."

Lily pushed up from where she had been lying in the middle of a pile of pillows and sat in the center of the bed. "You're not going to be around?"

"I haven't seen it yet, but I imagine that Mira sleeps in a sealed room for her protection. I'm either going to be sealed in the room or guarding the door from the outside. I won't be able to hang out tomorrow. I'm sorry."

Lily dropped her eyes to her hands in her lap, causing her dark hair to fall around her face. "These naturi she talked about . . ." she said in a low voice. "They hurt her?"

"Yes," I sighed. "A long time ago, they did some very horrible things to her, things she can never forget. She needs to feel safe. At least for one day."

"And you trust Gabriel and Matsui?" she said, lifting her head to look at me with a sharp, focused gaze.

"I don't know Matsui, but I know Gabriel and I trust him," I admitted, hoping that she wouldn't use this as a new excuse to run. I couldn't be in two places at once and Mira needed me. Unfortunately, if it came down to it, I wasn't sure that Mira had the strength and control she would need to hypnotize Lily into sleeping through the day the same way she had with Shelly when we were in Peru. If I was stuck, I could always see if Tristan could do it. "Gabriel has done a very good job of protecting Mira, and he will do whatever it takes to keep you safe tomorrow."

"All right," Lily said, with a nod. "She got a TV around this place?"

"I have no doubt that she's got one somewhere," I said, fighting back a grin. "Just don't go nosing into Tristan's stuff unless he says you can. I'd rather not worry about a vampire taking a nip at you because you ventured into his territory."

"Are they really territorial?" Lily asked.

"Can be."

"Have you been hunting vampires a long time?"

"Yes, a very long time."

"And now you're friends with them?" she pressed. I had to crush the smile that was trying to push onto my lips, her curiosity was so amusing.

"Not really," I hedged, pushing away from the doorjamb to stand with my legs spread. "We just have to work together on occasions to solve some bigger problems."

"And when it's solved, will you go back to hunting them?" she demanded.

"I don't know. Probably."

She shook her head at me, a frown crinkling in the corners of her eyes.

"It's nothing that you need to worry about," I said, wishing I could take away the concerned look on her face.

"But if you and Mira go back to being enemies, it means that I won't get to see you both. It means that you won't let me hang out with Tristan anymore. If Gabriel's Mira's bodyguard, then I probably won't see him again," she listed as her fears grew.

"It's nothing you need to worry about," I repeated, one corner of my mouth quirking in a smile. "We'll work it all out in a few days. I think we all have bigger things to worry about. Go downstairs and get something to eat. I need to check on Gabriel and Mira."

Lily still had a worried look on her face as she bounced off the bed and thundered down the stairs to the kitchen. I followed behind her at a slower pace, trying not to think about her questions. What were we going to do after this was all over? It was something that I had never had time to think about when I was involved with Mira before. Tomorrow was something we were never sure we were going to have, so such thoughts were never contemplated.

Now I wasn't sure what I was going to do. I knew my time with Themis was done. I had watched Ryan use and destroy people over the long years and had never done anything about it. I could no longer turn a blind eye to his actions. It was time to move on.

And in truth, I didn't think I had learned as much about nightwalkers as I would have hoped while I was at Themis. My short time with Mira had taught me that I was wrong about a lot of things, important things that could have easily decided whether a creature lived or died. It was time for me to move on. I had been with Themis for more than a couple of centuries, the longest I had ever bothered to stay in any one place. I had been a part of that institution before Ryan's arrival and now I felt that it was time for me to leave. I just didn't know where I would go next.

I followed Lily down the stairs and wandered into the kitchen to find Gabriel sitting at the table next to Lily and Matsui. The teenager was already halfway through her first slice of pizza while hammering Matsui with questions about vampires in Japan. Gabriel sat back in his chair, looking a little paler, but none the worse for wear.

"She's expecting you downstairs," Gabriel said when I entered the room. "The door is in the hall, under the staircase."

"Watch over Lily tomorrow. Get her some food," I stated as I reached over her and grabbed a slice of pizza.

"She'll be fine," Gabriel said with a faint smile.

"Ask Tristan's permission before you jump back on his computer and stay out of trouble tomorrow," I said around bites of pizza. I tapped Lily on the top of the head, getting her to look up at me.

"Gotcha," she said with a smile. "See you tomorrow night."

I nodded, grabbing a second slice of pizza before heading back through the house. It wasn't the greatest pizza I had ever had. The crust was a little soggy and there didn't seem to be enough cheese, but at that moment it was perfect. Like sleep, meals were something that were snuck in between catastrophes. Earlier today, I had managed to grab both breakfast and lunch with Lily because I knew that she needed food and it seemed to be an easy way to get her to open up a little bit to me about Abigail's attacker. Unfortunately, once the sun set, all my attention turned to Mira. But then she seemed to fill whatever room she entered, pushing out any other thought or action.

Downstairs looked like a place to have parties, with its full bar off to one side and pool table in the center of the room. A huge flat-panel TV dominated one wall, while the opposite wall had a pair of doors. They looked as if they could lead to a bathroom or storage. However, one of the doors was left open, revealing what appeared to a somewhat austere bedroom. There was a single chair off to the side and a queen-sized bed pushed up against the far wall.

Mira sat on the bed with her back pressed against the concrete wall. Her right leg was bent and the elbow of her left arm was resting on her knee as she held her head in her hand. The nightwalker looked worn, as if time were finally starting to catch up with her.

"Did you see Gabriel?" she asked in a low voice. "Is he okay?"

"He's fine," I confirmed, causing her shoulders to slump even more in relief. "It doesn't look like you took much."

"I didn't think I had, but after what happened with Tristan, I'm just not sure anymore . . ." she said, her voice trailing off.

"How do you feel?"

"Exhausted." She sighed before flashing a faint, wry grin that seemed to disappear before it could fully form on her lips.

"Then go to sleep," I said, as I reached over and pulled the door closed, then paused with my hand still on the doorknob. "What about Tristan?"

"He's got the next room," she replied, pushing off the bed and getting to her feet. "This used to be one big room, but last month I had it divided so that he could have his own room. It has the same security system as this one." Standing on the left side of the door, Mira opened the covering of a small gray box on the wall and typed in an eight-digit code in the keypad. A second later, a metal door slid out of the wall and covered the wood door. Mira smiled at me when I gave a little jump. "The entire room is concrete and steel. Nothing to burn." She frowned. "You're stuck in here now. No getting out until I'm awake again."

"I'll be fine."

"There's no bathroom in here. No food."

"I'll be fine," I repeated. "It's December. The days are shorter now. You'll be awake again soon enough."

Mira smirked over her shoulder as she returned to the bed. Placing her back against the wall, she stared at me as I leaned against the metal door that guarded the entrance into her secret lair. Her eyelids drifted shut after a few seconds, but she quickly jerked her head, her eyes popping open. I chuckled at her.

"Stop fighting it."

"Did you bring any weapons?" she asked.

"I'm always armed," I replied with a smile. Even when I didn't have a blade or a gun on me, I still had the ability to boil blood. "I'm not going anywhere. You're safe."

A small sigh escaped Mira as she slid down the wall and laid her head against the pillow. She closed her eyes and drew in a deep breath. "Thank you," she whispered, and then I felt it. It was as if she were no longer in the room with me. I could no longer sense her. It was still a few hours until sunrise, but exhaustion and Gabriel's blood had finally overcome the strength of Ryan's blood. She was deep in the sleep of the nightwalkers.

Pushing away from the wall, I walked over to the bed. Mira was dressed in a plain, white T-shirt and a pair of black shorts. Her dark red hair was spilled over the white pillowcases like a river of fresh blood. I bent over and picked up her legs, while at the same time, I pulled down the cover on the bed. I placed the blanket over the nightwalker, knowing that she would never feel it. Staring down at her, I realized that for the first time since I had met her, Mira finally looked like she was at peace. I just wished it would last.

Twenty-Eight

There are dreams that jump from one garish image to the next, blurring together memory and fantasy into one heart-wrenching nightmare. And then there are some that are just a mesh of sensations. Sometimes good. Sometimes bad. This one started with a pair of lips. There was no image, no smiling face; just a pair of soft, moist lips kissing my neck. My muscles tensed. I couldn't identify the temptress beyond these gentle lips moving up my neck with amazing care. These full lips paused at my earlobe, parting to draw that sensitive piece of flesh inside where it was caressed by the tip of her tongue.

I deeply exhaled, releasing a breath I hadn't realized I had been holding. My whole body relaxed, muscles unwinding from my shoulders to my calves. At the same time, a weight settled around me, almost hesitantly coming to rest in my lap. She was light like a butterfly and just as skittish. This creature with a gentle kiss and springtime scent would flee if I moved, so I hardly breathed as she dragged her lips up to my jaw.

She paused as she reached my lips, one small hand coming to rest against my chest. The first touch was light and faint, a soft brush of flesh as if testing me. Then again with more pressure, more demanding. She was slow, trying to memorize the contours of my lips before asking for more.

She shifted slightly, pressing closer, her knees coming to hug my hips a little tighter while the hand on my chest slid up to my left shoulder. Her other hand curled around my right biceps, a hint of nails biting flesh. Her lips brushed mine, parting so that the tip of her tongue ran along the seam of my lips. I opened my mouth, welcoming the invasion. This time there was nothing hesitant. Her tongue slipped into my mouth, tasting me.

I kissed her back, wanting to drown in the pleasure she was giving me. I pulled away, capturing her bottom lip in my teeth, tugging lightly. She came back, the kiss growing hotter, rougher. She tasted like nothing I could recall; warm and sweet. I was growing hard. I wanted more, but I was still afraid to move. Any wrong move and she might disappear.

She pressed her body more into mine. Her hands gripped my arm and shoulder a little tighter as she kissed me. A soft sound escaped her, a sweet mix of a sigh and a moan. Dragging her lips back across my jaw, she whispered, "Touch me, Danaus," in a husky voice. I knew that voice. I knew it, but I couldn't conjure up the matching face. It didn't matter. I lifted my hands and came in contact with her bare skin. I felt a shudder run through her and she sighed so softly I wouldn't have heard it if her lips hadn't been by my ear.

I moved my hands higher, over her thighs to her hips. Her skin felt like warm silk, so soft that her satin panties actually felt rough to the touch. I slid my fingers beneath the fabric, cupping her backside and pressing her tighter against my erection. She moaned my name, her lips brushing against my cheek. This time I recognized the voice. It was Mira, but it was wrong. This was a warm, vibrant woman. Mira . . . wasn't. I clung to that thought as I slid my hands up her waist. My thumbs rested on her ribs, just at the edge of her bra. I turned my head, recapturing her lips in a rough kiss that she eagerly returned. My tongue plunged into her mouth, tasting her, memorizing the contours of her mouth.

A sharp pain intruded on the moment, causing me to break off the kiss. I tasted blood. And in that horrible second I realized I wasn't dreaming. My eyes snapped open and in the dim light I found Mira watching me with hooded eyes and soft smile. Knowing now that I had been kissing Mira didn't cure my desire. A part of me had known from the first instant. It was that same part of me that wanted her and had wanted her since the first time I had seen her. She was too human, too beautiful and enticing: most of the time it was easy to forget that she was a vampire. She was just flamboyant, outlandish Mira with her biting sarcasm and fierce determination. But then her dark otherness would bleed through, obliterating all signs of humanity.

But for now, she was Mira—half naked and once again straddling my lap. I kept my eyes locked on her face, resisting the urge to take in the rest of her.

"Good evening, sleepyhead," she purred. The hand on my shoulder slid up to my neck. Her thumb ran along the line of my jaw in a gentle caress. She didn't move beyond that, seeming content to just sit and touch me, returning to the task of memorizing my features. I knew hers. I had burned her lines into my brain each time I watched her sleep. I knew the slope of her nose and the stubborn turn to her chin. I knew the soft, thick texture of her hair, and that she always smelled of lilacs.

"I'm not breakfast," I growled, desperate to remind myself that she was a vampire. A killer. And I was just food to her.

Mira's smile widened a little, but not enough to show her fangs. She had grown very careful about that around me. She leaned closer, rubbing her cheek against mine. I could have stopped her. My hands were still holding her thin waist, but I couldn't move them. My choices were to release her or slide them higher. Since neither was a solution I was currently comfortable with, they remained where they were.

"I wouldn't drink from you if you begged me," she said, her lips grazing my ear.

Had any other vampire said that I would have laughed. Yet when Mira pulled back and I gazed into her eyes, I be-

lieved her. Mira wasn't one to lie. To her, the truth tended to
be more shocking, which she in turn found amusing. Somewhere along the way, I had filled some strange niche in her
existence, become something I think she was still figuring
out. But it had officially moved me out of the food chain.

"What do you want?" I demanded, surprised at how
steady my voice sounded.

"The same thing you want," she replied. She pressed
her hips into me, moving close enough that her breasts now
brushed against my chest. There was no denying my desire—I was rock hard and holding her. I could have pushed
her off the moment I opened my eyes but I hadn't, and it was
taking all my self control not to lean forward that extra inch
and kiss her. Everything within me screamed for another
taste of her mouth.

Instead I did the only thing I thought would snap us both
out of this. "Is this how you pay everyone who protects
you?"

Mira leaned forward and brushed her lips against mine as
she spoke. "My relationship with Gabriel has nothing to do
with his job as my guardian."

"But you don't love him," I said, desperate to keep her
talking.

Mira pulled back suddenly and looked at me. Her smooth
brow furrowed and she cocked her head to the side in stunned
puzzlement. I was grasping at straws and we both knew it.

"Can you look me in the eye and tell me that you've loved
every woman that you've been with?" There was no mocking in her voice, just gentle amusement.

There had been more than one occasion where I had lied
to her, but even I couldn't convincingly lie about this. While
there had not been as many women as one would expect in
my 1,800-year lifespan, there had been enough. And not one
of them I would be as bold as to describe using the word
"love." To make matters worse, there had been more than
one that I been less emotionally involved with than Mira.

But I didn't have to say anything. My silence was damning enough. She leaned back into me, molding her lean body against mine. Her lips returned to mine, the tip of her tongue running along my bottom lip, entreating entrance. My hands tightened on her waist and I somehow managed to turn my head. Undaunted, she kissed my cheek, drawing a trail back down to my ear.

"Please, Danaus, touch me," she said. Her voice was like velvet, rubbing against every part of my body that she touched. "I need you."

I was drowning and with my last breath I finally managed to cut her. "Is this how you've acquired all your lovers? With begging?"

For an instant, I felt her whole body stiffen and then there was the shock of cold air where her warm body had been a second ago. I turned my head to look at her, but she was moving too fast. All I felt was Mira grab the front of my shirt and then I was flying through the air. Out of sheer luck, I hit the bed and bounced once. I'm sure she would have preferred it if I had gone through the concrete wall. I jerked into a sitting position, but the door had already been thrown open and she was gone.

I fell back against the bed, covering my face with my hands. I had regretted the words the second they left my lips. I hadn't meant it. I was drowning and desperate. If I had any real self-control, I would have pushed her away and left. I cursed Mira for pushing me and I cursed myself for wanting her more than air.

I could make excuses like she caught me off guard or that I was half asleep, or even that she got what she asked for, but it was a lie. I wanted her. I'd wanted her since our first encounter months ago in the abandoned house. Regardless of how lifeless she was during the day, at night she was more vibrant and alive than any other creature that I had ever met. She had no regrets about who or what she was. And when she was near, I wanted to wrap myself up in her energy. Her cool powers surrounded me, calming the anger and frustration that seemed to perpetually burn within me.

Reluctant, I pushed to my feet and trudged up the stairs to the first floor. I couldn't take the words back and nothing I could say would erase the pain. I walked through the rooms, and had finally settled in a chair in the living room when I heard the shower running on the second floor. Tristan wandered in with Lily following close on his heels. Both had matching expressions of concern and confusion.

"Mira said we are to meet her at the town house," Tristan announced when he was standing in front of me.

"I'm waiting for Mira. Will you take Lily to the town house?" I asked. I needed to talk to Mira. I needed to find some way to soothe her ego and feelings. Of course, I hadn't a clue as to how I was going to accomplish that mean feat, but I had to try.

Lily stepped around Tristan to come stand next to me. She crossed her arms over her chest and frowned down at me. "What did you do?" she demanded. I didn't need to know how she knew that this was my fault, though I wasn't willing to take all the blame for this matter. Maybe it was a female thing. They could sense when another of their kind had been slighted by a man.

"Nothing. It's a personal matter that I would rather handle privately," I said sharply, glaring up at her. A teenager didn't need to be involved in my personal life.

I clenched my eyes shut and gritted my teeth at that very thought. Mira wasn't a part of my personal life. She, like all other nightwalkers, was business. Nightwalkers were a part of my professional life, as I was a hunter. Or at least, I had been at one time. Now I didn't know what the hell was going on. Six months ago, I had hunted and killed nightwalkers with ease and a complete lack of remorse. Tonight, I'd kissed Mira and a part of me knew I would do it again if she gave me half a chance. I craved her like a vampire craved blood. She sustained me and gave me direction in a world that was growing more foreign to me with each passing night.

"I'll take her to the town house," Tristan confirmed, laying a hand on the teenager's stiff shoulder. "Mira should be down in a few minutes." With a little pressure, Tristan directed Lily away from me and back toward the kitchen. She didn't say anything as she walked away, content to just shake her head at me.

Mira reappeared downstairs thirty minutes later, but the sight of her was like a knife twisting in my chest. She was dressed in her usual black, but it was different. Instead of her typical tight-fitting leather and flashes of skin, she wore a pair of long cotton pants and a matching turtleneck sweater. Over that was a black leather jacket that fell to her thighs and a pair of soft leather gloves. In fact, only her face was visible and even that was in the shadow of the molten waves of her hair and a pair of large dark sunglasses. Mira was hiding not only from me, but also from the eyes of the world.

"Meet me back at the town house in an hour," she said then left, her heels clicking ominously across the hardwood floor before she slammed the front door shut. There had been no chance to apologize. No opportunity to offer up a lame explanation.

I knew where she was going. Feeding was the only thing at this point that would drown out the anger, pain, and humiliation. Normally, she wouldn't have to feed so soon after feasting on both Ryan and Gabriel the previous night, but I had left her with no other option. She would hunt tonight and it was my fault.

Flopping down in the chair I had been seated in only moments ago, I put my elbows on my knees and dropped my head into my hands. What a fucking mess!

"Women." A heavy voice sighed from above me. "Who understands them?"

I jerked upright, pushing out of the chair while I reached for the knife that should have been hanging at my side but was nowhere to be found. I had left it in the car last night so that I wouldn't upset Mira when I went in to initially speak to her. A short bald man with a potbelly stood before me in a rumpled white button-up shirt and wrinkled slacks. His hands were shoved into the pockets of his trousers and he shook his head at me as the corners of his mouth curled into a wicked grin. He didn't look particularly threatening. In fact, he looked downright pathetic with his patchy day's growth on his jaw and bleary, red-rimmed eyes. But he was also standing in the home of one of the most powerful night-walkers within the region and neither Mira nor I had heard him enter.

"Who the hell are you? What are you doing here?" I demanded, wishing I could back up a step, but the backs of my legs were already against the chair I had been sitting in. The living room was crowded with comfortable furniture, making this a poor choice of locations for a fight.

"I'm here to see you, Danaus," he announced. "Surely you've been expecting me."

"I have no idea who you are." As I spoke, I sent my powers out from my body with the intent of scanning him.

"But you do!" He took a step closer. "We spoke last night."

My brow furrowed. Last night, I met with Barrett, Gregor, and Nate. I distinctly remembered what each man looked like. I could recall the nightwalkers I had seen in the Dark Room. I had never seen this man before.

"No," I said at last after racking my brain.

"We spoke in the park after the Fire Starter left you," he said. A column of white mist flowered out of the man to his left and reformed into a slightly translucent image of the naturi I had seen last night. At the same time, the bald man blinked and looked slowly around as if he were coming out of a trance. The creature gave a hollow-sounding chuckle before flowing back into the man.

"Now you remember me," the man snickered, his brown eyes once again lit by a grim red light. "I'm sorry it has taken so long for us to have these moments together, but I have to admit that it's taken me a number of years to accumulate enough energy to push back into this world. I mean, prior to the few pathetic souls I've encountered in this wretched city, the last human I spoke to was your lovely mother."

"No," I whispered. I tried to take a step backward but hit the chair behind me and partially fell into it. I caught myself on the arm of the chair with my right hand.

"That's right," the man said. "Have a seat. We have a lot to talk about." He pointed at me and a burst of energy hit my left shoulder, knocking me into the chair. I watched as the creature slid over and settled on the sofa across from me. He sighed as he settled back against the cushions and placed his right foot on his left knee.

"Bori," I growled.

"Ahh . . . I didn't think we'd really need to state the obvious, but yes. Or rather, I'm a bori that is temporarily inhabiting this rather undesirable body, but then one does not complain about one's mode of transportation when one is desperate." The man folded his hands over his large stomach and smiled at me. "I am rather proud of how you've turned out. I've always considered myself your godfather of sorts, watching over you from a distance."

"You're the one that made the deal with my mother," I snarled as my too-slow brain finally started to function. He was the one that had held me damned in the afterlife. Pushing off the arms of the chair, I launched myself at the man, ready to wrap my hands around his meaty neck and choke the life out of him. I didn't think it would succeed in killing the bori, but then I wasn't thinking any longer. I just wanted the creature that had ruined my life to be gone from this earth permanently.

The bori simply chuckled as he raised his hand again. Another burst of energy hit me square in the chest, knocking me back into the chair.

"I appreciate your enthusiasm, but you really must stay seated," he said. "We're not done talking. Besides, you can't kill me. We bori cannot be destroyed."

I didn't believe him. Anything that lived could be killed, but I knew that I wouldn't be able to do it with my bare hands, considering that it seemed to be nothing more than a white mist. I also couldn't kill it with my powers, as I had already proven last night. If anything, I needed Mira, but then bori had the ability to control nightwalkers, as I had seen in Spain. I was trapped and there didn't seem to be any escape for me or the rest of Savannah.

"It really is a shame that you have to see me this way," Gaizka continued when I finally crossed my arms over my chest and appeared as if I was willing to remain seated in the chair and listen to his speech. "For your mother, I appeared as a strong Roman warrior. Almost god-like in stature. She really seemed impressed with me."

"In a body like that, why wouldn't she agree to give away the soul of her unborn child?" I snidely replied, barely able to unclench my teeth so I could speak.

The creature across from me threw back his head and laughed deeply. "Your dear mother was so set in her desire for revenge, nothing could have deterred her from her course. I could have appeared as an old crone and she would have still sold you to me. Or at the very least tried to."

"So in exchange for a little power, you got my soul," I sneered.

"You make it sound as if you got the short end of the stick in this deal," Gaizka said, slamming his right foot down on the floor. The bori wearing the large man shot across the room with more speed than I thought possible and grabbed me around the throat. His beefy hands crushed my windpipe, cutting off all air for a second before he threw me across the room. I slammed into a picture hanging on one wall, the glass splintering before my body and the picture crashed to the floor.

"I gave you amazing strength and powers. I extended your life more than a hundredfold. You're a god among men! And through all these years I've asked for nothing from you," Gaizka shouted.

"I never asked for any of this!" I shouted back at him, pushing to my knees. "I never wanted to be an outcast among humanity, to feel as if my very soul were damned to hell because my mother made a deal with a monster."

The creature again darted across the short distance that separated us. He kicked me in the ribs, breaking two as I fell back against the wall with a heavy grunt. "It was a gift," he bit out. "But we all know there's a price for everything in this world. It's time to pay the piper, as the saying goes."

"I don't owe you anything!" I snarled as my thoughts rose above the pain that beat at me. This thing was faster than any nightwalker I had encountered. I could try to use my power, but it would mean killing another innocent human being, and even then I wouldn't be rid of Gaizka's presence. It would still be in the house with me, able to finally crush me if it decided I wasn't worth the effort any longer.

"You owe me for the life you've lived!" he screamed. This time the back of his fist crashed into my jaw, snapping my head around before I could dodge the blow. I wasn't fast enough. I wasn't strong enough. I didn't have enough magical skill to defeat him.

"What do you want?" I growled, rubbing my jaw as I sat against the wall. Glass crunched against my back from the broken picture that was behind me.

"Like the naturi, I want out of my gilded cage," he said, flashing an evil grin at me that was reminiscent of the one I had seen on the face of the fake naturi.

"You are out," I snapped, motioning with my right hand toward the human body that he now inhabited.

"No, this is just temporary," he said, his smile fading into a frown. "I'm nearly out of the energy you and that wonderful nightwalker have sent my way. I need more, a lot more, if I'm going to permanently break free of my bonds and re-enter this world."

"Why would I ever send you more energy?" I demanded.

"Because you can't help yourself," he replied with a wide grin. "You've done it on numerous occasions already and I have no doubt that you'll do it again."

"What are you talking about?" I said, shaking my head

at his nonsense. I had never sent him any kind of energy. I would never willingly do such a thing.

"Come now, my boy," Gaizka chuckled. "You've been so helpful ever since you fashioned an alliance with the Fire Starter. I'll admit that creature has got me more than a little stumped as to her origin, but in the end it doesn't matter. You and she are the perfect match. I had always wondered how you would be able to finally help me, but you've found a way!"

"I've never helped you!" I shouted, resisting the urge to push to my feet. The bori seemed content to keep me on the floor at his feet.

"But you have," he whispered. Leaning down, he grabbed a fistful of my hair and jerked my head back so that I was forced to look him in the eye. I could now smell the horrid scent of rotting flesh that hung on him like a cologne. The bori inside of the human was slowly killing him, and he wouldn't be able to inhabit his current body for much longer.

"Whenever you combine your power with the nightwalker and kill naturi, you're sending their souls directly to me," he whispered in my ear before releasing my hair. "You're feeding me with the sweetest power that you could possibly find. I'm feasting off my enemy and they are extending my own powers."

I sat dumbfounded, staring straight ahead as he returned to his seat on the sofa, chuckling. In London, Mira and I had combined our powers for the first time and annihilated the horde of naturi that had come to destroy us. We thought we had destroyed their souls, but we had been wrong. Because of my link to this bori, we had sent the energy directly to Gaizka to feed off of. He had found a way to escape from his prison using the energy we had been sending him.

And then everything seemed to finally fit into place. "You killed Abigail Bradford," I murmured. I blinked a couple times, my gaze finally focusing on the bori that sat across from me. "You killed her, attempting to frame the naturi. You have been torturing Mira with images of Nerian. You've been pushing us to go after the naturi and wipe them out so that we'll send the energy to you."

"You've always been such a bright boy," Gaizka proudly crowed. "I knew you'd figure it out eventually, but I had to take a chance on the idea that you'd follow the breadcrumbs back to the naturi. Unfortunately, with the addition of that little girl, you've been led astray from the path that I've laid out for you. And I'm about out of time."

"I won't help you," I snapped, but he waved me off, ignoring my statement.

"I thank you for all your help, but you're not done just quite yet," Gaizka taunted. "You see, I'm running a bit low and I would really like to remain here. It's a nice place to stay and with the rest of my brethren still locked away, Earth is distinctly less crowded."

Horror filled my frame, tightening my muscles. A bori running loose in the world, able to feed off the billions of souls that filled the landscape with no other bori to compete with would quickly become a god. One would have no way of stopping it. "I won't help you," I repeated.

"I don't believe you're going to have a choice in this matter," Gaizka said, leaning forward on the sofa so that he could rest his forearms on his knees. "I will give you one last night to make some arrangements with the nightwalker. That will give you enough time to locate and destroy some naturi for me. If you fail to do that, tomorrow night I will stand on River Street and kill every human I see. But first, I will hunt down and slowly kill that little girl that you have so sweetly promised to protect."

"You can't!" I shouted, coming off the floor. This time, he didn't push me back down, but rose so that he was looking up at me from bloodshot eyes.

"I can and I will," he threatened, clenching his teeth. "Abigail Bradford was just a taste of what I am capable of. If I have to return to my cage, then I will destroy half of this city before I go. The nightwalkers will be exposed to the world. There will be no more hiding. They will become hunted by every creature on the face of the Earth. With that much bloodshed, you and the nightwalker will have no choice but to use your unique ability in order to survive. And then I will return regardless of your wishes. Do it my way, and the only ones hurt are the naturi."

"We won't do it," I said stubbornly. Mira and I wouldn't willingly help this creature that was potentially an even greater threat than the naturi could dream of being.

"You forget, you will have no choice but to help me. Your only choice lies in whether you will do it the hard way or the easy way. Think about it, Danaus, and then abide by my wishes. Kill the naturi. It will be easier for everyone."

Gaizka then exited the body of the bald man. He hovered in the air as a column of thick white mist before finally dissipating. The man blinked again and swayed on his feet as he shook his head to clear it from the fog that enveloped his thoughts.

"Where am I?" he said in a low, scratchy voice that was the polar opposite from the smooth, easy tones Gaizka had spoken in.

"You're in hell," I muttered, letting my eyes fall shut. We were all in the lower regions of hell.

Twenty-Nine

I hesitated outside of the town house, my hand on the doorknob, wondering how I was going to tell Mira that we were not only faced with a bori, but that it also planned to destroy her home and expose her. And in truth, I wasn't sure how we could actually succeed in destroying this enemy. I couldn't use my powers against it and I doubted Mira's fire would make much of an impact on a creature that seemed to be pure spirit. Sure, we could destroy the body that it inhabited, but what would stop it from grabbing another human?

Before he passed out at Mira's house, the man who had been briefly possessed spoke of encountering an angel with enormous white shining wings. Somehow the bori had convinced him that an angel needed access to his soul, which probably gave Gaizka access to the man's body for possession. I delivered the bald man to the nearest hospital prior to driving to the town house. From his gray pallor and trembling, I didn't think his odds of surviving the night were that good.

With a sigh, I opened the door and stepped into the house. Lily's laughter hit me first as it drifted down the hall from the living room. I followed the sound to find the teenager looking over Mira's shoulder as the nightwalker sat on the sofa holding something between both of her hands.

Lily turned at the sound of my footsteps, flashing me a broad smile. "Danaus!" she cried as she hooked a stray length of brown hair behind her left ear. "Look at what Mira bought me!"

Taking a step closer, I peered over Mira's shoulder to find her holding a small electronic device with a flashing movie screen. "What is it?" I asked.

"It's a PSP," Lily said in a voice that clearly indicated that I should have recognized such a thing. "It's a handheld gaming system," she continued when I just looked blankly at her.

"Danaus prefers to live in the Dark Ages," Mira coldly said, as she turned off the device and handed it back to Lily.

"I have a cell phone," I countered.

"Yeah, but do you know how to use it?" Mira glanced over her shoulder at me, one corner of her mouth turning higher in a smirk. She had me there and we both knew it. James had had to program all the necessary phone numbers into the phone and teach me how to use its most basic functions. Technology and I didn't always get along.

"Mira should have used her money to buy you some new clothes instead of toys," I criticized, trying to redirect the conversation away from me.

"But she did! Look!" Lily commanded. She took a step away from the sofa and threw out her arms before spinning around in place. She had on a pair of worn-looking jeans and a faded T-shirt over a black turtleneck sweater.

"They don't look new."

Lily gave a little snort.

"It's the style now," Mira informed me. "It's called distressed."

"Sounds like a rip-off to me," I muttered. Mira simply shrugged her shoulders as if to say "What did it matter?" And in truth, it didn't. Lily was happy.

"I only had time to pick up a couple outfits," Mira said. "I thought we could go shopping tonight for some more clothes and essentials."

It was a peace offering. Between the distinct pallor to her

cheeks and the fact that she had shopped for Lily, I knew the nightwalker had not hunted tonight. She had turned her focus to Lily, using the child as a way of distracting herself from the pain I had caused. I wasn't sure if she had actually forgiven me, but she was at least willing to call a truce.

At that moment, nothing sounded more appealing than trailing after Mira and Lily as they went on an intense shopping expedition, where we would encounter nothing more stressful than choosing between which pair of shoes to buy. No naturi. No bori. No coven and no Ryan. We could even stop and have a cozy dinner together at a restaurant. A normal night. A normal life.

"We can't tonight," I said, tearing my eyes from Lily's disappointed expression to Mira's look of concern. "Mira and I have some things that we need to take care of."

"It's that thing, isn't it?" Lily demanded, clutching her small gaming system to her chest as if I were threatening to take it away from her. "The monster I saw that killed that girl."

"Lily, would you please go upstairs and play with your new . . . PSP?" I asked. "I would like to speak to Mira."

"Hey, I saw this bastard first!" she said, raising her voice. "I should be involved in this. You can't push me out."

"Watch your language," I calmly replied, not allowing myself to be swayed by her outburst. Lily had spent most of her life on the streets. She had experienced enough horrible things in her short existence. She didn't need to be exposed to our world any more than she already had.

"No! I'm not going anywhere."

Mira rose from the sofa in the boneless fashion that seemed to be unique to nightwalkers. She turned around and stared down at the teenager coldly. "Lily, go upstairs," she said in a low, even voice. For a moment, I thought Mira was using her ability to control the girl's mind, but Lily soon proved me wrong.

"This is bullshit!" the teenager shouted, stomping her foot. "I should be involved."

"I promised that I would protect you," I countered. "This is me protecting you. You will go upstairs. Mira and I will take care of it."

Lily glared at Mira and me, then she whipped her gaze over to Tristan, sitting quietly in a chair in the corner with his own handheld gaming system. I flinched at the sight of him. My focus had been so trained on Mira and Lily that I hadn't even noticed him in the room. I was seriously losing my touch. Such a slipup would get me killed.

"Can Tristan come up with me?" she asked.

"Tristan is staying down here with us," Mira replied, surprising me. In most cases, she had not felt compelled to include the young nightwalker in our discussions. I had thought it was her decision to keep him protected against the growing threats in our world. Maybe she had realized that protecting was not helping him grow stronger. He wasn't learning how to protect himself, which had always been her grand plan when it came to her blood brother.

Lily let out a growl before she spun on her heel and stomped her way up the stairs to the second floor. Along the way, she muttered every curse word she knew while complaining about our combined stupidity. It was all I could do not to laugh.

"She reminds me of you," I murmured, looking over at Mira.

The nightwalker arched one brow at me as a slight smile lifted her full lips. "I can curse better." The smile fell from her face almost as quickly as it had formed as she turned serious again. "You saw it, didn't you?"

I let my eyes close as my mind replayed the vision of the mist pouring out of the man. This was the creature that had damned my soul for all eternity. "Yes, it appeared at your house. I—I don't know how we're going to fight it."

"What do you mean?" Tristan asked, pushing to his feet.

I turned my gaze from Tristan to Mira, who was intently watching me. "Have you ever encountered a bori?"

"No, but it's all spirit, isn't it?" she said, with a shake of her head.

"How did you know?" I demanded.

Mira sat down on the edge of the coffee table so that she could easily look at both Tristan and me. "With the naturi escaping from their prison, I started to think that maybe the cage that held the bori could be diminishing as well. Time erodes all things, right? So, before meeting up with Ryan, I flew to Venice and spoke to Jabari. He loaned me several journals regarding the bori. They included a description of the creature."

"The bori are the guardians of the soul?" Tristan asked.

"And our creators," Mira added, turning her head to look over at him. "Nightwalkers were created by the bori centuries ago to fight in the wars against the naturi. It's why we're dependent upon soul magic for our survival."

"What are they?" Tristan said, shaking his head. "You said it's all spirit. What did you mean?"

"A bori appears to be pure soul magic," I replied. "I don't think it has a body of its own. It can shapeshift into different forms, but it's at its physical strongest when it possesses the body of another creature. When Gaizka appeared at Mira's, it possessed the body of this middle-aged man."

"Gaizka?" Mira repeated.

"Yes, Gaizka. The part owner of my soul."

"Oh," she whispered, her shoulders slumping.

"What?" Tristan gasped, taking a step toward me.

"A bori owns part of my soul," I admitted. Normally, I would never have uttered such a thing aloud, and never to a nightwalker, but oddly enough, I trusted Tristan because Mira trusted him. I knew the young nightwalker would never reveal my secret to the world, even under threat of death.

"Oh," he murmured, sitting back down in his chair. "I guess that explains your . . . abilities."

"When you saw it tonight, what did it want?" Mira asked, drawing us back to the problem at hand.

"It wants us to go back to killing naturi," I replied.

Mira chuckled softly, flashing a brilliant smile up at me. "You make that sound like such a horrible thing."

"It is!" I snapped. "When we combine our powers and destroy the naturi, we're not destroying their souls like we thought. We're directly feeding Gaizka, making it stronger. It's how it managed to escape in the first place."

"Shit," Mira hissed, shoving both her hands through her hair, pushing it away from her face as she stared down at the floor. "Danaus, we weren't killing them that way because it was particularly fun. It was because we had no other choice. That weapon can't be stripped away now."

Coming around to the front of the sofa, I sat down on the arm. "But it has been. We can't give Gaizka any more power. We can't risk setting it loose in a world where it will have no other competition against other bori. I'm not sure exactly how they feed, but in a world filled with humans, getting energy from their souls can't be that hard. Gaizka would become a god among men."

"And we have enough to worry about with Aurora and the rest of the naturi running loose," Mira finished. The nightwalker drew in a deep breath and slowly released it, letting her shoulder slump. "All right. It's agreed. We don't combine our powers any more. The risk is too great, now that we understand what we're doing."

"Then you're in the clear," Tristan said, drawing our combined gaze over to him as he balanced on the edge of his chair. "If it's not getting any more power from you two, then it can't be a threat here."

"But it's got enough strength to create one more massacre and it plans to start tomorrow night if we don't kill the naturi soon," I argued. Looking down at my hands, I remembered the bori's threat. "Gaizka stated that if we don't kill naturi, it's going to start killing tourists on River Street tomorrow night. It will create a massacre large enough to shine a light on the nightwalker community, risking total exposure. It plans to start a war if it doesn't get freed. Gaizka believes that if we're forced into a war, we'll have no choice but to use our powers and it'll be freed regardless of our attempts to stop it now. But first, the bori said it will come after Lily before wreaking chaos on Savannah."

"No," Mira gasped.

"I should never have taken her from the police station," I muttered, mostly talking to myself. "It only succeeded in drawing more attention to her. If I hadn't promised to protect her, Gaizka might have finally lost interest in her. Whatever we try to protect is destroyed."

"That's not true," Tristan said firmly, drawing my eyes back over to him as he rose to his feet. "Both you and Mira have protected me on more than one occasion and I've survived. Lily will too."

"Then we fight it. We go looking for it tonight before it can destroy my city," Mira said, pushing to her feet. "We'll kill it tonight."

"How?"

"I don't know, but we'll find a way. We can go back to my place and search through the journals. Maybe there's something in there that will tell us how to send it back to its cage," Mira suggested. She was grasping at straws, desperate for anything that might protect that young girl who was currently pouting upstairs.

"We don't have time for that," I snapped, shoving to my feet so that I was standing in front of her. "Besides, I don't think we can beat it. I think it can control any nightwalker that it runs across the same way that the animal clan naturi can control the shifters. You wouldn't be able to stop it no matter how hard you tried. It's stronger and faster than anything I've ever encountered. It tossed me around like a rag doll."

"Then we'll get someone stronger."

"Who? The only people I know who are stronger than me are nightwalkers, and they are helpless against the thing.

The only natural predators the bori have are the naturi, and I don't know of any naturi that would help us take out Gaizka."

Mira turned and paced away from me, her hands fisting in her hair in frustration. We were trapped. We had nowhere to turn. "Aurora could beat it," Mira murmured.

"I don't know. You nearly beat her," Tristan said softly.

"Under very special circumstances," Mira pointed out quickly.

"I don't think Aurora would be willing to help us even if it means taking out a bori. Besides, we haven't a clue as to where we can find her," I reminded her.

"I-I don't know what to do," she stammered, shaking her head as she flopped down in her chair. "If this were any other problem, I would bring it before the coven. Let them handle it."

"But you're on the coven now and the nightwalkers can't fight the bori," I said. Frowning, I looked back over at Mira, who was staring at the ground. I didn't want to utter aloud the next few words, but I had no choice. It would break Mira's heart, particularly since her memories of Calla had been running so fresh in her mind during the past few days. "Lily can't stay here," I forced myself to say, finally.

"I know," Mira whispered. "It's not safe, not if it comes to fighting a bori that's going to use her as a bargaining chip. I was thinking that I could send her out to Alex in Portland for a few days, just until we get Gaizka taken care of."

Something in my chest tightened and I fought the urge to lay my hand on her shoulder. "I . . ." I started and then paused, trying to find the words. "I was thinking of something more permanent."

Mira jumped to her feet and paced away from me before spinning sharply on her heel to face me. Several feet of charged air separated us. We were squared off in the small living room and I just hoped that we wouldn't come to blows.

"What are you talking about?" she demanded, struggling to keep her voice from rising.

"I know you like Lily, Mira, but you can't raise her," I said calmly.

"You don't think I'm capable of raising a child?" she said, pointing toward her chest as she took a step forward. "I've already had one child and she was just fine under my care before I was taken. How could you possibly know what it takes to raise a child?"

I flinched. "I'm sure you could have raised a child just fine while you were human, but you're not any longer, Mira. You're a vampire. A nightwalker. You're limited in what you can do for her."

"I would be just fine!"

"What if she needed you during the day while she was at school?" I quickly countered, trying to leave her with nowhere she could run with her argument. "What if she was sick with a fever? What would you do? Nothing. There's nothing you could do to help her."

"I've got Gabriel. He could help," she said.

"You're going to turn your bodyguard into a nanny? How do you think he would feel about that?"

Mira growled at me as she paced a few feet away, but then quickly turned back to me. "Then I'll hire an actual nanny for a few years. Just to have someone around during the daylight hours."

"And what about Jabari? And the coven? What if they come calling? Don't you think she'll become a target? Isn't it enough that Tristan is in danger because of his association with you?"

"Don't drag me into this!" Tristan said, pointing at me. "I chose to be with Mira."

I ignored the young nightwalker's outburst and pressed on. "He can at least take care of himself against other nightwalkers. Lily can't."

"Then what do you propose?" Mira demanded, crossing

her arms over her chest as she closed herself off from me as I continued my attack. "Stick her with another so-called normal family? We've seen how well that works. She feels like an outcast, when she's really a precious gift. We see that. We understand her. We stick her with a normal human family and she's either going to feel like a freak when she reveals her gift, or worse, she's going to hide it from the world and never develop her talents."

"You're right in that we can't send her to a regular human family," I agreed, stunning Mira into silence. "She needs to be with people who will appreciate her gift and help her to expand her talents."

"What do you have in mind?" Mira slowly inquired, some of the tension slipping from her arms.

"Themis."

"Are you out of your mind?" Mira screamed, finally losing her hold on her temper. "You're taking her away from me so you can raise her with Ryan. Neither one of you knows anything about children. She would be a mess when you two were done with her."

"Do you consider James a mess?" I countered.

"What are you talking about?" Mira demanded, confused.

"Lily wouldn't be the first child Themis has taken in. While it's rare, it has happened in the past. James's parents were killed when he was only eight years old. Both were werewolves. They had been killed by a farmer who thought they were after his sheep one night. Unsure of whether James actually carried the shape-shifting gene, Themis offered to take him in and raise him in the event that he did grow up to be a lycanthrope."

"Why didn't his pack take him in?" Mira inquired.

Shoving my hands in the pockets of my pants, I shrugged my shoulders. "James's parents didn't belong to a pack. There are very few packs in the U.K. and none where James lived."

"Since I'm unfit to raise Lily, you plan to take her back to Themis so you can raise her among the researchers."

"I'm not going back to Themis."

A part of me had known for a while now that I wouldn't be going back, but actually saying the words out loud seemed to only solidify the idea, leaving me with no opportunity to change my mind. I maintained my usual outward calm, but on the inside my stomach was twisting into knots. I had no place to go, no place to call home after the long centuries with Themis. Anyone that I had once called a friend was now dead. I was truly alone in this world, beyond the people I called my enemies.

Tristan slowly returned to his chair as Mira's mouth hung open in shape of a perfect oval for a second before she found her voice again.

"What do you mean, you're not going back?" she said in a voice that barely carried across the room.

"It's time I left," I admitted. "I've known it was coming, but I always needed a reason. After what happened last night with Ryan, I can't go back to that place. I don't agree with his methods and I'm worried about his plans."

"So you want to send Lily into his clutches?" Mira demanded incredulously.

I knew it sounded crazy, but I had no doubt that my logic was sound. "It's the safest place I can think of. The naturi attacked Themis only when we were around. Ryan is a powerful warlock, well known in our respective communities. No one will cross him. With Themis, she will be out of the view of the coven."

"But she'll be with Ryan—the one man you trust the least on the face of the Earth," Mira quickly pointed out.

"I don't trust him, but I do know him very well," I admitted. I walked over and took Mira's arms in both of my hands. "The warlock needs you as an ally, not an enemy. If he's to get you on his side, he'll not touch a hair on Lily's head. In fact, he will work very hard to see that she's protected and happy. He will teach her to use her gift. He will see to it that she gets an excellent education and that she also learns about our world so that she is equipped to handle nightwalkers, lycanthropes, warlocks, naturi, and anything else the world decides to throw at her."

"I don't know," Mira hedged, looking down at my hands.

"Themis can offer her a somewhat normal life," I pressed. "We can't do that, no matter how hard we try."

I don't want to give her up, Mira whispered in my mind. I could feel the sorrow welling up within her. Lily had been her second chance at having a child, a second chance at living, and I was stealing that away from her. But then, I was losing her too.

I know. Neither do I, I replied as I leaned in and pressed a kiss to her temple. "We have to do what's best for her," I said out loud as I stepped away.

"Then let me stay!" Lily shouted as she burst into the room.

I stepped away from Mira and turned in time to see the teenager run across the room and grab my left arm. I could only guess that she had been listening from the stairs. After she had gone upstairs, I hadn't bothered to check to make sure that she stayed up there. Like I had told Mira, we weren't equipped to handle a child. A real parent would have checked to make sure they were alone when they started to discuss the fate of the child.

"We have to do what's best for you," I explained. "It's too dangerous for you to remain here. That creature that you saw, the bori, it plans to kill you if Mira and I don't do as it wishes. We have to send you somewhere you will be safe."

"I want to stay!" she pressed.

"It's too dangerous. We won't risk your life," Mira said, laying her hand on the girl's slim shoulder.

"Fine. Send me away, but let me come back once it's safe," she replied. "I like being here with you and Danaus and Tristan. You treat me like I'm normal."

"There is no such thing as safe when you are with Danaus and me. We can't risk your life," Mira said in a soft voice.

"The people that you are going to will treat you like you are normal," I stated. "Themis is a research facility that studies people like Mira and Tristan. There are others there that have abilities similar to yours. They will help you learn to strengthen your skills, something neither Mira nor I can teach you to do. At Themis, you will grow stronger. If you stay with Mira and me, you will only get hurt."

Lily pressed her lips into a firm, unyielding line as she looked from me to Mira. "Will I ever see you again?"

Mira gave a deep laugh that seemed to be half relief and half heartache as she threw her arms around Lily's shoulders and pulled her into a hug. "You'll see us again. Holidays. Summer break. Think of Themis as going away to school. You'll see us as often as possible, I promise."

Lily looked over at me for confirmation and I nodded, forcing a smile on my lips. I still didn't know where I was going to be after I left Themis, but I would do whatever I could to keep Lily in my life for just a few more years.

"Mira, could you call Ryan? We need to get her on a plane tonight," I said, dragging us back to the task at hand now that Lily was no longer fighting us.

"I'm leaving tonight? I—I don't have many clothes. Where is Themis?" she demanded, panic starting to creep inside of her voice.

"Themis is outside of London," Tristan interjected, pushing to his feet again. "If Mira can spare me, I'll accompany you to Themis. I've been there before. I can introduce you to some of the people and help you get settled."

"Please, Mira!" Lily pleaded, grabbing the Fire Starter's hand. "I can't leave the country alone. I've never even been on a plane before."

"That's fine with me." Mira nodded, giving Lily's hand a squeeze. "Gabriel, Matsui, and Tristan will accompany you. They will see that you are safely settled, and if there are any problems, they will bring you straight back to Savannah."

Mira slowly allowed Lily's hands to slide from hers before she walked out of the room and headed for her office so she could make a round of phone calls to settle things with Ryan, arrange the flight, and contact Gabriel.

Lily looked up at me as she stood in the center of the room, suddenly looking very alone. "This is for the best," I repeated.

The girl nodded, forcing a smile onto her lips though it didn't reach her eyes. "I've seen what vampires and werewolves are capable of. I heard about what that creature did to the girl. I know your world is dangerous. I still want to stay, but I know it's not safe. I know that this is for the best."

A smile finally lifted the corners of my own mouth. At least she believed me. Unfortunately, I was still trying to convince myself that this was all for the best. It just didn't feel like it.

Thirty

"I still don't see how she's going to be able to help us," Mira said for the third time since getting in the car. Yet, regardless of her doubts, the nightwalker pulled the flashy BMW into LaVina's long gravel driveway.

"When I met her this past summer, she already knew about the naturi. It stands to reason that she's heard of the bori," I patiently repeated for the third time. "We need to find out how to send this thing back to its cage and we don't have time to track down Jabari."

Mira gave a little snort as she slowed the car to a stop and threw it into park. "I doubt the Ancient would know," she replied. "I've read the journals. There's no mention of how the cage was formed."

Besides, I doubted Jabari would be willing to help us. I suspected the coven member would just snatch up Mira and disappear rather than risk her to the bori. He had to protect his interests now that he wielded controlling power on the coven. At least, I thought he did. Mira had never discovered where Elizabeth's loyalties truly lay. The other coven member's loyalties remained a mystery to us.

Even after parking the car and turning off the engine, Mira continued to sit, gripping the steering wheel. She was staring straight ahead, though I doubt she actually saw anything.

"She's fine," I said, resisting the urge to place my hand over hers.

"Yeah," she sighed. We had all left at the same time. Mira and I in one car for LaVina, and Tristan, Gabriel, Matsui, and Lily in another, for a private airfield where they would catch Mira's private jet for London. I knew that she was safe, but I was concerned about putting her in Ryan's hands. While I believed what I told Mira about the warlock, he still had the power to surprise me on occasion. I preferred to think he would not risk Mira's wrath by using the child as a pawn in his latest game.

With a shake of her head, Mira got out of the car as I did. Yet, she stopped me as I shut the door. "Did you call and tell her we were coming?" Mira inquired. The house was dark except for a single bare bulb burning away on the front porch.

"Not really." I hedged.

"What do you mean, 'Not really'?" she demanded, thumping the top of the car with her fist.

"No, I didn't call ahead. She wasn't exactly thrilled to see us the first time. I didn't want to give her the chance to say no," I admitted. "Let's just go. Everything will be fine."

Mira shoved both her hands through her hair and let out a low growl. "Danaus, you don't go surprising witches. And judging by the trouble she went to for the dirt in her basement, I'm willing to bet she's a powerful witch."

"I hope so," I muttered as I led the way up to the front porch. My footsteps up the wooden stairs were heavy, thundering in the silence that blanketed the area. Sure, I hadn't wanted her to know we were coming, but I didn't exactly want to surprise LaVina either. Mira hung back, moving as soundlessly as the wind.

Before I could ring the bell, a light was switched on in the front room, followed by another light in the main hall.

LaVina pulled aside the curtain on the door and frowned at me as she shook her head. But at least she unlocked and opened the door.

"We need your help," I opened before she could say anything.

"You get that one fed?" she demanded, jerking her head toward Mira, who was hovering behind my left shoulder.

"I've been properly fed," Mira purred, seeming to taunt the witch. LaVina only gave a little snort and opened the door the rest of the way so that we could enter her home. Upon stepping over the threshold, I saw that the old woman was wrapped in a soft floral robe over what appeared to be a white nightgown. On her feet were a pair of worn pink house slippers. We had obviously woken her up.

"Sorry about getting you out of bed," I murmured. It had never occurred to me that she wouldn't be awake. I had become so accustomed to dealing with creatures that roamed at night that I had lost touch with the majority of humanity that preferred the warm comfort of daylight.

"It happens from time to time. Come on in," she said, motioning for Mira to enter the house. After shutting and locking the door, LaVina shuffled down the main hall, leading us into the kitchen, where she flipped on a bright overhead light that left both Mira and me blinking as we struggled to adjust.

"Would you like a glass of iced tea? Or maybe you'd prefer some coffee?" LaVina offered, moving over to some honey-colored wood cabinets. "It'll take me just a minute to get a pot brewing."

"No, thank you. We're fine," Mira said. The nightwalker stepped forward and leaned her forearms on the island in the center of the kitchen. "We need to talk about the bori."

Leaning back against the counter that lined the back wall of the kitchen, I folded my arms over my chest and watched LaVina. Her old hands stilled on the paper filter. I could see a grim frown pull at one corner of her mouth.

"Is that the way the wind blows now?" she murmured, resuming the task of putting the filter in the coffeemaker.

"You don't sound surprised," I commented, but she didn't reply again until she had finished preparing the coffeemaker.

"Should I be?" she finally said, glancing over her shoulder at me as she pulled down a coffee mug with kittens on it. "From what I've been hearing, the naturi have already broken out of their cage. Something's obviously gone wrong with the spell that held them. Why shouldn't the bori be trying to break free as well?"

I looked over at Mira to find her staring down at her hands, her shoulders slumped under the weight of our failure. The naturi were running free because we failed to stop them. Rowe had been willing to take risks we hadn't foreseen. We weren't going to make the same mistake with Gaizka.

"I was contacted by a bori called Gaizka," I slid past her question. "He wants his freedom. Somehow he's here but he's not free. I don't exactly understand it."

"Are you going to tell him how it works, vampire?" LaVina demanded, settling her piercing gaze on Mira.

"The bori are little more than pure spirit energy," Mira began with a sigh. "If they want to interact with the world in some meaningful fashion, they have to have a host body, an avatar, a puppet."

"Like when it appeared at your house in the body of an older man?" I suggested.

"Sort of," she said with a grimace. Pushing off the counter, Mira stood upright and turned so that she could look at me. "That was only a temporary host. They can use a body for a short period of time, but their presence tends to contaminate the body, destroying the host. That man you saw is probably dead by now. However, a bori can prepare a body to be a permanent host so that it can use the body indefinitely. That's how we trapped them."

"What do you mean?" I inquired, a strange twisting in my gut caused me to take a step back away from her.

"The permanent human hosts for the bori were locked away in a magical cage," LaVina explained.

"Take away their permanent home, the main source of their energy, and they are trapped," Mira continued. "The bori had to follow their human hosts into the cage. We suspected they'd be able to slip out here and there for a short period of time under special circumstances, but they wouldn't be able to escape without preparing new permanent hosts—something they would never have the strength to do."

"Until we came along," I corrected.

"True," Mira sadly agreed.

I took a step back toward Mira as my thoughts shifted in a new direction. The floor creaked beneath my shifting weight, making the house seem to groan in the silence as night crawled past the midnight hour. "I don't understand. You said that you didn't know how they were caged."

"I don't know how they were caged or how the cage itself was created," Mira replied, shoving her hands into the pockets of her jeans. "I know what was caged: humans."

"Their human hosts," I said.

"Humans," Mira pressed, sending a chill down my back. "I think the bodies that these bori inhabit still possess the souls and consciousness of their original owners. We locked up humans in an attempt to save ourselves from the bori. The bori are nothing more than parasites attached to the human body. Just like nightwalkers."

"Innocent people are being tormented by these creatures?" I murmured, my brain struggling to wrap itself about this horrible thought.

"'Innocent' is a questionable word here," Mira said with a shrug. "They had to make some kind of deal with the bori in the first place. Sure, many were probably tricked, but I wouldn't paint most of these people as innocent. Of course, I doubt any one of them would have agreed to thousands of years of servitude to these creatures."

"And now you've got one with an interest in Danaus

there," LaVina added, drawing our combined gazes back to her thin frame. The old witch shuffled over to the refrigerator and pulled out a container of creamer. "Gaizka is going to go looking for your weak spot. He's going to find a way to force you into making a deal with him to protect something you care about. And when you do, he's finally going to be free."

"Unless you can tell us how to send him back," Mira quickly countered.

"What makes you think I know how to send a bori back to its cage?" LaVina snapped, putting the container of creamer on the counter with a little more force than was necessary. She filled her mug before putting the carafe back on the coffeemaker stand. "I've had no dealings with their kind."

"But I have no doubt that you know how to summon one," Mira said. LaVina turned around so that she could glare at the nightwalker, but Mira didn't flinch. I was beginning to wonder if this house was suddenly going to fall in on our heads. Mira didn't need to be pressing the buttons of yet another powerful creature. For an undead, the nightwalker had a death wish.

"You're a powerful witch," Mira said, leaning forward on the counter again. "Powerful enough to sense the different energies that come from different soil samples and how to mix them so that they work in harmony with your own skills. You may have never summoned up a bori, but I'm sure you know how the spell works. Someone of your ability would want to have the knowledge in her back pocket for emergencies."

"You're pressing your luck, vampire," LaVina warned, staring down at her coffee as creamer and sugar turned it pale brown.

"Maybe, but you know how," Mira said, a grin finally growing across her face. Some of the tension eased from my own frame as some of her own confidence returned. "We don't need you to summon one. We need you to tell us how you send one away again. The other half of that summoning spell has to be rattling around in your brain somewhere. We just need that bit."

"It's not as simple as you want it to be," LaVina admitted with a shake of her head.

"It doesn't matter whether it's simple or not. Just as long as you know how it's done. You're going to be the one that performs the spell tomorrow night," Mira said, to which LaVina let out a wonderful laugh, nearly sloshing her coffee out of her mug.

"You're not going to get me anywhere near that bori," she said, chuckling.

"Listen, witch—" Mira started, but I grabbed her elbow suddenly when something appeared on the periphery of my thoughts, something strong enough to cause the hairs on the back of my neck to stand on end.

"Are you cloaking me?" I demanded, but I had a feeling I already knew the answer to that question.

"What?" Mira asked, looking up at me with furrowed brow.

"Are you cloaking me? Blocking me from the sight of the naturi?" I repeated.

"No," she whispered. A tremble went through her frame, reaching my fingers through her arm. "I forgot. Shit. How many are there?"

"Eight, and they're getting close. Do you have a weapon?"

"A knife at my side, but my gun is in the car," she said, her expression growing grimmer. I could understand why, since her last few outings with the naturi hadn't gone well. The mixture of no sleep and Gaizka messing with her mind had left the nightwalker struggling with every battle, no longer sure of what was real and what was just a horrible nightmare. She had been unable to clearly see the world around her, leaving her vulnerable to the naturi.

"We can handle this. We're in your domain and you're

back to your full strength," I said, rubbing my thumb across her arm.

Mira gave a soft laugh as she stepped away from me, pulling her arm free of my grip. "Yeah, we've been in worse positions before, right? Just a walk in the park."

Only now our most effective weapon against the naturi had been stolen away. We could no longer combine our powers or we would be feeding Gaizka directly, putting it one step closer to freedom.

"LaVina, we'll take care of them. You might want to go hide in your basement for the time being," I advised.

"You think that's going to keep me safe?" she demanded, slamming her coffee mug on the counter.

Mira rolled her eyes as she turned her back on LaVina and started to walk out of the kitchen. "Just find a place out of the way. We'll take care of it," the nightwalker grumbled, the heels of her boots pounding on the floor and nearly drowning out her words.

Wordlessly, I followed Mira through the house to the front door. Anything I said was sure to anger one of the women and I wasn't about to step into the trap. Why should I get my face ripped off, when I still had to take on the naturi?

"Where are they?" Mira asked as she wrapped her long slender fingers around the front doorknob.

Standing directly behind her, I let my eyes drift shut as I finally sent my powers out of my body and searching through the area. I had become so attuned to searching for the naturi, it had become second nature for me and I was now doing it unconsciously. I could feel Mira's own powers spike in response to the touch of mine as if her body was reflexively protecting itself from me.

It took less than a second for my powers to pick out the bodies of eight naturi crossing the long front yard that led up to LaVina's two-story farmhouse. I couldn't tell which clan they were from or any other details beyond the fact that they were naturi. Their powers were like a glaring, cacophonous noise in contrast to the seemingly hypnotic melody that rose from Mira.

"Directly in front of us and slowly approaching," I replied, opening my eyes again. "They're spread out, so they're most likely on foot."

"I'm sorry about this," Mira murmured as her fist tightened around the knob. "I should have been—"

"Let it go. It's better we face them now rather than tomorrow with Gaizka," I said, cutting her off.

"Then let's clean up my domain," Mira said before jerking open the front door.

We stepped out onto the front porch and quickly spotted eight dark figures approaching from across the lawn. They were all tall and slim, wearing dark clothes that allowed them to blend in with the night. At the sight of them, my heart rate sped up and the muscles in my chest constricted. Adrenaline filled my veins at the promise of battle, while my thoughts slowed down to a precise point of focus. There was only my opponent and me. More than a thousand years of battle had filled my existence, and they all distilled down to that single moment of clarity before the first splash of blood. Until Mira had stepped into my life, even the fear had been drained from the fight. The nightwalker had been the first to remind me that there were worse things than death waiting for me.

"What clan do you think they're from?" I asked as I descended the stairs.

The nightwalker motioned with her head toward the sky, where dark clouds had begun to churn. "At least one is from the wind clan," she said as she pulled out a knife.

I frowned. The wind clan possessed the ability to control the weather, which meant they could also bring down strike after strike of lightning. From Mira's wariness of this particular clan, I was willing to bet that she didn't think she could survive a direct hit of lightning. I wasn't even sure I could. We would need to locate and take out the wind clan members as soon as possible.

"Do you want my gun?" I offered the weapon from a holster at my lower back. "I can make a run for the other gun in the glove compartment."

"Keep it," Mira said, shaking her head. "You're a better aim than me. I've got a couple of tricks." Taking the lead, the nightwalker stepped into the middle of the large yard under the limbs of a massive oak tree with her hands planted on her narrow hips. I hung back, ready to fire off a round of shots if they so much as flinched in our direction.

"You weren't invited into my domain," Mira called to the naturi.

"You aren't welcome in our world," one female naturi replied smugly, leaving my fingers itching to pull the trigger and bury a bullet in the middle of her forehead.

"Leave now, or we'll be forced to slaughter you all," Mira shouted. At the same time, she held her left hand out to her side and summoned up a fireball. While I was standing several feet away, I could feel the cool touch of her powers brushing against my face.

In response to Mira's obvious threat, three naturi also reached out their hands only to have them instantly engulfed in flames, matching Mira's stance. A ripple of laughter spread among the naturi. Not only did they outnumber us, but there were also light clan naturi among their numbers. That took away Mira's edge since they could counter any fire attacks that she could possibly summon.

"You're the one that started this fight," called one of the light clan naturi. "Those in the conservatory were no threat to you."

"Any naturi within my domain are a threat to my people," Mira shouted back.

The naturi gave a soft sniff, lifting her chin. "She warned us you may be unwilling to share." For a moment, I wondered whether she was referring to Cynnia or Aurora, but such thoughts were quickly shoved aside.

Danaus, shoot them now! Mira cried in my head.

In a single, smooth motion, I raised the gun with both hands and fired off three quick shots, landing two in the heads of the light clan naturi. Unfortunately, the third light clan member was already moving by the time and the bullet went slightly wide of its target, hitting her in the shoulder. Two naturi hit the ground with a hard thud.

A roll of thunder rumbled through the silence and the naturi charged. I squeezed off a couple rounds at the three that were headed toward me, but all the shots missed their marks as I was forced to dive for cover. Fireballs were flung at me in quick succession, backing me toward the house and away from Mira.

Instincts rose up to take control of my brain and I found myself reaching for my powers to boil their blood in their lithe bodies, but I fought the urge. I knew if Mira and I combined our powers, the souls of the dead would go directly to Gaizka, but I wasn't sure if the bori would benefit if I killed the naturi using my own powers alone. The bori had been the one to give me this ability, why should it not benefit?

With a growl, I rolled back to my feet, gun trained on the naturi as they closed in on me. Above, thunder exploded in the sky as the storm steadily grew in intensity. I turned my sights on the one naturi who was hanging back, controlling the growing storm. I tried to fire off a round of shots, but at that moment, he threw out a pair of white wings, catching the wind so that it carried him into the sky. I fired off two rounds, but only managed to clip some feathers before more fireballs came speeding at me.

I wasn't quick enough this time. One knot of flames slammed into my right hand, burning flesh and causing me to drop the gun in the grass. Tucking my right hand against my stomach as I tried to ignore the pain that beat at me, I picked up the gun with my left hand only to immediately drop it again. The metal burned my hand from when it had been heated by the fireball.

Running a few feet away from my predators, I grabbed

the knife I had attached to my belt. I turned, ready to take on my opponents. My heart pounded in my chest and a cold sweat was trickling down the back of my neck. For the first time in a very long time, I had begun to doubt my ability to get out of this fight alive. For too long I had relied on my powers to escape any situation against a dark creature without contemplating the potential consequences. Now that my powers had been removed from me by the threat of something darker, I was simply a human against creatures far more powerful than me.

"Boil them, Danaus!" Mira screamed. I caught a glimpse of her out of the corner of my eye, trapped in a firefight with three naturi encircling her. Soon, they would succeed in wearing her down.

"I can't! Gaizka!" I shouted back. "It'll gain strength!"

"Shit," Mira swore softly, following this with a grunt as she threw another fireball at a waiting naturi.

We were trapped. And then the lightning came. The naturi facing me backed off a couple steps just before a bolt of lightning slammed the ground a few feet away from where I had been standing. I jumped farther away from the spot. A cry of pain escaped me as I landed on my burned right hand, which was healing far too slowly for my liking. I rolled and quickly regained my feet. Another bolt of lightning smashed into a large oak tree, splitting it down the center. I threw my shoulder into the back of one naturi, knocking him to the ground. Wincing in excruciating pain, I wrapped my right arm around Mira's waist and carried her several feet before we both crashed to the ground. Behind us, the tree she had been standing under splintered and collapsed to the ground in a loud bang. Thin branches blanketed us as we failed to move out of the reach of the massive tree.

I groaned as I rolled onto my back, my body protesting every movement. "We need to get out of here," I said in a low voice, praying the naturi couldn't hear me utter the horrible words over the pounding rain that had begun to fall.

"Use your powers!" Mira snapped, sliding out from under my arm as she sat up. Her eyes glowed a vibrant lavender as energy pulsed around her in chilling waves like a cold arctic wind. "They are matching me fire for fire. I can't even get close enough to use my blade."

"Gaizka will get stronger," I said, sitting up as well while I kept my hand tucked against my stomach.

"You're hurt."

"It'll heal," I muttered, struggling to get back to my feet. The naturi were coming and it would be only a matter of seconds before the next bolt of lightning slammed into the exact spot where we were sitting.

"I've had enough of this," Mira snarled. Shoving herself to her feet, the nightwalker grabbed the knife from my left hand so that she now held a blade in each hand. Her shoulders were painfully rigid as she stalked the five naturi that remained on the ground. "Stay behind me," she called. The Fire Starter briefly glanced over her shoulder at me and I noted that her eyes now glowed an ominous red, something I had never seen her do before. Not even when she was lost in the heat of battle or wracked with pain from my pushing my powers through her body.

The naturi pummeled Mira with fireballs, but the flames seemed to wash harmlessly down her body. Her movements were a blur, yet each slice of the blade was precise in its execution. The naturi couldn't move fast enough to defend themselves. Within a couple seconds, the female naturi collapsed to the ground, her head rolling across the lawn while her insides spilled out of her body. Two rushed Mira, but just as quickly ended up in the same condition. A second later, she jerked to her left, dodging a lightning bolt that struck the spot she had been standing in. She hadn't even glanced up at the sky.

Something twisted in my gut as I watched her. I knew Mira's fighting style. I had fought her and spent nights watching her fight nightwalkers, lycanthropes, and naturi.

I had never seen her move like this. She was faster, more precise, more ruthless in her motions.

The nightwalker twisted around as she blocked one slash aimed at her heart, and threw out her left arm toward me. At the same time, a massive force slammed into my chest. It threw me backward several feet, sending me crashing back into the ground. Yet, before I hit the soggy earth, I saw a bolt of lightning slam into the spot I had been standing in.

The pounding of my heart returned and a knot grew in my throat. Mira couldn't move things with her mind. Between the red glow of her eyes and the increase speed and dexterity, something was controlling the nightwalker.

"Gaizka!" I shouted in the air, but received no answer. I could feel it now that I knew what I was looking for. There was a new power circling around us, filling the darkness that flickered and danced in the firelight. The bori had taken control of Mira.

As I regained my feet, the wind naturi who'd sprouted wings earlier lightly touched back down to the ground behind Mira as she battled the last two light clan naturi.

"No!" I bellowed, but I knew that Mira would not have enough time to react. She was surrounded. There was no second thought, no doubt in my mind. I summoned my powers and reached out for the wind naturi. He screamed in pain as he raised his blade, preparing to plunge it into Mira's back. He dropped the sword as he started to claw at his arms and chest. But it was too late. His blood blackened his flesh before finally bubbling through with an ominous pop and hiss.

A second later, Mira finished off the second of the two naturi. She blasted the creature with a massive wave of fire, lighting the night to the point where it seemed as if the sun had settled on the Earth between us. When she doused the flames, the naturi was reduced to a pile of ash.

With the threat destroyed, Mira collapsed to her knees, her body seeming to convulse. I ran over to her. My feet slid out from underneath me on the wet grass as I stopped beside her. I grabbed her shoulders, holding her upright so that I could look her in the face. The glow was completely gone from her eyes, but her irises had now expanded to the point of blotting out what purple there had been in her eyes. Terror had taken over.

"It—it was inside of me," she stammered, horror filling her tone. "I couldn't fight it. I could feel it in my head, in my body. Controlling everything. I tried to scream. I tried t-to reach for you. Couldn't do anything."

"It's gone now," I said, only to be instantly contradicted.

"Not quite, my boy," announced a scratchy, hollow voice that had become too familiar for my liking. I twisted around to find a ghostly figure standing just a few feet away. A teenager with spiked hair and baggy clothes that were criss-crossed with chains, it looked completely human other than the fact that we could see through it.

"Your hesitance to use your gifts is going to get you killed," Gaizka sneered. "If the nightwalker had not been here, I would not have been able to save you. I am disappointed that you didn't dispatch this riffraff properly. But then you'll get another chance to find some tomorrow night."

"We won't help you break free," I barked, my grip tightening on Mira's shaking shoulders. The rain was slowing, but the trembling wasn't from the bitter cold that bit into both of us. I could feel the fear that flooded her senses. She was looking at her creator, one of the creators of all nightwalkers. She was staring in the face of yet another creature that could control her. She couldn't even fight this one, like she could Jabari or me.

The bori laughed, sending a cold, bitter noise winging through the air. "I don't recall giving you a choice. Tomorrow night, I will finally be free of my cage, and you, my boy, are going to be my key."

"We w-won't help you," Mira bit out, struggling to stop her chattering teeth.

Gaizka laughed at us as we were suddenly torn apart, our

bodies flying through the air in separate directions. My back slammed into the side panel of Mira's car, while the vampire hit the trunk of an oak tree standing near the middle of the yard. I inwardly cringed, my heart nearly coming to a stop when I saw her slump there for a moment. One misplaced tree branch could have staked her in a second, sucking her life away before she could draw a breath to scream. Kneeling on my hands and knees in the mud, I watched Mira, waiting to see her move, anything to prove that she was still alive. The bori might need her alive, but that didn't mean it couldn't make an impulsive error.

After a couple seconds, Mira pushed to her hands and knees as well, allowing me to expel my pent-up breath. The vampire summoned up a ball of fire and attempted to throw it at the bori, but her arm stopped in mid-swing as if it had struck an invisible wall. Gaizka raised one hand and closed its fingers, causing Mira to extinguish the flame. For a moment, her eyes glowed red, but a terrified scream was still ripped from her chest as she fought it.

"Leave her alone!" I shouted, pushing to my feet. I summoned up my own powers and attempted to focus on the center of the energy that danced in the air. But all attempts to beat the creature back were useless. It had no body for me to attack. I had no way of fighting pure energy. I had no effective attack against a creature that was little more than a ghost.

"Listen to her screaming, Danaus," Gaizka said over the endless cries that escaped Mira, shattering the silence of the countryside. "The naturi are nothing in comparison to what I can do to her. Save her by doing as I wish. Set me free and you both will be protected."

The bori finally released Mira, and she flopped limply to the ground. Gaizka slowly faded from sight, leaving Mira sitting in the mud in LaVina's front yard. I ran over to her side and gathered her trembling body up in my arms. A large, broken tree smoldered beside us, while bodies of dead naturi lay scattered around the yard like broken ornaments. We had to find a way to stop the bori, but I had a growing fear that I wasn't going to survive this encounter if we were to succeed. What if, during the past thousand years, Gaizka had been simply preparing me to become his next permanent host?

Thirty-One

I leaned my shoulder against the stone wall outside of Abigail Bradford's apartment building, hidden in the shadows that blanketed Factors Walk. I was standing in almost the exact spot where Lily had first spotted Gaizka so many nights ago. The place where it had all started, and where the bori would finally appear. The sun had set nearly an hour ago, and above me, streetlamps popped on around Bay Street, creating a fresh cast of shadows in the narrow alley.

LaVina had reluctantly agreed to come when I stopped by her house that afternoon. Workers were still tooling around her front yard, cleaning up the debris from the felled tree. The old witch hadn't been particularly happy about the mess we made of her property, but relented as we focused on getting Mira out of her nearly catatonic state. The nightwalker had been faced with the naturi and the bori in less than six months—nightmares that had been banished from the Earth for centuries. And I had brought both into her life.

Mira had promised to meet me outside of Abigail Bradford's apartment, but a part of me wouldn't be surprised if she didn't show. She had been through enough. And in truth, this was my fight. I was beginning to fear that she would only be a target for Gaizka.

LaVina's steady, critical voice drifted down to me from where she sat on a bench near the railing above Factors Walk. I had left her there weaving Savannah roses with dried palm leaves. "You're late," she grumbled.

"Sorry," Mira snidely replied. "I stopped for a shower."

I looked up the stairs behind my left shoulder to see the nightwalker coming down wearing her typical garb of black leather. Strapped to her waist and legs were an assortment of blades. Her black leather duster danced slightly as she moved, while her leather boots were nearly silent on the concrete-and-stone sidewalk. She was ready for battle.

"Did you hear from Lily?" she asked in softer tones when she reached the bottom step.

"Tristan called me just about an hour ago to say that she was safe and that they were at the Compound," I replied, a half smile tugging at one corner of my mouth.

Mira nodded. "Tristan called before I left the house. Said he was going to stay on for a few days to make sure that she's settled properly."

"It'll give us time to get things settled here," I said.

Mira nodded, her lips pressed into a hard, thin line as she clenched her jaw. On the exterior, she was all cold rage and immoveable hatred, but I could sense the undercurrent of fear rippling through her. I reached up and moved a strand of hair that had blown in front of her eyes. I let my fingers stray across her cool cheek, cupping her face. For a moment, I regretted every chance I'd had to kiss her but didn't. I wanted to tell her to walk away. I wanted to tell her to get on a plane and fly as far from me as possible, but my throat closed up and I couldn't utter a sound.

To my surprise, Mira smiled at me before turning her face to press a kiss to the palm of my hand. "I want to be here. It's where I belong," she said. I shouldn't have been surprised. When we were close, we were constant ghosts in each other's minds.

I tightened my grip on her face and started to pull her close when the sound of approaching footsteps echoed off the high stone walls of the surrounding buildings. I hesitated then slowly released her, letting my hands fall back to my sides. Mira placed her hands on either side of my face and pulled me close, pressing her cool lips against mine in a kiss that left me drowning. But the touch was over almost as quickly as it had begun, as she stepped away from me, turning her attention to our newest companion.

Mira's shoulders slumped with relief, but a frown still marred her lips as she looked at the newcomer. I turned to find Emma Rose, the young lady who worked the trolley tours counter, coming up the hill to enter the wide alley.

"Emmy, you need to get out of here," Mira stated. The nightwalker tried to step around me, but I grabbed her left elbow, jerking her to a sharp stop. Something was wrong here. Emma Rose couldn't have known that Mira was up here and there was no way that the nightwalker would have told her friend where she was going to be when she was coming to meet a dangerous bori.

"What are you doing?" Mira demanded, trying to free her arm, but I refused to release her.

Sending my powers out from my body, I sensed the same energy I had felt at LaVina's last night lingering in the air.

As Emma Rose turned the corner, stepping into the shadow cast by a building, a red glow faintly lit her narrow eyes while a dark smile grew on her attractive face. Gaizka had taken possession of Emma Rose's body.

"No!" Mira screamed, finally jerking out of my grasp. She lurched forward a few steps before I got ahold of her arms again, keeping her from attacking the creature that had taken control of her friend. "Release her!" Mira cried in a choked voice, no longer struggling against my grasp.

"Or what?" chuckled a vaguely familiar voice, a mix of Emma Rose's soft voice and Gaizka's scratchy rasp. "You'll burn me out of her?"

I drew Mira back several feet, drawing her deeper into

the shadows that cloaked Factors Walk. Gaizka followed, moving around the building and out of the sight of anyone who might look up in our direction. The bori paused in front of the doorway that led up to Abigail Bradford's apartment. Laying its hand on the door, the creature turned its head toward us and smiled. "Good memories," Gaizka purred in Emma Rose's voice. "It's where it all started."

"How?" I asked, my eyes lingering on Emma Rose.

"The girl?" Gaizka said, putting out Emma's arms as if she were modeling a new dress. "She's a good girl. When an angel appeared before her at prayer, she didn't hesitate to accept my request for assistance." As the bori spoke, a pair of white, sparkling wings rose out of Emma Rose's back and a white glow spread all around her. But the illusion was gone almost as quickly as it had come, as if the bori didn't have the strength to maintain it.

"Emmy is a devote Catholic," Mira said, horrified. "She wouldn't have questioned . . ."

"What a pity," Gaizka murmured. "Of course, I must confess that things have not gone how I would have hoped. I thought by now you both would have destroyed a few naturi for me."

"We're not going to help you any longer," I said firmly, moving Mira behind me. "You'll not win your freedom through us."

"Are you willing to risk the lives of the people of Savannah on that stance?" Gaizka inquired, arching one brow at me while its grin grew wider.

"We won't allow you to harm anyone," I said, drawing a knife from my side. I couldn't use a gun while we were within the city limits. The noise would only attract a crowd and draw the attention of the police. The last thing we needed was a crowd gathered so that the bori could easily begin its massacre of the city.

I stared at Emma Rose's body, a lump growing in my throat. In order to stop Gaizka, I would have to kill her, something that sweet girl didn't deserve. I could easily imagine her watching this scene unfold, screaming on the inside, terrified, and I was going to make it worse by attacking her. I truly wished she couldn't feel the pain, but a part of me knew she would.

Gaizka threw back Emma Rose's head and let loose a wild, joyous laugh while crossing her arms over her thin stomach. "I am the least of your concerns."

At that second, I felt a shift in the power coursing through the alley as if a cold wind had slipped through me. I tightened my grip on my blade and prepared to step toward the bori when a sharp pain stabbed in my back, sending me to my knees. I cried out, nearly dropping my knife as I tried to reach back to find what had caused the excruciating pain. It shifted as I felt the blade being pulled from my back. I twisted around as best as I could to find Mira holding the knife in both hands, her fingers covered in my blood.

The nightwalker's face was completely blank, yet her eyes were once again glowing an ominous red. Gaizka was not only inhabiting Emma Rose's body, but had also taken control of Mira.

Gritting my teeth against the surge of pain, I rolled away from the nightwalker, putting myself directly between her and the bori. I pushed immediately to my feet, trying to ignore the flow of blood that was coursing down my spine. Mira had sliced through muscle and it felt like she had cut into one of my lungs as I struggled to catch my breath. The wound was healing, but it was only a matter of time before the nightwalker gave me a few more matching wounds until I was finally bled dry.

"Forcing me to kill Mira won't get you any closer to freedom," I snapped. "Without Mira, I can't help you at all." I circled to my right as Mira slowly approached me. The nightwalker still held the bloodstained knife in her hand. For now, Gaizka seemed content to allow us to slash at each other. It had not tapped into the nightwalker's ability to control fire. I had no defense against such an attack . . . unless I used my own ability to boil Mira's blood.

"Oh, my dear boy, you have no idea the many ways you can still help me." Gaizka chuckled softly. "Mira's not the only nightwalker that you can control. You've got bori energy flowing through your veins. I'm sure that, with a little practice, you can control any nightwalker you want."

"But not the same way I can control Mira," I bit out as I dodged a slash aimed at my throat. Mira reached down and grabbed a second blade from her side with her left hand. She slashed downward with the new knife, trying to draw the blade across my chest. I jerked out of the way, my heart thundering in my ears. I had to find a way to disarm her and knock her out so that the bori could no longer control her, removing her from danger. I didn't want to kill her, but I wasn't going to allow her to weaken me to the point where I had no choice but to abide by Gaizka's wishes.

"True," Gaizka purred softly. "Mira is the most efficient killer I've ever encountered, but if you won't use her then we have no need for her. She is simply a distraction from the main task at hand."

"So, you want me to kill her?" I asked, risking a glance over my shoulder at the bori.

"Yes," Gaizka hissed. The red glow in Emma Rose's eyes seemed to flare briefly before they returned to their normal glint. "And you won't do such just because I command it, so you kill her or she kills you."

"You won't do it," I said, lowering my knife to my side. I straightened from my defensive stance, facing Mira. The nightwalker seemed to pause for a moment and blink at me as if Gaizka had temporarily relinquished its hand on her. "You need me. You won't kill me."

"You do represent an eighteen-hundred-year investment, but I can make another like you. There are always more humans looking for a way to cheat death, gain massive strength and power. I'm immortal and very patient. I can wait," Gaizka taunted.

Mira's eyes returned to their former red glow just a second before she slashed at me again with the knife. I jumped backward, but the vampire was slightly faster, ripping the blade across my chest. My leather jacket took the brunt of the blow, but the tip of the blade raked across the opening in the jacket. It tore through my cotton shirt and cut a few millimeters deep into my flesh.

"No!" Mira cried out. The hand holding the knife trembled and she took a jerky half step backward.

"Mira! Obey me!" Gaizka commanded, raising its voice for the first time since stepping into the alley.

"Fight it, Mira!" I shouted.

"Can't," she groaned through clenched teeth just before bringing her blade down on me again. This time, I raised my own knife, blocking it from stabbing me in the heart. She seemed to be moving a little slower this time, as if she were finally fighting the bori. Beads of blood broke out on her forehead while a tear streaked down her cheek. Her body was trembling and her jaw was clenched. I had no doubt that she was fighting him with everything she had, but it wasn't enough.

"LaVina!" I shouted, as I struggled to push Mira away from me. "I could really use your help right about now."

"I can do nothing without Mira," the old witch said from somewhere behind me. She sounded somewhat closer, indicating that she had most likely come down the stairs to the alleyway. "You're going to need to free her."

"I don't see that happening, old woman," Gaizka mocked. "The nightwalker is mine to control."

"Danaus can do it," she said confidently. "Talk to her, hunter. Reach for her."

With a grunt, I finally pushed Mira away from me. Before she could move, I summoned up all my powers and quickly thrust into her mind. The nightwalker screamed and stumbled a couple steps backward, clutching her head with both hands still holding the knives.

Her mind was a gray swirling fog. At first, I couldn't even locate her. There were none of her usual chaotic thoughts, no cacophonous mix of emotions pulling one way or another. Then I found the thin trail of pain that led to greater and greater amounts of pain until the world seemed to go entirely red. In the middle of it all, I found Mira's thoughts huddled in a tight little ball.

Mira.

Oh, God, Danaus. Kill me now, she moaned.

Help me fight this!

Can't. Can't keep fighting it. So much pain. So tired. Watch out!

I pulled away from her thoughts just enough that I was also aware of my external surroundings. The nightwalker lunged at me. But now that I was in her mind, I could also hear the command. I dodged a blow that was aimed to impale me while blocking the second knife, which was aimed at my face. Grabbing both of her wrists as best I could with a knife still gripped in my right hand, I held her still as I plunged back into her thoughts. I would not kill Mira. I wouldn't allow the bori to force me into killing this woman, even if it meant risking my own life.

Help me fight this! Now! I ordered. At the same time, I pushed with all my strength against the thickening fog and the hum of power that sizzled through her thin, shaking frame. I pushed it until I finally felt it start to ebb. I could feel Mira beside me in her thoughts. She was no longer struggling to break free of my grip on her arms, but was focusing the last of her energy. As I asserted my authority within Mira's mind, both the nightwalker and Gaizka let out matching screams. Mira's legs collapsed, wrenching her arms from my grasp, but I didn't relent.

A powerful force knocked into me, throwing me into the nearby stone wall that lined Factors Walk. Releasing my hold on Mira, I turned my attention to the bori. Already in touch with my dark powers, I allowed them to easily flow from my body and seep into Emma Rose's body. The young woman screamed in pain, her body twisting to the left and then to the right as if struggling to escape some unseen attacker. I raised the temperature of her blood as quickly as possible, trying to rush the end. I didn't want to put her through this kind of pain, but I had no choice. I had to destroy the body Gaizka was using, hopefully forcing the bori to flee the area since I had already proven that I could eject it from Mira.

"No!" Mira screamed. However, I didn't have enough time to react. The blade buried itself in my abdomen, nearly pinning me to the wall as it ripped through organs, muscles, and tissue. I looked up to see Mira staring at me, tears running down her face. The red glow was gone from her eyes, and for a moment I believed that she had stabbed me in an effort to stop me from killing Emma Rose. A choked sob rose from Mira's throat as she threw out her right arm. Her friend was immediately engulfed in orange and yellow flames, lighting the entire alley in a massive fireball. Between our combined efforts, Emma Rose's body was reduced to a pile of ash. Her friend was gone, but finally free of her captor.

Mira slowly pulled out the blade she had embedded in my stomach. She pressed her free hand to my stomach in an effort to slow the bleeding. "I'm so sorry. I didn't want to. I tried to fight it," she kept repeating as she shook her head.

I dropped my knife on the ground and heaved a heavy sigh as I placed my right hand on the back of her head. I pulled her forward and pressed a kiss to the top of her head. "It's okay. It wasn't your fault."

Mira gave another choked cry, her hands trembling against me. She had lost a good friend to a bori and attacked me while under his control. To make matters worse, the bori was still running free.

"We're not through yet," Gaizka announced in the dark alley, its voice seeming to surround us. "I've still got at least one trick up my sleeve."

At the same time, a pair of footsteps echoed up the alley. Both Mira and I turned to see who was approaching this time. My heart stopped in my chest when I saw Tristan turn the corner, holding Lily by her collar as he pushed her ahead of him. Lily's face was swollen and bruised, while her cheeks were streaked with dirty tears. The collar of her shirt was torn and her clothes were dirty. A red glow lit Tristan's eyes, giving away Gaizka's presence within the nightwalker. Apparently, the bori had gotten control of the nightwalker before he and Lily could get on the plane. The unspoken question of whether Gabriel and Matsui were still alive hovered in the air.

"No," Mira whimpered beside me as she stared at the two creatures she had come to care greatly for. Gaizka was prepared to take everything away from her in the blink of an eye unless we started killing naturi and started feeding him the soul energy.

"Leave her out of this," I bit out, barely able to get the words through my clenched jaws.

"Danaus!" Lily cried. She tried to run for me and Mira, but Tristan held tight, keeping her pinned to his side. The nightwalker remained expressionless, staring straight ahead. And he was blind to the world around him, trapped in Gaizka's grasp. He had no choice but to obey.

"It's okay, Lily," Mira murmured in a shaky voice. "Everything is going to be okay."

Gaizka suddenly appeared before the young girl as an older woman with a kind, gentle face. The figure smiled at Lily, seeming for all the world as if she wouldn't harm a fly. "Mira is lying. It's not okay. She and Danaus are in terrible trouble," she said softly. "Only you can save them. Join with me and we will be strong enough to save them both."

"No!" I shouted. "Don't listen to it."

"Tristan, fight it!" Mira cried. "You've got to fight it. Release Lily. Let her run from here!"

Tristan didn't move, didn't even blink at Mira's words. I couldn't enter his mind like I could Mira's. I had no tie to this nightwalker. I could sense his soul floating about his body, but that was all. I couldn't push Gaizka out of Tristan, freeing him.

"I won't do it," Lily said in a trembling voice. "You're the one that's lying. You're the reason they're in trouble. You're the trouble." She lifted her chin slightly, though her whole body seemed to shake as she faced the creature that had haunted her for the past several days.

"This is your last chance, child," Gaizka warned. The bori's voice hardened, growing deeper and more ominous in its tone.

"Lily, no!" Mira screamed.

"No," Lily said in a strong voice, looking the monster dead in the eye.

"Very well," Gaizka said, shrugging the old woman's shoulders. "I have no use for you." The creature floated a couple feet away and waved his hand. Tristan tightened his grip on Lily's neck just before he picked her up and flung her small body into the wall that lined Factors Walk. There was no mistaking the sound of snapping bones and breaking rock. Her limp body fell to the ground in an awkward fashion, while a smear of blood coated the stones from where her head had slammed into the wall. She had died on impact.

"No!" Mira screamed, falling to her knees beside me. Neither one of us had had time to react. We hadn't had time to even move. In a flash of violence, Lily was dead.

Rage pumped through my veins as I lifted my hand, pointing it directly at Tristan, who had yet to show a flicker of emotion. Mira suddenly shoved to her feet as I summoned up my powers, grabbing my arm and forcing me to lower it. "Don't kill him! You can't kill him! Please! It's not his fault!" she begged. At the same time, she plunged her own energy into my body, forcing her way into my brain so that her pleading echoed there as well. She was heartbroken and desperate. She had already lost her surrogate daughter. It would shatter what was left of her to lose the creature she saw as both a brother and a son. "Please," she cried, tears streaming down her face.

In the instant that I hesitated, Gaizka flowed completely into Tristan and the nightwalker seemed to finally come to life. "You were warned!" the creature shouted, taking a step closer to us.

"And we won't cave," I snarled. Shaking off Mira, I picked up the pair of blades that Mira had dropped on the ground and charged the nightwalker. Tristan simply smiled at me as I plunged both blades through his stomach with enough force to pin him to the stone wall. The creature couldn't move. Blood poured from Tristan's body, but he just laughed. Behind me, Mira screamed. I had potentially killed Tristan as well. Gaizka had nowhere else to go. I pulled a third blade from my side and prepared to plunge it into Tristan's heart when the red glow faded from his eyes. He looked up at me with a haunted gaze. He was fully aware that he had been Lily's killer.

"Please," he whispered in a pained voice. "Please, kill me."

I hesitated. I didn't want to kill Tristan. As a nightwalker, he was harmless and I knew it. He was Mira's only true family and her staunch protector. He never meant to harm Lily. It wasn't his fault and he didn't deserve the death that now lingered on his horizon because of me.

"Leave the boy be," LaVina suddenly interjected, staying the final blow. "You've weakened the creature. It can no longer jump from body to body."

"Are you sure—" I started to say, but the rest of my sentence was cut off as something tightly grasped my ankles and pulled me. It slammed me into the hard ballast-stone road on my side, sending a shock wave of pain rippling through my body as I was dragged across the alley to where Emma Rose had been standing only moments ago. Her ashes still danced in the wind near me, but I was more concerned with what was holding on to me. I looked down at my ankles but saw nothing but the darkness of the night.

Twisting around on my back, I reached out toward Mira, reopening the wound on my stomach that was still trying to heal. "Mira! LaVina!" I shouted, pleading for the nightwalker and the witch to help me. Gaizka had me now and I feared it would take only a little effort on his part to make me his next and *permanent* host.

LaVina walked over to Mira with more ease and grace than I had ever seen her exhibit. As Mira ran toward me, the old witch grabbed a chunk of the nightwalker's hair and pulled her to a sharp halt, forcing her to kneel on the stones. LaVina bent over the nightwalker, wrapping one hand around her neck while she whispered something in Mira's ear. The nightwalker jerked and pulled against the witch, but surprisingly she couldn't break free.

I grabbed the large, smooth stones that made up the road and tried to pull myself free of Gaizka's grip, but I couldn't budge from where I now lay on my stomach, staring over at the nightwalker who was reaching for me.

"Mira!" I shouted. Muscles straining to the point that my arms began to shake while a cold sweat broke out on my brow, I found a sense of panic rising within me. I wouldn't be used like Emma Rose had been. I wouldn't be a puppet like Mira. "Mira!"

"Shout and scream all you want," snarled a dark voice in my right ear. A cold, bitter wind swept around me, biting at my limbs, causing my fingertips to go numb. "You'll not be free of me. I've waited too long. I want out of my cage and I will be out tonight."

"I'll not set you free," I bit out between clenched teeth

and tightened my grip around one large stone in the road, trying to inch closer to Mira and LaVina. "I won't be your next host."

"Soon, my boy. Soon," it hissed, sending another blast of cold air over my frame so that my teeth began to chatter.

The hand on my shoulder tightened, sending what felt like sharpened nails digging into my flesh. "Join with me now. Set me free, or I will grab the nightwalker again and set this town on fire."

"You can't!" I growled. "I forced you out once, I'll do it again. You're not as strong as you were. You're losing your powers."

"And you're useless if you're unconscious," Gaizka laughed.

Fear gripped me, clenching its fist around my heart. "Mira! Run!" I shouted, praying that she'd be able to escape Gaizka, knowing that it was unlikely. If I wasn't awake to push the bori out of Mira again, he would have no problem burning the city to the ground with Mira under his control.

Looking up, I found LaVina staring at me, a beautiful smile on her wrinkled face. Her whole body seemed to glow in the darkness, shining against Mira's black leather and deep red hair. The nightwalker had gone silent, but her hand was still outstretched toward me, her fingers noticeably trembling as they seemed to draw symbols in the air.

LaVina bent and whispered something in Mira's ear. The nightwalker flinched and then spoke a smattering of words that I neither recognized nor understood. But Gaizka did.

"No!" the bori screamed, tightening its grip on me until I cried out in pain. My whole right side was riddled with shooting pains and biting cold until I finally wished for my body to go numb.

On my left, a shaft of white light appeared, as if the very fabric of the open air had been torn. The opening remained just a slim slit in the night, but it was enough. I could feel a great pull in the air as if everything was being sucked into the opening. Gaizka screamed again and its nails scratched across my back as it searched for some kind of purchase against the gaping void it was being drawn into.

A hollow scream echoed through the night as the bori was drawn into the opening and finally trapped once again, back in its cage.

Mira uttered another set of words in a language I didn't recognize and the opening drew closed, mending perfectly as if it had never existed.

I exhaled a heavy breath, pushing all of the air out of my lungs, as I relaxed against the cold stones in the road. The bori was gone and Savannah was safe. If Mira and I could refrain from combining our powers when fighting, the bori should never be able to return again. We were safe at last.

My body shook from exhaustion and a dozen aches and pains that were only now beginning to heal. Blood was dried on my back and stomach from where Mira had stabbed me. The cold stones chilled my flesh, but in a way it all felt good. I was alive and I was free.

"Danaus!" Mira screamed.

I jerked my head up to look over at the nightwalker. Mira was straining against LaVina's hold, stretching her right hand out to me, desperate. I had seen fear reflected in Mira's eyes when she had been faced with Nerian and when she had been touched by Gaizka. Both were just a pale shadow to the terror that gripped her now.

"Danaus!" she screamed, her voice wavering. "Please, help me!"

"Sorry, hunter," LaVina said in a deep voice I had never heard before. A smile stretched across her face and danced in her eyes. "I've done my part. It's time for this wayward child to come home."

I pushed to my feet and started to reach for Mira, but she and LaVina disappeared before my eyes, leaving me alone in the dark. Mira was gone, grabbed by something far more powerful than any witch I had ever known, and I had no idea how to find her.

THE NIGHT HUNTRESS NOVELS FROM

JEANIENE FROST

✠ HALFWAY TO THE GRAVE ✠

978-0-06-124508-4

Before she can enjoy her newfound status as kick-ass demon hunter, half vampire Cat Crawfield and her sexy mentor, Bones, are pursued by a group of killers. Now Cat will have to choose a side…and Bones is turning out to be as tempting as any man with a heartbeat.

✠ ONE FOOT IN THE GRAVE ✠

978-0-06-124509-1

Cat Crawfield is now a special agent, working for the government to rid the world of the rogue undead. But when she's targeted for assassination she turns to her ex, the sexy and dangerous vampire Bones, to help her.

✠ AT GRAVE'S END ✠

978-0-06-158307-0

Caught in the crosshairs of a vengeful vamp, Cat's about to learn the true meaning of bad blood—just as she and Bones need to stop a lethal magic from being unleashed.

✠ DESTINED FOR AN EARLY GRAVE ✠

978-0-06-158321-6

Cat is having terrifying visions in her dreams of a vampire named Gregor who's more powerful than Bones.

Visit www.AuthorTracker.com for exclusive
information on your favorite HarperCollins authors.